The Red Queen Caper

Janet McDermott

DEDICATION

To Jake
The auspicious conversations we had about writing
and environment were fun!

ACKNOWLEDGEMENT:

I fully declare that my writing is a fictitious collection of thoughts and feelings that I have absorbed and accumulated over my lifetime. As a writer scribbling thoughts on the computer to the aspiring author finding a pathway to printing, there is a multitude of friends and places to recognize. To my hiking buddies who respect and understand the majesty of the Rocky Mountains and to all the people who freely shared a facet of insights on the internet or in person, thank you. My places, events, people and incidents come through my imagination then appear as my fiction. I also need to thank Craig Ebel for designing the clever book cover after listening to my comments. Plus, of course, a loving scratch goes out to my stouthearted Schnoodle who slept through the entire book! Thanks all!

CHAPTERS

CHAPTER 1

FAMILY AND FRACKING

"No. No. Nope. I am not going. I really can't stand to listen to dear Billy whine all week about what the family owes him. Give me a break, Dad." She finished sliding the door shut and shooing her herd of ranch dogs out of the barn then stared down at her father. Bernie's height had always worked in her favor when arguing with family; in romance not so much. Her gloved hands placed on her hips; her sharp green eyes staring directly at her father, created an image of pure defiance. The Holden clan was intense and that was a fact; she was no exception.

"Now honey, Billy will get over it like he always does. Your mother was better at cooling him down than I am but it will happen." Henry Holden ran his large hand through his graying red hair and focused his eyes on Bernie as she hurriedly walked toward the porch. The breeze coming up White

Earth Valley promised some relief from the summer heat. Still, it would be a hot one, he thought.

Bernie dropped her gloves on the porch table. She poured her dad and herself a glass of water from the cooler. It allowed her time to form the words that she wanted to express. Billy had never given his family the consideration that he should in her mind. She eyed Henry closely." Will he? Billy smells more money. He has always lived in the moment and it smells sweet to him right now. North Dakota's pot of gold is there for his taking. Has Billy written your will yet?" She paused and watched her dad's reaction to the question before she sat down in the wooden rocker. She was disgusted with both her father and Billy. "What the hell is wrong with Billy?" she muttered trying to control her temper. Her gaze watched the dogs finding the shade for naps. Bernie took a deep breath and calmed herself.

"Don't go there, Bernie. He's your brother, damn it. Whether we like it or not fracking is here to stay. Billy didn't create the mess. You can't blame him for wanting to better his life financially. Hell the mines are all over the place now days like jack rabbits," Henry added while lowering his body into the old chair with a creak. "Hard times create hard decisions no matter. Your mother and I were always lucky. Money dried up with the drought and most folks were hurting. Damn government let bankers go wild. Mortgages weren't the only thing worth shit. Selling mineral rights was the only way out for lots of ranchers," his voice trailed off into other memories. "We was lucky that I could afford to wait that's all," he finished.

Bernie placed a strand of her red hair behind her ear in a quick motion and thought about what her father was saying. Still, selling the land's soul was selling to the devil, past or present; the devil wanted the minerals to be sucked like blood….how true she thought. Yet, Bernie could understand need and had always understood her father's philosophy. She wondered how her mother had really felt back then. Did Mom stay silent like a good ranch wife or did she agree? Hard to know; her mother's thoughts on that subject were carried to the grave.

Bernie considered again. She understood that during the first depression ranchers sold to survive, however, Billy's actions, at this time, seemed sinister. There weren't children to feed with farm prices plummeting for him. He had his portion of the family ranch and livestock prices were at a premium. Billy was set, that is, if he wanted to be a rancher. She sighed. Why did his decisions smell so much like greed to her?

Should she just keep quiet and see how it all played out? Hell, it would affect all four of the Holden children. How would John and Lydia react to Billy's decision? Bernie shook her head then frowned; she waited for her dad to continue.

"Shit, Bernie, this is the family vacation I'm talking about. One week out of the year when family leaves it all behind and travels. Get in those old RVs and go. Get away from all the work and spend time together. Tradition keeps the family solid. Campfire conversation calms folks and clears the air. Did you know that it's been ten years for all of us; we done it for ten years. Your mother knew the value right up until she died," Henry's voice softened. It was an unfair comment, he knew, but Bernie had to go. Second oldest at 55 she was the rock of the family. John, the first born, was too hard headed to always think clearly. Bernie was born one year later and brought all the common sense with her. No, she was the rock. Bernie would somehow keep the family together. She would have to eventually take his place as the peacemaker. At eighty, Henry had to wonder if he would be around much longer to maintain the family's common ground. Who knew? The duty would have to fall to Bernie some day soon.

She petted one of the dogs and thought about her decision. "Are John and Lydia okay with the plans?" Bernie asked.

"Lydia has already changed the dates twice so she's now satisfied. The kids are able to come. John postponed the cattle auction until the week after so yes it's set. We're now waiting for your blessing." Henry held his breath. Bernie could be so damn stubborn when she wasn't comfortable with the situation. Lord knew he understood her frustration. Billy was asking more of the family than they really wanted to give at this point.

Henry did know the implications for the whole Holden clan including his grandkids. Surely Bernie must know that he had thought it out. Compromise was such a difficult issue. More than anything else, Henry wanted his children to follow their dreams. What else could an old man really want? Billy's contrary decision was just poor timing. Why had he waited until right before their vacation to spring on them that he was selling his mineral rights, Henry wondered? Was it a smart move or a stupid one? Being the youngest child had always been hard for Billy. He was never really satisfied with following along; never really satisfied period.

"You've made the reservation for when?" Bernie asked. She was caving in like she knew she would. "Damn," she mumbled.

"June 27th through July 5th. That way we'll be right back after the holiday. Well, honey, let me know soon. We're all counting on you." He pulled himself up out of the chair and searched for his truck keys in his jean pockets. Henry felt that he'd done all he could. She'd come around. Where else could she corner Billy into talking about his decision? Yep, she'd come around.

***

Later on, after a full day of fence mending, Bernie finished the dinner dishes. She paused to stare out the kitchen window at the sunset. North Dakota prairie lands were so incredible. The blue haze veiled the distant land and summer smells traveled through the open window as the temperature began to cool. Her house was small and neat. Just big enough to clean quickly so that you could get back outside for what really mattered.

When she had it built, the location had been most important to her. Sunrise and sunset filled the windows daily. Her house was her sundial. Bernie glanced at her hammer sitting on the kitchen counter. Spatula and hammer seemed always to be side by side.

As she opened the front screen door to sit and relax, Bernie noticed a trail of dust coming up the road. Company? A few minutes later she recognized the truck. What was John up to tonight? Had her dad convinced John to push the camping issue? Interesting to say the least, she thought. Bernie walked out to greet John as he applied the brakes. "Evening, John; everything okay?" She rested her hands on the passenger side window of her brother's truck.

"Fine with me and you? Life treating you good?" John leaned up as he rested his arms over the steering wheel. John was shorter than her father but his red hair and facial features mirrored the photos of her dad thirty years ago.

"Other than Dad pushing the vacation button this morning, it's been a good week. I've fixed the north fence between our properties. It was my turn right?"

"Yeah, I guess it was. Say, would you want to take a ride with me? There are some folks I'd like you to meet. It seems kind of important to me right now. You got a couple of hours to spare?"

It was an unusual request coming from John. For him to be out on the roads at night was unique so Bernie acquiesced. "Where are we going?" she asked.

"Down the valley a-ways closer to Tioga than here, the Jensen Farm. You ever met them; been on their property?" he asked. "It's about forty miles down the road."

Bernie looked back at the house and decided to

leave it open. Rarely did anyone come by the place at night unless they were invited. If they weren't invited, she figured if the door was unlocked they wouldn't break a window. Anyway, John could help if need be.

"Yeah. Let's go." Bernie jumped up into the cab of the truck and settled. "Think I met the wife maybe four years ago at the mining meetings. What a waste of time that was. Remember? Seems like decades ago." She eyed the tall burning tower off in the far distance that burned 24 hours a day. It was her constant reminder about the mining invasion.

"Pretty sure Ashley attended all of those meetings," John said. "Think they built their house about that time. I've kept in touch with them since then. She and Kevin built a beautiful home where they fully intended to raise their two children." John stopped there; he didn't want to influence Bernie's reaction. You didn't preach to Bernie; you showed her. He did continue to paint the picture of the family farm somewhat. "They went the agricultural route raising wheat, alfalfa, flax and corn. Pretty ambitious considering there were grape vines on the property to take care of already when they inherited the old farm. It just shouted for more produce, Kevin told me. Hell they're young and can handle it. Pretty damn good start. Two years later Hydraulic Fracturing came to call. See his grandparents sold the mineral rights during hard times." John was quiet then being content to play 'Show and Tell.'

They traveled through the valley on highway 93 and out onto 124 about 15 miles to where the presence of mining was far more apparent. Bernie had intentionally avoided driving this way. She'd seen the images on television of the toxic filter socks left along the back roads in old junk trucks. When the *Gazetteer* placed the picture of the abandoned gas station filled with the sock debris on their editorial page, it was a complete eye opener; discarded horrible trash from the fracking industry left for the locals to clean up. Their media now called this part of North Dakota, 'Kuwait on the Prairie.' Was it worth it, she pondered? The state politicians were now bragging about North Dakota's employment numbers being highest in the U.S. Plus, the unfathomable growth of population was amazing to her. Could people with their incomes soaring comprehend how the prairie was disappearing? So many questions left unanswered.

They descended down a long sloping hill. On the left of 124 was a large billboard announcing J Meyer Petro. There, unfortunately, was the North Dakota legacy, she thought. Bernie had a very short time to process that scene. From the corner of her eye she saw a huge mining truck, camouflaged in dust, barreling down the newly bulldozed road. She realized almost too late that the driver had no intention of braking at the stop sign onto 124. He was going to round the corner wide so he could get a fast start on the hill.

"John, watch out!" she screamed.

John quickly swerved onto the right shoulder and hit the brakes. The truck making a wide turn at top speed roared down the road without any hesitation. John applied the horn and a finger in the direction of the driver. Finally when the dust had settled, they both let out a thankful sigh. At least fate had been with them. John pulled his truck back onto the highway and proceeded.

Within 50 feet he slowed down at a miniature tractor mailbox which announced that the Jensen clan did indeed live there. The driveway was lined with dusty brown grapevines clinging to the long fence that escorted their truck to the Jensen home. Absent from the vines were any signs of life or fruit. He pointed toward a field of stunted corn stocks; the lack of water had hindered their growth also. The farm house was seated with a little haze hovering around it.

It wasn't natural, Bernie thought. No, it was somehow a different atmosphere. The difference became apparent as they got out of the truck. There was an odd ammonia smell that dominated the air. As they walked up the path toward the house, loud voices broke the evening quiet. The screen door sailed off its' hinges and landed in the yard. Three men flew out the doorway in an explosion of testosterone. Kids from inside screamed.

"Get out of my house you fucking criminals! Haven't you taken enough from us? My kids are sick from the damn stink! Where are my rights? State protects your rights but don't give a shit about my damn rights," Jensen bellowed!

"Mr. Jensen, you are under contract," the guy in the suit yelled! "His 'muscle man' pried Jensen's fists off the lapels of the 'suit guy.' Then for good measure 'Muscles' proceeded to mash Jensen's nose into pulp.

John flew into the fray trying to separate the thug from Kevin. His slight build was no match. 'Muscles' threw John across the yard like a doll.

'Suit' shrieked, "Have we got an understanding yet, Jensen?"

Ashley Jensen charged out the doorway with a frying pan in her hand. She wacked 'Muscles' on the back of his crew cut head. The guy melted into a heap on the ground. "Like my husband said, get off our property, you piece of trash! The contract's maybe on your side but in this house, we respect what rights we have left. Now take your briefcase and crawl back under the rock you came from, lawyer man."

The Jensen children silently blocked the entrance to the house.

'Suit' nudged 'Muscles' with his wing tip shoe and got the beginning of a response. 'Muscles,' half crawling, began moving toward their Land Rover. "You haven't heard the last of this! The company has the mineral rights remember that," 'Suit' shouted safely from the driver's seat. 'Muscles' fell into the passenger side rubbing his head. The Land Rover sped out of the driveway leaving only exhaust in its' wake.

Bernie was in the middle of tending to John. From all apparent signs there weren't any broken bones. Little bruised pride maybe but hopefully nothing was broken. "John, you okay? Move a little so I know you're all right."

"I'm okay. Well, that was a surprise. I'm in it now up close and personal," John said while staggering to his feet.

"Good riddance to bad rubbish!" Ashley Jensen yelled as she helped Kevin stand up. She had gotten a washcloth for his bleeding nose and was tending to other small wounds. "Coffee?" she asked the Holdens.

"Yes," they both answered.

Indeed Bernie calculated as they entered the Jensen home, the Holden clan was now officially in it. Those guys would do some checking and figure out who John was. Life had just gotten a little more complicated. Hopefully, their life wouldn't be as ugly as the poor Jensen clan. Kevin and Ashley were trapped by those legal contracts. Like so many families their grandparents had been enticed by the availability of easy money. Back then the established homesteaders had laughed at oil companies. Their thinking was that those investors couldn't be serious about digging miles below the surface. The ranchers and farmers thought it was like taking candy from a baby. They had no idea back then.

CHAPTER 2

PREPARATIONS TO TRAVEL

Carol Bixler, nicknamed Bix at birth, let Simon out the screen door. She watched as he rustled around in the front yard. The miniature schnoodle, with nose down, checked out the front yard in a flurry. Some type of critter had passed through during the night, Bix thought. During the summer season, wildlife was active in the Colorado Rocky Mountains. Bix loved living in her Blue River home at this time of year. The locals called it Blue Shiver during the winter snows but the summer was stellar. Extreme weather conditions brought extreme beauty; it was hard to beat a high of 75 degrees. Bix smiled as she decided that Blue River was true air conditioning. Opening the windows and doors was so therapeutic.

She slipped into the house and poured her coffee then proceeded back outside to sit on the small deck and watch her dog. The little guy might get into trouble if she didn't keep an eye on him. Bix didn't really know what Simon would do if he ran into a bear which was always a possibility. Deer, moose, fox and bear were highly active in June. Since her property was along the river area and away from the highway, the wildlife could pursue their migratory routes freely. Keeping your property clear of food temptations was the main idea so the wildlife would pass right through.

"No digging, Simon," Bix yelled. Vole mounds were ever present in the front yard and Simon was enthusiastic about their removal. The little critters burrowed and ate their way through the yard every summer. The cat litter box remains had been a natural deterrent but now that the cat was off in Denver with her ex-partner, the Vole activity was excessive. Bix didn't miss the cat hair but she did miss the cat.

Breaking up with her partner had been a traumatic separation. Now for the first time in five years, Bix was truly by herself. There was an extraordinary sense of freedom and relief sprouting. Taking a camping trip in the RV by herself was one step toward that independence. Well she wasn't totally alone; she had her little black co-pilot for company. Yep, pulling the trailer out to pack was truly exciting and Simon was watching intently.

"Come on, Simon, let's get to work, little buddy." She tossed her coffee remains on the daylilies and headed for the garage. Bix pulled the Ford Ranger out and backed it up to the hitch on the 13' Scamp Trailer. It took a few tries of course to get it straight and coupled. The safety chain connected was the next step. Bix then measured to see that the electrical plug was long enough and easy to connect to the truck for travel. Simon followed her around like he was memorizing the process. He wasn't going to let her out of his sight. Bix tossed Simon into the truck and pulled forward a couple feet just to assure herself that things were good to go.

***

Bernie Holden, back in North Dakota, leaned under the hood of her Rialta Winnebago and found the oil dip stick. She pulled it out and eyed the marker. It figured that a little oil was needed. Hell, the Winnie was nineteen years old with 85,000 miles on it. She had bought the thing from a neighbor who had decided to move before fracking dominated White Earth Valley. The price for the motor home had been good at 4,000 bucks. Bernie had traveled to the Buena Vista, Colorado, family reunion for the last five years in it.

Before that time she had been holed up in her parents' second bedroom in their 30' Keystone. She liked to keep her privacy now that she had gotten older. Besides Lydia and Jim had taken over the second bedroom as their kids grew into teenagers. They had surrendered to the kids the pop-up trailer. It all made sense now that her mother had passed on and the kids had gotten bigger and louder. Her dad probably liked having the couple with him during the vacation.

So the plans had been made. John and his wife, Mattie, would travel in their fairly new Jayco 26' palace. Stock shows all year long and the rodeo circuit with Mathew, their son, had made their motor home a necessity. Now, Mathew was studying at CSU and had decided to enroll for the summer session. It was still questionable if he could join them for the long July 4th weekend. Still, to have the tribe of cousins back together would be nice; it was always amusing to watch the grandkids. Bernie had to admit the whole family experience was good for the soul. Hell, the Holden clan with their Colorado cousins, took up half of High Mountain Vista RV Park.

Bernie shut the hood on the Winnebago then circled the trailer checking the tire pressure. She had the compressor ready to add some air knowing that the winter always did its' thing. Satisfied, Bernie began the inventory of equipment. She smiled to herself as she sorted through the outside storage compartment. RV people sure were equipment freaks she thought. You had to love it.

***

Bix was in the middle of sorting her clothes for packing. She ran a hand through her short sandy hair, eyes intent on the sorting when her smart phone rang.

"Hello?"

"This is the High Mountain Vista RV Park," Chelsea Bailey said. "We do have a site open for you and Simon. It's the little campsite near the back with full service available from June 29th to July 5th. The group from Iowa cancelled because we couldn't fit all their trailers in next to each other. We have a large party coming in from North Dakota that takes up over half the park. They're not rowdy but it is a family reunion. There will be commotion. Are you okay with that?" she asked. You would need to check in on Sunday around 11:00. Sound okay?"

"Terrific," Bix said. "The Denver traffic will be going east and we'll be going west. It works for me."

"Then we'll see you Sunday, Bix. Don't need to tell you about the cancellation policy right?" Chelsea hesitated for a moment and then added, "Sure glad to see you're traveling again. It's been awhile."

"I know," Bix murmured. Her acute blue eyes starred off into space gathering thoughts. "A lot has happened; I'll tell you all about it over coffee. I'm buying," Bix added. "See you Sunday then?"

"Definitely. Safe travels, my friend," Chelsea added before she disconnected.

It was a good omen getting that site near the back. Being on the outskirts of the RV community suited Bix just fine. Her first trip as an independent lady was a definite go. Thank heavens she could take advantage of a Sunday beginning. No job to go back to on Monday. Retiring from teaching after 34 years was such a gift. It was incredible to get up out of bed in the mornings and not rush to work. Anyone who said retirement was terrible was crazy and misguided. Retired to Bix meant freedom to be active and not collapsing into a damn chair. Hell life wasn't over; in her mind it was just beginning anew. Another vacation was unfolding. Hot damn!

She had been thinking about writing again. Throughout her life a few attempts had happened in that field; a bad book then an average musical with a friend unfolded. They had presented the musical once; however, time and work washed away that motivation. But now she truly had time. Maybe she could stop being just a writer and become an author. Lord knew she'd read enough mysteries in her lifetime to come up with something worth publishing. It was a great feeling to get another opportunity to try. Retirement was truly a blessing.

The Scamp trailer was part of the whole picture. Traveling to collect experiences from different RV parks was part of her plan. Bix glanced at Simon who had settled at the foot of the bed in the sunlight that streamed in the tall windows of the room. He was reclining on his tummy with feet pointing out. She wondered how he would feel about going. The Scamp was a compact comfortable rig with all the amenities; shower, toilet, heat, air-conditioning, refrigerator and stove. Made in Minnesota the little trailer was very well done; it resembled a marshmallow on wheels. Bix began to feel the seed of enthusiasm sprouting. "Hey Simon, go find one of your toy babies. We're packing for adventure!" Simon shot off the bed to retrieve; play time ever present in his mind.

CHAPTER 3

TRAVELING I-70 COLORADO

Bernie was on the home stretch. The Winnie was pulling the elevation slowly but surely. The Holden caravan had all cleared Denver. They had pulled over and met at the Downieville Exit. Filling up with gas and letting the trailer engines cool during a lunch break was always a smart move. Too many hoods up campers along this stretch of Highway I-70 told a different story. Cooling off the motor was an important part of their traveling routine. The family would also allow 5 minutes between rigs so other motorists wouldn't run into a cluster of slow movers. Courtesy was a good thing Bernie remembered her mother saying many years ago. Why not? They were on vacation.

The clan had been on the road for three days. After years of driving this way, their over nights were at the same parks. Yep, they did have their routine down.

Bernie had been relieved that during the last weeks no visit from the mining company had occurred. John hadn't said anything but she could feel his concern. Keeping an eye out had been an ever present and unspoken bond between them since the Jensen visit. Maybe the company had their hands full what with lawyers and the Jensen family. For whatever reason, it was quiet. Thank heavens, Bernie thought.

John and Mattie were up front in their Jayco somewhere probably approaching the Eisenhower Tunnel by now. After that it was all downhill. They had climbed the worst in elevation and now would descend Loveland Pass. As if on cue a call came in from Mattie's cell. Bernie flipped on the cab speaker. "Hey, you guys at the tunnel yet?" she asked.

"Just calling to tell you that we've been stopped for a thirty minute rock mitigation delay. CDOT has finished the blasting and are cleaning up with a bulldozer as we speak. Actually, it's sort of entertaining and far better than to be under some of those boulders. I'm reading my book and John's got the hood up tinkering. You know how he is."

"Good to know what's happening. I'm not too far behind you and just now had to stop. Want me to contact Dad and Lydia?" Bernie asked.

"Sure. My book is just getting good. See you in a bit."

Bernie turned off the Winnie and got out to stretch. She looked out at the view. Colorado Mountains never ceased to amaze her. There was a little snow still present at over eleven thousand feet.

It was the end of June for heaven's sake; must have been an incredible winter she thought. The sky was crystal clear and so deep in color that it took your breath away. Well there could be lots worse places to be held up in traffic. People had begun to get out of their cars to fritter away time.

The air had definitely cooled off since Denver's 92 degrees. Bernie opened a couple of windows. "Nice," she mumbled. She searched the refrigerator for a bottle of tea then pulled out a lawn chair and sat down outside. Lydia was probably riding with Dad she thought. It would be a better ride than plugging along with Jim and the kids. Bernie activated her phone and waited. "Hey Sis, have you had to stop yet?" she asked.

"Just. What's happening?"

"Mattie says rock mitigation up ahead so relax. Has Billy called you yet? Would be great to know what's going on with him. Always some type of drama, I know."

Lydia hesitated for a moment then put her hand over the phone and said to her dad, "You want to stretch your legs and go tell Jim that the highway department is doing rock mitigation?" There was a pause while Henry must have gotten out and left. "Well the gossip has it that Billy's bringing a lady and has rented some new rig so he can impress Miss Date. I do believe that they are hitting Denver night life and Blackhawk Casino. He called me late last night when he knew everyone would be asleep."

"You're kidding?" Bernie shrieked and then reconsidered. "On second thought that's just what he's doing. Drops a bombshell about selling his mineral rights and upsets the hell out of John then pulls this stunt. Nothing like pissing off the whole damn bunch," Bernie added. She took a drink of the chilled tea while processing. "Unbelievable."

Lydia laughed then said, "Believable. Once again darling Billy has found a way to be on center stage. Once the baby; always the baby. Mother knew how to rein in my baby brother. Dad just seems to let him go wherever," she added.

"Ain't that the truth. I asked Dad if Billy had changed the inheritance clause in his most recent will. Of course Dad ignored the comment which I found rather scary to say the least."

"It wouldn't surprise me if Billy's gotten that shyster of a lawyer involved somehow. What's the guy's name? I only know him by his reputation from high school and that's horrible enough. John always said that he lived under a rock," Lydia chuckled.

"Bellows," Bernie said. "Guess what that idiot is working on now?" I know exactly why he came back to North Dakota after all these years. What do you suppose he wants?"

"Don't know but I'm sure you'll tell me."

"If that slime has his way the oil companies will take over the Missouri River shoreline all the way through North Dakota. Now there's a disaster about to happen. I had the displeasure of listening to him during one of the state hearings last month. Lord help us all," Bernie grumbled. "But hey, we're on vacation; don't get me started." Bernie decided that a different tact was in order. Why rain on this parade now? It would all come out later one way or

21

another she was sure. "On a better note, do we know if Mathew is coming up from CSU? Sort of hope he is. I haven't seen him since Christmas. He always brings a positive view of the future. I like that."

"I heard that he's going to come up before the Fourth. Apparently, he has a hot date on campus for the Fourth which is nice to hear. Mattie told me that he was into dating one young lady in particular. Kid deserves the best."

"Agreed," Bernie added. "Well Sis, looks like it's time to get a move on. The cars are starting their engines up ahead so I'll talk to you later. Been real. Bye." Bernie disconnected and threw her lawn chair in storage. Other than hearing about Billy, she had enjoyed the view and the weather. She shut the windows and started up the Winnie.

The traffic slowly began to creep forward. Some cars jumped into the outer lane so they could be the first to charge forward into the Eisenhower Tunnel. Bernie could see the top of John's Jayco up ahead now. He was just entering the tunnel. There were probably 15 cars between them at this point. Bernie flipped on her lights as she entered the dark tunnel; she could smell the pent up gas fumes coming through the vents. Out of nowhere a SUV careened around her dangerously close to the Winnie. It was completely oblivious of the traffic rules; fifty miles an hour and no lane changes. The black streak viciously honked and jockeyed for position in traffic up ahead. Let that damn car out of here, she thought. As if on cue the sunlight announced the opening. The tunnel poured the impatient traffic out into Summit County.

It was an incredible vista to process as she emerged from the mountain's inner body. There was nothing like being in the clouds at twelve thousand feet while beginning the descent. It left your heart in your throat with the sheer beauty and power of what God could imagine.

Bernie turned off her lights and shifted the Winnie down in gear so she wouldn't have to break constantly. Descent was emergency lights blinking and slower speeds for RVs' and semi-trucks in the far right lane. Should be a nice slow go, she thought with relief. It was a great change in routine.

CHAPTER 4

CRASH

Bernie checked the road up ahead to see where John was at this point. The Jayco was slowly progressing down the grade in the far right lane. John had on the emergency lights and was snuggled in back of two trucks carrying heavy loads. The procession was two switchbacks ahead in the distance and entering into a long straight decline.

As Bernie cleared the two switchbacks, she saw that damn black SUV again. The car swerved from one lane to the other as it accelerated through traffic. It was moving like a defense missile seeking a target. Bernie suddenly realized that the target was John's Jayco! She grabbed her cell. Before the call connected, Bernie began screaming, "Mattie! Watch out! The car on you left!" Bernie watched in horror.

John felt the impact of the car butting his RV! The sound echoed through the rig creating a mammoth growl. The back of the Jayco began to fishtail dangerously. Its' wheels lifted off the road into a dance of balance. Both Mattie and John screamed in unison; neither one aware of their howl! Mattie covered her face and prepared for the inevitable.

John, fortunately, saw the emergency truck exit ramp up ahead. He swerved the steering wheel right and prayed. The gravel ramp replaced the smooth highway pavement. He could hear the rocks pelting the windows. The tires began straining as they spit out gravel. The RV sped up the steep grade grabbing for any and all support. John applied pressure on the brakes as the rig finally slowed to a stop.

Mattie reached over and touched his shoulder. "Dear Lord," she whispered.

Finally, John allowed himself the luxury of breathing again. The Jayco had survived the attack. He slowly shifted the motor into reverse and crept down the incline. It had taken at least thirty feet of distance to stop the rig's momentum. The relief began to flow through John's body. At the bottom of the exit, he put the rig in park and turned the motor off.

"Unbelievable. What was that guy doing? Road rage?" John speculated as he hugged Mattie. They melted together for a few seconds in silence. Safe and together was all that mattered.

Bernie had pulled over as quickly as she could. The highway had some shoulder space 50 feet down from the emergency exit. She leaped out and started backtracking to John and Mattie. It seemed Bernie was moving in slow motion as she tried to hurry up the slope. Her lungs began straining for any oxygen they could get. John and Mattie opened the doors of the RV to inspect the damage as Bernie arrived too out of breath to say anything immediately. She was physically exhausted and emotionally spent.

John was now standing with his hands on his hips staring at the large ugly dent located around the left back wheel. The gash had black paint mixed in with the metal exposure. "Damn," he mumbled.

Bernie could hear some relief in John's tone. He put his arm around her and gave a reassuring hug.

"Whew," was the only comment she could muster. The air was slowly returning to her lungs. Mattie placed a hand on Bernie's shoulder in commiseration. They stood close while watching John. He crawled under the Jayco to check the axle and wheels for damage. John appeared a few minutes later. Mattie and Bernie waited for the prognosis. "I think we got lucky," he stated. Mattie, how about calling for a tow? Tell them to tow us into Silverthorne to the nearest mechanic that can check it all out and realign the wheels. Better safe than sorry before we continue down the road. As Mattie disappeared into the RV, John glanced at Bernie. "What do you think happened?"

"I think it was intentional. I caught sight of that SUV in the tunnel. He passed all of us like a bat out of hell. John, he was after you. I think he targeted you. That car jumped both lanes and made a beeline for the Jayco. There was nothing wrong with his car; it was intentional. We need to report this accident to the police and have them try to find a black Chevy. I didn't catch the license plate of course. It all happened so damn fast."

"Well I'll have plenty of time this afternoon to chat with the highway patrol. Of course the guy will be in Utah before anyone actually looks for him. All we have to go on is the dent and paint he received from the Jayco."

Mattie walked toward them finishing the call. "Yes, we're on the first emergency truck ramp. The rig is green and tan." She listened for a few seconds then added, "Thanks." She flipped her cell phone shut and looked at the expressions on their faces. "What?"

"Bernie doesn't think it was an accident. That car headed right for us," John said shifting his position to stare at Mattie.

"Why?" Mattie began to process what he was saying as the thought occurred to her, the fight; she was now on the same page. "You two think it has to do with the Jensen encounter, right?" Mattie looked at them. She interpreted the silence as a yes. "What happens now?" she asked.

"Why don't you go with Bernie and get us checked in at Buena Vista. I'll be there as soon as I can. It certainly is over for today. If you two go ahead, Dad and Lydia won't worry so much. Maybe give them a call as you go down the road and tell them I had a minor accident and will catch up. If I'm still on the roadside when they pass, tell them to go on. No need to cause another accident on this busy highway."

Mattie hesitated, tossed her black hair back and looked deeply into John's eyes.

"Please?" John asked.

"You will be careful?" Bernie said. She got a nod from John.

They stopped at the Jayco so Mattie could pick up a few items and then started down the grade to the Winnie. Mattie became silent as they walked. Bernie felt a tightening in her stomach. Their vacation had just taken on an evil turn. Would the family be safe at High Mountain Vista this summer? Hopefully, John's close call would be the end of any attempt against the Holden family. She couldn't convince herself of that concept as she got into the Winnie and unlocked the passenger side for Mattie. Bernie resolved to tell the whole family what had actually happened. No sugar coating this time. They all had to be aware of any danger that might come their way. What would her dad say and what the hell was Billy thinking? Would there be more information added to the picture? Bernie didn't know, but she was ready to find out.

Mattie and Bernie were busy for the rest of the trip. Mattie's brown eyes grew large as she talked on speaker phone with Lydia. The adrenaline was still intense as she answered all of Lydia's detailed questions.

Finally, Lydia was satisfied and in agreement with Bernie about having a family meeting. "The sooner the better," she said. "This family has been keeping secrets entirely too long lately. Billy finally called this afternoon. He and the girlfriend will be arriving tonight after dinner. I say hit him early before the beer makes him comatose and before Henry goes to bed. Let's plan this event for 7:00," Lydia reconnoitered. "I'll talk Jim into taking the kids for ice cream. I can fill him in later."

"I think that sounds good to me," Mattie agreed. "Bernie?" she glanced over for her sister-in law's reaction.

Bernie nodded and turned onto Highway 24 at Copper Mountain. They had to go through Leadville then the next stop was Buena Vista. Did the black SUV know where they were going? Was it already there making plans? Bernie began to keep a watchful eye. Fortunately, there was only 34 miles to go. Bernie settled back for the last of this trip. She was really glad that Lydia was organizing the family meeting. Billy had a hard time saying no to Lydia. Those two were the curly redheads; they should have been twins, Bernie thought. They always had this silent communication between each other. Lydia could always get Billy to come clean and confess whatever he was doing. She and John were close but not like Lydia and Billy. Thank heavens Lydia also saw Billy's short comings. She had a great grasp on reality.

CHAPTER 5

SETTLING IN

Mattie Holden had sent Bernie toward the High Mountain Vista Office. Since John was busy she had given Bernie the task of checking in for the whole family. Mattie stayed in the Winnie being entirely content to simply sit and process her feelings while she waited. Poor John, she thought. Such a hassle the whole day had been. John had called to say he was starting down the road; Mattie was relieved. As she settled back to wait, a large tinted window rig had just turned in from the road. It sped past not stopping at the office. Probably went into town for groceries she imagined. Not a care in the world, she thought with envy. However, they were going too fast for the RV community. She checked for kids in the road but didn't see any. Good. There had been enough excitement today for anyone's vacation.

How in the world was all this happening to her

family? They were ranchers for heaven sakes raising children and trying to be good people. Being run off the road was crazy. Mattie could feel the tension growing; she inhaled slowly and tried to calmed herself. It was over she told herself. The dust would settle and life would go on; she would now stop being an alarmist. "Time to relax, Mattie, just relax," she mumbled to herself out loud. Life would get back to normal Mattie hoped. She watched Bernie open the screen door and disappear into the office.

The room had a welcoming atmosphere Bernie thought as she closed the door. It was a sunny office with a long counter adorned with tourist curios. Small bear statues in different poses smiled a welcome. The room had supplies in freezer and refrigerator units along the far wall. An additional little fridge stood ten feet from the others with a 'worms' sign. At least the bait wasn't next to the milk Bernie thought as she rang the bell. She picked up a site map of the camp and waited for Chelsea or Bob Bailey to come out of the back where the family residence was located.

"Hey Bernie, long time no see," Chelsea said with a big friendly smile. "Got you the sites Henry wanted. Are you the first to get here?"

"Yep. Two rigs are right behind me and then John will pull in later. He had a fender-bender coming out of the tunnel so he'll be in later. And, you know Billy will be his usual late self."

"Sorry to hear about John's mishap. If he needs a mechanic or any help, my Bob can give him a hand. We can recommend a mechanic in Buena Vista if need be."

"Thanks Chelsea. I'll make sure he knows. How's business been?"

"Good. We had quite a few hunters last fall and we can't complain about summer business. Lots of folks coming back for another summer plus new reservations are up. Amazing what nice weather can do."

"And it might be that you two run a nice place," Bernie said as she signed the register and paid for the week with cash. She had the total amount for the immediate family. John usually did the honors so Mattie had given Bernie the envelope on the way from Silverthorne. "I'll remind everyone to come on up and sign in sometime this evening," she added.

Henry had always taken the responsibility to pay for everyone. The family didn't argue with him about the money. He did it because it was his family obligation and it would have insulted him if someone dared to try and pay. John had given up trying years ago. First trailer in carried the money in cash from Henry including a generous tip naturally.

Mattie helped Bernie set up as they settle in E15. It was the last full site in a long line that ran from north to south, 1 to 16. Each site had a narrow expanse of grass with picnic table plus a tree. The Holden clan from both North Dakota and Colorado occupied almost all the D and E sites. They were the second group of spaces east of the office. The Community Center was on the east side of their sites snuggled in with the permanent trailer residences. There were quite a few folks who chose to stay in the park full time because of the incredible environment. Bernie could see why as she looked around at the trees and how well the area was maintained. Her site was as far south from the road as the park went. There was one lot farther south and it was half the size of her space, E16. Bernie wondered what rig would occupy that site; a pop-up maybe?

It took them a half hour to set up. Full hook ups meant water, sewer and electrical either 30 or 50 amps. The rest of the family began pulling in on the north of Bernie's Winnebago. Site 14 was where Henry pulled in his Keystone Cougar. His large unit would shade Bernie during the afternoon. She helped her dad park and hook-up the facilities while Mattie went up the line to E11 where Jim and Lydia pulled in the pop- up trailer. John and Billy's trailers would occupy E12 and 13. It was a busy afternoon.

Bernie had made it a point to tell everyone about the 7:00 PM meeting. Hopefully, Billy would pull in sometime soon. At 5:30 most of the work was done and everyone retreated to their rigs for a little privacy. Mattie went to Henry's unit and made him dinner. She knew John would also be hungry when he arrived.

"So what's happening?" Henry asked Mattie as he set the table at the dinette. "You and Bernie have been awfully quiet about John's accident. What happened?"

"Dad, quite honestly John and Bernie don't think it was an accident."

"Why? What do you mean? What made them think that?"

"Bernie saw the SUV head directly for our Jayco. It crossed two lanes then hit us." Mattie placed the plate of grilled cheese sandwiches on the table and turned back to the stove for the tomato soup. She had left two sandwiches off the grill and would cook them when John appeared. "Thank heavens that John saw the emergency exit. I don't know what would have happened if it hadn't been there."

Henry paused, spoon in hand, and looked at Mattie. It was hard to process that the family had been attacked. It just didn't make sense. Who would hurt them and for what reason he wondered? It was truly hard to grasp.

Mattie sat down and stared at him for a few seconds. She was debating what else to say at this point. "Dad, John feels that it has to do with the assault that happened at the Jensen Farm. He'll explain when he gets here."

Henry became slightly afraid for his family. Brothers and sisters were in disagreement about the future. This whole damn mineral rights thing was taking such an ugly turn for them. Hell, if the mining companies had stayed out of North Dakota, life would have been so much simpler. The ranch life should be all that existed; nothing else should matter. He wished that Margaret was still alive and could help him decide what to do and how to council everyone. Life had gotten so complicated lately.

CHAPTER 6

FAMILY FEUD AT 7:00

"You son of a bitch, the ranch is the family. You act like big oil has all the damn answers! You can't get enough can you, Billy?" When does it stop? When do you stop?" John yelled pointing an accusing finger in Billy's face.

"The future is fracking," Billy yelled at John and moved forward. "Haven't you figured that out yet? Holy shit most of the ranchers in the valley see the writing on the wall. You either get in financially or dry up in your old ways. The American Indians tried that route and look what it got them? Wake up, John!"

"Now Billy, slow down," said Henry as he placed his hand on Billy's shoulder. Stopping his youngest son had never been easy. Henry turned to John and said,

"You need to listen to what Billy is saying. You may not like it but you need to listen."

"Why, Dad? Where do you stand in all of this? What's your part in this greedy mess?" John retaliated.

"I'm standing with the family and family interests, John. Billy has a right to feel the way he does. Just like you have a right."

"He can, with your blessing, sell his mineral rights and destroy ranching for the rest of us? Is that what you're saying? I can't believe it. It's the *Red Queen Syndrome* coming to destroy all of us whether we want it or not." John threw up his arms and alternated his cold-eyed glare from Billy to Henry.

"What do you mean by that?" Billy asked with a smirk.

"Come on that's bullshit, Billy. You know damn well what the *Red Queen Syndrome* means. It's a testament to oil production greed right out of *Alice through the Looking Glass*. It says, and I quote, 'It takes all the running you can do to keep in the same place.' Big oil adopted that quotation because they need to drill 6,000 new wells per year to just keep up with oil demand. They're going to suck North Dakota dry then move on and we're going down with all the rest of the ranchers. Wait until they export our damn oil to other countries and then say they need more. You can't be serious?"

"It's my inheritance and I can do what I damn well please thank-you-very-much. Truth is, I don't want to be a rancher for my whole life! Enough is enough!" Billy screamed. "Dad has released me from the mineral part of the deed. In fact, he has signed over his mineral rights for half of his ranch to me so stop acting like you control the fucking future! The family fortune is not all yours; being the oldest son doesn't make it so!" Billy grabbed John, spun him around and glowered; his anger skyrocketing into emotions that would never be forgiven or forgotten.

Lydia gasped and jumped between them before it was too late!

"Enough!" Bernie thundered. She stood up, fists clenched, as she sought control. "You are brothers and you will not forget that." Bernie turned to confront Henry. "Dad, I want to know if you have created a new will." Her earnest gaze now demanded an answer from her father; Bernie waited. Henry wouldn't look at her. She persistently continued, "Have you given all these mineral rights to Billy without telling the rest of us or is it just in the works?" The family waited for the answer.

"I haven't signed it yet," he hedged. "Billy and I have been talking...." Henry fell into a chair and looked at the floor.

"With the help of Bellows? That man's reputation in White Earth ought to speak volumes!" Bernie blurted.

"Who's Bellows?" Mattie questioned.

"A snake of a man that I went to high school with before he disappeared back East to get his degree," John answered.

"He's a good lawyer! You just hate him because he's smart enough to work for the oil companies," Billy shouted. "He understands the future."

"No Billy, working for big money doesn't make Bellows smart. It makes him greedy and ambitious," Bernie answered. "You know that he's working with the oil industry to purchase all the ranches along the Missouri River shoreline, don't you? If they are successful, the river will be polluted all the way through North Dakota. Hell why stop at the border. They'll make a run for the gulf. You know that don't you?"

"Well…." Billy choked. He didn't look at Bernie either.

"You don't care?" she asked with her hands on her hips.

The defiant look on Billy's face said it all. "I care as much as all the other ranchers making $80,000 a month for selling mineral rights. Let them lease it for 25 years then I get my ranch back. I can then sit on my porch and hire all the help I'd need. Like a…like a plantation."

"Is that what you want, Billy?" John asked. "There was a lot of blood spilled on those plantations that you think were so great. Lots of folks died and the country went to war over that nightmare. Brother against brother. In the end their world of luxury collapsed. You haven't heard the last of this, little brother and neither have you, Dad. The talking ain't done," John hissed as he took his rage outside.

Mattie started after John but then turned back to look at Henry. "How could you make such a huge decision and then keep it to yourself? Is that what you call good for the family?" She left the RV shaking her head in disbelief.

Bernie looked back and forth from her father to Billy. "Shame on both of you." With that comment

Bernie went back to the Winnie to wrestle with her own convictions.

Lydia said softly, "Gentlemen, you need to talk and make this right. I'm spending the night with the kids in the pop-up. At least they're honest about what they think." With that comment she left.

Billy and Henry were left to consider their dilemma in a very quiet RV. Henry knew that Lydia was correct. He did need to make things right. How? Now that was a big question. "I'll talk with you tomorrow, Billy. Right now I'm really tired and not feeling well." Billy opened his mouth to say something but Henry held up a hand in warning. It was over for tonight. Their family meeting had exploded into a disaster. What was done was done.

CHAPTER 7

SUNDAY PLANNING

It was Sunday and *The Summit* was tossed on the kitchen counter. It was time to take a break Bix decided. She had just finished adding all the food to the trailer. Her list was completed. She unfolded the newspaper to checkout the front page. It read, 'Recreational Vehicle is forced off I-70 near Tunnel!' Wow. Not totally surprising, she thought. Every summer there seemed to be so much more road construction and tourist travel. It was a good and bad scenario. Sure the economy was blossoming but there was a price to pay. Bix tried to limit her trips east to Denver because of the construction and the heat of summer. Being retired she could choose. One of the major perks of retirement she thought. Still people did have to travel eventually.

Bix sat down on the couch and decided to read the article before she pulled out to go to High

Mountain Vista. There was time. It would take maybe an hour and a half to get there and she couldn't check in until 11:00. Simon Schnoodle jumped up on the couch also. He could always catch a little nap between events. She began to read the article which made it sound more like road rage than fatigue. That was scary for anyone traveling the road. It made no sense to her; what were they hurrying for, their death? After the day's horoscope and local articles, Bix took the paper out to the trailer. It would now become fire starter in its' next life.

She came back in and began going through her to-do list one more time. Closing up the house and making sure that being gone a week wouldn't cause problems was an important detail. A few minutes later after checking all the lights one more time, Bix locked the front door. She checked her watch. "Perfect timing, little guy," she told Simon as he turned his head to the side and watched with interest. Bix tossed him in the truck passenger seat and gave his head a scratch before she shut the door. They pulled the Ford Ranger and Scamp Trailer out of the yard and turned south on highway 9 joining the Sunday traffic. A stellar day Bix noticed as they began the climb through the far south end of Summit County.

The Ford Ranger slowly crawled over Hoosier Pass with Bix shifting into third gear then second gear then first gear then repeating the process. Pulling the Scamp through the tight switchbacks of Hoosier Pass was a challenge for anyone. She relaxed her muscles as she approached the summit and started the decline into Mosquito Gulch. Through Alma then Fairplay and west on 285 toward Buena Vista was the game plan. Arid sage and yucca replaced spruce and pine within 20 miles of her home. From alpine to arid was always a breath taking change. Bix had no idea how immense the change would become for everyone at High Mountain Vista.

***

Sunday morning broke with cooler tempers for the Holden family. Stubborn silence dominated the men folk Bernie noticed. She was not surprised. Fortunately, Billy had left his date in the rented King of the Road Fifth Wheel last night. It would have been one hell of an introduction for her to the Holdens. An awkward silence was better at this point.

Bernie stood by her trailer watching Lydia approach. They had decided to meet and walk along the old railroad tracks at the far south end of the park. It was isolated back there and would give the sisters some privacy to talk. They fell into a comfortable hiking tempo in silence for the first quarter mile putting the camp behind them. "Thanks for stepping in last night. I was too shocked to move at first," Bernie confessed. "It has been decades since I've seen John and Billy get into it like that. And Dad, taking sides with Billy over John. He's always been at least fair on the surface. I know things changed after Mom died but I didn't realize how much."

"How long do you suppose Billy and Dad have been planning this bombshell?" Lydia asked. "Billy has been spending lots of time with Dad. I figured it was because he saw how lonely Dad was."

"I'll bet you it's since Billy met Bellows and his business partners. I'm sure there's some type of bonus in this for Billy. He not only lives comfortably for the rest of his life with the lease but he gets a gift of some sort. Something that makes it so he can't turn it down but he can turn against family. I wonder," Bernie pondered.

"The whole thing makes me sick, Bernie. I hate to see the family relationship destroyed. I thought Billy saw Dad's loneliness and decided to take up the slack after Mom died. The rest of us were so busy that we probably did neglect Dad. I so wanted to believe that Billy's intentions had been good."

Bernie began to feel anger again. "Good? How do you steal from family and turn it into some cockeyed notion where, you believe, that they owe you? That's not reality but out and out bullshit," Bernie said. She had stopped walking and stared at Lydia. Bernie knew that she had been harsh but to gloss over Billy's devious scheme was totally incomprehensible. The truth had to be faced now; Lydia couldn't twist the facts to protect Billy. They were beyond that nonsense.

The frustration had been building in Lydia also. She sputtered out in a frustrated cry, "You know how I feel about Billy Now, I really don't understand what he's thinking. It hurts. Damn it," she cried. "He's intentionally blocking me out," Lydia added through the tears that had started falling. She had been brave and held it together last night but today with just Bernie the flood gates opened.

Bernie's heart broke for Lydia. Billy had been Lydia's confidant. She and Lydia were sisters but were so different in what they needed from life. Close and yet so far apart she thought. There were secrets in that closet. Things that had never been said out loud yet probably understood. Hell, Bernie hated to see any woman cry. "Lydia, I'm sorry. I should have realized that this is much more for you." The word 'betrayed' came into Bernie's mind. Poor Lydia was suffering the betrayal by her best friend. How cruel. "What did Jim think after you told him last night?"

"He's devastated. We both have worked so hard on the ranch. Ever since I met him in 4H in high school, I knew how much he loved the land. We both know that mineral rights dominant surface rights and that's the law. Billy has no idea and I'm not sure he will ever understand the true meaning. What it would mean to lose the prairies. It would be like cutting our hearts out. It could destroy Jim; I can't stand that," she sobbed.

Lydia fell into Bernie's arms with the flood of tears shaking both of their bodies. Bernie shut her eyes and breathed in unison with Lydia. She held on as tight as she could. Comfort was such a nebulous quantity in life. What to do when you feel a person's heart shatter in your arms? What can you truly offer, she thought? Finally the tide of tears finished and left Lydia with hiccups. Hiccup then silent then hiccup was the natural conclusion. Lydia put her hand over her mouth and whispered an embarrassed, "Sorry."

"For what?" Bernie asked. "We're in a ton of hurt here."

They began to walk back. Both women lost in their own thoughts. Then as women will do and have done for centuries, they began the inherent process of solving the dilemma. Their mother wasn't here to help but they would take on the job of mending the family; ranch women did that.

Hell all women possessed that instinct, Bernie realized. "What can we do, Lydia?"

"I am going to question Billy so I can figure out what he is truly planning and why," Lydia said. "Deep down inside he can't be happy with the pain he is causing. Maybe I can talk some sense into him."

"Guess I could talk with Dad and try to find out how deep he is into Billy's plan and why," Bernie added.

As they entered the campgrounds the two women split without another word; both lost in thought about accomplishing their goal. Trying to bring the family back together would be no easy task.

CHAPTER 8

IN SEARCH OF COMMON GROUND

Bix had checked in and wheeled on down to site E16. The site was small in size but had the most privacy. She had always been a person who liked to be on the outskirts of a community. It gave one the option of joining or just watching. Bix liked to study people and that was a given.

She had just opened the door of the truck and taken Simon out to put him on his leash. Right as she leaned down, Simon sprinted off toward a tall lady with short red hair coming up from the old abandoned railroad tracks.

Simon headed directly forward as if he had known her all his life. Dogs were equal opportunity critters; they just assume everyone will love them. This was one of those times. "Simon," Bix yelled to no avail.

She began walking over to the lady to retrieve her dog. Simon was lost in the enthusiasm of finding a new friend.

"Sorry. He can't help himself," Bix chuckled.

"It's okay. I already miss my ranch dogs. Didn't bring a one this year and I do need my dog hit," Bernie said standing up with Simon in her arms. "Simon, you say? Cute little guy. Usually not crazy about little dogs but I can definitely make an exception for this one. Right, Simon?" He stared at her with all the adoration that he could muster. My name is Bernie Holden from North Dakota," she commented continuing to scratch under Simon's ear.

"Bix or Carol Bixler and I hale from Blue River, Colorado. Glad to meet you. And, this is Simon Schnoodle; half schnauzer half poodle"

"He is too cute and a very nice dog. She patted his head while Simon panted. You don't live far from here then?" Bernie questioned. "Changing environment I assume?" She put out her hand for the leash and attached it to Simon who now complied with no problem. Bernie put him down. The little dog calmed down and stared up at her. He was delighted with the new friend he had made.

"Yep. Nice to travel over the pass and enjoy this RV camp," Bix added.

"Bix? Must be a nickname then?" Bernie questioned.

"One of the first words that I learned to say. My father and mother never really thought I was a Carol. My grandmother wanted the family name 'Carol' so they christened me then proceeded to call me Bix. It all worked out."

"Bix it is then," Bernie said. "I was wondering

what kind of rig would occupy that site. Your Scamp is a perfect fit. 30 amp?"

"Yep," Bix said as they walked toward the trailer, her white marshmallow. "Got all the comforts I need: shower, air conditioning, toilet and kitchen."

"Nice. How long is it, twelve feet?" Bernie asked.

"13 feet and 1300 pounds so my Ranger can do the job," Bix said.

"Good combo. I'm in the Winnie over there," Bernie pointed. "So neighbor, I'll see you later."

"Sounds like a plan," Bix answered then walked back to begin the process of hook-up. She tied Simon to the truck bumper on his longer leash and tossed his doggie bed under the truck in the shade.

Part of the RV tradition was to be quick and efficient in your setup process. With tool box out and ready for action, Bix began the routine. First, she plugged in the 30 amp connector to the electrical box on site 16 to get the refrigerator and lights going. For the second task, Bix pulled on her gloves. The tubing for the toilet and the grey water tubing from the sink joined into a Y connection that emptied into the sewer disposal ground opening. Finished with that ugly task, she tossed off her gloves and got the white drinking water hose attached to the site spigot. Bix was left with turning on the propane tank and lighting the hot water tank. Lighting the heater wasn't too hard after one figured out what the pilot looked like. Bix used one of those propane lighters with the longer wick so she could reach it easily. A sigh of relief escaped from her mouth when the task was finished.

She knew that there were at least five men watching her to see if she needed help. They would have been glad to assist. That was the way of life in RV parks. People were open to establishing new friends and experiences. People would meet once and then move on. There was a little gypsy in all of them, she thought. These well meaning gestures were nice except her ego wouldn't allow it. If you were going to haul a trailer then you needed to know how to hook-up the rig yourself. Hopefully, the guys were impressed with her handy work. Simon raised his head as Bix tossed the last of the tools back into the box; he didn't seem too impressed as he rolled onto his back to sleep. Oh well, she thought.

As Bix prepared to go inside the trailer, she noticed a lady with curly red hair come out of a pop-up and go toward a huge King of the Road Fifth Wheel. The rig had to be over 30 feet in length. Bix could see that Bernie had to be related to this lady. The red hair was a dead give-away.

Simon, by this time, was up and wanting to come in the trailer. They disappeared into the Scamp to organize the place for their stay

***

Lydia knocked on Billy's door once. When nothing happened she pounded louder. Her insistence was finally met with a sleepy Billy peeking out. His hair was standing on end.

"We need to talk now, Billy. I am not going

away," Lydia announced.

Billy shrugged and opened the door. "Suit yourself, Sis." he said. Billy turned back into the trailer and plopped on the couch while finishing a yawn. "Guess you couldn't wait any longer?" he sneered.

"How long have you known what you were going to do? Seems to me we all have waited long enough to be informed of your decision. I think you know how disappointed I am." Lydia sat down across from Billy and waited.

Billy glanced at the bedroom door then got up and closed it quietly. "Why would I tell you? I knew that you and Jim would have a fit. When it comes to the land, you go ballistic. We can't talk about the ranch without you losing it. I'm fucking tired of ranching. Do you understand how trapped I feel? There has to be more for me than cattle and crops. Dad knows that about me. I'm surprised that you don't," he added.

"It doesn't make it right, Billy. You could have come to us and talked about selling your part of the ranch to us."

"You think you guys could make an offer that would even come close to what the oil companies are offering for just mineral rights? Come on, Lydia, you know better."

"We should have at least gotten the opportunity to put something together. Maybe not all at once but over time."

"I want my money now before I'm old. I have plans damn it. And trust me, they don't include ranching. Coffee?" Billy pulled himself off the couch and went toward the kitchen intentionally putting space between himself and Lydia. Arguing with her had never been easy.

As if on cue the bedroom door opened. A woman who Lydia had never seen before came out partially dressed. She was older than Billy by maybe ten years Lydia judged. Her blond hair was right out of the bottle. Eeeeeek, Lydia thought.

"What's going on, Billy honey?" Blondie asked.

"This is my sister. She isn't too happy with my ranch decisions," Billy grumbled. "Never too early or inconvenient to argue with family, right, Lydia?" he added.

Lydia ignored Billy for the moment and offered her hand. "Hi, I'm Lydia Robertson."

"Bethany Bellows," the lady offered while watching Billy lost in the activity of making coffee. "Nice to meet you, I think. Everyone calls me BB by the way." Billy ignored the obvious social faux pas of no introductions. She accepted Lydia's hand with a wet noodle shake. "Think I'll visit the bathroom and try to tidy up before someone else comes knocking on the door." With that, BB disappeared into the bathroom.

"Is that Bellows as in the lawyer's daughter?" Lydia asked. Her head was spinning. The pieces of Billy's decision were all coming together in her mind. Now she knew what he was thinking or at least she thought she did.

"That would be correct." Billy turned around and faced Lydia. "What of it?"

"What of it? Is she the reason that you're ready to sell out your family? Oh Billy, please," Lydia sighed.

"Look, stay out of my personal life. I don't need your blessing. I want off of the fucking ranch. BB and I are maybe in love and for once I'm feeling positive about my future. Just one day without cow shit on my shoes would be fantastic. Surely you can understand that, Lydia? Don't you ever sit back and think about something more than the land?" Billy hissed.

"At what price, Billy? You'd sell your family down the river for what you want." Lydia could feel herself holding back tears. "You know mining will not only destroy every living thing on your ranch but the air will begin smelling like ammonia and the well water will ignite with a match. The cattle will die from the chemical laden dust on their feed. Not to mention someone will get killed on the roads. You got any idea how many kids have been killed on the Indian Reservation roads? How about your niece and nephews? There will be trucks roaring down the roads with no care for the living. My God, Billy, surely you are aware of the repercussions. Is your decision worth all of that?"

"Have you ever thought about the fact that it's no big deal; all hearsay. It will all come back in time like everyone says; the environment ain't lost forever. You don't like the fact that gas is 20 percent less expensive now days because of fracking? That North Dakota doesn't have unemployment lines like the rest of the country? That leases are the way of the future for ranchers? The good outweighs the bad in my mind. Bruised feelings aren't near as important as energy independence for the US of A, Lydia. I'm past caring," he said and threw his spoon into the sink.

"Caring about what?" BB asked as she appeared from the bathroom. Her makeup applied was a considerable improvement Lydia assessed. "You okay, honey?" BB said as she established her claim on Billy by grasping his arm and staring intently at Lydia. "Could we calm down a little here? Coffee almost ready, sweetie?" she asked. BB retreated into the kitchen and busied herself while pretending that she was at home in a kitchen Lydia observed.

"So, BB, how much pressure are you and your daddy putting on my brother?" Lydia asked. She didn't feel like wasting anytime avoiding the issue. It was a dead on strike for her.

BB whirled around, hands on hips, brown eyes piercing, she then sneered, "This must be hard for you to understand but Billy is doing what he wants to do. You haven't noticed that he's not ranch material, sweetie?"

"Don't call me sweetie." Lydia flew up off the couch with her eyes blazing. "My name is Lydia and I'm touchy that way," she hissed.

"Be careful, BB, my family is pretty prickly. They don't waste punches on being civil. Hell why bother when there's ranch work to do, right Sis?" Billy said with a glare.

"Do you have any family loyalty left, Billy? Any decency left for the people you grew up with and raised you?" Lydia shot back.

"Yeah, I got decency for Dad. At least he's trying to make it right. But the rest of us are in competition or haven't you noticed? When the land was divided, John got the biggest bite plus water right there on his property. When the best views were offered, Bernie ruled. You and Jim got equal land to me but you got the prime herd of cattle. I got the land nearest to the road with Dad and Mom breathing down my neck. What the hell was that all about?"

"Dad and Mom wanted to be able to help you, Billy, as best they could. You went away to college remember? They took care of your land during that time for free. It was easier for them when it was closer to their ranch. Not to mention that they financed your education. The herd went to Jim and me because we were going to have a large family. John is the oldest Holden with a wife and son. Bernie wanted to build her house on top of the hill. Are you really feeling so hurt? You're the one who had the college opportunity. Give me a break," Lydia said realizing that for the hundredth time she and Billy were having this conversation. "What is your fair share, Billy?"

"Does it really matter? What's done is done," BB inserted in the conversation while returning from the kitchen with her own cup of coffee. "I can't believe that all of this wasn't settled years ago."

"And I can't believe that you think it is any of your business," Lydia retaliated.

"We're engaged," BB said with a self satisfied look on her face. "It is my business, Lydia!" BB plopped down on the couch and stirred her coffee hiding her smug expression. The bombshell had been landed, she thought, and with success.

Lydia noticed that Billy was beginning to feel a

little uncomfortable. There was a long pause as she began to comprehend how out of hand this situation had gotten. How could she have missed the clues? "I'm beginning to understand just how this whole situation occurred," Lydia said. "How in the world did you rope Dad into agreeing with you, Billy?"

"He knows how unhappy I've been. At least Dad and I talk these days," Billy said while staring at Lydia. His comment was implying much more than what he said.

There it was, Lydia thought. She had been so damn busy with the kids, the ranch and Jim. When was the last time she had gone over to see Billy? Lydia had to admit it had been months; obviously too long. BB and her lawyer father had shuffled right in and set up camp. Working on Billy's loneliness and frustrations had worked. Was Billy really in love? Lydia wondered how in love either one of them happened to be or was it all convenience. Lydia was about to find out just how convenient the situation had become as events developed.

CHAPTER 9

TRYING TO UNDERSTAND

"Oh there you are," said Chelsea. "Been looking for you, Bernie. Bob and I are building a campfire tonight at the pit. I've talked with Mattie and John and most of your clan. All are invited. You are my last stop."

"Sounds nice; I'll be there. Have you knocked on my dad's door yet," she asked?

"Actually I saw him first. He's over at the Commons cooking up a huge pot of chili for the occasion," Chelsea giggled. "I couldn't stop him if I tried. He's found the biggest pot I've got over there and the chili pepper is a-flying."

"He loves doing things like that. Since Mom died he hasn't done as much cooking so I'm sure this is good for him. Think I'll go over and give him a hand," Bernie added.

"Probably not a bad idea," Chelsea said. "Well got to get going. Need to deliver some mail. See you tonight?"

"Good. John and I are heading into town later for supplies. Anything you need, Chelsea?"

"Nope we're good. Say, would you mind if I asked the lady in the smaller trailer down your way to come by for chili and conversation tonight?" Chelsea asked. "Have you met Bix yet?'

"I did and that would be fine. Tell her to bring Simon."

"Will do," Chelsea said then headed toward the permanent trailers in row B.

Bernie hadn't talked yet with her dad so this was probably as good a time as ever. People would be in and out of the Commons but there were always quiet intervals between showers and laundry. How to approach 'the Billy subject' would be tricky she thought. She didn't want to get him angry before the conversation ever started. Bernie needed all the facts before she and Lydia talked again. Easy does it, she thought.

Bernie walked toward the Commons and could smell the chili ten trailer sites away. Henry was cooking for sure, she thought happily. Thank heavens that the easy life of RVing could over shadow many of the problems. People were more approachable and that included her father. Good. As she opened the screen door, a blond lady was exiting. Bernie said, "Hi," and she was ignored. Well, most people were nice in the RV parks; Bernie readjusted her thinking slightly. She saw her dad clad in cowboy boots, hat and apron as she entered. Henry Holden was twirling his wooden spoon in a five gallon pot of sauce. There was a pile of fried venison meat and onions ready to add to the brew.

"Hey, Dad, it smells mighty good in here. You got quite a project going here," Bernie said.

"Yep, it's going to taste pretty damn good by this evening. What are you up to?" he asked. Henry cupped his hands and began putting the mixture of onions and various meats into the pot. The smells were almost overwhelming.

"Came by to see if you need any help? Chelsea did the invitation thing about the campfire a few minutes ago. She steered me this way to see how you were doing."

"She did huh? I figured she was getting worried about too much hot chili. I bet when she's had a couple beers, she'll eat her fill. What do you think?" Henry eyed Bernie closely. His meaning was obviously going somewhere else. He had something he needed to tell Bernie and this time was as good as any. "Say I got this concoction pretty much together. Let's go sit in the shade outside. I got something to say."

They silently cleaned up the counter then put the dirty dishes in the dishwasher. Bernie found the soap and added it. Henry left his wooden spoon on the counter in a saucer so he could taste the flavor during the afternoon. Tasting of course was crucial. Kitchen cleaned, they moved out under the shade trees where the picnic table sat. Henry reached in his back jean pocket and pulled out his chew as he swung his leg over the bench and sat.

Bernie sat down also and leaned her elbows on the weathered wood of the table.

"Know you hate the tobacco habit but there are times when I got to…this is one of them. John's accident and the hot tempers last night have set me on edge."

Bernie nodded and sat silently waiting for her dad to get to his point. He rarely chewed in front of her anymore so she could tell he was nervous about something. His index finger deposited the tobacco wad into his cheek.

"About last night I feel that I owe you and John an explanation and apology. Want you to talk with John for me. We both know that he's too hot right now for me to tell him anything. Will you do that?" he ventured.

Bernie nodded then said, "You know that eventually you and John will need to clear the air?"

"I know, honey. I will bring up the subject with him but distance is better right now. This whole thing is weighing on me to the point that my stomach is giving me fits. Naturally, I'm not sleeping like I should. Life ain't balanced right now. So will you settle things with John for me? I'll be better in awhile; promise. Will you help me, Bernie?"

"I'll try, Dad," she reluctantly answered. "It does depend on what I hear of course." Bernie shifted her weight on the bench and again waited for her dad to talk. She had to admit John might not be able to control his temper right now. Billy also seemed out of control. Where was his compassion and loyalty? It all seemed so convoluted at this point. The family had to find common ground somewhere so they could at least talk. Consensus was miles away. The only thing Bernie did know was that she had to control herself so that her dad would open up to her. "So what have you got to say?" Bernie asked in a quiet determined tone.

"I honestly feel that I do owe Billy something." Henry raised his hand to stop Bernie from saying anything. "Hear me out, honey, before you judge. Margaret and I pushed him into going to college. Lord knows that at the time he didn't want to leave home. Billy was having fun drinking and running around with the wrong crowd. We figured he'd get someone pregnant and that would have been a disaster. College was the best idea we could come up with so off he went. Speaking of disaster, that was one. The boy hated college but he did hang on because of the lifestyle. The only trouble was he came home with a degree but still no direction to his life. Common sense was never a strong suit for Billy. The land he got was not the best as you well know and he knew that."

"He could have made the ranch into something, Dad. I don't exactly buy that argument," Bernie ventured. "We all have lifetime water leases from John's ranch. With irrigation and attention Billy could be successful."

"Ain't disputing that, Bernie. But there wasn't any motivation there. Billy hadn't found his direction until now…."

Bernie's breath caught in her throat. She sensed that what was coming wouldn't settle with her at all. What in the hell could be Billy's defense against destroying the family legacy?

Henry spit into one of the empty bean cans that

he had saved and then said, "He's going to run for the senate."

Bernie felt the tightening of her stomach muscles. "You can't be serious?" was all she could muster to say.

Henry ignored her reaction and kept on talking. "Politics takes lots of money as you well know. With Billy and me selling our mineral rights he can build the capital that he needs. Bellows has set him up with political contacts and the support of the oil men. Billy is really excited about something for the first time in his life. Margaret would be relieved to see him finally happy."

"At the expense of the whole family? I don't think so, Dad," Bernie said. "You're leasing all your mineral rights?"

"Well not all. I'll still have half of them around the house and my road. My ranching days are over, honey. Getting too old and tired. Lord knows, I've been tired lately."

Henry ran his hand through his graying hair and truly did look beat, Bernie thought. She weighed her reaction to all this bleak information; it was a lot to process. How do you tell a parent that their decision is just wrong? Bernie was sensing the inevitable time in life when parent and child reverse their roles. Her dad wasn't seeing the entire picture. The future, for God's sake, had to be taken into account. Billy was only one piece of the family puzzle. There was another generation of Holdens to think about. In the long run the land belonged to them. Billy's scenario would kill the future legacy.

The Holden land would die from unnatural

causes. Fire was one thing but mass destruction by chemicals was totally another. Plus, Billy had never found anything that could keep his attention long enough to be successful. How in the hell could he change? Consistency and motivation weren't in Billy's vocabulary. The oil companies would have two more pieces of the Missouri River shoreline in their coffers. The implications were staggering.

Bernie took a deep breath and then asked, "Have you signed the papers? Have you signed it all away, Dad?" Bernie placed her hands on her father's and stared at him intensely. Her eyes penetrated Henry's heart as she waited.

"Well…no. I forgot to bring in the title for Bellows so it's only halfway done but I did give my word on the matter. Not yet but when we get back…." Henry mumbled turning his gaze away from Bernie's eyes. "Billy has a chance for happiness," he added lamely. "I need to feel all my kids are set for the future."

Bernie felt like exploding but instead she asked, "Will you promise me something?" Henry seemed far away as he gazed off into the distance. "Dad, look at me. Will you promise me something?" Bernie said again and waited for her dad to focus.

"What?" he finally asked.

Now that she had his attention Bernie went on, "That you will not sign anything more until I have had a chance to talk with Lydia and John. There might be another way to help Billy. Please give me a chance… I need a little time to talk with the rest of the family. It is only fair."

Henry mulled over what she had said. He let out

a long sigh and then said, "All right. But the offer won't last much longer. I'll need to let Billy know by the time we get back. Fair enough?"

"Fair enough," Bernie said. How long could a miracle take anyway she mused. Common ground when tempers are flaring would be incredibly difficult. What in the world could bring them together? First of all, did everyone know all the facts? And after everyone did understand, could any type of agreement happen? It sounded like they had one week to save their land; one week to save the legacy. Hopefully, God might be able to give a hand and compromise might be reached. Bernie could only hope.

CHAPTER 10

NEGOTIATIONS

Bix decided to wander up toward the office just on the chance that she could buy some milk without having to go into town. As she came up on the Jayco, she noticed Bob helping a man disconnect the rear bumper and wheel cover. "Looks like you guys have your work cut out for you," she said.

"Hi Bix," Bob Bailey said as he went to the toolbox for another socket. The RV camp co-owner and handyman was busy helping his clientele. "Yep, did you read *The Summit* about John's untimely accident? Chelsea probably has yesterday's paper," he added. He dusted off the knees of his trousers then went back to work. He put an extra crank on the wrench. His tanned face turned red with the effort. The bolt gave way. "Damn that sucker was on there. Oh, Bix have you met John Holden here?" he asked now that the dented pieces were lying on the ground like a discarded carcass.

"Can't say that I have," Bix answered. "I've met your sister, Bernie. She resides down my way." Bix pointed toward the Scamp.

"Yeah, Bernie gets around," John chuckled. "Come sit down a spell." He gestured toward a vacant lawn chair. "Mattie, my wife, is bringing out coffee. We done here, Bob? Need anymore parts before we call it done?" John asked.

"No that takes care of what I can fix in the shop. I will be able to take out the dents and put a primer on so things won't rust on your way home. Sorry that I can't spray paint for you but by the time I ordered the paint and got it sent, you could be home."

"Hey this is just fine. I can take in the rig and leave it with the dealer when I get back. No time limit after the trip's over. Sure appreciate your help, Bob."

"Don't mention it." Bob placed the pieces gently in the back of his truck on top of an old blanket. He had come prepared.

"Can you sit for awhile and have coffee with us, Bob?" John asked.

"Better not. Chelsea has a rather long list for me today. My spare time is limited. No breaks for this worker. Do want to have time left to gather a little more wood for tonight's campfire. Sure can't forget to do that."

"Want some help later in the day with wood?" John asked. "I brought my 18 volt saw this year knowing the Holdens do like to burn your wood."

"Sure. Come by the shop around 4:00 and bring that saw," Bob said. "See you then," he added.

John reached out and shook Bob's hand. The deal was signed between these two, Bix thought. She could tell that John and Bob liked each other's company; working together was what they did best. The Holdens watched Bob get in his truck and drive toward his shop behind the permanent trailers.

"Mattie," John yelled toward the trailer, "come meet Bix our nearest neighbor who ain't related. Good thing, huh?" John said with a wink for Bix. "Here comes Mattie now and her tray has plenty of mugs. "Need help, honey" John said then got up and took the heavy tray. He placed it gently on the table for Mattie.

"Nice to meet you, Bix. Bernie said that she met you and your little black dog. Where's your doggie?" Mattie asked looking from side to side.

"Left Simon napping. Figured I'd be back soon enough until I got offered coffee." Bix pointed at John. "Hope that's all right?"

"Wouldn't have it any other way," Mattie replied as she brushed her black hair back before serving. "Sugar, milk or none of the above?" Mattie asked.

"None of the above. Thanks," Bix said taking a full mug from Mattie. "Smells great."

They all sipped in quiet appreciation for a few moments. It was a glorious morning. The Collegiate Peaks were clearly in view and there was a minimum breeze. Mattie broke the silence. "Bob okay with fixing the dents?" she asked John.

"Seems so."

"From what I read in the paper before I left home that collision had to have been quite a scare," Bix said. "Of course the paper toned it down some to keep the tourists from having worries. Still, one could tell it was ugly."

"Sure was intentional as far as we could tell," said John as he crossed his legs and settled. "I'm afraid that we might have brought our troubles with us."

"Road rage then?" Bix asked.

"We're thinking so. Keep your eyes out for a black SUV with a grudge." He amended his statement after a second. "You know that North Dakota is experiencing growing pains with our new economy? They don't call us Kuwait on the Prairie for nothing. Ranching in the Bakken Shale Area has changed life to say the least. It's a sad state of affairs."

Bix wasn't sure if she should ask or not.

Mattie filled in the details for her. "Fracking can make life hell in more ways than one. Bernie and John met a young lawyer and his thug at a friend's farm. The event wasn't pretty. Ranchers and farmers are feeling both the hyperbaric bombing underground plus the intense social pressure on the surface. Our lifestyle is changing right before our eyes. You got to worry about fracking in this area, Bix?"

"So far no. Summit County has white gold that people ski down. I guess there was major mining until the 1940s. However, lately the mines are fairly well closed down for environmental reasons and lack of ore. We do hear about some of the events in North Dakota but not all. Sounds worse than what we're hearing."

"Well it's not a pretty picture if you happen to

love the open prairies. Power and control seem to be major topics. Our family is going through the drama of having different opinions. Some of us like the fracking change more than others," said John.

"You can say that again," said a new voice coming into the conversation. "I'm Lydia Robertson, the third oldest in the Holden second generation represented in this here conclave." She held out her hand to Bix. Introductions done, Lydia slid into a chair and crossed her legs. "And you are our neighbor. Correct?"

"Correct."

"Lydia held out her hand for the coffee mug that Mattie gave her. "You're a brave woman to reserve a spot near this rowdy crowd."

"Can't complain yet. Of course the court is out on that one. I'd better wait until after the campfire tonight. I hear tell you folks get crazy."

The Holdens smiled in unison. John chuckled then said, "We have been known to enjoy the time. You know that this row of sites and the next row are all in some way related. You are the honorary token of said stranger. Careful," he quipped. "Yep, I think it's fair to say that the majority of our Colorado cousins made it this summer. They hale from Gunnison and Grand Junction mostly. I guess some of the kids are now living in Eagle. Don't think we've got any Breckenridge folks though."

"Eagle is pretty close. You're spreading my way," Bix said.

"Do you ski, Bix?" Mattie asked as she added seconds on coffee to all.

"Not since they started wearing helmets and

going 90 miles an hour down the hill. I decided that I really didn't want any broken bones. I do cross country ski and snowshoe some. But the downhill is just too crazy for me. I'm a retired teacher now trying to write my first book. We'll see how that goes. Really love to take the trailer out and visit areas around Colorado. Maybe eventually I'll venture out of Colorado but so far this is just fine."

"What's the refrigerator magnet say, "'I'm a teacher so you can't scare me.' Something like that," Lydia said with a smile. "I'd much rather brand a bull than face a bunch of kids in a classroom. No thank you."

"Me neither," said Mattie and shivered dramatically. "Do you like country music, Bix?"

"I have been known to enjoy it. Why?"

"There's enough family here to make a pretty good band. Have you met our dad, Henry?"

"Not yet," Bix said.

"He plays a mean fiddle. Dad gets the crowd hopping providing he feels like playing," Mattie added eyeing John and Lydia.

Lydia sat her coffee down and looked at Mattie for a second. "Is he feeling better? Bernie told me he seems pretty tired after the trip. Hasn't bounced back yet."

"I'll check on him today," Mattie said. "I can smell the chili from here so I figure he is feeling a little better. Fiddle and chili have been Dad's contributions for as far back as I can remember," Mattie said and smiled in Bix's direction. "Oh he'll get it together," she added assuring herself and the family. She nodded and then concluded, "His fiddle makes the magic. And, if I'm lucky, somebody will ask me to dance." Mattie shot a look at John. "Somebody better not be too tired for that. Even Chelsea can get a dance out of Bob."

"What else happens around the fire?" Bix asked becoming more curious by the minute.

"Well the Grand Junction ladies set up a couple tables for bridge early. They quit only when it's so dark they can't see. The little kids do hide- and-seek and the teenagers text each other like crazy then a few folks do some fireworks that don't upset Buena Vista law. Sparklers and worms are the main event. Just the usual stuff for the 4th of July weekend," Mattie said.

Lydia stared into her coffee then added, "Wonder if Billy will sing this year? Our little brother has an angel of a tenor voice. That's where the angel part ends by the way. Have any of you met his fiancé?"

"His what?" Mattie shrieked.

"You heard me. Blonde as the bottle it came from and probably ten years older than his majesty. Charlie Bellows, the snake, has a daughter. She crawled out from underneath the family rock," Lydia said.

"Oh my God," Mattie's hand flew up to cover her mouth. The surprise on both John and Mattie's face was classic. Bix could tell that Lydia had scored a direct hit. It was met with a shocked silence. It became obvious that all was not well in the Holden family. Things could be coming to a boil, she mused.

"You'll have to excuse us, Bix. I apologize.

Vacations should be for relaxing. It does appear that we brought our problems with us this summer," John added. "The Red Queen strikes again," he mumbled.

"No need for an apology. Life happens no matter where we are. Well folks, I am sure glad to meet you and I am looking forward to the campfire. See you tonight." With that, Bix placed her empty cup on the table and headed on up to the office for milk. Her head was spinning from what the Holdens had said. People sure had a difficult time keeping their family together. Society's problems were all so intertwined; Wall Street, bank mortgage frauds and fossil fuel land disputes. The common denominator was money whether it was in North Dakota or Colorado. What did John mean about the Red Queen? She weighed the possibilities as she opened the office door.

CHAPTER 11

A FESTIVAL OF FAMILY

The three o'clock hour started with the deer wandering through the park munching on an occasional stock of grass or clover. It was obvious that they were used to this environment. They knew when the tourists disappeared into their trailers to eat or rest. A doe and her two fawns had the routine down. The deer family moved slowly from campsite to campsite checking for any stray morsels under the picnic tables. They wandered toward the back of the camp near the woods.

Simon had his front paws on the top of the couch and stood up on his back feet so he could see the deer. He twisted his neck back and forth so as not to miss any activity. The little guy was respectful of their space and height, Bix thought. She had just finished feeding him inside and settled down to check her email. Simon was guarding them against any animal attacks obviously. The deer seemed docile, however, and so was Simon; she gave his head a pet. As the deer strolled off into the woods, John and Bob pulled up in a truck. Simon began watching them unload wood at the fire pit. It looked like more than one night's entertainment Bix reconnoitered.

They began stacking it to one side. Bob went to the pit and began to build the structure for his starting fire. It would stand until later when they would light it up.

She sat down on the couch and clicked on the computer. She had become fairly curious about John and Mattie Holden's accident. Bix went back to *The Summit* article on the computer and read it thoroughly. Flipping over to the police reports she found no mention of finding the car. In fact, she looked at today's paper and found no mention of any arrests. So the car flew on down I-70 heading God knows where. Case was closed from the local stand point. Wonder if the car drove right into Buena Vista, she pondered. Could check a few mechanics for a damaged black car, she thought. Can't be too many repair shops in Buena Vista right?

Bix got out her notebook and began writing down as many of the names and places that she had heard about today. Bakken Shale could be researched. Actually, the lawyer named Bellows could be investigated right here on the computer. What were his major cases? Bix hoped that she could figure out if his practice was reputable or not? Facts were facts; the internet was so nice. From a little trailer in the middle of the mountains, a person could do some extensive research. Pretty amazing she thought.

The topics just kept rolling on. Surface and mineral rights on any private land was something that also screamed for investigation. Lord knows everyone should find out what they did own and the difference in mineral and surface rights. What really was eminent domain? No one had discussed that topic today but it seemed important to the whole context. Were both surface and mineral rights under the rule of eminent domain? Wow. Bix sat back for a second and took a deep breath. From the little that the Holdens had shared, she knew a lot could be gleamed. Bix set up her notes under the topics: people, property rights, fracking and state of North Dakota. This research was interesting to say the least, she decided.

***

Late afternoon began with the Grand Junction ladies who talked Bix into a dozen games of bridge before she could escape. Dusk wrapped around the tables until no one could see and the cards were put away. Bob's magnificent campfire had taken center stage. Darkness beckoned the kids into playing their games interrupted by occasional fireworks. The chili was excellent; it was hot but actually had a great balance of spices. Lots of folks brought side dishes. Bix had thrown together a fruit salad that seemed popular; it was gone early. Makes for a lighter dish to carry home, she thought.

The band began to tune up. Henry Holden had

not come forward to pick up his fiddle yet. It leaned forlornly on the center chair. The guitars, drums and bass gathered around in a half circle. Expectations were so high that Bix could feel it. Tenuously, the band began to move from individual tune-up into a combination of blending sounds that then burst into a song.

Henry suddenly appeared and took center stage with the band. "One set is all I got in me tonight. Hope you enjoy," he said. And, enjoy they did. Henry's fiddle fused body and soul into music. Mattie motioned John out of his chair while Bob guided Chelsea toward the dance. The bridge ladies also were brought forth by their husbands. Human shadows locked together as they glided through the night. The beat was almost primitive as the couples circled the campfire, Bix thought. Simon was awakened by the new activity. He seemed to think the two-step was okay. People who remained seated had begun to clap in rhythm. The atmosphere became electric.

Billy then appeared from the crowd. Jumped up onto the small makeshift stage and began to sing. The audience melted with the mixture of fiddle and voice. The smooth tones blended warmly into perfect harmony. Anyone in the Holden family had to be aware of this special connection between father and son, Bix thought. No wonder Billy was able to persuade his father about mineral rights. The situation all fell into place for Bix. Family dynamics were always so mysterious.

The falling stars finally replaced the band for entertainment; people were slowly disappearing into their campers. Bix found herself sitting with Bernie close to the remaining campfire. The evening temperature had dropped probably fifteen degrees. There were red embers glowing with an occasional flame reaching for the sky. Bob would once and awhile toss on another piece of wood. He had brought out the water hose earlier during the red hot times. Now the embers occasionally shot sparks into the night while maintaining a welcome glow.

"Really a nice evening," Bix said to Bernie. "When you get a chance, please tell your family how much I did enjoy it. I may have been the token stranger but I felt right at home. And the food…that was amazing. I didn't understand Henry's chili until it sneaked up on me. At first you don't realize how hot it is but then you start stuffing in all the side dishes so you won't burn up. I felt my ears growing red at one point," Bix gasped.

Bernie laughed thinking back to eating her dad's chili when she was a kid. "I can remember my first bowl," she told Bix. "I had grown enough that summer that I could reach the sink faucet. I'm not sure what would have happened if I couldn't have gotten to the water. Lordy! You do get used to it, however," Bernie added.

Bix petted Simon's head. He had jumped up in her lap when the evening cooled. She glanced over at Bernie then ventured on into their conversation. "So Bernie, I have something to ask you and I hope you're not offended. Colorado's a pretty open state for such things so I'm going to ask. All you need to say is 'yes or no." Bix eyed Bernie closely waiting for permission.

"Go ahead and ask," Bernie said.

"I have a feeling that you might be a lesbian like I am so I have to ask. My curiosity is killing me."

There was a long pause while Bix could feel Bernie deciding what to say. "Yes. In North Dakota though I am so far in the closet that the door is locked shut. Had a girlfriend a couple of years ago. She had a little girl so people didn't think much about us spending so much time together. Amy came to Tioba to drive one of the water well disposal trucks. Pays way better than anything else; you can actually begin a saving's account with that salary. Unheard of in most of the Midwest as you well know. Amy and her daughter finally left the area when she had saved enough money to go after a college degree. You end up breathing in lots of chemicals so you don't want to stay in the fracking field too long. It was a good decision especially if you have children. She did ask me to come with her; I love the land so that wasn't going to happen. Kinda lost track of her after that," Bernie finished. "What's your story?" she asked.

"Five years with the wrong lady. It was either make a change or continue feeling old and trapped. I had to leave the situation." The two ladies sat quietly staring at the fire.

Bix and Bernie settled back to enjoy the last embers. Obviously, the family troubles had been placed on the back burner. The Holdens had been doing what they did best by celebrating each other and living life in the moment. Accepting the gifts of family, Bix thought. "Nice," she whispered as she reached down for the metal poker near the fire pit and huddled the embers together to encourage warmth.

CHAPTER 12

FLASH IN THE DARK

It was the low growl from Simon that woke Bix from her deep sleep. The night held a half moon with partial light. Bix raised herself up on her elbow next to Simon and stared out the trailer window. The little dog was standing on his back legs with front paws on the screen. The dark shadows were stretching the length of the trees. Bix glanced at the clock on the wall; 2:45 it glowed.

"What's there, Simon?" Bix asked in a whisper. She was expecting to see a deer or raccoon shuffling through the trash dumpster. Maybe a bear she then thought? She inspected the yard light areas of the campground then stared more intensely at the entire scene.

Simon was standing closely by her and their eyes in unison caught sight of a slow quiet moving car coming down the road with lights off. Makes sense she thought if you were coming home at this hour you wouldn't want to disturb folks. Yet, something felt funny. Things seemed too quiet and eerie. Simon growled again; he didn't blast her ears with barking. It was like he sensed something too. They watched quietly.

The car eased to a stop across from John's Jayco trailer and the passenger door opened without a sound. Bix caught a glimpse of both men in the car. One shadow driving while the other stepped out on solid ground from the passenger seat. Without any hesitation the passenger flicked on a lighter and held it under a cylinder shaped object. He waited for the lighter to ignite the object. Suddenly like a huge sparkler, the cylinder flashed alive! The flames skyrocketed through the night air. The man quickly threw the lethal flare toward the front of the trailer. Then as quickly as possible he jumped in and slammed the door. The car sped down the road toward Simon and Bix. She ducked down and held Simon. The black car swerved left and charged toward the permanent residences and was gone. Just like that. Gone!

Bix shot up and looked out the window. The emergency flare was increasing in size and oh so close to John's propane tank. She had very little time to get there before the whole trailer would simply blow up. Bix knew that magnesium flares were incredibly dangerous once lit.

She threw the trailer door open and sprinted toward the noxious flames. She was aware that Simon was at her side barking the alarm. The gravel gnawed at her bare feet. The distance seemed to grow longer as she ran. Bix grabbed the metal poker at the fire pit while she raced toward the flames. She had to move the damn thing into the road! One crazy lady and a little black dog racing in slow motion flashed into her mind. The lethal flames seemed so far away yet so close to the propane tank. Panic was in full force; her focus was on stopping this disaster.

Bix wasn't aware that the trailer lights had come on all around her. People cloaked in shadows began to emerge from the opening doors. Their eyes slowly adjusting to the night darkness; their minds were trying to comprehend what in the world was going on. Voices exploded into questions and a riot ensued!

Bix reached the trailer and batted the blazing flare into the middle of the road. She could smell the acid odor of burning magnesium in her nostrils.

She threw dirt and gravel on the dissipating flames and yelled, "Help!" A crowd of people were now throwing dirt and rocks at the damn thing. After their vigorous assault, the flare surrendered into a smoldering powerless mass.

Suddenly a water hose began to spray Bix and the propane tank. She hadn't realized that her night shirt was on fire. Bix dropped to the ground and rolled as the coldest water that she had ever experienced drowned out the flames. John finished dowsing her and Mattie then covered Bix with a blanket. "Damn that's cold!" she shrieked.

Simon sprinted to take shelter under one of the trailers. He yelped as he raced away from the chaos! Bix was aware that Bernie followed him. There must have been at least fifty people rushing around with good intentions. A well meaning soul was carrying a bucket and shovel ready to remove the dead flare.

"Help is on the way!" Lydia yelled. "Jim has called the police and an ambulance."

"Ambulance? What? No!" Bix wailed. "I'm okay. A hospital I don't need. Some salve, yes."

Chelsea and Bob came running down the road with two huge flashlights. Kids from all the families near the incident were running around just to add more bedlam to the scene.

Bix yelled out a big, "Stop! The evidence! Don't mess up the tire tracks for heaven's sake. Leave the flare where it is." Bodies stopped moving and stared at the ground. The gentleman with a bucket and shovel froze seconds before tossing the flare into his bucket. A couple of kids near Bix's trailer yelled, "They went that-a-way." The tribe of kids in unison pointed down toward the residence trailers while lifting their feet off the tire tracks like they were walking in mud.

Well at least the tracks and flare would be there for the police, Bix thought. That was one good sign. Maybe the police could now make something out of this whole mess. The emergency flare could have blown up one trailer and those flames could then have destroyed the park. The implications began to take on larger proportions for Bix. It was far greater than just fracking and family squabbling at this point. It had taken on a more sinister tone. These events were not simply coincidences. They were adding up to attempted murder charges. Bix began to realize how these developments would involve everyone at High Mountain Vista RV Park.

***

After much conversation the ambulance call was cancelled and Bix was piled into Lydia and Jim's car. Jim Robertson had taken charge of the situation and driven her to the Regional Medical Center in Buena Vista. Chelsea had called ahead to get Bix medical assistance. A nurse practitioner named Linda Benson opened the door of the clinic as they got out. If Bix was any judge of the situation, it was her feet that hurt the most.

"Come on in. Let me get the lights going and we'll take a look at you." Bix was escorted into an examining room. Linda shut the door and began inspecting Bix's back. "How does it feel?" Linda said while touching various spots gently. She whipped out her stethoscope and listened to Bix's heart front and back.

"I'll live," Bix said. "I may not lean back in a comfy chair for a while but that's to be expected."

"Let's check your blood pressure while we're at it," Linda said. "Chelsea said that it was a flare huh? You are very lucky that the temperature didn't burn your skin right off your hands," Linda said as she rapped the blood pressure cuff on Bix's arm.

"I got there right before the whole thing was in total flames. Used the fire pit poker for batting practice. It still seemed hotter than hell," Bix said.

"Well your blood pressure and heart are fine. Now let me see your hands." Linda examined Bix closely. "Going to apply an antibiotic cream on your hands and back just for precaution. I think you did get very lucky. Your feet do need some care. I noticed you're limping?"

"Bare foot running on gravel was not a good thing either," Bix said.

"I'll need to pick some debris from the ball of your foot and that could be uncomfortable." Linda cleaned Bix's feet then removed small bits of gravel and checked the cuts gently.

"My prognosis is that you're going to want to keep the burn surfaces cool and clean if possible. I don't think there will be any blisters but you might get a few. The feet just need to heal so wear scandals and these small bandages for today. Wait a day before showering but use this lotion on your burns when you become uncomfortable. Think I'll give you a shot to make sure that there is no infection. Can you come back in on Tuesday?" Linda asked.

"Sure." Bix felt immense relief that she had survived with minimal damage. "How long do I need the lotion?" she asked.

"Use the tube up if you need it. It certainly won't hurt to apply. If you need more, call the clinic. Your feet will heal fairly quickly providing that you don't go for long hikes. Sitting in the shade for a while sounds like the ticket. Tell Chelsea to serve ice tea and pamper you. That would be an order. I'll give her a call tonight. I know that she is terribly concerned. What in the world is going on down there?" Linda asked.

Bix explained what she could but kept it pretty mild at this time figuring the police would want less said to the public. Linda seemed pretty stable but gossip is such an easy thing to grow. Chelsea would be the judge of that situation not Bix. She was thankful for the lotion and the prognosis. The rest of the adventure would now be in the hands of the police she hoped.

On the way back to High Mountain Vista she and Jim were both feeling conflicting emotions. "I really don't understand how all this is happening. Billy is being a jerk but he's not trying to kill John," Jim said as he turned out on Highway 24. "They are brothers for Pete's sake.

I've known them both since grade school. Billy was born dissatisfied but he's not a killer. John, well he's a careful kind man. There has to be an outside source here. It ain't family!" Jim emphasized his last sentence and then fell silent. The cool Buena Vista breeze came in through the windows. They navigated the stop light and traveled to their turnoff.

"I keep coming back to the premise that it couldn't be a coincidence," Bix stated. "Is fracking such a huge controversy that John is truly in danger for his life? And why, John? What would make him a target?" Bix asked.

Jim ran his right hand through his blond hair. "From what I know so far is that the fracking industry has a strong financial backing in North Dakota. Having said that, I can't see them killing people. Murder would end up being totally inconvenient and time consuming thanks to the legal system. Right now, the state is content to let the fracking industry have its way with the environment. Murder?" Jim shifted his position while shaking his head. "Why bother with something that slows down drilling? No. The oil industry operates above the law paying pollution fees when they get caught and slipping cash to the lobbyists who then pay the politicians. The Red Queen Syndrome works quite nicely for them."

"What does that mean exactly?" Bix asked. "John mentioned the Red Queen a couple days ago."

"From *Through the Looking Glass,* the Red Queen said, 'it takes all the running you can do to keep in the same place.' The oil industry will never admit to getting ahead of demand and so they call it, jokingly, the Red Queen Syndrome. They will drill 6,000 new wells per year at the cost of 35 billion to maintain. They'll suck North Dakota dry then move on. Hell, they'll begin to export oil to other countries and still tell us that we need to drill for more. The appetite for oil is nonstop. Of course that's my opinion," he added.

Jim put the blinker on and turned into High Mountain Vista. He drove on down to Bix's home on wheels. He stopped at her door and came around to the passenger side and leaned in the window. "Sorry that you got in the middle of this cowboy tale. I haven't thanked you personally for saving John and Mattie's life. I need to do that." Jim opened the door and helped Bix get out. Her feet were tender but it didn't seem to matter now that she was back.

"Thanks, Jim. Somehow I don't think your family wanted any of this either. You know people have a tendency to stick their heads in the sand. The problem is that if you ignore trouble, the event will bite you big time. Somehow at sometime, fracking had to interrupt my life. I think these events are a wake-up call and that's my opinion." Bix limped to the door and found it unlocked. Jim helped her get up the steps and inside. "Thanks for the ride," Bix said.

"Well anyway, Lydia and I are sure glad that you're okay and that you had the fortitude to get involved. You're my hero." With that, Jim left before Bix could see his eyes watering up.

She limped over to the kitchen sink splashed some water on her face and glanced out the window. Bix noticed that a beautiful day was dawning. She would appreciate the peace and quiet of this morning and some coffee. She prepared the brew then opened the window for fresh air. It would be a 75 degree day and she was still on vacation. As she sat down, an impatient bark came from outside the door.

"Can we come in?" Bernie asked.

"Sure. Door's open. If you don't mind I won't get up right now."

Bernie opened the door and Simon bounded in. He flew from the floor to Bix's lap at the speed of light with his tongue hanging out and sparkling eyes. "Hey guy, good to see you too. Been a long night hasn't it?" Bix scratched him behind his ears. "Come on in and sit down, Bernie. It's good to be home."

"I bet. He's been a good dog since you left. I thought he might put up a fuss but he's been great.

Of course the dog treats did help. I borrowed some from my cousins down the way," Bernie sheepishly said. "Hope you don't mind." Bernie slide into the chair on the other side of the table.

"Not at all," Bix said.

"I take it you weren't burned bad? You gave us quite a scare."

"Good to go. A little sore but I'll make it. Police still here or have they come and gone?" Bix asked.

"Come and gone but they will be back to talk with you later today. I think they generally see this whole thing correctly. Of course they want to talk more with Billy and Henry separately but they put a search out for the car and don't believe it left the state. The Chief said that they would be talking with the Silverthorne police today also."

"Chief?" Bix asked.

"Police Chief, James Marten, is handling the case. He's going to send a patrol car through High Mountain Vista every couple of hours tonight. Think I'll sleep better knowing that. Naturally, Chelsea and Bob feel absolutely awful. Like it is their fault that we brought our troubles to High Mountain Vista." Bernie shook her head. "You know I'm so sorry that you got dragged into our troubles. You truly didn't deserve what happened last night."

"Quite frankly it was Simon's fault. He's the one who woke up first. I'm sure if he had thumbs, he would have thrown the flare away. Little guy did put up a racket though. Were the police able to get the tire tracks and flare remains into evidence?"

"Done and done. Now the investigation can

begin. It will put a clamp on everyone's vacation time but that's the way it goes. By the way, my family would like to invite you over this evening for dinner. The Holdens really want to thank you properly. Can I come and get you around 5:00?" Bernie asked.

"Sounds wonderful. I can't imagine cooking tonight. Simon and I would be delighted."

"Good. Oh I almost forgot one of the bridge ladies from Grand Junction sent over a spare cane if you need it. I left it outside by the door. Although you don't look like you're familiar with such stuff."

Bix chuckled, "No I am a hiker and usually do a couple miles each day. My exercise schedule will be a little more limited this week. I don't think Simon will mind too much. Do you get a chance to hike in North Dakota?"

"Horse back is usually my mode of recreation. Unfortunately, I find myself herding cattle or fixing fences most of the time. Ranch life is constant exercise if you know what I mean."

"Are there any, obviously, gay ranchers?" Bix asked just a little curious. "Riding the range holding hands?"

"Not in the White Earth Valley that I know of but people are starting to be more open to the idea, I think. Kind of like the rest of the country, North Dakota is changing. I can go into the city and find places to meet women but I don't go too often. I find myself on the computer though. Trouble is that many of the computer ladies are just that, computer partners. They aren't interested in living with someone out on a ranch. Having a relationship with a rancher gal ain't easy."

"What's your family think?" Bix asked.

"They don't. I never have brought it up and no one has asked. I know Lydia and Mattie have guessed but the men just rather talk ranch and that's what we do. Since I've hit my 50's I'm pretty used to being alone. You said you had a relationship?"

"Had a partner but it didn't work out for the long run. Our personal goals and lives became very different. Somehow you have to feel safe in their arms and if that isn't happening then you drift apart. Don't get me wrong, I still hope to find my soul mate. How about you?"

"Sort of have given up but who knows. I think lesbians have a heck of a time finding good relationships. I don't do bars and that brings down the social possibilities. Straight men and women have it so much easier when it comes to the social things. There was no mother or father saying find the right girl and get married in my life; they said, 'find a man and have children.' Where's the blessing in that for someone who is gay? Oh well, don't get me started." Bernie's sigh was long and spoke volumes.

True, Bix thought. "You ever come into Denver for the gay Pride Parade and Festival?"

"Nope."

"How about joining me next year? There's something about seeing over 350,000 gay people all coming together to celebrate; it does the soul good. You're not alone, Bernie, whether you're on a deserted ranch or a deserted island. It's amazing what email can really do. If you promise me you'll show, I'll keep in touch and make sure that you're there. Deal?"

"You betcha." Bernie smiled and sealed the deal with a hand shake. "Why do I feel like I was just adopted?'

"Because you were. Strength is in numbers. Plus the money world is beginning to figure out that gays do spend cash. We contribute our fair share to this nation. We are your neighbor with or without children. So, back to this morning…"

Bix would meet the Buena Vista Police Chief and his officers fairly soon. The complex situation would bring forward a whole new set of problems for the town's chief. He would find himself entangled in the fracking industry and the Holden family dispute. It would have far reaching effects that no one could anticipate.

CHAPTER 13

DETAILS REMEMBERED

Chief James Marten knocked on Bix's door three hours later. She and Simon had snuggled up for a nice well deserved nap. When she was awakened, it was not unexpected. "Chief Marten?" Bix inquired. She opened the door.

"Thanks for seeing us, Miss Bixler. Sorry that it has to be under these circumstances. Your actions were certainly brave. I wish there had been no danger; it was a very unfortunate situation to say the least. May we talk with you?" he asked. James Marten's demeanor was authoritative but warm. His brown hair was cut short and his uniform was neatly ironed to precision. Marten's body was stocky like a stuffed teddy bear with compassionate blue eyes. "Just so you know there are two detectives, Burger and Smith, on the case plus Sergeant Holly and myself. Our group of four will be conducting all the interviews today."

Bix thought that he was probably retired military. He was definitely not a country bumpkin. "No problem," she said. The young lady with him was equally as neat in appearance. Her long black hair was gathered in a ponytail so that her intense brown eyes became her most dominate feature. She was beautiful. Bix's gaydar sensed that Sergeant Holly was probably a lesbian. Nice.

"Shall we sit outside here?" Chief Marten extended his hand in a motion to escort Bix to the picnic table. The Scamp trailer would have held all three of them but it would have been a stretch. Confined quarters to say the least, Bix thought. She placed Simon on his outside leash and settled at the table. Simon jumped up on Bix's side of the bench and looked at their company.

"Sergeant Holly began the interview; she was ready to take notes on an ipad. "So what time did you become aware that something was happening?"

"I have a digital clock in the trailer. It was 2:45 when Simon woke me." She petted him affectionately.

***

Detectives Smith and Burger knocked on Billy Holden's door.

They were met with, "What?" Billy peered out the window then rolled his eyes. He released an audible sigh then moved to open the door. "Let's get this over with," he snapped. Billy motioned them into the living room. A lady, who was smoking a cigarette, sat rigidly in a large lounge chair. Her hostile expression mirrored Holden's obvious contempt, Burger noticed. Billy then collapsed into the other lounge chair. The couch was left for the two detectives. Smith brought out a pad and pen for the interview while Burger tried to make small talk in an attempt to bring down the tension.

"Sorry to intrude but your brother and his wife had quite a scare during the night. We have been asked to investigate the incident. I am Detective Burger and this is Detective Smith. There are two other policemen who will work this case, Chief Marten and Sergeant Holly. Our presence in the RV camp hopefully will not intrude too much but an investigation must be done." Burger waited for some sort of recognition and found that it was not going to come so he continued, "Since your trailer is on the opposite side of John Holden's trailer, we need to talk with you." Burger shifted his large frame so that he could watch the couple. He almost felt like he had to apologize for asking them questions. What was that all about, he thought? Smith, his partner, was not making eye contact with these disagreeable people either. Both detectives waited...and waited for any type of response.

Finally, Billy gave in and said, "We were asleep naturally until all hell broke out. The lady from down the way and her dog started shrieking to high heaven. We glanced out the bedroom window and then grabbed some clothes. We ran out. By the time we understood what was happening, it was over."

From Billy's point of view there was nothing else to say. He was surprised when the detective asked the next question.

"What time was that?" Burger asked.

BB answered, "Sometime before 3:00 in the morning. Way too early for all of this."

"And you are?" Burger inquired.

"Mr. Holden's fiancé, BB Bellows. I am also from North Dakota," she added. BB shifted her position like a nesting bird and fluttered.

"And your occupation is?"

"What's that got to do with anything?" she asked indignantly.

"Merely background, ma'am. We need to have the information for our records," Burger stated. Smith's blond head shot up with pen poised.

"I work for my father in his law offices. I'm the head secretary if you must know." She fluttered again.

"Thank you," Burger said a bit annoyed. It was like pulling teeth with these two to get answers. "How long have you and Mr. Holden known each other and where did you meet?"

"Three months and some change," Billy answered. "I met BB socially and then again when I went to meet with her father."

"May I ask why you needed a lawyer?"

"If you must know, I am in the process of selling the mineral rights for my ranch."

"May I ask why?" Burger kept pushing.

"Because like the rest of the intelligent ranchers in the state, I want the damn money. The rest of the family are purists when it comes to the land; they're holding out."

"Would you explain that comment, please?" Detective Burger felt that maybe they were getting somewhere now. He and Smith exchanged glances as he dug a little deeper. "Then your family isn't happy with your decision?"

BB suddenly let it slip, "Well that's an understatement."

***

"So you saw two figures in the car?" Sgt. Holly asked to clarify.

"Correct. It was dark but I know that there were only two shadows in the car. Both men I think. At least the shadows had short hair and fairly wide shoulders," Bix added.

"Any other distinguishing features?"

Bix shut her eyes for a second and envisioned the scene one more time. "You know now that I think about it, the passenger wore glasses but that's all I saw. It was mostly shadows."

Sgt. Holly added more to her comments on the ipad. Chief Marten thought for a moment and asked, "Have you heard anything said by the Holdens that struck you as unusual or different?"

"Other than they're really a nice group of people? They have their problems like any family but this fracking thing really is awful for them to deal with."

"In what way?" he asked leaning closer on his elbows so that he didn't miss a word.

"From what I have heard, as a third party, Billy

Holden is selling his mineral rights to the fracking company. It would seem to be a problem for the rest of the family other than Henry, the father. I think Henry is selling his rights also so that Billy can go into politics. Bernie Holden and Jim, Lydia's husband, have been talking with me; the family has quite a lot to resolve."

"Did they know anything about Billy's decision before the trip to Colorado?" Sgt. Holly asked.

"That, I don't know."

"What color was the car that tossed the flare?" Chief Marten asked.

"It was either blue or black. Darkness made it impossible to identify. Sorry."

"Did you see anything on the car that would distinguish it or maybe something missing?" the Chief asked. His eyes focused on Bix closely.

"Missing? I hadn't thought about anything missing." Bix shifted her body on the hard bench and closed her eyes for a couple of seconds. She saw the image of the car itself. Dark and shadows…then the door opened and there was a splash of light to see…what? Amazingly, another detail came to Bix. "There was no front bumper visible. I should have seen the horizontal silver on the front of the car and I didn't. I saw some grille but no front bumper. The flare did light up the area enough to be sure of what I could see."

"Thank you that's helpful," Sgt. Holly said as she thought of another question to ask. "Did the car passengers seem to know what trailer they were looking for?"

"Good question…hmmm. I would have to

say…yes," Bix answered. "Yes, the car approached so slowly that it was as if they were either counting the number of trailers or were looking for a Jayco trailer now that I think about it." The pieces were falling in place; the men knew what they were looking for. It had all been planned she realized. It was no accident but a deliberate attempt on John and Mattie! "Wow," was all Bix could say.

***

"Please explain why you believe the family wasn't happy about your fracking plans, Mr. Holden?" Burger asked.

BB suddenly stood up and stomped her cigarette out in the ashtray on the table. "Because they just don't get it!" she hissed in disgust. "Why not keep your damn land and sell what's below the surface? What in the hell can that hurt? $80,000 a month ain't chunk change anywhere these days. Daddy says that all these ranchers will sooner or later sell. It will just take time for these stupid people to come around!" BB caught herself and reined in her temper. She sat back down in her chair and stared out the window. Obviously, she was done on that subject.

Smith suddenly asked BB a direct question as if he had to get his notes completed. "Where were you during the chili party the other night, Miss Bellows? We just need to know where everyone was. It's departmental procedure you know."

"I was in here making business phone calls for Billy. His family hasn't exactly opened up with warmth toward me so we decided not to push it. Billy checked on my progress when he brought me chili," she added.

Burger figured that was the only thing they hadn't pushed. He turned his attention back to Billy. "Miss Bellows is correct that you stopped by?"

"Several times during the evening," Billy answered. "Naturally, I checked in often. She is my fiancé."

"By the way, what did you need $80,000 a month for exactly? "Were you planning to spend all of the money on your campaign?" Burger ventured.

Billy put his hands in his pockets and weighed the situation. He wanted to think about how much he should say here. Had they said too much to these detectives? Was a lawyer necessary before he or BB went on? Billy paused to consider. Cautiously he answered, "I plan to run for the senate come this fall. The money would help stage my campaign and support us. Naturally getting married is also costly," he threw in casually.

Burger observed Billy's countenance transform into self-importance. The young man was definitely proud of himself right or wrong and BB was right there patting him on the back. Interesting, he thought. "And does your father feel the same way about your future?" Burger asked.

"My father is perfectly happy with my decision. In fact he has offered to sell his mineral rights on half of his ranch to help me. No dad and I are right on the same page," he added.

"Then your brother and sisters are the only barriers here? Why is John then the only target do you think?" Smith suddenly asked. "What other financial prospects are in the picture here?"

Billy and BB both whipped their attention from Burger to Smith and stared for a few seconds. Again there was a pause in the conversation.

"I have no idea," Billy finally said. "Maybe these attacks have nothing to do with my campaign. Maybe it is something totally different," he said with a smirk. "You better ask John. Maybe there's more going on here than meets the eye."

"We have no damn idea what's going on," BB added.

Smith stared at her for a moment and then asked for the record, "What is your first name?"

"Bethany," BB said in a huff.

***

"So, Miss Bixler, did you notice anything odd during the chili get-together last night?" Chief James Marten asked.

"No. Everything was really nicely done and I felt right at home. Billy and Henry can really entertain. Lots of relatives were there. How incredible to be able to get so many people together at one time. These people have known each other for a long time and I'm sure that will make your task harder in some ways."

"Have you met BB Bellows?" Sgt. Holly asked. Her brown eyes flashed with curiosity.

"You know I haven't. She wasn't at the festivities or at least I didn't see her. Most of the Holdens are red heads; I guess she's a blond. Or a bottle blond as Lydia said. Kind of surprised that I didn't see her when Billy started singing. Henry was sure proud of him; the young man has talent," Bix added. "Might make a better singer than politician. Who knows?"

"I have one last question," Chief Marten said. "Did you recognize what make of car the men used to throw the flare?"

"I believe it was an SUV. I didn't catch the make. Sorry," Bix said and she was truly sorry.

***

"Couple more questions for now, Burger said. "Where were you two when John had his accident near the Eisenhower Tunnel?"

"We were sleeping it off after enjoying a night of losing money at Blackhawk. I didn't crash into my brother if that's what you are implying," Billy said. "That's totally bullshit."

Burger sucked it up and pretended to ignore the snide remark. To get this interview over would be wonderful news, he thought. "I'd like to go back to your comment, Miss Bellows, about your relationship with the family."

"They don't like either one of us right now," Billy interrupted. "They'll get over it eventually," he added.

"If you don't mind, Mr. Holden, I will need you to not interrupt or we can finish this interview at the station. Please let Miss Bellows answer the question for herself."

Billy sighed and then settled back in silence.

BB pulled out another cigarette and took her time lighting it since none of the males in the room were going to assist. After the first long inhale, she blew out the smoke then stared directly at Burger. "Lydia is jealous of my relationship with Billy not to mention that her loyalty is to ranching. She, obviously, sees me as an intruder who is talking Billy into something he doesn't want to do. Speaking of total bullshit," she chided then threw a hot ash toward her ashtray. "Billy has told me many times how he wants out of ranching. Politics will suit both of us."

"Have you threatened or been threatened by any of the Holden family?" Burger asked.

"If you count Lydia Robertson calling me a slut; I would call that an attack," BB hissed. "The bitch called me that right to my face." Her lower lip began to pout, Burger noticed.

"Were you afraid for your life?" Burger ventured.

"Well no but they could have been a little more civil with their welcome into the family." She was in full pout now.

"How does Henry Holden feel about you? Do you get along with him?" Burger asked while trying to hide his annoyance.

"Henry and I get along fine. We have talked a lot about the leasing of mineral rights and Billy's future in politics. Henry understands that Billy will make a super candidate; he gets it. Billy has my father's support also. Billy can't lose what with all the financial support he'll have. Money buys elections, you betcha," BB said smugly and crossed her arms under her ample breasts. A gesture that both Burger and Smith didn't miss.

"So your father is fine with your decisions. Is that correct, Mr. Holden?" he asked now staring at Billy for confirmation of what BB had clarified.

"It took a little while but Dad has come around. Yes, he is on our side in this matter," Billy said. "Anything else? We need to get busy and make some phone calls. Campaigns don't go on vacation," he asserted.

"We're almost finished for the day. Miss Bellows, you haven't mentioned Bernie Holden yet. As the oldest daughter and a land owner, how is she taking all of this?"

"She's a dyke," BB sneered. "What about her?"

"BB, cut it out," Billy shot back. "Get off of it." Billy looked at Burger then and said, "Bernie has sided with John, naturally, as she always does. My dad feels that he can bring her around. She does have a fair sense of understanding."

"John doesn't?" Burger inquired casually throwing a glance at Smith.

Billy opened his mouth to say something, obviously negative, but thought better of it and said, "You'll have to talk with John about that."

Burger could see that maybe Billy would actually make it as a politician; he was totally indecisive. They had left shortly after the last round of questions. The rest of the family needed to be interviewed. This case was going to be a challenge.

"How much pressure do you think those two applied to the old man?" Smith asked as they walked back to their car.

"Plenty," Burger mumbled.

CHAPTER 14

TAKING IN REALITY

The day had slipped away from Bix. After the police had left, there was a quiet that settled over the camp. She checked the time and saw that they could go for a short walk. Simon needed to be aired and Bix needed to step back from last night's anxiety. The trailer just wasn't big enough for all her thoughts. Bix wanted to understand how close the danger had intruded; she wanted to acknowledge how lucky their response had been. Thankful, was the only word that Bix could process at the moment. She put on her sunglasses, sandals and got the leash. Simon exploded into excitement; dogs always know.

She decided to take the path that Lydia and Bernie had taken the previous Sunday. they locked up and Bix grabbed the cane Bernie had left outside her door. "Okay guy, we have time to hobble down the trail." Bix checked to see if she had doggie bags still in her pocket. Good to go.

It was slower with the cane but well worth the effort. Bix let Simon off his leash. They came around a turn maybe half a mile from the camp and the quiet of a beautiful sunny day surrounded them. The pungent scent of pine and sage mixed together in a pure recipe that filled Bix's lungs. She inhaled deeply and stood still lost in the moment. Sometimes she just couldn't stop inhaling fresh air; it was a cathartic release. Simon took on his schnauzer stance and was quiet. "What a wonderful day, guy. We almost missed it didn't we?" Bix purred.

For a few short moments she was captivated by the vision of the Collegiate Peaks that bordered the valley floor. They were more rugged and vertical than Quandary Mountain in Summit County. Quandary Mountain lumbered along leisurely capturing as much ground as it needed. The majority of the Collegiate Peaks simply shot up into the sky. How incredible was that, she mused?

The terrain was gradual and fairly flat as she moved along the path letting the afternoon clear her mind. Lots of sage and yucca covered the sandy ground. Once in awhile a piece of weathered wood sat near a grove of trees. There were a few bushes and sparkling graphite flakes spotting the trail. Simon was hiking with his nose down sniffing for telltale scents. Bix was sure the coyotes and deer covered this area each night. During the day small Skink Lizards peeked out from under rocks. It was glorious.

Lady and dog traveled together as they put

distance between themselves and the camp. Simon inspected both sides of the path traveling twice as far as Bix. A half mile lapsed into a mile. Her eyes followed the gulley lines. She began to let the environment drain away her fears. God's temple surrounded them. They hiked ten minutes more then turned back toward the park. "Ready to join the human race again, Simon?" she said to her dog. Bix reached down and attached the leash just before they entered camp. Somehow, life began looking brighter to her; she could almost trust the future again. Once again….

***

Bernie knocked on the door precisely at 5:00. "Dinner time, you two. Simon is coming isn't he? The family considers him to be a hero, you know. He can have some snacks I hope?"

"He can just as long as I can too," Bix said as she opened the door. "I don't think he'd let me leave him home." Bix grabbed a jacket for the evening while Simon sat at the door ready to be the first out. They exited together and then Bix locked up. "This is really nice of your family by the way," she commented.

"Well we really appreciate what you guys did. It's always great to get a chance to experience the good side of humanity. Let us celebrate that moment, lady." The three walked along the road side by side.

"All is well," Bernie added thoughtfully. "Mattie finally called their son, Mathew, and he's coming down from CSU right now. He needed to know what was happening. He should be here at dinner. Another set of watchful eyes will be a good thing. They're relieved that he's coming even though John is acting like a tough guy," Bernie added rolling her eyes. "It's a male thing."

As the three walked toward the Jayco Trailer, the smell of dinner cooking was over the top. "Smells wonderful," Bix announced as they arrived to find the Holdens seated in lawn chairs. The family jumped up to welcome them happily; it would be a celebration. A beer was placed in Bix's hand, a toast was initiated and Simon was given a bone to gnaw. He immediately settled in the group making happy chomping noises.

"Well I certainly am glad to thank you two. Mattie and I are still in shock over last night's chaos," John admitted.

"When you think about what could have happened, it takes my breath away," Mattie added. Her eyes watered slightly and she fought back the tears. John placed a reassuring arm around her shoulders.

There was a thoughtful pause in the conversation while everyone sat back down and included Bix in the circle.

Jim Robertson broke the somber mood. "Here comes the potato salad. Anybody hungry cause Lydia made enough for a small army again!" He glanced around and noticed the quiet. "Am I interrupting something? Hey this is a party. No 'gloomy-Gus' faces allowed. Come on folks; where's the beer?"

"This way," John said as he walked over and opened the cooler. The family relaxed. The chatter focused around how good everything looked on the table. Bix noticed a Jello bowl, homemade bread, a huge lettuce salad and now the crowning potato salad. John's pork roast was still smoking in the cooker. From the smell, Bix figured dinner was ready.

Lydia came up escorted by a tall red haired young man, a taller image of John with Mattie's freckles. "Look who I found?" she said beaming. John and Mattie quickly got up to greet their son.

Mathew went around the circle in welcome. When he came to Bix he said, "This must be the lady of honor that I have heard about. Thank you. I'd miss these folks if anything happened." He gave Bix a grateful smile. He petted Simon warmly as his eyes scanned the gathering. "Where's Gramps?" he asked looking around the group a second time.

John answered sheepishly, "Well, I think he'll be here. We've had a lot of excitement and not any of it positive. Dad's feelings are pretty torn up right now. Mattie went over this morning and invited him but he hasn't shown up yet. He was still sleeping can you believe that? He was okay by noon."

Matt thought about that for a moment then said, "I'll go get him." With that, he turned and headed for the Keystone Cougar in search of Henry Holden.

Lydia Robertson sat down across from Bix and clarified, "Mathew and Dad have always been close. He's the first grandchild and Dad thought the sun and moon rotated around Matt when he was born. Well, that's your family history for tonight,

Bix," she commented. "Hope Matt can get Dad off the couch this evening. He really hasn't been feeling a hundred percent lately. Then addressing Bix again, "And speaking of feeling better, how are your burns?" she asked.

"Much better actually. Went for a short walk and it helped. Did you take your kids fishing today? Is that what I heard earlier?"

"Oh you mean the yelling and turmoil around noon? We don't seem to do anything quietly anymore. I guess that comes with the pre-teen years times three. Yes. Caught a few small ones but nothing spectacular. That's such a beautiful little lake. "

"You mean Cottonwood Lake?" Bix asked.

"Exactly. Hey look who is coming over with Matt. Good. Now we can eat," Lydia got up and yelled for the kids.

As Matt and Henry approached, the kids piled food on their plates then walked back to the pop-up trailer. Lydia had set up a card table near their trailer for the kids. Matt brought his grandfather to a chair. The group smiled approvingly. Lydia then addressed Bix, "As our celebrated lady of honor please dig in. We wish that we could do more in return for the favor."

Bix got up and announced, "Thank you all for being so gracious. I am indeed honored and let's eat." Bernie followed her and so began the adult procession around the table. Simon followed Bix in anticipation. He was fifteen pounds of hopeful dog.

"Looks good doesn't it, Gramps? Can I get you a plate?" With a nod of approval from Henry,

Mathew went over to the food.

Bix had returned to the table with her plate amply filled; it all looked so good. Of course Simon would help her. She was seated across from Henry. "Glad you can join us," Bix said. "This is quite a spread in my honor. I really appreciate it."

"And I truly appreciate what you did. I hear that your little dog there was responsible for the heads up?"

"That's correct, sir. Simon keeps his ears tuned no matter what time. For a little guy he's quite a watch dog."

"I see," he said. And as if on cue Simon went over to meet Henry, his stub of a tail waging furiously. They both made greeting noises. Eventually, Matt came over with Henry's plate and went back for his own.

Henry's eyes followed Matt approvingly; he then stared at John. "Looks wonderful, John." Henry made a point of making sure that John heard him. There seemed to be a truce in effect, Bix thought. Good.

Dinner was wonderful. Both the pork and Mattie's corn had been cooked on the grill. People slathered butter on the corn and made happy noises. Eventually, they leisurely moved back out to the chairs with either a beer or coffee in their hands. Bix had her second beer which she knew would send her right to sleep tonight. Mathew and John started a little campfire in a portable fire pit. The family settled back in no hurry to rush home. Henry asked for a soda instead of a beer.

"You feeling okay, Gramps?" Matt asked.

"Sour stomach and a slight headache for the last couple of days," Henry answered. "I'll get over it. Might be all the excitement we're experiencing or high altitude," he added.

On cue the family eyed a police car moving slowly down the road. It passed them with the officer waving when he saw the group. Matt opened the conversation after the patrol car was out of sight. "Are they going to come by a few times tonight?" he asked. He took a long drink of his beer.

John answered, "That's the plan. I know I'll feel better since we don't know who's responsible."

"Well I know it's not Billy doing this," Henry said. "We talked yesterday after all the investigation noise settled down. Billy couldn't hurt you, John, and you know that down deep," he added. "He's got a hot temper but he's not a murderer. He's family; we're family."

"You sure he's not involved, Gramps?" Matt asked.

Henry stared intently at Mathew before he answered. There was no animosity in his words; his words came from the heart. "Billy's dealing with his ambitions. I haven't seen him this excited for years. His intentions are good."

"Politicians have a tendency to get involved in power and the money of Washington. It's a big world out there, Dad. Sure Billy could handle that?" Bernie asked.

"As well as any of us," Henry said to Bernie. "His family should help him find his way." Henry's point was not lost on anyone.

"Will his intentions take into account what is

good for ranchers, family and North Dakota?" John asked. "I can't see the ranchers or family being content with fracking in the backyard. North Dakota might feel economic relief now but what happens after all these wells run dry?"

"Rumor has it that the wells will be gone in less than twenty years. What do you think, Mathew?" Mattie asked her son.

Matt glanced around to see if his opinion was welcome before he began. Even Henry gave him a nod. "I've been taking a course this last semester on water rights and the agricultural future. Obviously, water rights are a timely subject for ranchers and the oil companies. 80 percent of the liquid the miners use in fracking is water that ends up contaminated. The big question out there is can contaminated water be transformed back into drinking water? It hasn't happened yet so the competition for water will be huge in this decade," Mathew said. He could tell that the family wanted him to continue. Simon sensing the mood jumped into Bix's lap and retired.

Matt poked the fire then continued, "Pennsylvania is having real problems with toxic water supplies. In some parts of that state their drinking water is suffering. How much do these water stress problems affect the droughts in Oklahoma and California is another question. Scientists just don't know. Obviously, research needs to be done and the landowners and miners need to listen. Their prejudices on either side of the controversy have got to stop. People have got to listen to scientific findings. Science is not some political conspiracy out there. It's the only real road map we have. Not politics as usual or quick money. People owe their children an informed future." Matt looked around to see how his comments were being received. "Sorry, Gramps, but that's the way I see it. Yes, we need the fossil fuels right now but we don't need to export to other countries for profit and we don't need anyone stifling solar energy research," Matt put his hand on the old man's shoulder and smiled warmly. "There's enough room for all these components."

"Don't be sorry, son. We old people need to know where you young folks stand," Henry said then quietly mulled over Matt's explanation for a few moments. Everyone sipped their beverage and watched the fire which decided to crackle and then spark.

Lydia sat up in her chair and said, "Well, if Henry's right and it's not Billy, where do we need to look?"

There was plenty of speculation and it always came back to fracking. Bix noticed that Mathew became strangely silent and only listened at this point. From his expression she could tell that he had something on his mind but wasn't sure if he wanted to share it now. Finally the group decided to process the information later and get some sleep tonight. Tomorrow would be soon enough for more discussion.

Around 10:00 the group broke up and began to pack the food away. Mathew and Henry offered to walk Bix back to her trailer. She liked that idea; she still had some questions about fracking. As they slowly followed the beams of their flashlights, Bix began her own research. "So Mathew, isn't there some kind of solution to the fracking controversy?"

"Well, it's probably years off but scientists believe that there could be dry fracking. If the government got involved like they should to protect the environment, research toward that goal would be financed."

"They'd stop using water in the process then?" Henry asked. He had stopped walking and waited for the answer.

Matt turned toward him and said, "Yes but it would take new guidelines and regulations also. Corporations sometimes need to be forced into taking the right direction."

Bix thought about that as they continued down the road. Simon on leash was weaving back and forth totally enjoying himself. "So water is the bottom line, huh?" she said. "Aren't they setting up a plan to use the Missouri River water?"

"They have to win the lawsuit being presented to the State Supreme Court. The lawyers are in debate as we speak. It's not a done deal by any means," Matt added. "I think it will end up in the higher court eventually after appeals have been issued."

"What if oil loses?" asked Bix.

"They need a plan B then," Matt said looking directly at his grandfather. "And Gramps, that's what scares me the most about Billy selling the leases. My dad has the major water well on his property. The family leases water freely from our land. You gave him the well when you and grandmother divided the land for your kids. What happens when the mining company needs water, Gramps? Do they use Billy's lease on my dad's well?"

Henry stopped in his tracks again and stared at Mathew. Bix could see Henry beginning to comprehend where his grandson was taking the discussion. "You mean that the attempts on John's life could be because of the well water?"

"Yes I do. I haven't talked to Dad about it yet but I need to. What do you think?"

"I think you may have caught on to what's really going on here," Henry confessed. "Two older generations totally missed that point."

"And that's why we educate our children," Bix added as a retired teacher echoing philosophy. "We teach to create solutions. Well done, Mathew. Makes me proud of you and I only met you," she announced.

"Well, if I am right there's another piece here. I truly don't think Billy understands the implications of water stress either. He could easily have fallen into a situation where he's being used also."

Henry felt the weight of the problem and it was squarely on his shoulders. Bix knew Henry hadn't wanted any of this controversy but here it was staring him in the face. She ventured forth a suggestion. "Henry, maybe you and Matt could talk with Billy together? With your heart and Matt's knowledge, you two make a great team. "

"What do you think, Gramps? I'm willing to try if you think it sounds like a good plan," Matt said. "If you think Uncle Billy would listen to me?"

"I thought you'd never ask," Henry answered

with a slight smile. "Let's go now. If we wait to do it, I won't sleep again tonight. Let's get the job done." Matt nodded.

Henry without hesitation took Bix in his arms and gave her a great big bear hug. "Thank you for your suggestion. You must have been a hell of a teacher. Thanks."

"You're welcome. Good night you two and good luck," Bix said then opened the trailer and signaled for Simon to hop in. She glanced at the two men walking back down the road. It was so interesting how life unfolded. Hopefully, Henry and Matt could really get Billy to listen. Maybe the dilemma would be unraveled after all, she mused. Bix shortly after getting home collapsed into bed to read her book. Sleep, however, subtly cast a soothing spell over her and the pages remained unread. Simon snuggled in next to Bix; he could always sleep.

***

Matt and Henry approached Billy's trailer. They stood outside for a few moments to make sure that Billy was still awake. Henry finally knocked softly at the door. "Billy, it's me. Are you up?" Henry asked softly.

Billy swung the door open to find his father and nephew seeking a late night visit. When he saw the two, Billy let out a sigh and moved to one side so they could enter. "What in the world brings you two out at this time of night? Hell, it's darker than shit out there," Billy said as he glanced at his watch. It was obvious that he had fallen asleep watching television. He went over to the set and turned it off then motioned for them to sit. As Billy finished a yawn, BB came out of the bedroom. She looked at Matt and realized that he was someone she did not know.

"Hi, I'm Matt, Billy's nephew. Sorry to wake you all up but Gramps wanted to have a conversation with Billy this evening."

"It's a little late to call this evening," BB announced to all of them.

"It's okay BB. Go back to sleep; I'll take care of this," Billy said. "Beer or anything?" he offered holding the refrigerator open.

"I really don't know how you can be so damn civil at this time of night. It's rude," she mumbled.

"Easy BB," Billy said. "I'll take care of this. Go to bed will you?"

"I still think-"

"Then don't think. Get the hell to bed and let me talk with my father and nephew all by myself!" Billy ordered loudly. His stare at BB was fairly hostile.

Needless to say, it was obvious that things weren't going lovingly this evening in Billy's household. In fact Matt was afraid that Billy would start throwing things if she didn't back off. Billy's reaction surely wasn't just over their arrival. There had to be another agenda going on here. Something must have happened earlier to ignite the situation.

"Well when Daddy gets here, you won't act so damn almighty, mister." With that comment hurled across the room, BB rushed into the bedroom and slammed the door. The whole trailer vibrated with the bang of the door. It became suddenly quiet as all three men stared at the closed door. It was like the anger vacuumed right out of the living room.

"Sit," Billy announced. "I'm having a beer after that shit. Can you believe it; her dad is coming here? BB thinks I need a lawyer against my family. That's crazy." He opened his beer and tossed the cap in the sink then took a nice long drink. Billy then slowed down and returned to his recliner where he had been when they knocked. "Okay, what's up?"

"I've been talking with Matt about the leases. Think we need to take another listen here, Billy." Henry eyed the bedroom door. "I'm thinking without the Bellows in the conversation. Billy got up and made sure the bedroom door was indeed shut even though trailers were not sound proof. Henry then continued, "Matt's just finished a course that deals with water rights. I think there's some stuff you need to hear and then we need to ask more questions. I ain't changed my mind, son, but take a listen and see what you think."

Matt and Billy talked for the next couple of hours. The give and take was good, Henry thought. Matt could see where Billy was going with the political angle. If the state could get more ranchers and farmers into politics then maybe the state's direction would not be controlled by city folks. The state government had to reach a balance. Billy was rather shocked to think that John's water well might be the reason for the attacks. He was willing to entertain the importance of the water needs for business and ranchers. State Supreme Court delays struck a cord with him.

For the first time in months Henry had hope that a compromise could be reached. Seeing two generations working together did Henry's old heart some good even though the cloud of depression hadn't completely lifted. Issues still needed to be resolved. The point was that the family had begun to talk with each other again. It was a new beginning.

Later that night when Henry finally arrived at his trailer, he did feel some relief. Bernie had called Billy a greedy kid last week. She would have been proud watching Billy and Matt talk tonight. And Mathew was so powerful in his knowledge. He was turning into such a strong gentle man.

Maybe the family could live together again. Lydia and Jim could move back in with him here at the park. The trailer was so empty tonight. Henry could handle the loneliness on the ranch because there was so much to do. But here it was vacation and having Lydia baby him was nice. He hadn't used the trailer bedrooms since she went back to sleep in the pop-up with the kids. He missed Lydia fussing over him and teasing him; he missed Mattie coming over to check on him each morning. He wanted life to return to normal; hell, he wanted Margaret, his wife, back with him. Henry had to admit that he was truly thankful that his children were doing well; he knew that Margaret was watching over them. Now if they could just find common ground in this fracking mess, things would be good again.

Henry suddenly felt really thirsty. The evening

had taken something out of him. It was hard work mending family fences without Margaret. He went over to the refrigerator and found a new half gallon of cherry fruit juice. Now who had left that for him? Returning to the couch Henry gulped down half the bottle. It tasted so good and sweet; he closed his eyes for a second. He finally leaned back and turned on the television. Henry had decided to calm himself. Let his mind escape. David Letterman was on; he watched intently.

Fifteen minutes later his stomach began to ache something terrible. Hell, not even the juice would settle his indigestion. He didn't feel good at all. Henry felt his breathing become labored. It felt like he just couldn't get enough air in his lungs. He placed his hand on his chest. It began to feel like his heart was going to jump right out of his chest! Henry realized that maybe he couldn't wait until he got home to get a check-up. He needed a doctor this very minute.

Hyperventilation was in full swing now. Henry knew that he had to call someone and get help. Bernie would help him; tell him what to do. Get him to the hospital.

He slowly got up and felt like he had run miles. His chest pounded and his breath rushed from his lungs. The pain was horrible! Henry felt like he was going to explode! He grabbed one of the chair backs then collapsed losing consciousness.

His body began to jerk like shocks of electricity were attacking his nervous system. Henry's legs shot straight out; his whole body began to convulse. He thrashed around on the floor like a fish out of water; his eyes rolled up in his head during one last morbid seizure. Passed comatose; passed resistance. A strange gasp escaped his throat as his body organs shut down.

The room became still while his soul slipped away to find Margaret. David Letterman droned on talking to an empty room.

CHAPTER 15

UNBELIEVABLE

The birds awoke and flew from their nests with the urgency of a short summer climate. There were baby chicks to feed and a deep blue sky to travel. The morning sun had just dawned over the peaks to spread light through the valley. Cool temperatures were being chased out of High Mountain Vista RV Park. The touch of frost evaporated from leaves and windows. It was a great time to snuggle down deeper in your covers for another hour of luxurious sleep.

The piercing scream shot through the camp like a stray bullet ripping apart tranquility! It shocked hearts into jumping a beat and brought cold chills. Confused and disoriented, people leaped out of their beds.

Bix and Simon jumped. Bix grabbed shorts and shirt and hopped toward the door never, slowing down. They scrambled out and saw Bernie emerging from her trailer. Their eyes met for a second in confusion.

Another scream indicated the direction. Bernie pointed then joined Bix in a full run. Mattie, John and Mathew leaped down the steps from their Jayco joining the crowd.

Billy and BB peeked around the corner while Jim came rushing toward everyone as he yelled, "Lydia, where are you?" Jim's face was pure panic. His eyes leaped from each camp site to the next and then down the road. He cupped his hands in front of his mouth and yelled again, "Lydia, where are you? Answer me, honey!"

Lydia flew out the door from Henry's trailer. Her eyes were wild and large. Her face was beet red as she rushed into Jim's arms. "It's Dad. Oh God, he's dead!" Lydia buried her face in Jim's shoulder and sobbed. The world stopped for the Holden family as their reality suddenly crashed then changed forever.

John and Matt rushed into Henry's trailer returning a few minutes later; their faces said it all. Matt stumbled past the family and walked back to his parent's trailer. Bix could see the tears in his eyes as he moved away. John simply held Mattie and buried his face in her hair. Bix watched the repercussions of sudden death pierce this strong family. Their hearts broken unexpectedly; grief pounding in their pulse. There would be no ritual grieving for them where they could reconcile with the inevitable; Henry Holden had abruptly vanished. Gone forever.

Bernie then moved toward Henry's trailer. She needed to see for herself. Billy moved in behind her and they went in. Even BB gave Lydia a nervous hug and stood in sympathy for a few moments. The group, like statues, stared at the exterior of the trailer. Finally they began to talk quietly. Bix could hear the wail of a siren coming down the highway. Matt must have called the police. She felt that the Holden family's private conflict was going to suddenly become public knowledge. The sirens would truly open the door and unintentionally create the media frenzy. The whole park was now news worthy.

Bix decided to go find Chelsea and Bob to see if they needed any help. Surely they had heard the sirens and wondered. As she came around the back of Billy's fifth wheel, BB was lifting a trash bag into their garbage tub as if she was getting ready for the intrusion of people. She looked up and nodded at Bix. "So sad," BB mumbled. "Hard to believe that just yesterday, he was…." She didn't finish her comment knowing that Bix knew. Instead BB closed the trash container and walked back into Billy's trailer. "So sad," she said again to no one in particular. Bix hurried on and met Chelsea and Bob halfway up the road. The three stood and watched the drama unfold.

"Don't touch anything just in case," Bernie said to Billy as they entered the trailer. He had reached down to straighten Henry's shoes into a pair. It was a gesture that he had done for his dad a thousand times. The trouble was that Henry would no longer appreciate the care. Bernie stared down at her father. The body lay rigid on the floor. It was apparent that he had been in pain from the expression on his face. His eyes were open in shock; the lifeless stare was hollow and vacant. There was some type of stain on the carpet in front of the couch waiting for Henry to clean it up. The trouble was Henry would no longer be able to do so.

Billy grasped Bernie's hand as he had instinctively done when they were kids. Brother and sister stood together processing. This stark vision would haunt them many times during their lives. There was no way of blocking out death. Billy whispered to Bernie as if not to wake his dad, "Matt and Dad came to talk last night, Sis. We were working things out. Dad was so full of hope last night; this just doesn't make sense. We'll never finish that conversation. It just seems so…crazy. Sis, I've got to get out of here," Billy said giving her hand an extra squeeze. He then released his hold, patted her back and headed for the door. Billy shut the door carefully as he left.

Bernie was frozen in one spot staring at the grizzly scene. She began to reenact what her father had done before his death. What were the logical steps that he had taken? Her eyes focused on the table. There was a spilled bottle of antacid that had drained and dried on the table's surface. He must have hit the table and chair somehow. His phone was on the floor in back of the table. The television was still on.

Had he been really sick in the last moments? She examined the stain on the rug. Had he been drinking something and if so, where was the container? She didn't see any glass or bottle. Bernie didn't want to touch the refrigerator door. Maybe her dad had put the container away. Was his death of natural causes? She suddenly became afraid. Bernie's hand flew up to her mouth, "Oh my God." Cold horror spread through her body as it occurred to her that just maybe her father had been murdered. Bernie was going to demand that a full autopsy be done. The family needed to know the truth before this case was over. Right now, however, she had to leave the trailer; the warmth of her dad was gone forever.

As she left and began walking away she knew that her life would never be the same. Memory would bring this vision back to the surface time and time again. She couldn't imagine the grieving process that her family would have to experience. Her father had no chronic illness. No warning signs. They were just dropped into grief. Bernie realized that it would be a very long time before she could truly close the door on this chapter of her life.

***

The day produced a parade of police officers. They marked off the area around the trailer with yellow crime scene tape and had one officer keeping family and other curious tourists away. Burger and Smith were leading the crime analysis on the trailer. Every available officer had been ordered to High Mountain Vista. There were at least six police cars parked on the gravel road.

The car lights were rotating with a solemn rhythm of silent alarm. Chief James Marten and Sergeant Holly were talking with various family members. They had set up a temporary office on two picnic tables under a cluster of Aspen shade trees.

Bix moved about her camp site giving a wide berth to the scene. She couldn't help but notice that investigating a death was such a gigantic undertaking. Was it a crime? Bix had just assumed that it was. Could have been a heart attack but for some reason, her mind didn't buy that conclusion. Granted, there had been plenty of stress on Henry but last night he was so full of life. He and Matt had walked away with a positive outlook. It would have been great to be a fly on the wall during their conversation with Billy. She had so been looking forward to asking Henry today how they had done. Now the family dilemma was put on hold or was it, she mused?

Chelsea came up from the back to find Bix. She placed her hand on Bix's shoulder as they both stared at the drama unfolding. "What a horrible morning," Chelsea said. "I really enjoy having the Holdens come here each summer. Now, the memories will probably be too much for them. It just wouldn't be a vacation anymore. I can't blame them at all. I wish it wasn't so awful but it can't be avoided."

"You never know. They may decide that it becomes a way to be with Henry," Bix said. "Even with all the sorrow, you have to account for the music and joy these folks share. It really is something special."

"I hadn't thought about it that way, Bix." Chelsea eyed her as if there was more to say. "I hate how Bernie carries her grief; I wish that I could help her. Being the only gay member of the family seems so unfair at times like this. She won't open up."

"You knew?" Bix asked with the surprise registering on her face.

"Her mother, Margaret, and I sat in the office years ago and talked about how worried she was for Bernie. The differences between the kids had been apparent to her. Bernie had always been so strong yet aloof and Margaret did understand what being in the closet truly meant. It really was Bernie's own personal closet with the door shut. Different type of environment for sure," Chelsea said.

Both women were watching the interviews taking place. Their eyes were intent on all the investigative activity. Bix finally said, "I'll see if Bernie wants to talk later. Maybe I can help. Grief counselor I am not but a friend I can be."

"Thanks." Chelsea patted Bix on the back then went on about her errands.

Finally, the coroner was on the scene. The body was removed and sent to Salida, the county seat, for the autopsy. Eventually, Sergeant Holly wandered down to Bix's site. "So Bix, what did you see and hear?" she asked?"

"Well I should tell you that Henry was a happy man last night." Bix went on to make sure that her little piece of the action was described thoroughly. At this time who knew what was important and how it all would fit together. What would the puzzle reveal?

Sgt. Holly informed the Holden family and Bix that they were not to leave town at this point.

Chelsea and Bob had been informed also. Bob was calling up their reservations for next week and explaining the situation. It would take half a row of sites to accommodate the Holdens for as long as the police would need. The Baileys were not going to charge anyone for extra time if it was needed. Bix would, of course, ask if she could pay; Chelsea and Bob would absolutely refuse to take any extra money. That was the way it was going to be but she had to try.

Hopefully by the Fourth of July, it all would be sorted out whether Henry's death was a crime or of natural causes. Bix was hoping for the Holden's sake that he had died of natural causes. She couldn't imagine what it would be like to find out that murder had become part of the family's history. That was a really cruel ending that she wished on no one.

Apparently, any of them could go into town so it wasn't exactly a terrible situation. It was a wait and see process at this point. Life would go on for the Holdens.

They would start living without Henry. Getting through the rest of the week would be difficult. Sitting and waiting for the answer was going to be awful. A little diversion would be helpful. That left the hot springs as an option. Getting out of here for a couple hours tomorrow was a good plan. Bix wondered if Bernie would come. It certainly would do both of them a world of good. She wandered toward Bernie's Winnie to ask.

CHAPTER 16

TALKING

Wednesday dawned with the prediction of showers arriving sometime late afternoon. It was normal high altitude weather. Colorado brought warmth during the clear morning then began the subtle piling of thunder clouds in the mountain biome. Rain would finally spill onto the thirsty ground for awhile then the sun would do a repeat performance for the waning afternoon. The temperatures would eventually drop to chilly for the evening. Locals would layer their wardrobe while tourists had a tendency to struggle. Took a little education but it all worked out eventually.

Midmorning found Bix and Bernie sprawled in the sand along the shallow shoreline of the Arkansas River; their heads resting on smooth large river stones. The warm water from the natural hot springs washed around them then meandered into the current of the river. People had creatively arranged the large rocks to make borders for small individual pools. Visitors could either choose the cement pools and lawn chairs above or climb down to the more rustic environment along the river shoreline. You paid your money either way.

It seemed like a fitting place to rest and escape from all the chaos that surrounded High Mountain Vista. The police were still there interviewing and searching for clues. It was like a dreary cloud hovering over that lovely place. The mental repercussions of the last four days had torn the heart out of the Holden family. Tension had taken control.

Bix could feel Bernie relaxing just a little. It was obvious that she was exhausted. Bix realized that the grief was just beginning for this strong woman. Maybe some of the tension would wash down the river today. One could hope.

Bernie raised her foot from the water and wiggled her toes examining them. Her countenance was thoughtful. "So what do you think happened to my dad?" she asked.

"Why don't you tell me what you're thinking before I answer your question? In many ways it's not my business; I don't want to presume."

There was a slight pause while Bernie mulled over Bix's response. She lowered her foot back into the warm water and turned her eyes toward her friend. "I think he was murdered; in fact, I think he was poisoned," she said.

Bix thought about that for a few seconds before she replied, "I've been wondering. Henry just didn't act like suicide was an option and no one has mentioned any health problems. What are the police saying at this point?"

"Chief Marten says it looks like natural causes. Of course that's without the autopsy results. He says that no one broke the lock on the door and nothing seems to be taken. My dad's wallet was on the dresser with two hundred dollars in it. Credit cards were there too. No one heard any late night disturbances either. Anyway, that's what the police assumption happens to be right now. I'm not satisfied with that easy conclusion. I keep thinking back to all the sour stomach comments. What if he was being poisoned a little bit at a time?" Bernie speculated.

"Why Henry then? John's the one who has been the focus up until this time. Henry was going to lease his mineral rights and help Billy. What's the motive and who?" Bix took a drink of water from the bottle in her backpack as she thought about it. "Has anyone seen any evidence of that SUV again? They would have to be in the camp already to have poisoned your dad. An inside job as they say. Wonder if the guest list might offer some clues? Maybe it would be a guest who you don't know but with North Dakota license plates?"

They both looked at each other. "Maybe we need to ask Chelsea?" Bernie said. "I just can't sit back and accept natural causes right now. Maybe I'm overreacting but I can't help it. What's the good in that?"

"Well, if it makes you feel better, neither could I. Couldn't hurt to check out a few things. What would be on our list…if say…we looked into the possibility of murder?"

"Well…there was a stain on the rug in front of the couch as if Dad had spilled a drink before he died. I didn't open the refrigerator to see what he had on hand. It wasn't the same color as the spilled antacid bottle on the table. I'd like to know what made the stain on the carpet. Maybe we could find some remains of the poison."

"What about the chili the other night?" Bix asked.

"We all ate that. Wait a minute…Dad was continuously sampling the chili over in the Commons. You suppose?"

Bernie had more to say she could tell. Bix brought up her hands in a questioning pose. "What?"

"He used a big old wooden spoon. When Dad and I put the dishes away later, I don't remember seeing that spoon. Interesting."

"So first we need to prove that there might be evidence pointing toward poison?"

"I think so," Bernie nodded. "Still your question of why murder is huge. Why my dad? Like you said he was leaning toward selling his leases. Why now?"

"All good questions but maybe we ought to take one step at a time. How he died seems to be a priority for you right now. What if I talk with Chelsea this evening and you look for the spoon? Wonder when we could get into Henry's trailer? Wonder when they'll be done in there?"

"What if we sneaked over late tonight and

checked the trailer? I have a key. I could show you what I saw. I'd like to know what you might see that I missed. Of course that is if you wouldn't mind. I know my request is a lot to ask of a new friend but-"

"Isn't that what friends are for?" Bix interrupted. "I certainly haven't felt like an outsider since you all adopted me that first night. Even Chelsea wanted me to check on you and make sure you were okay. You are okay, right? I just figure action is the best solution right now. At least for me it would be. I guess I am presuming that it works for you."

Bernie gave Bix's a slight smile and said, "Funny thing is that it does work for me. Thanks for understanding what I need. Guess that's what good friends are for. At least friends that stick around in bad times."

"Permanence is the bottom line isn't it?" Bix said as she looked at Bernie across the small rock pool. "True friends need to have the ability to listen when life is crucial. I would think that right now what you have to do should be priority. Lead on oh new permanent friend. We have obviously met for a reason. I figure if I needed help, you'd be there," Bix stated.

Bernie didn't even hesitate, "Sure. I'd go into your trailer of trouble anytime."

"Then I say we head back to High Mountain Vista and dig into finding the proof so that we can establish the motive of poison."

***

Bix and Bernie had just turned into High
Mountain Vista behind a blue Cadillac with North
Dakota plates. The Caddy had stopped at the office
and was honking for attention as if the place offered
roadside assistance. Bob Bailey came out of the
office door with a wry smirk on his face. He strolled
slowly around the Caddy and leaned in the driver's
window. Finally, he pointed down the Holden row
of sites and crossed his arms while watching the car
creep down the road.

He saw Bix's truck and began shaking his head.
He came over to them smiling. "I believe Princess
BB's father, the lawyer, has arrived. Oh hi, Bernie,"
Bob said as he peeked over to see who was with
Bix. "Glad to see you out and about. I'm so sorry; it
couldn't have happened at a worst time to a great
family. Just doesn't make sense."

"Hi, Bob," Bernie said. "Thanks for all your
help. I just wish we could have gotten home before
all this trouble started. You and Chelsea certainly
don't deserve our problems."

"Don't you fret. We're here to help in anyway
that we can," Bob said while rubbing Bix's arm
warmly then noticing their wet hair. "Been to the
hot springs I assume?"

"Yep," Bix answered. "Amazing what a little
relaxing can do; we both needed that. So Mr.
Bellows has arrived." She began to speculate out
loud, "What for, I wonder? To take BB back to
North Dakota.?"

"He didn't say but if arrogance counts for
anything that would seem like his inclination." Bob
stepped back from the Ranger's window and swung

his arm bowing with a courtly gesture. "You may enter, ladies. There's always room for royalty."

"Thank you, sir," Bix replied. "Oh, Bob, is Chelsea going to be around this evening? Need to talk with her after dinner."

"I'll tell her. Maybe around 7:00 at the office?"

"That would be great. Thanks," Bix added.

They drove slowly down the road and watched as BB rushed out to give her daddy a big old hug. A screech erupted from her mouth echoing through the camp. Billy, with arms crossed, watched from the trailer door. Charlie Bellow's light tan suit definitely looked out of place at the High Mountain Vista. He was a portly short man with graying hair. The two Bellows whispered to each other in a quick communication. With the plan established, Charlie released BB and headed toward Billy with his hand extended for a shake. Billy came down the steps and gave the man his hand. They disappeared into the trailer shortly after.

Bix and Bernie had watched the meeting with interest. Their resolve to investigate Henry Holden's death had changed their perspective. From now on they would make sure that whatever happened was recorded in their memories. Somewhere in this camp there were answers even if the facts were buried in North Dakota. Hopefully, they could be of some help as the clues unfolded. Bix let Bernie off at her Winnie and then proceeded down to give Simon his long awaited hugs and treat. She glanced up at the clouds forming to the west and figured she and Simon could take a quick walk before the rain shower started.

Bix opened the trailer to an explosion of yelps and prancing feet. Simon leaped out the door as if he had been in bondage for days. His little head leaned to one side as it did when he was in stress. She held him until the chaos stopped and grabbed his leash off the hook inside the trailer door. "Come on guy, let's get some walking in." Her feet felt much better plus the hot springs had helped with the other aches and pains. There was still some sun left; they would come back when the clouds began to truly threaten the sky. Maybe a nap at that point before dinner, she thought. Wear Simon out then nap in or read sounded super. Hell, she was on vacation, right?

CHAPTER 17

DEALING WITH QUESTIONS

"And what exactly do you want, Billy? We're talking here about being a senator in the next two years. Who knows where all this stops?" Charlie Bellows hitched up his pants with a self-important gesture. "You have big money behind you, boy. Big money," he finished his thought by holding out his hand for BB to give him a coffee cup. Charlie sat down on the couch and blew on his newly acquired drink.

"Of course I want to get into politics. However, I would like to represent North Dakota which also means the ranchers point of view." Billy's eyes fluttered hesitantly.

BB could tell that Billy was purely testing the water here. He was so easy to convince that she still felt confident. "Billy honey, that ain't where the money is; you got to follow the money."

Charlie sent her a 'butt out' look. His voice took

on a soft manipulative tone as he spoke, "Politics takes big money. The days when a man ran on honesty are long gone, Billy. When the media and technology took hold of us, the times changed. Surely you can't think that standing on a corner with twenty people nodding their heads cuts it anymore? You'll be run over by the money flooding in from back East and out West. Billy, don't lose your focus here. Keep your eyes on the ball, son."

Billy stared at him intently for a few seconds; he knew it was good business sense hitting him in the face. What he didn't like was that he truly was selling out his family. Matt had made the environmental picture clear. Surely there had to be a compromise. Could a candidate run on compromise or would the money folks simply slander him until his message was a moot point? Maybe it was best to keep quiet at this time and seek out the money then, eventually, back dry fracking research. It was certain that the country was hell bent on using up all the fossil fuels. Would the fuel companies dig huge tunnels under everything until sink holes devoured entire towns? When would people finally say enough is enough? Where could he find the solar and wind backers?

Suddenly, he wanted to talk with John and Matt. Maybe between them he'd get some names to contact. Until then it was best to acquiesce to good old Charlie. The man was brilliant at making money there was no doubt. Wait your turn, Billy. Don't say anything more, he thought.

"Well, Charlie, I know you're right. I do want to be a senator and then some," he said with a smile.

"Life is good I have to admit. I'll stay the course, Charlie," Billy confirmed and at the same time realized that indeed he was becoming a politician after all. What he actually believed didn't need to come out until he made his first speech and maybe not even then. The shit could hit the fan when he was ready. There was time to plan his actual campaign strategy.

Suddenly a wave of unexpected grief shook Billy; he couldn't help but feel jealousy and loss. BB was so relieved and happy to see Charlie. Billy couldn't help but miss his own dad; he would have given anything to be able to talk with him again. Billy wanted to do something that Henry would have been proud of; some action that would have made him a stronger man instead of a pawn playing gutless games. Maybe the family was all he did have; in reality, BB was daddy's girl. He looked at her with new eyes as if all the glamour and privilege was falling away. There was a dividing line between having class and being cheap he thought; Billy's mind began to see the difference. "Okay, I'm in," he lied like a true politician.

"Good," Charlie nodded. He put his coffee cup down and pulled himself up out of the chair. "Now where is the police station? I need to go have a chat with the chief. Did I hear his name is James Marten?"

Obviously Charlie had done his homework, Billy thought. "Yep that's the right guy. Do you want to go somewhere for lunch first?" Billy asked.

Charlie checked his gold watch and said, "How about after my conversation with him? I want to check in at the motel also."

"But Daddy we have an extra bedroom. You can stay here," BB said quickly.

Billy held his breath while Charlie made his decision. Sure you can stay with us," Billy said with his fingers secretly crossed hoping that fate would not bring Charlie into his trailer.

"Nope. I need to set up my office computers and phones. Room to spread out is important. Not this time, honey." He patted her shoulder and kissed her cheek. "Let's eat around two," he said.

Fate, unfortunately, had other plans for these people. Charlie did leave and go check into his motel. However, when he arrived at the police station the two detectives, Smith and Burger, were on their way to High Mountain Vista. They were under orders to bring back to the station a person of interest. The autopsy report had come back and there were traces of poison. Henry Holden had been poisoned. Chief Marten had just finished talking with the coroner. There was no doubt that Ethylene Glycol was found in Henry's body. It looked like antifreeze was the culprit.

***

BB noticed the police car first as it parked outside of their trailer. "Billy, the police are here again. It's those two damn idiots from last time," she yelled toward the bathroom door.

"In a minute damn it," Billy retorted.

There came a loud knock at their door. "Coming," she said slightly nervous. She opened the door.

"Is Billy Holden here?" Detective Burger asked. There was a hint of urgency in his voice. Both detectives invited themselves in looking around for Billy.

"He's in the can. Hang on will ya. Billy, get out here," BB demanded. She banged on the bathroom door to make sure the police could see that she was complying.

"What?" Billy flushed and then swung the door open while hitching up his pants.

"We would like you to come with us down to the police station. There have been new developments in your father's death."

"What?'" Billy said again.

"We need to discuss the details with you at the station."

"No. I don't think so. I think we'll discuss the details right here, right now before I go anywhere. Unless, I am under arrest?"

"Why would you think that?" Smith asked.

"Because you are acting like I did something. I need to know if I need a lawyer."

"Not at this point," Smith replied.

Billy held his ground looking at them. He wanted BB to hear anything that took place here in case he needed a witness. "BB and I both need to know what this is all about. As a citizen in good standing I deserve to know." He crossed his arms and leaned back waiting.

Burger was the one who answered his question, "Your father was murdered. We got the autopsy report back. You are at this time a person of interest and a formal interrogation needs to take place now. If you believe that you need a lawyer that is of course your right," Burger added. "You are not under arrest but need to come in for questioning. We also have a search warrant coming for this trailer. Miss Bellows, you will need to stay outside until after the officers finish."

Billy checked his watch and said, "My lawyer is probably at the station or on his way. BB, call your dad and make sure that he knows. Let's go." Billy went out the door first and waited by their car. John and Mattie came out of their Jayco and watched.

"You need anything, Billy?" John yelled.

"No. I'll talk with you later when I get back. Providing I get back," Billy said and got in the car.

Another police car arrived. Sgt. Holly and two other officers proceeded into the trailer. Sgt. Holly gave BB the warrant on her way in.

As soon as the car drove off with Billy, BB screeched hysterically, "Son of bitch, they're arresting Billy. My God, do something!" she demanded of John. She dialed her phone with shaking hands, "Daddy, they took Billy and are searching the trailer!" During the pause BB began to settle down. "Yes, they have a search warrant; no, the warrant says for traces of poison." Charlie Bellows was obviously giving calming advice. She sat down in a lawn chair still clutching the paper. "Well no, they didn't say arrest but something about person of…interest that was it." There was a pause while she listened and nodded her head. "Okay…okay I won't. You're there?" Another pause in the conversation ensued. "Okay I will.

Bye." She disconnected.

BB looked up suddenly and remembered that Mattie and John were waiting. "Daddy's there with Billy. They now think Henry was murdered. That's ridiculous. I'm going over to my dad's motel room and watch television until these jerks are done. This is crazy," she said and stomped off toward her rented BMW. BB began making calls on her cell as she left them standing with more questions than answers.

"What do you suppose?" John said to Mattie. "Murder? How in the world could that have happened?"

"If Billy's a person of interest then maybe the police believe that he actually was involved. You don't suppose?" Mattie's question was left unanswered when John's phone rang.

"Hello. Yes this is he. Yes, Chief Marten, we're both here." He listened and put the speaker on so Mattie could hear. They grabbed each other's hand when Chief Marten uttered the word, 'murder.' The couple sat down together and let the situation soak in. "Then Billy is a person of interest only? You haven't charged him? He didn't do it, Chief. We may disagree but family doesn't murder family. Can I tell my son what has occurred?" Chief Marten gave his permission for the parents to inform their son.

As John disconnected he knew that things were going to be difficult. It would remain up to the police to spread the word and tell everyone about the new set of interrogations. John began thinking about telling Matt. What a way to remember your grandfather, he thought. It left a hollow feeling in his stomach to say the least.

Mattie sensed his thoughts, "You want me to tell Matt?"

John weighed the offer. "Let's do it now and together, honey."

"Fair enough," Mattie said. They walked hand in hand toward the Commons where Matt was doing his laundry. The boy was a young college student enjoying the university life and concentrating on his future, Mattie mused. Unfortunately, she now realized that Matt's world was abruptly going to change forever; murder would destroy any innocence he had left. It would steal from Matt a part of his grandfather's memory; the evil shadow would always persist. Immense anger and confusion exploded into her consciousness. Who would do such a thing and why? What a good honest man Henry had been. The bitter reality of murder would scar so many people forever; it was despicable.

As if reading her thoughts, John said, "Such a good man. He didn't deserve this kind of an ending. How will we get through this?"

"We will, John." Mattie gave his hand a reassuring squeeze.

"Will what?" Matt asked as he carried a huge load of laundry out the screen door.

"We need to talk privately back at the trailer," John said. They divided the load of laundry and walked back in silence. Finally they arrived at the picnic table outside of the Jayco site.

Matt could tell that whatever had happened was

bad. He braced himself. He quickly tossed the laundry into his car trunk and sat down with them. "So what's going on?" he asked while looking from face to face.

"Matt, there's no pretty way to say this…your grandfather was murdered. The police just called and told us. How? We don't know yet. The whole mess has gotten pretty ugly," John finished.

Mattie added the rest of the information. "The police came by earlier and picked up Billy. He's now a person of interest so they say. BB's father is here so Billy has a lawyer thank heavens."

Matt's heart broke with the sheer weight of the situation. He had not only lost his mentor and confidant but now the police were trying to take away his uncle. Matt gulped down his sorrow and said, "He didn't do it. Uncle Billy had pretty much changed his mind last night when we talked. He really loved Gramps. Uncle Billy didn't do it anymore than I did. This is crazy. We're family."

Mattie smiled at her son seeing the man surface and the boy fading farther into the background. She would miss the boy terribly but Mattie was so proud of the man sitting with them here at the table. "I'm sure it will work out somehow," she said. "Henry won't let anything happen to Billy I know."

Matt glanced at his grandfather's trailer for a moment. "You know I have to admit that I wondered about murder from the start. Gramps was strong. There's no way that it was suicide and his heart was good. He had a physical a couple of months ago. The doctor told him that he was in good shape. At least that's what he told me. I didn't totally buy what the police have said from the start."

"I have to confess that I've been holding back some doubt about his death since the beginning," Mattie said. "I haven't gone so far as to think murder but I haven't been satisfied with any answers yet. It was so sudden."

John looked at both of them and shook his head. "You two have been holding out on me. I just figured that you never know when something is going to happen. If anyone would meet an untimely demise, I thought it would be me. Dad was falling in line with the oil money. What's the motive here?"

"Don't talk about your death that way," Mattie said. "Don't put it out there. I don't know what I would do," She grabbed John's hand and held it tight. "We've got to take care of each other."

Three heads nodded in unison. John suddenly noticed that Matt had laid a large spoon on the table beside him. He recognized it as his dad's. It had the Holden brand burned in the handle. He pointed at the spoon and asked, "Why do you have Dad's spoon?"

"What? Oh I forgot. Bernie was over in the Commons looking under and over everything. She was looking for this spoon. I found it behind the washing machine when I turned on the hot water handle. Somebody must have thrown it back there. Weird."

"Equally as weird as why was Bernie looking for it in the first place? How did she know it was in the Commons and/or missing? You want to go get the answers to those questions and let us know? We'll go talk with Lydia and Jim. I'm sure the police have notified them by now. We'll meet you back here later?" John said.

"Sounds like a plan." Matt got up and went toward the Winnie in search of Aunt Bernie while John and Mattie went in the opposite direction to find the Robertsons.

By nightfall the Holden clan would all know the cause of death. The bleak reality became so much more to process; murder was not something easy to handle.

***

"Aunt Bernie? You home?" Matt said while knocking softly on her door. "Found that spoon for you. You're not going to believe where I found it."

"I just might," Bernie said as she opened the door and motioned him inside. They sat at the kitchen table. "Where was it?"

"Well I went to open the hot water faucet for more force. Leaned over and there behind the washing machine was the spoon on the floor. You can't miss the brand on it." He handed it to her.

"Damn we probably lost the finger prints," Bernie said as she got out a plastic bag and deposited the spoon.

"Finger prints?" Matt asked. "Then you knew that Gramps was murdered before the police? Chief Marten called Dad and told him only that the autopsy was back but didn't mention a cause to us. Have they called you yet to set up an interview?"

"No but I'm sure I'll hear soon. I'm really not

surprised by the news. Actually, Bix and I talked today at the hot springs. We both think that Dad must have been poisoned."

"Poisoned? Nobody has said anything about poison. What brought that idea to the surface?" Matt asked.

"It just made sense to us. Remember your grandfather's comments about his sour stomach and headaches? I probably have watched too much television crime but antifreeze has similar symptoms. Granted, it would also sound like an ulcer but that seemed less likely to us. Anyway, we began to think about how poison could have been given to him. I remembered Dad tasting his chili and leaving that spoon on the counter in the Commons. We were in and out of there like many people that day. Later, Dad and I put the dirty dishes in the dishwasher and I remembered that I hadn't seen the spoon. Funny how things occur to you later after the fact. Could be I'm crazy and then again who knows," she said holding up the bag with the spoon. "I just hope there's something on this old spoon other than the brand and ugly old chili residue."

"Me too," Matt said. "Wish I had been here earlier in the week. Maybe I could have picked up on what was going on."

"Don't punish yourself, Matt. Things happen when they happen. You can't play the game of 'what if.' I'd say you were lucky to have missed your dad and uncle's fight over fracking. Billy informed the family that he was selling us out. I thought your dad would have a fit. Everyone was pretty steamed."

"They didn't throw any punches did they?" Matt asked.

"No. No, but the words flew and then there was BB announcing her engagement to your uncle the next morning. I thought Lydia was going to explode. She and I went for a hike that day. Your Aunt Lydia was really unhappy that Billy hadn't confided in her. You know they were always the two closest kids, right?" Bernie added. She grabbed the coffee pot and poured two cups then offered sugar and milk to Matt.

"You know when Gramps and I went over to Uncle Billy's that night after the dinner, he was listening to us. I could see the wheels turning. I don't think it would be a bad thing for Uncle Billy to get into politics if he stays informed. Ranchers need someone at the state level for sure."

"What makes you think that he'd represent the ranchers? Way I see it Billy is hell bent on making money and marrying that bitch, BB. We don't need a Bellows in the family trust me on that one."

"Well, it may be their relationship is a good thing right now what with Uncle Billy being taken to the police station," Matt said taking some of the cookies in Bernie's jar to top off his coffee.

"What? I hadn't heard about that!" Bernie leaned in closer.

"Probably shouldn't have said anything and let the police tell you, but damn he's family," Matt said. "They took him down to the station as a person of interest and Bellows is there with him."

"All this just happened?" she asked.

"Yep. Probably about an hour ago. I was still over doing my laundry when Mom and Dad came over. It was maybe 40 minutes after you had left." Matt halted his cookie on the way to his mouth and looked at Bernie. "I don't think that Billy was involved. A pawn maybe but he wasn't involved. Gramps and I were changing his perspective; I'm sure of that. I could feel it."

Bernie looked out the window for a few moments as she processed what Matt had said. "Matt, I'll agree with you about Billy. He loved his dad and really respected him. Dad meant everything to him so he wouldn't intentionally hurt him. He might lie to him but not hurt him."

"Agreed. So that leaves whoever tried to take my father off the road for our prime suspect. There's got to be more involved than just family…."

"It would make sense," Bernie said getting more comfortable with the idea every minute. "We would need to prove that of course but maybe this spoon will reveal its secrets." Bernie tapped the spoon in the bag and Matt finished his cookie. "Bix is going to ask Chelsea if she can take a look at the registration book. We're thinking maybe someone else from North Dakota checked in and has been hiding out somewhere in the other two rows of trailers."

"Sounds like a good idea," Matt said. "Anything I can do to help?"

"Well the plan is for Bix and I to go into Dad's trailer tonight and look around. I think Bix might help me piece together what I saw and who knows, she might see something else."

"You want me to keep an eye out for you two while you search? I could hang around outside. What time?"

"We're thinking 11:00 since quiet time begins at 10:00."

"I'll be sitting at the picnic table then at 11:00 just to add my two cents worth. Are you going to tell the police what you ladies are thinking?"

"Well I'll need to give them the spoon and explain where I got it eventually. Hope I can delay my interview until tomorrow. That way we can get the trailer search done." Bernie smiled at Matt. "Thanks kiddo for offering your help. I'm sure Bix will agree with including you in the plan."

"Let me know anytime I can help. I would like to be included," Matt said as he got up to leave. "Maybe we can help the police from the family viewpoint. I just need to do something. Do you mind if I tell my parents what we're doing?"

"I would have no problem with that. Besides they'll probably hear us snooping around tonight anyway."

"True. Okay, be careful and I hope you do find something. Some evidence that will help free Uncle Billy would be great. Thanks, Aunt Bernie."

"Anytime. Besides, what's family for?"

Matt felt better as he walked back to the family trailer. To sit back and do nothing just wasn't an alternative for him either. He would so miss his grandfather and the sooner they could clear the family name and set things right the better. He had decided to stay at High Mountain Vista until Uncle Billy was back with the family. Until they could have Gramps taken back to North Dakota and this whole horrible situation over; Matt felt an obligation to stay. There would be no closure for him until this murder was solved. One had to pray that the investigation wouldn't go on for years. Hopefully, the evidence would help to solve the murder quickly. Closure would then mean that Matt could grieve and remember the good. Henry Holden had been a great man and a role model for Matt. "Think of the good," he vowed out loud to himself as he walked. "Think of the good."

CHAPTER 18

SEARCHING

"Hey Chelsea, can I come in?" Bix asked as she peeked into the family room off of the office.

"Sure come on back. Want some tea? I just sat down after dishes and dinner. Whew, busy day. What's on your mind, lady?" Chelsea asked. The TV was quietly playing in the background as Chelsea leaned back in her lounger and crossed her legs. The cup of tea was warming her hands as she blew on it.

"I'll take a rain check on the tea but thanks. Really hate to bother you but Bernie and I have a favor to ask," Bix said hesitantly as she sat down in a comfy chair. "Can I check the registration book for visitors... say for the last two weeks?"

"What are you thinking?" Chelsea asked while placing her tea on the side table after a sip.

"Do you remember any other visitors from North Dakota who weren't part of the Holden group?"

"Let me think…. Actually there was a big rig that came in right before Bernie and Mattie on the first day. I remember the rig because the trailer had Denver plates but the car being towed had North Dakota plates. I thought it was an odd combination. Come to Denver and then rent a rig so you can stay here? Just some trivia that sticks in your head you know. They booked the reservation at the last moment. We had one site left up front by the road. Most people won't rent that spot because of the road noise. Let me go get the book and we'll look for the name." Chelsea began to get up.

"No, sit! Can I go get the book for you?" Bix said and jumped up.

"It's right below the counter out there so it's handy."

Bix brought the book back and handed it to Chelsea who started turning the pages. "Here is the name, Jones? John Jones. That is a strange name now that I think about it," Chelsea mumbled. She grabbed a note pad from the table drawer and wrote down the license plate. "Says here that there were two people in that trailer for a three day stay. They pulled out yesterday. Not a couple but two men, John and Robert Jones. I assumed the Jones's might be brothers." She looked up at Bix with questions in her eyes. "What are you two thinking?"

"We're thinking that just maybe there were other people here who were concerned with the family's activities. Obviously, the people that ran John off the road had to have hid somewhere. Why not right under our noses?"

"So you have heard about the autopsy results?"

Chelsea asked. "It all is so hard to take right now. High Vista is becoming famous for the wrong reasons. Chief Marten has requested that Bob and I do not allow any of the media from Denver to camp here. Since all the sites are taken for the 4th there's no problem with his request. Murder is such an unheard of word for Buena Vista. We're just not used to the repercussions at all. It's bad enough with Henry gone but to have it be murder is unbelievable. If Bob and I can in any way help you, let us know."

"You just have. Did you see these guys during their stay at the camp?"

"Not really. They kept to themselves as far as I could tell. I'll ask Bob if he saw or heard anything from those guys. He seems to meet most of our guests at some point or another as he goes about his work."

"Thanks, Chelsea. I'm sure Bernie will appreciate your help." Bix got up to leave.

Chelsea eyed Bix closely and then asked, "Is Bernie okay?"

"I think so. As long as she feels that she can help in the investigation, she'll be fine."

"Good. Let me know what else I can do, Bix." Chelsea got up and walked Bix back to the office. "Be careful please. Don't want anything to happen to you two ladies."

"We'll be careful. See you later." Bix walked back toward her trailer. So High Mountain Vista did have some visitors that could have been watching the family. The site Chelsea was talking about was close to the Commons also. It would have been easy to add poison somehow as you walked through to the laundry or showers. Bix decided to eat dinner and relax with Simon before her eleven o'clock meeting. Maybe take a shower and do some normal things. She didn't want to watch the local news though. One of the big stories would be about High Mountain Vista and probably not accurate. Denver would be adding their personal opinions to any facts that they might have. Way over the top for Bix at this point.

As she walked toward her trailer, Billy arrived back at the park accompanied by BB and Charlie Bellows. The Cadillac slowly pulled up to a stop in front of their site. Bix noticed that they all looked tired. There was no doubt that it had been a long day for those three. Well, at least Billy was being released and the family would feel some relief. Having Bellows arrive was definitely a good thing for Billy. Bix wondered if Billy was still on the short list for the police. It was time to look at all the possibilities and especially outside of the family, she thought.

***

Bernie knocked on the door promptly at 10:45. She looked prepared with a flashlight and dark clothes. Bix also noticed that Bernie had a gun holstered to her waist. She hadn't expected that move.

"We have some help tonight. Matt is going to sit at the picnic table outside and keep an eye on the camp for us. I didn't think you'd mind so I gave him the go ahead. He found the spoon by the way. I have it in a plastic bag for safe keeping."

"Good on all counts. I'm taking Simon with us. His nose might be a bonus for us as we rustle around in there. Surprises we don't need." Bix glanced at the gun and decided to say something. "You think the gun is needed?"

"I have no idea but my Glock is a precaution that seems natural in a North Dakota kind of way. It's a whole different environment that we're dealing with when it comes to murder. I simply feel safer. It's just there in case we get in over our heads. What did you find out from Chelsea?"

Bix decided to let it go at that; different folks, different strokes. She could very well be out of her element tonight. "Chelsea said that there had been a rig pull in earlier on Sunday. The trailer had Denver plates and the towed car had North Dakota plates. Two guys named Jones. They left yesterday so they're in the wind," Bix said as she placed her baseball hat on her head and grabbed some gloves. "You ready, Simon?" The little dog twisted his head to the side thoughtfully and moved toward the door. Bix turned off the lights as they exited her trailer.

"What county was the North Dakota car plates from?" Bernie asked.

"It was Williams County. Chelsea wrote down the number for me. We can check the specifics when we get back to my trailer if you like."

"That would be close to the city of Tioba where the mining companies operate. It could be another piece of our puzzle," Bernie said as she unlocked the trailer door and removed the yellow crime tap.

She waved at Matt who was already seated at the table as they entered the rig. They climbed into the trailer, turned on the lights and shut the door. Simon began to sniff around as all dogs will do.

Bernie shivered as she stared at the floor where Henry had been found. The pang of grief was hard to control; she took a deep breath as the vision of his body flashed into her mind. Life gone from Henry's body had been so incredibly difficult for her. Quickly, Bernie put her feelings aside and began explaining to Bix what she had seen. They noticed that the carpet with the stain had been cut out by the police. The place was a mess with finger print powder and police going through all the drawers. "Wow," Bernie mumbled as she looked around. It doesn't seem like they could have missed much. I think I'll start in the kitchen," she said and moved in that direction.

"Hey, Bernie, did your dad ever hide stuff for safe keeping in here?" Bix asked.

Bernie stopped inspecting kitchen utensils and thought for a moment. "I'm sure he did. At home at the ranch he and mom always had little cubby holes where important papers and money were kept. I wonder where he'd figure was a good place in here? Maybe out in the storage spaces somewhere." She continued sorting the utensils and looking under the mats in the kitchen drawers.

Simon followed Bix into the bedroom. She turned on the light and saw that the mattress had been taken off the bed. Nothing under the bed was worth noticing. She went over to see what had been found and left in the dresser. Simon began sniffing at the corner of the rug over in the small clothes closet. He began to dig. "Simon, stop. We're not here to make a bigger mess." Then she began to wonder exactly what he did smell.

The trailer was new enough that rodents hadn't taken up residence. She turned on her flashlight and went into the closet. She pulled the corner of the carpet up carefully and sure enough there were papers under the rug. "Bernie," she called.

"What did you find?" Bernie rushed in and began to shuffle through the documents. "It's an agreement between Billy and my dad. It gives Billy the mineral rights on half of my dad's property. Looks like he had not signed the agreement." Bernie took the papers into the kitchen and sat down to look at them.

Bix patted Simon on the head and adorned him with praise. She lifted him up for a hug. "You're a good boy." She placed him back down on the floor and finished her search of the bedroom. "Nothing else in here that I can see," Bix said as she came back into the kitchen.

"I was thinking I'll check the top cabinets in here next. Not sure why," Bernie said. "Looks like the police took even the flour and sugar with them. The top cabinets still have some things in them." Bernie opened the high cabinet over the kitchen sink.

From Bix's view at 5'5" she could see the bottom of the shelf only. Her eyes caught something on the back corner on the bottom of the shelf. Something only a short person could see. "Bernie, feel under the shelf at the back corner," she said.

Bernie brought out a small black plastic item.

"What in the world is this?" She examined it closely then showed it to Bix. "Do you think it's a bug of some sort? Please don't tell me that my dad's place is wired?"

Bix eyed the object and concluded that it was a surveillance device. "Yep, I think so. Wonder if there are more of these little gems?" She began to start feeling around with her fingers. Bernie with her height started checking out the ceiling panels.

"Bingo," Bernie extracted another one from above the ceiling panel in the far corner of the living room. She replaced the panel and went on searching.

Bix found another one stuffed in a small pillow back in the bedroom. "So who do you suppose is listening?" she asked.

Simon began to growl. Not anything loud but a warning as if he smelled something outside. Bix was just going to comment about him when a bullet exploded the kitchen window. Shattered shards of glass burst through their atmosphere! In quick order another bullet pierced into the cabinet next to Bernie's head propelling splinters into the ceiling. Both women hit the floor praying that there wouldn't be a barrage of bullets while Simon barked furiously. Bix grabbed him and held him close.

The door flew open and Matt ran in keeping low as he moved. He also was carrying a hand gun. Sounds like a rifle doesn't it, Matt?" Bernie said. Her voice trembled as she flipped the light switch off. They sat on the floor and waited.

"Yeah a rifle from some distance away," Matt

added. Maybe they're sitting in the woods."

Bernie crawled over to the bedroom door and reached an arm up to flick off that light. The darkness seemed almost friendly as they listened to the silence. Time halted and left them motionless with only thoughts racing through their heads. The night settled bringing them an eerie peace. They waited.

Suddenly there was a rush of footsteps approaching the door. John's voice came booming from the other side. "Everybody okay?" he yelled.

"Fine, Dad. Be careful. I think it was a sharpshooter from somewhere to the south. One of the windows is shattered but that's it. Bernie had one hell of a close call with the second shot. We're okay. I'm coming out," Matt said and crawled to the door. He looked back and smiled slightly. "Want to join me ladies?"

"Sounds like a plan," Bernie whispered. They all exited the trailer without using any lights. John led them to his trailer and whispered to Mattie to unlock the door.

"No lights," he emphasized. John then went immediately to one of the overhead cabinets and brought out a rifle. "I think it's over. Matt, lets you and I go down toward the dumpsters and see if there's anything there. Bernie, are you okay with protecting this trailer?" She nodded her head in agreement. "Mattie, call the police." Matt and John left quickly. Bix produced the wire devices that she had grasped and placed them on the table. Bernie took the documents out of her back pocket and added them to the pile. They waited quietly until

Mattie was off the phone.

The three women sat huddled in a circle on the floor with Simon in the center getting attention. "This is really getting scary," Mattie whispered. "How long do you think Matt and John will be gone? I pray that the gun fire is over."

"I'd say they'll be back pretty quick. You can hear people waking up in the other rigs. Pretty soon the place will be busy and that should stop this nonsense," Bernie said. About five minutes later the sirens could be heard in the distance. Doors around the camp sites began to open and close. People were yelling from all different directions. High Mountain Vista had come alive one more time for all the wrong reasons.

Billy and BB knocked on the door loudly. They had a flashlight aimed at the window searching for anyone. "Everything okay?" he yelled.

Mattie sighed and then turned on the lights. "We're fine, Billy. We're all just a little shaken by the shots." She opened the door as a crowd of family rushed in to check on everything. The questions were like bullets firing at the three. Bernie began explaining the events to the crowd. Finally the chaos stopped when John and Matt came back. The family focused on them for more answers.

"Everything is clear," John said. "There are some empty cartridges by the dumpster out back. Matt and I probably hurried their departure. We tried not to walk where there were footprints."

With the lights on Bix noticed that Bernie had some small cuts from the spraying bullet splinters. "Bernie, let's go get your head cleaned off. There is some blood on your forehead," she said.

"We'll talk with the police first then send them your way, Bix, if that's okay?" John suggested.

"Thank you. Please give the police those papers and the bugs we found." With that the two ladies exited leaving the cluster of family to examine their findings. Bix was sure that Matt and John could explain what had happened and, quite frankly, she was still in shell shock. Bernie didn't look any better either she noticed.

"Thanks," Bernie said as they walked toward Bix's trailer. "I really need to sit down and catch my breath."

"Me too," Bix whispered. She unlocked the door, grabbed her bourbon off the shelf and poured them both a stiff drink. Bix took a generous swallow of the warming liquor and then went to another cabinet for Band-Aids plus antiseptic. She offered Bernie a cold washcloth for her forehead. "I think you might be lucky that nothing hit your eyes. Thank heavens you were quick hitting the floor. I've never seen a tall lady move so fast," Bix said then smiled.

"I can move when I have to," Bernie chuckled. The bourbon had really done the trick. It was exactly what she had needed. She finished her glass and felt her tense body unwind.

Bix had just finished applying the Band-Aids when Sergeant Holly knocked on the door. "Come on in," Bix yelled.

Sgt. Holly entered. She checked out the bourbon bottle and smiled. "You ladies okay? Quite an evening I would bet."

"Come on in. A little bourbon to calm the nerves

at this point," Bix said. "I'd offer you some but you guys will be busy tonight I'm sure."

Sgt. Holly sat down at the table and pulled out a small tape recorder. She paused before she turned it on. "Can I first say that you two were damn lucky tonight and should leave the investigation to the police. My boss is not happy. I think that's why he sent me to interview you. His temper might get the best of him right now. You do understand?"

Both ladies nodded sending the message that they did indeed understand. Neither of them was totally convinced to stop, however. Their determination had grown since they had found the surveillance devices. It just made them angry to say the least. Bernie shot a glance at Bix and could tell that they were on the same page.

"Now let's begin," Sgt. Holly said.

Bernie began with telling Sgt. Holly about the spoon. The sergeant listened closely as they told how Henry had felt nauseous and was having headaches then Bernie described where Matt had found the spoon. The word 'poison' caught Holly by surprise; they had her full attention now.

Bix added her information about the rig from North Dakota. Sgt. Holly became intrigued as the ladies began weaving the trailer of strangers into the equation.

"You see," Bernie said, "Williams County plates meant that they could be from Tioba which is a rather large city where the oil companies reside. I'm sure John has told you about our meeting with the oil company's muscle in White Earth before we left for vacation?"

"Yes, he did in our first interview with him. At this time, it all is purely conjecture, you realize?" Holly said. Bernie and Bix nodded. "Proof has to surface before we can tie it all to what happened in North Dakota. Did you file a complaint with the police when the two men harassed you?" Holly asked Bernie.

"Well no. At the time it didn't seemed important to get the police involved. We just dismissed it as the way things are, you know? It's a push and shove environment there right now; people are fighting for property and power. It's a ranch community basically. Very cowboy oriented," she added.

"Well, there you have it. We need to find the proof," Holly said.

Bix offered the information about the devices in the trailer from this evening hoping to sway Sgt. Holly's further investigation.

"I will go talk with Bob and Chelsea tonight and see what else we can discover about the mysterious rig. However, I would like to get a promise from you two that you'll leave the investigation to us?" Sgt. Holly looked from one face to the other. There was a long pause while her words settled.

"It's up to Bernie," Bix said.

"I need to keep moving forward. My father is dead and right now you have no idea how I feel. I owe it to him to keep searching for answers. My family is a clan that sticks together. And by the way, Billy is not the murderer here. He loved his dad and would never hurt him. You are barking up the wrong tree. As for Bix, she needs to make her own decision here," Bernie said and then looked at

Bix.

Bix eyed them both before she said, "I'm with Bernie on this one. Whoever is attacking their family deserves to be brought to justice. They are placing a lot of folks in harm's way including myself. No. I'm with Bernie on this. Besides if I ever want to get back home, we had better solve this crime. I need to get home and water the plants," she said with a slight smile.

"You do realize you two could be charged with obstructing justice? Please be very careful. Helpful is one thing but obstruction is another; there is a thin line between the two. You understand?" Sgt. Holly said.

Both ladies nodded in unison.

CHAPTER 19

COMMON GROUND

John was glad that he and Billy had decided to meet early this morning before everyone got up. He knew that his relationship with Billy had to change and, hopefully, for the better. There had been some pretty bitter words said in the last year and it needed to stop. As the oldest brother he needed to get it stopped. Their family dynamics were in the process of changing because Dad was gone.

'Gone?' That sounded like Dad had stepped out the door and would be returning. It was hard to come to terms with the reality of the situation, John thought. Of course they all needed to get used to it. The word 'dead' stuck in his throat. He wondered how soon a person got used to the idea and then felt comfortable saying it. "Dead," John whispered out loud. There really was no other suitable word. Were there other ways to communicate the fact? John doubted it.

He and Billy needed to find common ground at this point. They were the surviving brothers who owned fifty percent of the family estate. Bernie and Lydia had always been able to get along but he and Billy were another issue. Dad had always been the referee between his boys. Now they had to learn to control themselves. John waited outside Billy's trailer trying to be as quiet as he could.

He couldn't help but notice what a clear beautiful morning it was. There was no traffic noise; the birds were in full chorus scouring the camp for abandoned morsels. There was a slight chill in the air and he inhaled the pine tree scent. Colorado had given them a weather gift this morning. John decided that he would make the most of it and settle with Billy.

"Hey," Billy said as he quietly opened and closed the door. He had put on his jacket and boots. "Want to take a walk? I could sure use some fresh scenery and a little peace and quiet."

"Sure. Shall we walk up the road? It's pretty quiet out here," John said. "After all the craziness in the back of the camp last night, I'd rather walk where there is no yellow crime tape."

"Good plan," Billy popped some gum in his mouth and offered John a piece just like when they were kids. Some things never changed. They chewed silently as they put some distance between themselves and High Mountain Vista.

"Billy, I'm sorry that we have been at each other's throats lately. The land controversy just makes me crazy," John said. "It just seems like such a sacrifice for wealth to me. I have a hard time getting past that concept."

"And I have a hard time getting past the concept that my life is boxed into ranching. It's claustrophobic to me; I'm strangling here," Billy added.

They walked awhile in silence. Neither brother wanted to say anything that they would regret later. When they were young fighting words meant just that. A physical fight would ensue. All hell would break loose.

Their mother had learned the art of peacemaker and, if nothing else worked, she'd dose them with water. Cold hose water had a way of cooling tempers. It was a concrete method that brought the dispute to a halt. A truce would then be reached or no supper, Dad's rule.

Hesitantly, the brothers would then reach some agreement. Food had been a priority at their young age but not now.

"Then you really need to do something other than ranching?" John asked. "You know it was always assumed that we all would ranch. Dad never had any other thoughts that I knew of when it came to the land. That's why it's so hard for me to understand how he changed his mind about your future," John said.

"And it took me years to convince him that I had to be happy to be satisfied. Dad and I went round-and-round. I just kept talking and finally he started listening. I think it had something to do with mother's death. Dad began to understand that life wasn't forever. You know he had their retirement all figured out with his kids working the ranch.

Mom and Dad would grow old together sitting on the porch watching the ranch grow and prosper. Then oil came in and Dad saw his neighbors changing and he saw me changing. He didn't like it at first, but then he did start listening," Billy said. "Sometimes people have just got to listen so life can change and rearrange."

He had stopped walking and looked directly at John. Their eyes locked in understanding for the first time in years. Billy's demeanor was so intense that John couldn't help but sense the strength and resolve. His little brother was desperately trying to make him understand. There didn't need to be any referee at this moment. Just real human empathy tossed into the mix. A truce had been reached.

John sighed and looked up at the Collegiate Peaks. His eyes scanned the mountains perceiving their strength and purpose. They had been there for millions of years and looked like they had not changed a bit yet he knew that weather and time had modified them. Mother Nature constantly created rock slides and avalanches to alter their terrain faces. Yes, there were subtle changes but the peaks still existed equally as strong. They just rearranged.

"Politics?" John asked.

"Politics," Billy said and then started walking again. Billy was so relieved that he and John were finally going to talk and not yell. He put his hands in his pockets and upped the pace. He could feel his dad in the atmosphere smiling. His boys might have a chance to get along after all. Thanks, Dad, Billy thought. "It is a challenge for me, John. I love trying to convince an audience; it's like I was singing to them. But instead, I am selling them a concept and telling them what I could do if they voted for me. It's a whole new way of life and I need to try. I need to follow this path and see if I can find my purpose. Not your purpose or Dad's but mine. All mine. It's what I think I am supposed to do with my life."

"What's BB's role in your decision?" John asked carefully. He looked at Billy out of the corner of his eye hoping that the question was okay.

Billy let out a long sigh before he answered, "I think that BB and I will eventually part ways. I'm not sure if it's before I am elected or after. I have to admit that there's a part of the politician in me that's not pretty. Yeah, I'm going to use her daddy's money. I'll admit it. Does the end justify the means? I don't know. Money, however, is a necessary evil of politics. I'll need it for my ride."

"What if we got the ranchers behind you? I mean, lots of ranchers that desperately need to have a say in the state government? You know, all the little guys working together and working for you. What if you hire a hell of a computer tech crew who are able to create the right kind of network? Your speeches would be on the internet and broadcast on the radio that ranchers listen to when they're working. What if a new radio station is created just for your purposes?" John's vision began to take on a life of its' own. He could sense his enthusiasm growing and even some hope. "You know, I am a firm believer that words can buy votes better than money. You just have to be good. And Billy, I know that you'd be excellent with the right message."

They had stopped walking again and were staring at each other. John was shocked by the vision that he had proposed and Billy was shocked by John's compliment. Two brothers both sensed that life just might be changing. It felt exciting and in some ways incredible. Billy stared down at his feet and shuffled the dirt, considering what he would say. Finally, he decided to take a chance and tell John about his latest theories. What the hell, Billy thought, as he went for broke. "You know the Harvard Magazine just did an article on the future of fracking. Dry fracking is the future being considered. Taking the water out of the fracking equation would certainly be better for the land. Ranchers and farmers could use the water and the oil companies would make less of a mess. Contamination is a huge issue right now as you well know. A politician could demand that the oil companies must place a percentage of their profits into dry fracking research and green energy solutions before creating any new wells. It could work for all concerned eventually. You'd have to make them do it. It sure is a better solution than just not permitting fracking. You need lots of money for research and development. Why not demand that big oil contributes?"

"You've talked with Matt then?" John asked.

"Yeah, we were up late the other night. He might just be able to convince me to take a chance. What with my brother behind me, maybe we could change the future a little bit," Billy added. "Let me really think about it. I could end up just another failed candidate running on a far-fetched platform full of dreams."

"Do you really think that there are no backers out there for someone who has taken an educated look at the future? Billy, we have no idea what a progressive candidate is worth at present on the open market. Maybe we need to look into the money that backs new technologies. I'll bet you that Matt could ask around on campus and find out who we need to contact."

"Wow. Let me think on this. Right now I need to get the police off my back. They could destroy any future that I might have in politics," He said.

"I agree with you. Maybe we need to figure out just who or what is behind Dad's murder. Right now that's got to be a priority. The family name must be cleared and Dad must rest in peace," John said while placing his arm around his brother's shoulder just like he had done when they were kids.

They turned around and began the walk back to High Mountain Vista united for the first time in years. Even their mother must have been smiling through the atmosphere along with their dad. It was for certain that these two men might have found a truce. The future would tell.

***

Bix got up around 9:00 the following morning. She was diddling around in the kitchen doing a little cleaning and a little eating. That was a-okay with Simon. He was still lounging in bed watching her every movement. The sun warmed his body and that topped off a good night's sleep for him. Simon liked the trailer because he didn't have to go from room-to-room to keep track of Bix. He could just be lazy in his vigilance.

Trailers were such an incredibly convenient and efficient mode of travel, Bix thought as she cleaned. The words 'what am I taking' took on a whole new meaning. Your stuff all touched in a confined living space instead of being separated by room barriers. Life was simple if one could locate a needed article. Then again, one could become unglued if an item escaped from your arrangement! Bix avoided those times as much as possible. You had to put things away just like your mother had told you or else. The other downfall was acquiring too many items when traveling. A person had to be careful. She knew by first hand experience that there could be too much of a good thing in a trailer environment.

This morning seemed glorious because of the sunshine and normality. It was her timeout from a very intense situation. Bix always needed a timeout so she could process. Finally, she sat at the table poured her coffee and examined her writing research. In the last couple of days, her notes had become two distinct files.

One file was the murder data and the other was her impressions of High Mountain Vista. Bix promised herself that some day soon, her book would be written. She had begun to store the notes in a cabinet where her laptop resided. It was now labeled the research shelf. The extra toothpaste and cleaning soaps were demoted to a lower shelf. It was yet another necessary arrangement for orderly living. She hadn't gotten quite to the point that notes were taken on her laptop. That stretch would be another learning tool for later. Old folks may learn slowly but they do learn, Bix thought with a chuckle. However, Bix couldn't quite bring herself to defining 'old folks.' Interesting, she thought.

Her contemplations were interrupted by a knock at the door. Bix found Bob Bailey standing outside. She wondered if Bob might know something about the Jones brothers. Hopefully, there was more to the story than the license plates. That would be a stroke of luck. "Good morning, Bob. What's up?" Bix said as she moved out to the picnic table. Bix left the door open so Simon could have a choice. He naturally gravitated out to Bob for some morning attention. "Want some coffee?" she asked.

"No, I'm fine. Chelsea and I always have two mugs before we emerge. The reason I stopped by is those guys in the rig? Chelsea said you ladies were interested. I told Chief Marten but he didn't say I couldn't tell anyone else. Seems to me, the more people who keep an eye out for them the better. Chelsea is calling around to the other parks in case they have just changed their location. I told her the police were probably doing the same thing, but it sure doesn't hurt to inquire," Bob said. He scratched his chin and looked out into the distance as though the answers hid in the woods. "You know they found a cigarette butt next to those cartridges at the dumpster. Who knows, maybe the police will get lucky on that one."

"I sure hope so. So far the bad guys have made all the moves. If this keeps up, the Holdens could lose another family member. It has to come to a stop," Bix said. "We all need to watch for these people."

"What do you think they heard on their devices?" Bob asked.

"More of a question might be why Henry?" Bix added.

"Good point," Bob mumbled. "Well anyway, the Jones brothers really kept to themselves over there. They rarely came out. However, the day that they left, the Carter kids next door were playing around with their smart phones. The oldest girl, Sara, took a picture of her dog with those guys in the background. They were outside packing up. One of the Jones brothers went crazy and demanded that she delete the photo. Sara's dad got into the disagreement and did tell her to delete it which she acted like she did. Later she saw me working and came over to talk. This was after the guys left. Sara told me that she had actually placed the picture in her archives. The Chief is putting in a call to the Carters and having them email the picture. Hopefully, someone will recognize those jokers from somewhere else."

"Excellent," Bix said. "I guess we are making progress."

"Guess so. Well, I best get to work. The place doesn't take care of itself especially when there's a ruckus." With a sigh, Bob got up and checked his list of projects. "See you later." He walked down the road toward his shed.

Bix and Simon disappeared back into the Scamp Trailer. Simon wanted a nap and Bix decided to check her email just to see what her friends had been up to for the last week. She enjoyed the pictures and articles that her face book group posted. There was nothing wrong with social media if you didn't go crazy. It did provide a little escape from the present at this point. Half an hour later the emails were read and answered. It was time to organize her day.

She felt that the whole ordeal at High Mountain Vista had really taken over. It was time to separate herself a little and maybe do a hike on the trail up the side of Princeton Mountain today. The trail she had picked was fairly isolated but accessible by vehicle two miles from the trailhead. Not many people used the trail and so it was just fine for her today. Bix began to place food in her pack along with the water. A little picnic lunch would be great.

On her way out of the park, Bix saw Matt sitting in a chair studying. She stopped and told him about Bob's information so he could tell the family. They all needed to make sure that the information was heard by all members. Bix felt better after telling Matt and letting someone know where she was going. After all, it didn't hurt to make sure your neighbors knew where you had gone. Bix didn't know how important that type of information could become until later.

CHAPTER 20

THE CHASE

Sgt. Jennifer Holly had taken the morning off after working overtime all week. She had sixty hours in and really didn't know how many to officially declare. The Chief, with a smile on his face, had told her to get the hell out of the station this morning. She didn't have to be told twice. This last weekend she had missed her usual dinner with her mother. Sunday had been their day. Jen would drive the thirty minutes over to Leadville and take her mother out to eat. Both of them worked entirely too much and never had time for their personal life it seemed. They had religiously carved out Sunday afternoon for meeting. Sunday had come and gone this week; here it was Thursday. "Well, better late then never," Jen mumbled as she slipped on her sunglasses.

Her mother, Arlene Holly, had bought an old vacant store on the main street in Leadville using her divorce settlement money. The foreclosure mortgage mess had left several stately old buildings vacant again in Leadville and Arlene had seen the opportunity plus a chance to amend her life. It was just like her mom to take a chance and invest, she thought. So The Single Canvas Art Gallery had been thriving for the last couple of years. It had a great location and was safely nestled between two antique stores. With her gray hair immaculately groomed, Arlene bravely stated that she was indeed the only antique working in her store. Arlene had gone from having too much time on her hands to having no time, just like her daughter the policewoman.

Even her bridge club was now on the back burner; she said that the ladies were up in arms. Jen had even heard that the ladies were considering a bridge intervention where they arrived at the gallery armed with tables and cards. It would be a genial revolt adorned with appetizers. Jen thought the whole idea was crazy fun. Maybe they'd recruit more bridge club players that way. It just had to make her smile.

She jumped in her Chevy Caprice and thought for a second about going home to change clothes. Just for a second though. If something happened and they could reach her in Buena Vista, she would be back on duty. Best to get the hell out of town and on the highway to Leadville, she decided even if she stayed in her cruiser. Fortunately, Highway 24 was the main street in Buena Vista so Jen just headed north. One stop signal and open road was before her. Well, maybe thirty minutes between the two

towns wasn't much but it would place her farther
down the list for active duty. Right now that's all
that mattered. Hot damn, a morning off at last!
What could go wrong, right?

As she drove in the sunshine, she checked her
scanner and then turned the volume way down.
Cops were never totally off duty. She turned on the
local radio station for music; the announcer was
chattering about the snow pack last winter. "Music
please," she mumbled.

Some day she'd take up skiing but right now
juggling her life was enough. Jen's goal of making
detective next year meant lots of volunteer hours
and study for her. She had intentionally arranged
her apartment living so she could shower and go.
No lawn to mow; no flowers to water. More time
for work she figured. Through Colorado Mountain
College she could take the courses on line. At least
there were no physical classes that required her
attendance this semester. When she had to attend a
class, her weekends were shot to hell. Denver was
quite a commute to say the least. They did schedule
courses on the weekends, because cops could get a
couple weekends off a month. Still, her goal was
quite ambitious.

Jen's cruiser was closing in on a black car half a
mile ahead. Highway 24 had been fairly clear of
traffic at this morning hour. Jen's ardent brown eyes
focused on the black SUV; it was going maybe 40
mph in a 50 mph zone. Curious, she thought. Was
the car going slow because something was wrong
with it or were the two individuals deliberately
going slow? Jen then noticed that the license plate

was from North Dakota. Well, it didn't hurt to check, she thought.

Jen turned off the local radio and turned up the volume on her police scanner to call the plate in just for curiosity. Barb picked up on the other end and began the process of running the plate. Sgt. Holly stayed back from the car while she waited. Barb came back on line.

"Jen, it could be the car with a 10-29-W on it. It could be the John Holden incident in Silverthorne. We don't have plate numbers for identification on Holden's accident. This car's plates are clean as far as I can tell. Any chance that you can see body damage on the car?"

"I will need to pass the car to find out. Here comes a two lane opening for the ascent. Hang on I'll pass them if they get over in the slow lane. Yeah, they just moved over. 10-23, stand by." Jen pulled into the left lane and slowly passed the car. She intentionally did not look at them but went past. She flipped on her turn signal and pulled into a turnout a mile ahead then positioned the cruiser to face the oncoming traffic. It would look like her police car was getting ready to set up a speed trap, she hoped.

As the SUV approached, Sgt. Holly could see that the right front wheel well had considerable damage plus there was no front fender! This car could definitely be the one that crashed into John Holden and had tossed the early morning flare. "10-54," Jen called into the radio and waited to hear the response. She could call it 'suspicious' but needed confirmation from the Chief to do more. Best way to play it, she knew.

Barb called back, "10-29V." Holly now had the okay to follow a suspicious vehicle that might be connected with the crime. She flipped on her turn signal and got back on the highway a quarter mile back from the SUV. She proceeded to follow keeping her distance.

"Officer assistance, 11-99, heading toward Leadville. 10 miles out of Buena Vista going north," Jen called. "10-29V and in pursuit, code 2." No lights and no siren in a quiet pursuit mode suited Holly just fine.

Barb came back on. "10-77, 10 minutes out. Calling Leadville for 10-93, blockade."

"10-4," Jen said. She followed letting the distance between the two cars stay at a quarter mile. She could see them and would know if there were any direction changes. As she came over the top of a hill, the SUV must have decided that they were being followed. It sped up to over 90mph. At this point there was nothing to do but become more aggressive. "Code 3!" Jen called on her radio. The hot pursuit was reality and she couldn't stop it!

Both cars began to fly down highway 24. The cars were cascading over the crest of hills with wheels barely on the road then both cars accelerated down the descent. Jen got no closer in distance so that any traffic would have a chance if they encountered the SUV. Hopefully, the suspects would be surprised by the Leadville blockade; that scenario was the most positive end to this chase in Jen's mind. However, fate decided the issue.

Unfortunately, she could see a slow semi truck

crawling up the next ascent about a half mile ahead of the SUV. They must have seen it also and decided to avoid passing on the top of a hill. All options considered or not, the SUV hit its' brakes and swerved a right turn onto County Road 371; tires hitting the gravel with a fury!

"10-20, east, on 371," Sgt. Holly yelled into her radio over the siren that she had turned on. Well, Leadville was now out of the question, Jen thought. She had hoped that assistance would appear before they made her car but it wasn't to be. The chase was on and road conditions would become one huge factor in the outcome, Jen knew. 371 was an incredibly beautiful county road. Her cruiser flew over the railroad tracks. Jen ignored the stop sign for speed's sake then passed the cozy Burlington train car house. She had always wanted to check out the interior just for fun. Some day she thought. No time now.

Gravel was flying and Jen did a mental assessment of her situation. Both cars were going over 60mph on a gravel road that was posted at 35mph. The SUV could take one of the side roads and disappear into wilderness if she wasn't careful. Granted, the Arkansas River on the right kept their choices less fluid; the red cathedral cliffs on the left threatened them only with occasional tumbling rocks. Still, Jen had to keep the car in view. There was also the possibility that they could crash into an oncoming local who had no idea about the pursuit. It was her hope that Barb was doing some reverse calling to the locals. The gravel was creating enough of a challenge at this point; she let Barb handle any alerts that went out.

Suddenly, the SUV slowed slightly and turned right onto CR375 then quickly sped up. Jen followed. She said good-bye to the aspen groves and river and got ready for lush green pastures. Her mind reeling with all the new possibilities at this point; 375 was a pretty damn rough road. Oh boy, here we go, she thought. "10-20 now right on 375," she yelled into the radio.

"10-4," called Barb. "10-77 assistance 10 minutes out!"

Right now it could be 5 hours out, Jen thought!

"Right now would be a good time for some help!" she mumbled to herself. She began to create a picture of the road ahead in her mind. As far as she could remember the road became narrow with washboard ruts starting about now!

Chrome trim flew off the vibrating SUV and viciously threatened the Chevy Caprice windows. Jen swerved just in time to avoid the deadly silver spears. The debris sailed around her car and somersaulted on the gravel road behind her. She swallowed the bile that had come up in her throat and let out a sigh of relief. "Thank you, Lord," she whispered.

Jen then remembered that there was a hell of a cattle guard coming up. That guard, if she remembered correctly, would rattle their teeth right out of their heads! She watched the car in front battle with the ruts. It had started swaying back and forth trying to stabilize. Now the fun starts, she thought. Undaunted, the car sped up again to 55mph. "Wait until you hit the cattle guard, sucker.

It's going to be a big surprise!" she yelled to no one in particular.

Jen slowed to 45mph and followed cautiously. The dust and gravel was enough to deal with at this time. She was able to keep herself on the road and that would have to do. Besides, at this point their speed might just take care of them! And, low and behold, it did. The SUV hit the cattle guard with a vengeance. Wham-bang the car, like a helpless body, flew off the road, hit the creek bed, tumbled over twice and finally landed belly-up!

Jen eased down on her brakes and watched with fascination. The wheels were silently turning as if they were still propelling down the road. There was an eerie quiet settling in over the pasture. A few cows were grazing near by. They raised their stoic heads as they checked out their new neighbor. Jen could tell that the cows weren't impressed by fate's sudden turn; they just kept on munching away.

It was a surreal scene until one guy crawled out the window of the driver's side with his gun firing!

"Stop! Police!" Sgt. Holly yelled as she released her hand gun from its holster. She jumped out the door, took cover behind the car, aimed and waited to see what the guy would do.

The suspect suddenly took off on foot passing the cows and heading into the San Isabel Wilderness Area. Jen scrambled to the wrecked car and checked on the other occupant. He had a pulse but it was weak. There was a huge amount of blood forming on the seat next to the suspect. The wound on his right temple was bleeding profusely.

Holly called two more requests into her hand

radio; a 10-52 for an ambulance and a 10-32 for the man with a gun. Chief James Marten came on the radio. "Sergeant, stand down. Stay with the injured man and do not pursue the fleeing suspect until backup gets there. Repeat, do not pursue armed suspect at this time. Do you read me?"

"10-4." Jen said and began to check the car. She could smell gasoline so she quickly pulled the injured suspect out through the window. As she dragged him far enough away, Jen saw two police cars flying over the crest of the last hill. In the distance she could also hear the ambulance coming. Sgt. Holly went back to the SUV and reached into the driver's side window. She completely turned off the car then pulled out the keys hoping that a fire could be avoided. Any time of the year, a small fire could become a forest fire in the mountains. Maybe there'd be a fire truck in the parade of vehicles arriving on the scene, she hoped.

Jen grabbed a towel from the back seat before she returned to the suspect. She began applying pressure to his wound in hopes of stopping the bleeding. He was breathing but out cold. The guy was maybe fifty and well built. His physical condition might help him heal from this accident. Jen was sure that he had a story to tell and the sooner they heard it, the better. The clamorous parade was barreling down the hill; they were seconds away. The cows now decided to seek a quieter ambience for dining; they strolled away from the imminent turmoil. Well she had gotten within twenty miles of Leadville. Almost home, she thought. Almost.

***

Bix and Simon were on the first trail. She had parked the truck to the side of the switchback to add distance to the hike. They started out on a short two mile trail that would intertwine with the road in a round-about where hikers parked. Bix figured it would then be a four mile ascent and then back down. She had never been a hiker on a timeline. Those people had personal agendas. Her agenda had always been the stellar view and conversation if she was hiking with a friend. Why rush a good thing? Hiking was like yoga to Bix; you stretched your endurance and your mind. A rain jacket eliminated any need for rushing unless you were caught above tree line in lightning. All bets were off at that point.

The sun was shining now but she did notice some clouds starting to collect over the top of Mt. Princeton. It looked like they had a couple of hours to hike before it would threaten with an afternoon rain shower. Lunch at the top of the second trail and then start back would probably do the trick. It was warm enough that the pine and sage scent was strong and wonderful.

Simon was off leash and happy to check out an occasional animal hole as they walked. In the distance off trail, the pica were out talking happily in chirp language. It was a busy morning in the woods for the animals, Bix decided. Maybe they would see marmots before the day was over; she so loved those critters. You had accomplished altitude when the marmots gathered to bitch and squeak at your intrusion. It was pure joy to say the least. People, however, seemed few and far between this morning. Nice.

Bix had seen some tire tracks on the road after the switchback. It could mean that a camper had been pulled up to the trailhead. They would have to go around that area if they saw the rig. One simply had to be polite and avoid stomping through a campsite. Just good hiking etiquette, she thought. Keeping Simon from being a total snoop when they reached the area would be a challenge though. Dogs were driven to smell everything and everyone! Even now Simon was circling over the road area making sure that he knew just exactly what had traveled before them. Bix was glad that she had remembered his canvas water bowl. He was going to be thirsty pretty quick at his pace.

The trail was fairly smooth with some rocks surfacing just to keep you attentive. It always seemed so pure and intense on a mountain hike. The afternoon showers constantly cleansed the rocks and smoothed the trail. A friend had once asked Bix why she hiked. There was, of course, the obvious explanation of keeping in good physical shape but that was such a cop-out. No. It was more than that. High altitude hiking became instant therapy. Was it an addiction? Sure.

There was now iron pyrite sparkling in the sun on the trail. Evidence of a life almost forgotten, Bix pondered. The search for pyrite's cousin, gold so motivating. You couldn't help but think that high mountain miners were super crazy humans; they packed into the mountains canned goods, bricks for their smelters and numerous bottles of booze. It must have been an incredibly lonely life waiting for the snow to melt off your claim. It was hard to breathe and hard to live in an atmosphere so large that your mind just couldn't rap around it. Miners had to be a little maniacal to risk their sanity for gold. It was truly a lottery filled with adventure. Even merely hiking could be a risky adventure depending on the challenge of course.

They were nearing the trailhead at this point. Bix put Simon on his leash. It had always amused her that he never seemed to mind the change. For Simon, it was like someone else doing the driving and sharing their view with him. As they approached the trailhead, the view revealed a campsite. There were a couple of chairs out and a card table loaded with supplies. A large antenna outfit was mounted on a stand to the side of the rig. In her hydration pack Bix carried a small pair of binoculars. She pulled them out and inspected the trailer more closely. The license plate was from Denver and she could tell that it was a rental from the lettering.

Hadn't Chelsea said that the Jones brothers had a rental trailer? There was a car parked there also. However, the camp did look deserted right now. Bix weighed the options of hiking past or going closer. 'Damn.'

In her mind all the factors were blinking caution. Nevertheless, the urge to know flashed a green light. Bix could feel her body tensing. Simon immediately picked up on the change in her countenance. He let out a small bark as if asking what was happening. His eyes intensely stared up at her; she gave his head a rub that calmed him. Bix inched her way forward and raised the binoculars again. She found herself crouching low behind a cluster of tall wild rose bushes. Bix glanced back at the trail to make sure that nothing was approaching. She moved closer again. Her binoculars focused in on an ammunition box on the table. Bullets! They could be hunters shooting out of season but why the antenna? You certainly couldn't get TV out here. What in the hell were they after? Bix's mind was spinning.

She had to see the license plate on the car located behind the trailer. What if they were from North Dakota? That would be more than a coincidence; that would be reason enough to call the police. Bix took out her smart phone and discovered that there was no signal. "Of course," she mumbled. Well, if they were going to backtrack to the truck for reception, Bix wanted to be certain of what she was seeing. They moved in closer and circled the trailer from 50 feet out. Sure enough the plate said North Dakota. She didn't quite remember the exact number. It was written down back in her trailer. Still, this sure didn't feel like a coincidence. The point was that they were from North Dakota. Bix checked out the box on the table a second time then made her decision.

One quick look into the trailer could be made without disturbing anything. She and Simon would then hightail it back to the truck and call the police. Bix wanted to click a picture of all the details before these guys left or got rid of any evidence. It always took time to request a search warrant. Anyway, it did in the movies. She began taking pictures with her phone.

Bix kept Simon close to her side as they crept closer to the rig. It was a large luxury model with plenty of windows. In her head she had figured out that if anyone was there, she would say that she had lost another little dog? Had they seen a little tan dog? The excuse sounded pretty lame but it just might work. Bix voiced a greeting, "Hello? Anyone home?" She was shocked to hear her own voice and hoped that she didn't sound too nervous. "Hello?" she called again, then knocked on the door. No one answered.

Bix let out a breath in relief. She tried the door. Locked. She cupped her hands around her eyes and leaned on the door glass to look inside. She saw maps of Colorado and, specifically, Buena Vista with markers indicating High Mountain Vista on them. The name of Holden was written on the top of a list of names. She even could see a location map of the trailer park sites with the names on each site. Yeah, these guys were using the trailer as their headquarters. There were computers with a receiver and other transmission type paraphernalia on the desk. Looked like surveillance stuff to her, sitting right there in plain sight. Bix placed her phone camera flat against the window and took a couple quick pictures.

Suddenly, Simon started to growl in a low unfriendly tone. Bix had been so focus on taking pictures that she had become unaware of her surroundings.

Her head whipped around at the exact moment that a big burly guy yelled, "Hey!" He was standing in the trailhead clearing.

Another guy equally as big joined him and pointed at Bix. "Ain't that the bitch from the park?"

CHAPTER 21

PURSUIT

Chief James Marten surveyed the overturned SUV on road 375. The scene was crawling with men and women doing their individual jobs efficiently, he thought. The Crime Scene folks were dusting and vacuuming up every crumb and piece of evidence they could find in the SUV. It did look like the suspects had been living in the car for awhile. The tow truck was waiting to haul out the car when all evidence and pictures were done. They would then tow it back to the station garage so that the paint from John Holden's rig could be matched to the front end damage on the car.

Marten was pretty certain that this had to be the right SUV. It was really the first good material evidence to be found. No rifle cartridges in the car to match the sniper at the trailer incident, but they did have prints, the SUV and a suspect in custody at this time. Jen had done a hell of job with pursuit and orders in this situation. He wouldn't forget it. The evidence would come together including the suspect in the woods. They'd get him.

The Chief had issued an APB out on that guy. Head start or not, they would apprehend him. Marten could hear the helicopter from Denver starting to search the area. Eventually, they would get a sighting and know where to start the manhunt. Fortunately, there had been two sets of hiking boots with socks in the SUV. Their ambulance suspect wore the size eleven boots; the one in the woods would sure like to have his size twelve boots on right about now. Bad choice for escape, James mused; good choice for the cops. "Score one for the good guys," he mumbled.

***

Chief Marten had chosen the search team including Jerry and his dog, Tyler. The chief was holding one evidence bag with a lone sock in it; a present for the dog so the scent would be fresh. He had just informed his three most physically fit officers to prepare for a couple of days in the woods. They would carry packs with sleeping bags plus dehydrated foods. That meant Detective Bill Smith, Deputy Jerry Neal and Sgt. Jen Holly would pursue the suspect into San Isabel and Pike National Forest. The official manhunt would begin within the hour. Unless the escapee was a trained runner or retired Marine like Jerry, they would catch him soon. Might take a couple of days but they would catch him unless he had arranged to meet another suspect.

To assume that there were only two individuals was not the best option. The Chief was open to all possibilities at this point. It was an all points bulletin manhunt. Barb had ordered any available officers to stake out the trailheads including Lynch, North Salt, Rich and Buffalo Peak. She had sent Ernie Burger over to the Forest Service Office to alert them and be advised on the terrain. He certainly hoped that the town council wouldn't demand his head for all the overtime. If the suspect got over into Weston Pass terrain, the search would then include all three counties; Park, Lake, Chaffee. Hopefully, the helicopter would help limit the forest area to search; otherwise, it would be overwhelming.

The Chief's list was getting longer at this point. He had also just gotten the photo from the fourteen year old girl, Sara Carter. She took a smart phone picture of the Jones brothers before her family departed High Mountain Vista. The suspect that they just loaded into the ambulance was in the picture. Their forest runner probably was suspect number two or there were more suspects involved. Marten would bet on the later. He was thinking four or more men at this time. Hell, a whole colony from North Dakota could have invaded! God help the budget, he mused.

Chief Marten could now see another cruiser coming down the road. His three officers were just about ready to begin. They jumped out of the cruiser and shouldered their packs. Each officer was well armed with police issued rifle and their own hand gun. The Chief knew that he could have waited for SWAT to be recruited. In his judgment the three standing before him knew the area, knew the situation and were extremely capable. There was no need to wait. Time was a priority. Chief Marten calculated that if he had to widen the manhunt then a SWAT team could be recruited. He had left that order on stand-by for now.

Tyler, one anxious dog, eyed the evidence bag intently. German Shepherds were so into that word 'pursuit;' it was their life in many cases. Tyler was the best. Marten handed the sock bag to Jerry Neal. "Our friend out there wears a size twelve and has headed into the forest in tennis shoes. Hope Tyler enjoys his new sock-toy. Give it to him when you guys land," the Chief yelled over the top of the approaching copter noise.

"Where are we heading?" Jerry shouted as he slipped the bag into his fatigue pant pocket.

Marten looked back at the officer manning the radio for the answer. The young man read the data cupped his hands around his mouth then yelled, "Marshall Creek Trailhead. "ETA 10 minutes." They all nodded and then turned their attention to the whirlwind beginning overhead.

The helicopter headed for the clearing where the cows had been dining. As the copter landed, dust swirled from the blades and the ground began to vibrate. The three looked at the Chief for any last minute instructions before boarding. "Go get the son of a bitch and be careful," he yelled then saluted.

The three returned the salute then ran toward the

helicopter. Tyler ran with them and didn't even hesitate when he jumped aboard. They waved and vanished in a cloud of dust and fury. The Chief began to feel a little guilty sending his three best officers on this mission. He said a silent prayer as he turned back to work on the crime scene. Lots to do and many decisions to make, Chief Marten considered. Damn, he felt like an old mother hen.

All three put the headphones on in the back of the copter. Jerry placed earplugs on Tyler to keep him calm. There wasn't any real need for conversation or commands at this point. They had talked and planned the expedition in the car. The team had divided the necessary weight. Jen would carry the mess kit and hydrated food for all, Bill Smith would carry the radio equipment and Jerry Neal would pack all the ammunition. Now all three, lost in their own thoughts, simply watched the terrain pass below the helicopter.

Sgt. Jen Holly couldn't help but feel proud that she was on this team. She had trained at least four years for this type of assignment to happen. It was a privilege to be among the team chosen. She knew that it was the first time a woman had been on a Wilderness Pursuit Team with the Buena Vista Police Force. Therefore, it was crucial that she make wise choices during this assignment. She meticulously went over her list of items and weight in her pack. Jen could leave something in the copter if she didn't truly need it.

Recently, she had purchased a solo backpacking tent that crunched her budget for the month. It would be well worth it at less than two pounds of weight and especially if it rained at night. Jen had left the thermo-rest pad at home. Comfort was not priority in this pursuit assignment. Yes, she had brought; toilet paper, hygiene kit, headlamp, sleeping bag, matches, water purifier, socks, small first aid kit, rain jacket and a vest. She did also pack some protein bars for herself. Might be a luxury but she had to snack to keep the pace. Besides, the copter could drop a care package if the hunt went more than three days. Fact was that they were more equipped for survival than their suspect. Could he go without food and purified water for more than three days? Jen hoped not.

The helicopter had spotted the trailhead. There was a fairly large open space to land. The team hit the ground running getting out from under the helicopter blades quickly. They watched it ascend and head back toward Buena Vista. Couple of minutes later the copter was a very small speck in the sky. The silence became a welcome friend at this time. Bill with earphones was listening to the radio GPS instructions. He pointed southeast and nodded his head. Jerry pulled out the sock and let Tyler have a long sniff. His nose immediately hit the ground; he circled the Marshall Trailhead and did indeed take off in a southeast direction.

"Shall we begin?" Jerry said. They left the trailhead doing a slow jog with Tyler in the lead.

***

A shot ricocheted off of the trailer near Bix's head. These guys weren't going to ask questions

first. They were going to kill her if they could. Bix
ran around to the back of the trailer with Simon in
tow. They ran into the forest off trail. She hadn't
much time to disappear into the underbrush. Bix
could hear them yelling and running; they were now
at the trailer. Did she go up or go down? Up she
decided quickly. The hope being that these guys
weren't in the greatest physical shape. Up meant
they had to work to follow this old lady, she
thought. The truck was down the slope but
they would expect her to head there. No she would
need to ascend for now and try to lose them. Maybe
these guys would eventually give up and trek back
to her truck. Who knew what would go through
their heads. One of them fired off a lazy shot into
the trees. Not real menacing, she thought, but
motivating! Bix took the leash off of Simon and
gave a strong, "Come," command to him.

Right now these men were following as far as
she could tell. Simon was looking at her when they
would stop for breath. His eyes wondering but he
was keeping quiet. Thank heavens! She petted him
hoping to calm him. "Concentrate on the climb,
boy, only the climb," she whispered. Bix looked up
the side of the ascent and tried to map in her mind
how to scale the height without being seen.
Switchbacks were the only way to climb higher she
knew.

There was an aspen grove maybe 100 feet above
her. From there they could move undetected she
hoped. The ascent was slow and tedious. Simon's
tongue was hanging out and she felt the fatigue that
this chosen path had produced. It felt as if they were

crawling in slow motion. Their progress, however, was accomplishing the goal. "One step at a time," she whispered to Simon.

Bix had now gotten them into the aspen. She stopped and gave Simon water and some to herself. Better to remain hydrated than to faint because of the exertion. Her mind began to calculate the climb with more clarity. She could see two approaches to the top. One would really be scary and could produce a heart attack. Nope, the longer ascent would be safer for them. She noticed that the mountain goat tracks verified her decision. The goats traveled this path to the top. They would follow the hooves. Maybe she could get a cell phone signal at the top. A hopeful thought, to say the least.

***

Matt Holden closed his book and checked his watch again. Bix should have been back by now. He wondered if she had gotten carried away and gone farther on her hike. Matt decided that maybe Aunt Bernie might shed some light on the situation. As he rounded the corner toward Bernie's Winnie, he saw that Detective Burger was talking with her. Matt increased his pace to join them.

"Are you sure, Miss Holden?" said Det. Burger.

"I'm sure. The picture is of the muscle guy from the Jensen's Farm. He and Kevin Jensen started throwing punches at each other then he started rearranging Kevin's nose. John finally decided that Kevin could use some help. The whole scene is pretty damn clear in my mind. Have you shown the picture to John yet?" she asked. Bernie glanced up and saw Matt approaching. "Hey, Matt, have you seen Bob?"

"I think he is in the shop working on Dad's fender. So this is one of the guys?" Matt took the picture and looked at it closely. "Can't say that I've ever seen him," he said. "But I haven't been home for maybe six months." He handed the picture back to Burger.

"Well it happened in the last month so I'm not surprised you haven't seen him," Bernie said. "Did your Dad tell you about the fight?"

"Oh you know him, he just mentioned it. He said that you two had quite a surprise when you arrived at the Jensen Farm. No details about a physical fight. Dad doesn't get into fights very often," Matt added looking at Burger.

"So this occasion was pretty unusual?" Burger asked.

"Very," Bernie said.

"Will you tell me what the dispute was about? Some details might be related to this crime," Burger said as he pulled his notepad out.

"Well as you know fracking has become the most important economic boon in North Dakota," said Bernie.

"Generations of ranchers have discovered that their mineral rights are owned by the oil industry. Of course there are many ranchers who see this growth as another positive way to make money. Needless to say, people don't always agree on the situation.

The Jensen Farm is now owned by the younger generation who had decided to farm. Ashley and Kevin had not included fracking into their plans. Because of their family's past decisions, the young couple is now experiencing the industry first hand. Their crops are dying and the excessive use of water for mining has dried up their drinking water well. I also need to mention that the ammonia smell from the chemicals has now made their kids sick. It's a pretty sorry state of affairs," she added sadly.

"When the legal team came by to give them a copy of the mineral rights contract again, Kevin must have hit the ceiling. John and I arrived in time to see Kevin and the guy in the picture fly out the door of the Jensen's home. I wondered at the time if our family would end up in the same type of trouble."

"Why did you feel that this event could threaten the Holden family?" Burger asked.

"My younger brother has decided to run for the senate and he needs the money. Billy has planned to sell the mineral rights under his property and my dad's. Trust me; the oil industry would then spill over on the rest of us. Lydia, John and I couldn't help but be involved. You have to wonder if somebody with an interest in fracking is applying the pressure."

"How do the Bellows figure into all of this?" Burger asked.

"I'm not totally sure. I do know that Mr. Bellows has represented the mining companies in several buy-outs," Bernie added. "Plus, you need to ask John about Charlie Bellows' childhood. They were in the same grade in high school. I just know that he had a big mouth and got a lucky scholarship. Bellows then left the area; he has now returned to make his fortune."

"How does BB figure into this?" Burger inquired.

"She has latched onto Billy for whatever reasons. Your guess is as good as mine," Bernie finished.

"Then she is a new item?" Burger asked.

"First time I have ever met her is on this trip. BB has been a surprise to all of us. Lydia might be able to tell you more. She and Billy always have been close. I know Lydia did talk with Billy about BB. I haven't."

"Well, thanks for the information. I think that we'll probably have more questions to ask as we keep investigating," Detective Burger said. "Now I need to get some paint samples and photos from Bob, then I will talk with John." Ernie slipped his notepad back in his pocket as he finished his interview.

"Did we hear that the police had a lead on the SUV?" Matt asked.

Burger thought for a moment and considered what he could and should say about the situation. He knew that the newspaper would have the full story out today in a special addition. Hell, it was big news so why not tell them, he thought. "Sgt. Holly chased the SUV which ended, belly up, in a gully north of town. One of the guys was injured and was taken to the hospital; the other guy took off in the woods. We have three officers in pursuit at this time. Naturally there's an APB out on the suspect so it is only so much time before he will be apprehended. I'd say today or tomorrow but that's my personal opinion. Don't quote me."

"That's great news," said Matt. "Is the guy in the picture one of those suspects?"

"Yes," Burger verified.

"Are there more guys involved?" Matt asked.

"That is a possibility. I would love to look at their surveillance equipment in that trailer if we can prove those two are involved," Burger added.

"I do wonder if there's more to this," Bernie suggested. "Poison is such a close and personal weapon. Why not just use a gun if it was one of these hired thugs?" Bernie questioned. "Sorry, Matt, just thinking out loud," Bernie added and touched Matt's arm.

"It's okay, Aunt Bernie. You're right."

"My thoughts exactly," said Burger. He left his words hanging in the air for the moment. "Well thank you and I'll see you later."

"You know where the shop is, Detective Burger?" Bernie asked.

"Pretty sure I can find it. Thanks, Miss Holden. I appreciate your cooperation."

They watched him walk off in silence. Matt and Bernie both were thinking about what he had said. It did really look like the North Dakota problems were the cause of what had happened. The implications were huge. Bernie began to examine the whole picture. How were the Bellows involved? She'd have to ask Bix what she thought.

"So have you seen Bix?" Matt asked.

"No. Why?" Bernie asked.

CHAPTER 22

UP CLOSE AND PERSONAL

Four hours had passed and the dog, Tyler, seemed to be still on the trail. So far the suspect had stayed on the path and not gone off into the bush. Jen figured that they were definitely moving faster than he was. The team had not stopped at all. Marshall Trail was a twenty mile loop which would end up back at the beginning. There were two trails off it. Mason Trail would come out on highway 285 between Fairplay and Buena Vista. The other trail was Salt Lick Trail and would end near Leadville. The suspect would make the choice. Tyler would be the one to determine what direction the guy took.

The radio began to squawk. Bill stopped to connect. "Yeah, we're heading toward the division on Marshall," he verified. "Thanks. We'll see what Tyler thinks when we get there. About three miles you say?" he listened intently. "Okay, 10-4. They said that the guy is heading for Leadville on the Salt Lick Trail. I guess we're about three miles behind him now and one mile from where the trail divides."

Jerry had gotten out water for Tyler. The Marshall Trail hadn't provided any streams to drink from for the dog yet. Jen was downing water also and had taken a couple bites of a protein bar. They rested for a few minutes and checked their location by GPS plus map. "You know we just may catch him in the next three hours," Jerry said. "Everybody locked and loaded?"

The team nodded and began their pace again. Three miles later Salt Lick Trail was also Tyler's choice. It was slower on trail at this point because of the ascent. Jen figured that they were probably at 10,000 feet in elevation at this location. It looked like the summit was around 10,500. They would eventually be heading down hill at a run providing the trail terrain wasn't too rocky. Tyler on leash now was pulling Jerry up as they went. He was definitely on scent and it was becoming stronger. Jen wondered if the suspect realized that they were following him. Tyler wasn't like a beagle that would howl in excitement. He steadily pursued; there was no time for anything else. He possessed a quiet determination.

As they reached the summit, Jerry stopped and began to study the terrain below them. Bill got out a small pair of binoculars and methodically scanned the terrain. "There," he pointed. The suspect was probably a mile ahead. He was moving at a pretty good clip since it was downhill at this point.

"Let's rest and drink some water then work our

way down as quickly as we can," Jen suggested. "If possible it would be to our advantage to silently catch up with him. Maybe he hasn't figured out how close we are. Ready?" she asked.

Jerry considered the situation and said, "Be careful and if he begins to shoot, divide up and find cover. In that case, I'll try to get in front of him. Jen go to the left and Bill, right."

"Sounds like a plan," Jen said. "Jerry, let's divide some of the ammunition up so if we need to separate completely we can." They each tucked a box of ammunition into their pockets. "See you at the bottom," Jen whispered and took off at a fairly fast pace.

The team was proceeding in a run. Rifles were carried across their bodies. They concentrated on their descent. The path was a maze of protruding twisted and gnarled roots. In some places it was almost like a dance, Jen thought. Their boots weren't the best footwear for a two-step but the trail would change eventually.

She could feel the wear on her knees about halfway down. The ground seemed to be flying past as in a fast-paced movie. At each switchback turn, Jen began to feel trepidation; the expectation that she would suddenly round a corner and find him staring at her with his rifle aimed was ominous. She wondered if he could hear them approaching? Tension was building throughout her body; not exactly fear, but an anticipation of combat raised its ugly head.

＊

Matt and Bernie headed for Bob's garage ten minutes later. They had gone to Bix's trailer and found no one there. It just felt uncomfortable right now. Bernie had a feeling that something wasn't right; Matt felt the same way. Sure wouldn't hurt to mention it to Burger, Matt thought. He knew where the trailhead was that Bix had taken. Better safe than sorry was the bottom line here.

"Hello? Bob? Detective Burger?" Bernie shouted as she opened the door and stared into darkness; her eyes began adjusting from sun to shade.

"Over here, Bernie," Bob said and waved his hand. "What's up?" he asked. Burger was beside him watching Bob sanding a table for the Commons; the polyurethane was soon to follow in this project.

"Well, we actually came to find Det. Burger," Matt said. "It's maybe nothing but we're both feeling a little edgy about Bix's hike. She should have been back an hour ago."

"I haven't known Bix long but I find her to be punctual," Bernie added.

"You don't say?" Burger said. He didn't seem too concerned as he watched Bob test the smoothness of the sanded surface with his hand. After a pause in the conversation, he asked, "Where is she hiking? Maybe I can send a car by the trailhead. We're kind of short of officers at this time but someone could swing by. Might not be for an hour or so…."

The timing of the call was impeccable. Bernie's phone rang in her pocket. It startled them all.

"Hello?" she said. Her eyes got larger and she looked at Matt then Burger. "Where? I'll tell the police. Det. Burger is right here. Bix, be careful please." She listened carefully then handed the phone to Burger. "She wants to talk with you."

Burger listened and took down the instructions. His body language had changed; his focus concentrated on the call. "I'll send a team immediately. Stay put, okay? They can't see you, right?" There was a pause as he listened. "We'll block the trailer if they head back. If they begin to climb the ledge, climb to where there's a phone signal if you can. Please don't be a hero, Miss Bixler; keep your dog and yourself safe. I mean it. An officer will wave at you when it's safe to come down. You can get down from there, right?" He listened again intently. "We're coming right now. I am going to transfer your call to Barb so she can monitor what's happening. Okay?" His eyes scanned the tools on Bob's work bench as he listened. Bernie could tell that Burger was now all business. "Good. See you soon," Burger said then gave the phone back to Bernie with a nod and left the garage without another word.

"Wow, it just doesn't get better does it?" Matt said looking at both Bernie and Bob Bailey.

"At least we followed our instincts," Bernie added.

"So where is she?" Bob asked.

"Princeton Trail," Bernie answered.

"I could take my ATV over to that trail faster than they will get there," Bob said with a twinkle in his eye. "Just to check out the situation, of course."

He rubbed the stubble on his chin as he calculated the route.

"Of course," Matt said. "Can I ride along?"

"Let's go. Bernie, will you tell Chelsea where we're going and promise her that I won't do anything stupid. Okay? We'll just watch."

"Consider it done," Bernie answered as she left the garage.

Like two school boys playing hooky, Bob and Matt jumped on the ATV and sped out of the garage back door. Matt hanging on for dear life as Bob increased the speed and ascended the trail. Obviously, they were going over the top and down into the next gulch. Fortunately, Bob had two helmets; Matt thanked his lucky stars as they careened over the path. He wondered how far the distance was but knew that he couldn't be heard over the motor. Guess it was time to hang on and go, Matt decided.

The route was an incredibly beautiful experience that Matt would have enjoyed if they hadn't been on a mission. As they descended into the next gulch, Matt spotted a water fall that tumbled into the condensed creek bed then roared beneath the bridge that they crossed. The rocks on the sides of the creek bed forced the fast moving water into fountains of extreme energy. Quickly the scene changed as they climbed the other side.

The ascension trail of the gulch was cluttered with large rocks. They lumbered and crawled slowly over them. Bob would steer them wide of the larger boulders. Still, the ride was like holding onto a bucking bronco.

Matt knew something about that kind of ride. He had missed that thrill this summer. Staying at CSU had cramped his rodeo style and the circuit now had left without him. He did miss the rodeo, but this trip was certainly making up for the loss of bumps and bruises.

Descending down the other side of the gulch was a quick streak of speed; Bob sure as hell knew what he was doing. Matt could definitely testify to that. The sign on their right announced that Princeton Trail was up ahead. When they came to the trailhead there was a rig camped; Bob slowed down and got a better look at the trailer. They were idling as he examined the situation.

"Well, I'll be. Hope we're not too late. Damn that's the Jones brothers' trailer. I definitely know that rig. So this is what Bix found. No wonder they're chasing her. She can take the lid off their whole damn scheme." He applied the brake on the ATV and went over to the door of the trailer. From his vantage point, he could see plenty of reconnaissance type equipment. It was a perfect setup for listening to the conversation in Henry's rig. What there was to hear was another question, Bob thought. Did they need to keep tabs on Henry's conversation with Billy and make sure that he would will his mineral rights? Bob had no idea but he hoped that these guys had left enough evidence recorded so the Chief could prove their intent. "Come here and have a look, Matt. These guys aren't fooling around."

Matt went over and checked out the interior. He was amazed at how the trailer was set up as an office. It certainly was not a recreational rig, that was for sure. Matt moved around the area until he found a signal and dialed Aunt Bernie.

"What did you find?" she asked immediately.

"So far we found the trailer which is one and the same with the Jones boys. It's fully equipped with spy ware. Really amazing, Aunt Bernie. We'll head on up toward the summit and see what we can find out. You and I were right about getting the police involved. Burger isn't here yet, however."

"Find Bix," Bernie commanded.

"We're on our way now. I'll check in later," Matt said then pocketed his phone and looked at Bob expectantly.

"Let's take the ATV up further and see if we can find these jerks. You think that they were firing at Bix?"

"Yes, sir, I do," Matt answered.

They throttled up and returned to the trail. Both men watched the road for any signs of Bix or the men. Matt's eyes scanned the summit's ledge carefully just in case he could spot Bix. If she had found a way to climb that high, Matt was pretty sure that the guys hadn't followed her. Somehow, he didn't feel that these guys were experienced climbers. No, they were from North Dakota. Flatlanders. Hired help he speculated.

Suddenly Matt saw Bix perched near the top of the summit. From directly below a person probably wouldn't see her. Matt's distance worked to an advantage. He placed his hand on Bob's shoulder; Bob slowed down. Matt pointed. Bob stretched and looked in the direction that Matt had indicated.

"Yeah, there she is. That's quite a ways up," Bob estimated. "Not sure that I could do that. Bix and the mountain goats huh?" he said then shook his head. "Now let's see if we can figure out where those jerks are." They moved a little farther up the trail. Bob shut off the ATV and listened to see if there was anything to hear. In the distance they could hear one loud conversation taking place. The men were coming back down the trail; it was obvious that they had given up on their pursuit and were totally pissed that Bix had gotten away. In the distance, Matt heard faintly the wail of a police car on the highway.

Bob and Matt got back on the ATV and turned around. They headed down the trail using their same tracks. Bob had decided to head back to the place where Bix had parked the truck and stay put until the police showed up. That way the guys couldn't destroy the truck or get out of the gulch. Maybe they could add some extra support to the authorities. They pulled in next to the Ford Ranger and waited. Not more than five minutes lapsed before two police cars arrived. Bob leaned into the first car's window and was greeted by Det. Burger himself.

"Thought we'd go for an ATV ride while we waited. Bix is up on the south rim of the summit and not too far from the top. The men are about half a mile from their rig on the trail. They're doubling back probably thinking about heading down out of here at this point," Bob finished. "Think we'll just sit here and enjoy the view," he said then smiled.

"Yeah, not a bad idea to keep track of Bix's

truck. I assume you two are done playing cowboy?"

"Yes sir we are," said Matt.

"I'll call you when we have Miss Bixler down and all is clear," he said. The police cars drove up the road to gather in the suspects using no sirens this time.

When they arrived at the trailer the two men were breaking camp in a hurry. The police blocked the road, jumped out and aimed their weapons at them. Detective Burger yelled, "Hands up and behind your heads! You are under arrest. Get down on the ground. Down!" The suspects dropped their weapons and complied. It was quick and simple at this point. They were placed in the second patrol car with an officer; Burger and two of the police team took off toward the summit.

Sure enough Miss Bixler was sitting near the top with her little dog in her lap. It was a good 1000 feet above the path. Burger raised his megaphone that he kept in the trunk of his car. "Miss Bixler, are you okay? Can we assist you on your descent?"

Bix cupped her hands and yelled, "We're on our way down. Did you get them?"

"We did. Two of my officers will wait right here until you are down. Matt and Bob are waiting at your truck. You want me to call them?"

"Please and thank you," she yelled.

"You're welcome." Burger turned and walked back to the waiting car. He dialed Bob then the Chief before heading back to the station with the suspects.

This week had really been a busy one. The people of Buena Vista were in shock because of all

the media coverage and homicide news. Ernie
Burger's wife couldn't wait until he got home each
night to find out what had developed that day. Just
as long as she got the information before the
newspaper, she was happy. There was new life in
their marriage and that certainly was nice as far as
he was concerned. So there was a positive side to all
of this. Folks would at least take an interest for
awhile; that old, 'good news-bad news syndrome'.

Granted, the police department was being
stretched to the limit. James Marten was an
excellent Chief, Burger thought. He was able to
stretch the budget as far as the limits would allow.
Burger couldn't imagine having to justify spending
money to the town council. The Chief could have
that part of his job for sure. Actually, the Chief
could have all the political hassle and leadership
responsibilities of his job.

Doing a detective's job was best for Ernie. He
was very satisfied to work with Bill Smith who
could out run a majority of suspects. That was truly
handy since Ernie was a year from retirement. They
made quite a team with Ernie's experience and
Bill's physical talents. In some ways it was like
working with your son, Ernie concluded.

He opened the car door and settled in without a
word; the driver put on the police lights and started
down the road toward the station. Burger waved as
he passed Matt and Bob giving them thumbs-up and
a tired smile. Interrogations would be a long and
arduous process. Well, it could be worse, Ernie
thought. He could be trying to keep up with Bill on
the trails. Lord knew that would be a nightmare for

him; he wasn't in that kind of physical shape.

***

As they descended through the forest floor, the police team transformed the manhunt from tracking to apprehension and arrest strategy. Jerry had commanded his dog, Tyler, to follow them and wait for further commands. It was apparent that the adrenaline of combat was molding all of them. Bill and Jerry moved in unison behind Jen; all thoughts focusing on the moment. Sgt. Jen Holly felt ready for the confrontation; her body was tense and acute. The inevitable afternoon shower had covered the ground with a damp cloak. In her mind a surreal silence prickled with tension; the forest atmosphere almost became alive. She had waited all her life to reach this plateau where keen instincts and skills melted together into action.

The soft thumping of their boots on the moist trail jammed her consciousness. Jen's heart beat pounded in her ears sending the message of perception whirling through her body. It was real and yet unreal to her. How the team had arrived here had to be some type of irony. Three people trapped within their own minds now sharing the same significant moment. It was a moment that would create their history; balancing between stories of jubilation or tragedy. There was no going back or rewrites, she knew. It was here; it was now. It was simply a profound moment.

Destiny began quickly and simply. Near the last

switchback a rifle bullet ripped branches off an aspen tree near Jen's shoulder. The team dropped to the ground. On cue Jerry and Tyler slipped into the grove of aspen and disappeared from view. Jen began moving to the left in quick rushes of speed between trees. Bill had gone the opposite direction. Jen decided to aim directly at a large boulder where his first shot had originated. She lowered her rifle and aimed. Her shot ricocheted off the rock in front of him and flew into the trees leaving small green confetti floating to the ground.

Another shot sought out her position; the shooter was tracking her actions at this point. Jen was his focus. He was coming closer to her position and he seemed to anticipate her direction. The guy was good she thought; combat action was her guess. The question was, did he realize that there were three of them or did they have him fooled? So far Bill and Jerry had stayed quiet in their pursuit. Each man systematically stalking the suspect from outside the perimeter that Jen had established. She was beginning to feel like a deer targeted; the suspect obviously had a decent scope on his rifle.

Jen figured it was time to fake a retreat and pull him into the center of their pursuit area. She popped up from her position and let four shots off in quick succession creating a small frenzy. Spinning around through the nearest grove of pine, she zig-zagged in retreat praying that it had been quick enough to surprise him and give her that few seconds of cover. He had bought it. There were at least half a dozen bullets flying over her head wildly. It was now her hope that he would follow her leaving Bill and Jerry free to move in undetected.

So far they were spinning the web without detection. The deeper into the circle he moved, the easier it would be to make a clean arrest. It had been a good plan until Bill accidently tripped. The suspect fired two rounds in his direction. Jen heard the yelp from Bill as he went down to the ground with a thud. Bile came up in her throat as her stomach muscles tensed in fear. Suddenly flashes of Bill dying forced their way into her mind. Another cop funeral on television! Not a killing dear Lord; I will be positive she thought. He will be alive. Her goal began to change now. It was time to get to Bill before the suspect could.

Jen leaped over some weathered wood stumps and backtracked quickly. Now she could hear the suspect in the process of reloading his rifle. His preparation would give her time to find Bill's position. Jen dipped lower to the ground and ran another 20 feet nearer. Bill wasn't moving as far as she could tell. His body was draped over the radio which was a good thing. The suspect needed to be kept from getting their communication device. Bill's life could depend on that. She crept closer hoping that her position couldn't be seen.

Two shots hit the trees in front of her. Well there went that hope right out the window, she thought. Jen was now crawling toward Bill; she was staying as low as she possibly could without digging a tunnel. More shots ricocheted off the ground ahead of her. There had to be a way to make this work, she calculated. What was Jerry thinking at this point, she considered? Tyler the dog answered all the questions as he burst through the underbrush and ran straight for Bill. Jen took advantage of the situation and followed quickly keeping her cover as much as she could. Finally, she was at Bill's side and feeling for a pulse.

Jerry let out a war whoop that sent Tyler off in pursuit of the suspect, leaving Jen there to rescue both Bill and the radio. She could hear Jerry running after the retreating suspect. The pursuit was on again. Thankfully, Bill moaned as Jen found his pulse. It looked like the bullet had gone into his calf muscle. She quickly applied a tourniquet to stop the blood flow. Bill screamed as she tightened it.

"Holy shit that hurts!" he yelped.

"Better than bleeding to death," she said with a smile on her face. It was great to hear him complaining. People who were alive complained! Relief sprung into her body; Bill would make it, she knew.

"So get moving, Sgt. Holly." Bill felt a late afternoon chill settling into the woods. It would be getting dark soon; he had to push her into pursuit. "Jerry is going to need help and I'm going to need more help than you can give me. I can radio my position quite nicely all by myself. Now git! Hurry. You ain't that good of a nurse. Leave me some water?" he added hopefully.

"Can do." Jen reached back on her pack strap and pulled off a water bottle. "Make sure that the radio does work before I go, Bill."

He pulled himself up and wedged his upper body on a rock so he could sit. He flipped on the radio which crackled in response. "This is team one; we have a man down," he said.

Barb came on immediately. "Life Light from Denver will be notified. I have your location. Who is it?" she asked.

Jen stayed around long enough to hear Bill's answer, "Well, I'm afraid it's me."

They now heard a volley of rifle fire up ahead. Jen figured Jerry was 10 minutes out. Off trail of course which would make the whole apprehension harder. Jerry and Tyler's diversion had worked. Jen now grabbed one of the small battery radios then looked back at Bill. All was good to go. He gave a weak smile and waved good-bye as Jen determined the direction of her pursuit.

Somehow she doubted that the suspect would just be running. It probably had turned into a game of stalking and her presence would change the balance. Jen and Bill both heard the echo of distant shots; they silently assessed the direction and inevitable dusk.

"Get going, Jen. I'll be okay. Do us proud," he added then winked. "Get that son of a bitch in the morning light!"

Jen nodded and began her pursuit.

***

Bill had just begun to feel lonely as dusk settled around him. He could no longer hear Jen and the symptoms of shock had begun; he was cold and dizzy. Bill calculated that it had been an hour since Jen had left. Why did it feel like days? His vision was becoming blurred now.

Barb would come back on the radio every few minutes and check on him; her voice was his lifeline. She assured him that help was on the way. Barb would ask him to listen real closely. "They're on their way, Bill; watch the skies. You hang in there, buddy. Everyone is counting on you here at the station. Any minute now," she said.

And sure enough, he did begin to hear the giant propellers rhythmically slicing through the quiet. Bill let out a huge sigh of relief. He was ready to place his life in the hands of the medical staff. How many times had he helped load an injured climber into the copter's emergency facilities? It was part of his job. The helicopter hovered above Bill's position searching for a potential landing field.

He had never expected that their mission would be to pick up his sorry ass. Now, the expectations were very personal for him. What a strange concession that was, Bill thought. The helicopter found a meadow close by where they could land. He truly appreciated the wonderful scene of two medics rushing toward him.

Jen's tourniquet had held, allowing his body time to wait. The whole scenario took on a new meaning. He would live. How simple those three words were to say and yet so immensely complicated, so magnificent. He murmured, "Thank you."

Bill lapsed into a convoluted state of semiconscious. He released the reins of reality and floated into the sky. Somehow, he was looking down now on his own rescue. He could see the medics working on him. In slow motion, they were checking his vitals and preparing to load him on a stretcher. Bill had witnessed this scene so many times in the past from the outside looking in and now he witnessed from the inside looking out. How incredible was that? The immense miracle was not lost on Bill.

As the copter finally ascended toward Denver, it cut the darkness with an eerie spotlight and then cast a whirling wind into the forest. Their passenger was 15 minutes from his destination. The pilot made radio contact and cleared their flight plan for the hospital. He also alerted the emergency ward that Bill was coming. They would schedule surgery right after he arrived. Officer Smith would make it but he had a long road to recovery.

Below the helicopter now was highway I-70 winding its way toward the east. People traveling would look up and see the familiar blue and yellow colors of Life Light. They would figure that some poor schmuck had hiked too high, slipped off a ledge or had a heart attack. The state population knew that helicopter.

A few minutes later, Chief Marten got the news about his officer's condition. He let out a sigh of relief. Smith was a damn good officer and Marten was like an old mother hen when it came to the safety of his staff. He would notify Bill's wife and make sure that one of his officers would escort her to Denver. James made a note to call his wife and see if she could maybe go along to the hospital then he could pick her up tomorrow. Bill would need all the support that he could get after surgery and Marten was going to make sure that his staff was available. Maybe they could spare one officer each day to be with him; it sounded like a plan.

***

The Pursuit Team had weathered the first assault and come out alive. Jen would use that thought as motivation tonight. She jogged, like a crazy woman, for three hours through the woods heading north into the forest darkness. The silence now told her that either both men were resting or the confrontation was over for tonight. Jen would only let her mind focus on the first alternative in this pursuit. It was obvious that she and Jerry would spend the night separately. Jen knew that the pursuit had needed to halt; it was safer to wait until first light for both men. Obviously, stumbling through the woods was stupidly dangerous. No, everyone had stopped for rest, she told herself.

Tonight, the stars were her companion. The sky became immense as promised, sending an occasional falling star. Nature's reality brought comfort to her somehow. It was time to throw into the atmosphere a prayer and hope for Bill that he was resting safely in a hospital tonight. Jen had radioed her position and now relaxed. She lay with her head outside the tent; it just seemed safer that way. Her mind and body subtly closed down into a deep sleep brought on by exhaustion. She hadn't given herself permission, but it had happened anyway.

Six hours later light began to return and her eyes popped open. She was starving!

CHAPTER 23

HALFWAY THERE

Bix and Simon began edging their way down the cliff. The narrow path was just wide enough to accommodate her boots. Simon paused and looked back at her to make sure all was well. His little eyes intensely searching her face with concern; his under bite whites protruding. "It's okay, buddy, I'm going to make it down," she assured him and smiled. Bix followed the mountain goat tracks carefully; it wasn't exactly a conspicuous path but did have ample switchbacks.

Simon rendezvoused with a small stream crossing the path. From his satisfaction, Bix knew the water was cool and satisfying. He lay down and rested his tummy in the small stream. She knew that Simon would be more at home descending this area after his pool break.

Finally, they proceeded down and reached an easier section 15 minutes later. The clouds were beginning to cluster together in anticipation of the approaching mountain shower Bix noticed. It was so good to be almost down and safe. Bix gave herself permission to let the anxiety dissipate.

The two police officers began to rush up the trail. She could see the relief mirrored on their faces. Bix was glad that the trek down was finally over. The whole ordeal had been ambitious, but it had worked. She began to wonder if the police officers had thought her climb crazy. However, these criminals hadn't been kidding. Rifle shots got the point across to her. She didn't have to be told twice!

"Very good job, Miss Bixler. Our hats are off to you! Great escape technique! I've never seen anyone climb that area other than goats. Your nephew and Bob are waiting for you at your truck. You ready to go meet them?"

"Gladly," she said. They got in the police car and drove down. The officers offered water as they filled her in on the arrest. As they passed the trailer, the crime scene investigators were combing the grounds. Bix guessed that it would be an all day process. They had a stack of guns displayed on the table outside. Needless to say, these two criminals had been prepared. Her police escort said that she could wait until tomorrow for her statement. Good, she thought. Enough was enough.

As the police car approached Bix's truck, she noticed that the welcoming committee had grown. John and Billy were both leaning up against her truck busy talking with Matt and Bob who leaned on the ATV. It had become a guy thing. Matt was illustrating some event. His hand was going up and down like rolling storm waves, and she could tell that he was enjoying the storytelling. The guys were engrossed in his description. When the police car stopped, they flew open the door. Matt grabbed Simon and gave him a huge hug that brought on tail waging. Bob hugged Bix and kissed the top of her head with equal enthusiasm.

"So glad to see you, Bix! You keep getting into the right place at the wrong time," Bob said. "That trailer was unbelievable. These guys weren't kidding. A shitload of guns!"

Billy couldn't keep quiet any longer. "Hell woman, how in the world did you climb that cliff? No wonder you lost them. My hat is off to you!"

"I was lucky to find a small path. Thank heavens for the mountain goats. Not that I would have gone there on my own today or any day," Bix said, then smiled at Billy. There was something new about his countenance; she studied him closely. John moved over close to Billy and patted him on his back. Good, Bix thought. They have had a chance to talk and maybe started reconciling the family situation. Bix had to wonder how the Bellows figured into this new scenario.

She then glanced at Matt who held Simon up in the air and inspected the little guy. Simon obviously didn't mind the attention at all. Matt then pulled Simon back in for another hug. Simon was totally enjoying being on eye level with the grown ups. His little head twisted to the side as he listened intently. Bix so loved Simon's dark eyes peering out from under his schnauzer brow and Muppet hairdo. What would she do without him? Unimaginable. She pushed those thoughts away and let the appreciation flow. After all, he was her copilot!

The guys pulled the ATV into the back of John's truck and piled into the double cab letting Bix have the passenger's seat of honor. Matt followed them in Bix's truck. There was an atmosphere of celebration taking hold of their moods. Matt had suggested that they should go have a beer in Buena Vista in celebration. Bix really couldn't find any reason to go hide out in her trailer. The Den seemed like the bar to frequent. Everyone agreed.

The late afternoon shower cleaned the ground as they pulled up to the Den. It was decided by all that the outside patio was a great idea. Simon had his own chair of course. After the first beer and three toasts to a quick solution to the case, Bob suggested that the ladies needed to be included. The phone call was made and chairs were added.

Half an hour later, the owner had cooked up enough for an army. Bix found that she was surprisingly hungry. She was almost finished with her burger when Mattie, Lydia, Chelsea and Bernie arrived. The ladies approached with hands on hips and a few skeptical looks then they relented when they noticed Simon sitting in his chair and Bix eating. Cell phone pictures were taken and another round was ordered.

Lydia and Bernie moved their chairs closer to Bix for the entire story. They asked questions and listened intently. Both ladies wanted the full description. Bix tried to relate details. The conversation brought fear to the surface of her mind again; Bix had no doubt that she would continue to see these images flashing before her eyes for months. Naturally, she was very thankful for the beer at this point. It was almost too much to imagine right now. Bix needed to change the conversation's direction. She looked around the table and suddenly asked, "Where's BB?"

Bernie looked at Lydia to supply the answer to that one. Lydia had a slight smile on her face as she whispered her answer, "It would seem that BB has retreated to her daddy's motel." She glanced in Billy's direction. He was caught up in a conversation with Mattie and John so she could elaborate. "I haven't asked Billy but he did drive her there this morning. Being the watchful sister that I am, I did notice a suitcase was tossed into the backseat. Billy's attitude has gotten considerably better lately. Have you noticed, Bernie?"

"Yes. Actually I have," Bernie commented.

With a burst of laughter the group's conversation converged on Matt's ATV ride. What hadn't seemed funny then, now had the markings of a true storytelling event and Matt was creating the tale as he spoke, "Oh yeah, this quiet kind man transforms into a raving, crazy damn monster on that machine! Shit we leaped streams, jumped boulders and just kept going higher. A jet plane hasn't got anything on this guy coming downhill. Hell, I thought my teeth would fly out! The rodeo ain't no challenge next to this maniac! My butt has never been so sore. He gets off the damn machine and transforms back to silent kind Bob! And, he says softly in a whisper, 'Well, that was a ride.' "That was a ride?" Matt howled placing emphasis on the word 'ride.'

"Man, I wondered if we could have beat Bix up the mountain! Faster than the speed of light! Who taught this guy to drive an ATV?" Matt added.

"I did," came a little voice from Chelsea in confession. She was laughing more than anyone else. Bob was turning beet red from ears down. She jumped on his lap and gave him a huge kiss.

Billy grinning had to ask, "So is he this crazy in bed, Chelsea? A wild man or faster than the speed of light?" The group let out a collective howl.

"Billy!" yelled Lydia as she had done since they were kids. "Leave it be, boy!"

"Too fun," Chelsea exclaimed with a huge smile. "Glad we could have this meeting today and go a little crazy. However, there's no one taking care of the park. I locked it up and put the 'Out on the grounds' sign on the door. The guests would have to look pretty far and wide to find one of us right now. Best get back," Chelsea said then finished her beer in two gulps. She added an after thought, "Best brush my teeth when I get back."

"I'll go with Chelsea back to the park. I assume you gentlemen will haul my ATV back to the garage after you get done discussing my bedside manners?" Bob groused.

"Consider it done, my friend," said John saluting Bob with the last of his beer. "And by way, thank you for bringing my son and friend back to us in one piece."

"My pleasure," said Bob as he took hold of Chelsea's hand. "So glad I could be of help today. See you later, folks." They left holding hands.

Billy watched them leave feeling a little jealous

of what they had. "I'd say his bedside manners must be just fine." The group chuckled then mellowed into the last round of beers.

Bernie who hadn't been able to talk to Bix since she arrived now found the opportunity. "So what made you look into that trailer?"

"I'm not sure, Bernie. I was standing there thinking that maybe I could phone it in and then run back to the truck. My head said retreat but my feet just kept walking forward."

"Geez Bix, you know that was crazy? Granted, I will admit that there are times when you just have to go with the flow. I'm not sure what I would have done. Really doesn't matter, does it?" Bernie added.

Bix thought for a moment then said, "No it actually doesn't and would I do it again, probably. I really needed to look into that window. Actually, I was going to take off and do my civic duty after my look-see but the rifle shots sort of decided the whole issue. I was surprised that I could still think after the first round of shots. Climbing higher seemed the only solution."

"I heard tell that those idiots had quite an arsenal with sights mounted on every damn rifle?"

"Luckily, the aspen grove had covered the peak. It grew spotty at the top but there were boulders to hide around up high. Never so thankful in my life for small paths made by wildlife. I got lucky and Simon was in tune to the situation. Dogs are so intuitive that it's mind-boggling. He just went right up the slope with me. Did he know that the higher we went, the safer we were? I have no idea. I just know that we were intent on our goal." Bix gave

Simon's back a loving rub in his chair. He was curled up in his customary tight ball sleeping soundly and resembling a little black cushion. Exhausted, she thought; as she would be later when there was time to process the day.

"Got to tell you that I was really worried this morning when Matt mentioned that you were late getting back to camp. I surely wouldn't have wanted anything to happen to you," Bernie said then reached out for Bix's hand; she held it tightly. "Sometimes people just naturally become part of another family. I looked around today and realize that all the Holdens have quietly adopted you. Welcome to the family," Bernie said staring into Bix's eyes.

***

"Sit down in that chair, you fuck, and shut-up," yelled Detective Burger. This suspect had been obnoxious during the ride back to the station. Burger had little patience with any man who would shoot at an unarmed woman. Making a hunting game out of the situation just didn't play well with him. Plus, Barb had just told him about Bill being taken to Denver by Life Light. Ernie had no doubt that these jerks would have finished their game with a kill. Murder was too easy for a whole lot of jerks.

Burger had searched both suspects and found out that their drivers licenses said North Dakota and identified them as not the Jones brothers. Barb was running the names right now. Real names? The finger prints would tell. Ernie had just left Travis

Norton's interrogation room. He was standing in the hallway trying to simmer down. Norton had a real mouth on him; it was obvious that he had played the legal system before. Barb had found out that 'coma-guy' was Walt Mason and wasn't expected to wake up anytime soon. No, these two were the only hope for information right now.

The quiet guy was, supposedly, Brad Holt. He had watched his partner go arrogant and just sat there silently. Could be the guy had a case of the nerves. Burger needed to get Holt's mouth open. Let Holt sit and stew for awhile, Burger thought. Now that Bill Smith would be spending time in the hospital, it was Ernie's show. He considered what strategy to use. Obviously, he had to play these jerks against each other. Barb opened the door from her inner sanctum and wiggled her finger at Burger. There was a smirk on her face. Ernie approached her quickly.

She took a deep breath and began, "So, Holt has an arrest sheet littered with petty crime. Nothing huge that would send him away to a federal prison. Doesn't look like he's packing a lot of brains, I might venture to say. Now Norton is poised for his third strike and a nice long federal stay. He likes shooting at people and probably has connected a couple of times. Just hasn't been caught. Robbery, burglary and assault are his stellar accomplishments up to this date. One accessory to murder didn't stick but he was close to going up for a long time on that one. A good lawyer and a few brains here might have helped." Barb handed Ernie the documentation papers then continued, "Hired guns I suppose.

Doesn't look like they cooked this one up on their own; they needed help. I'm checking their bank accounts as we speak. Let you know what I find out pretty quick." With that comment Barb disappeared back into her office. Ernie stared at the papers in his hand and thanked the Lord for computers and Barb, of course.

So Norton probably brought Holt into this job and they set out from North Dakota with specific orders. The question was who and what were those instructions? Was murder among the possibilities or were they just for the surveillance part of this con? Did the SUV suspects even know these two? Good question. Ernie had one in the woods, 'coma-guy' in the hospital and these two jerks for immediate answers.

Detective Burger took a moment to review the list of crimes before he re-entered either one of the interrogation rooms: Henry Holden's murder, attempted murder of John Holden twice, attempted murder of Ms. Bixler, assault of Bix and Bernie, wiretapping, arson. The list just kept getting longer. Go for the jugular right off the bat was Ernie's assessment. He decided to choose Norton first. He, obviously, would soon ask for a lawyer. Maybe Norton would shed some light on what the defense might look like. "Door number one," Ernie mumbled.

"Okay Norton, you have been read your rights. Is that correct or shall I repeat them for the camera?"

"You mean my rights for all these trumped up charges? Hell yes." Norton leaned back in the chair with a sneer on his face. His mustache twitched slightly, Burger notice. Not all a picture of total confidence, Ernie observed. "Attempted murder of a helpless woman in the woods and then stalking her will be an easy conviction, you shit." Burger leaned over the table and got right in Norton's face. "The closeness of Burger's advance didn't faze Norton.

He waited a few seconds then said, "If it was a woman? All I saw was someone trying to break into our trailer. I don't take kindly to robbery."

"You have got to be kidding? You need your eyes tested. I don't think you could miss the fact that it was a woman. Nevertheless, what did you do after you noticed 'someone' at your trailer?"

"We yelled at the person to leave it alone. The individual told us to fuck ourselves and promptly headed into the woods. This person moved so quickly that I couldn't determine who it was, total blur." The sneer returned to his face. He was very satisfied with his testimony so far.

"What did you notice about this person? Anything?" Burger backed off somewhat and sat down. Easy does it, he calculated. Maybe he could pull a little more information out of him before the lawyer talk.

"Looked like a transient to me, backpack and all. Those people are always hungry for items to pawn plus food. You can't be too careful these days," he added for embellishment. Norton had taken on a quiet confident tone now. His web of lies conveniently created.

Burger could feel the steam coming out of his ears. He told himself to maintain a little longer. The sacred words to 'lawyer up' hadn't been murmured yet. Reel in as much information as possible, he thought. "As this person retreated into the woods, you decided to follow. Why?"

"I don't take lightly to bad language and attempted robbery. A citizen's arrest was the only option. I would hate to see a criminal get away." The pure joy of his last answer shown in his eyes. Burger could feel Norton's ego growing by the minute. The more he lied, the more enjoyment he was getting. Norton was sure that the country yokel sitting across the table was buying some of his story.

Keep playing the game, Burger thought. Watch out for the 'pronoun game' that Norton was playing about gender. Stay neutral, he carefully thought.

"And what did you do then?" Burger asked objectively. Norton was starting to make his skin crawl. What a cretin, he thought.

"Why, we did what any concerned citizens would do. We gave chase hoping that we would be able to catch up with the crook. We merely shot some rounds over the head of the guy to scare the shit out of him." Norton was playing it carefully.

"So you admit to firing at the individual in question?" Burger asked to establish the presence of rifle fire. "How many shots did you and Holt fire?"

"How the hell should I know? It was fun. The little shit was running and it was fun. I couldn't say. I wasn't counting. I was hoping that the transient would shit his pants. A little scare sure as hell didn't hurt."

"And how much of a scare did you two feel was enough? Did you have cell phones?"

"Sure, but we got caught up in the moment."

"So instead of calling the police at any time, you kept in pursuit of this person, enjoying firing at them and stalking them?"

"I never used the word stalking. We were protecting our property and decided to chase the guy. Last I checked, robbery was a crime." Norton squirmed a little in his chair.

Just a slight movement of discomfort Burger noticed. Now he thought; jugular time. "So you're so fucking blind that you didn't see breasts on this woman? Yep, guys always wear yellow shorts and a flowered tee shirt. You didn't see the little black dog that surely must have passed your trailer on the way to the Commons at High Mountain Vista Park? That's funny because people saw you! Who the hell do you think you're kidding?"

"I didn't recognize her! I told you that!" Norton fired back.

"But you knew that you were firing round after round at a woman who had been at the same park as you? An unarmed woman to boot!"

Norton opened and then closed his mouth like a hooked fish flopping on the dock and said the sacred words, "I want a lawyer."

CHAPTER 24

ASSAULT

Dehydrated eggs and brown rice, yummy! Jen gulped them down almost choking in her haste. She could feel the eggs hitting the bottom of her stomach or thought she did. And then a large gulp of water and Sgt. Holly almost felt human again. She then began to concentrate on the morning sounds. Any disturbance coming from anywhere would have a story to tell. Jen listened hoping for direction. The pop of a shot cut the morning silence. The game was on! Her mind and body merged into the morning's goal, pursuit then capture. Nothing else would matter until this suspect was in custody. Time to move! She threw everything in her pack and left quickly.

Jen felt the branches lashing at her arms and face as she covered the first mile toward Jerry and Tyler.

She could see that 200 feet ahead the trees finally became sparse due to rock formations. She began to think about her approach into this combat. Jen was hoping that she could use surprise as a tool. Her tactic had to be clandestine; the element of surprise might just produce a quick arrest. Jerry was probably less than a fourth of mile ahead now.

The pursuit had slowed down. The volley of bullets indicated that it was more a fight than pursuit. It was possible that Jerry had the suspect cornered somewhere. Jen paused for a second and broadcast her position into the radio before she moved farther back into the canyon that was now opening before her. Unfortunately, she was met with a static response. Naturally, the immerging cliffs on her right had disrupted her transmission. "Shit," she mumbled. The red soil and rocks had now completely changed the complexion of her environment. Jen left the radio on but turned the volume down. It was possible that Barb could get some type of signal to verify location. It was worth a try, she speculated.

Sgt. Holly became aware of the Arkansas River current noise to the right of her position. The current was extremely powerful because of this season's immense run off. So, it was now river basin and cliffs? Yes, she began to envision this area near Salt Lick Trail. In fact, it was all coming back to her; she had been here before. The Salt Lick Trail would have meandered gracefully down to the river and finished at the trailhead. They had to be maybe 300 feet above and heading into one of the cathedral cliff canyons. If she was correct, the pursuit would end in a cul-de-sac of sharp cliffs and a small parcel of land.

It was one of the hikes that Jen had taken last summer. She had decided to become more familiar with the various camping areas around Buena Vista. Probably her third or fourth hike had involved this area. It became apparent to her that the suspect would eventually have no place to go. Nice, she thought. The guy was running right into nature's trap. Jen wondered if Jerry was familiar with the area. Her bet was that he knew exactly where they were. Well, the plot was thickening. Her guess was that Jerry was herding the suspect right into the canyon. How cool was that? She paused for a moment to decide how it was best to approach. Obviously, her position could determine where their arrest would take place. It wasn't a question of would they arrest this guy but when and how. A little planning would be good, she calculated.

As she proceeded into the canyon area, Jen realized that Jerry was located to her left. She began climbing the cliff to the second tier so that she could look down on the action. It seemed to be a two volley then movement strategy at this time. Jerry approached then fired to force the suspect back further. She timed her advancement by moving when Jerry would shoot. The guy had to then be positioned behind some type of cover. The suspect would then jump up and locate where Jerry was and shoot if he had a target. Sgt. Holly moved to the right cautiously crawling on her belly. Jen felt that she had two options: timing could make it possible that she would be able to get the guy in her sights for a clear shot or she might be able to work her way around from the back. The problem with the second tactic was that he might be able to slip through and run toward the river. Jerry had become more stationary at this point; he seemed content to hold the suspect in the canyon. Someone had to make a move eventually, Jen thought.

So whose move was it? Surely the suspect had looked around and could see his situation. Another option occurred to Jen. Wouldn't the guy finally decide to advance on her position and be unaware of her presence? Wouldn't he eventually try to come through the entrance to the canyon near her? How to let Jerry know that she was here was the question? Her mind began to spin. Surely there was a way. Jen looked around wondering what might work. There certainly wasn't any noise in the canyon other than a few crows circling above. Throwing a rock would be a dead giveaway.

Then Jen remembered a time at the station when she and the guys were practicing their bird calls during down time. Man, those days seemed so far away at this point. Wow, the normal days, she thought. Her crow call had been a point of contention and laughter. Jerry and Burger had argued over how bad it really sounded. Burger thought it must have been the mating call of a very frustrated bird while Jerry felt it was totally not crow in nature. Well, it might have been totally awful then, but who knew what it would do now? It was worth a try.

Jen waited until the crows circled again. She timed her call to begin right after the crows had finished their conversation. She took a breath crowed and hoped. Now she waited.

Two shots as usual and then Jen heard Jerry's magpie call. It was soft as if the bird was in the distance. Fortunately, the crows circled back and added a few more calls to the morning. It all seemed so natural. Jen had heard Jerry's magpie call that silly day at the station; it was excellent of course. Jen knew for a fact that Jerry had initiated the call a few seconds ago; her ears had memorized his technique. Now what, she thought?

Jerry began to move forward pushing the suspect toward her position. She hunkered down hoping to use surprise as a weapon. The suspect was now running full speed in her direction. He would pause now and then and aim a bullet toward Jerry. It was obvious that he was making his break.

Tyler suddenly began stalking the guy. The shepherd crawled to the top of a boulder and was ready to bounce as the suspect rushed down a crevasse. Tyler timed his jump perfectly. The only problem was that the guy became aware of the dog too soon. The suspect leaped up onto another boulder and took aim at Tyler.

Jen came up out of her position and fired to protect the dog. The shot ricocheted off the rocks but had been very close to a hit! Tyler was able to run back to Jerry who was whistling for his return. Now the guy could figure out that he was being trapped! "Shit," she mumbled for the second time.

Out of nowhere the suspect unexpectedly heaved a hand grenade in Jen's direction and then pulled the pin out of second grenade sailing it toward Jerry. There was an extreme flash of light then the blasts!

Jen was thrown back into the brush by the force. She covered her eyes with her arms; her body had crumbled to the ground. The sensation was like a rag doll being heaved across a room by an angry child. The debris peppered her body; the explosive roar flooded her ears. The massive force sent an earth shattering trauma up her spine. Pain shot through her whole body; a scream erupted from her mouth in climax then darkness. The grenades shocked and devastated her world for the longest moment of her life then it was over. Her eyes opened.

The havoc left as quickly as it had come. Her surroundings became incredibly calm. The explosions reverberated off the cliff walls echoing from side-to-side through the canyon into the distance. She was still conscious; she was alive. The blast had been so unexpected, powerful and final and yet the shrapnel had missed her. The debris had floated down and rested some distance away. Relief spread through Jen's bruised body. The guy had way more ammunition than they had thought. He had won this round but they would meet again, she knew.

Sgt. Holly began pushing the fuzz from her mind now concentrating on movement; she ignored the possible signs of a slight concussion. Hell, who wouldn't have a slight concussion? "Jeez," she mumbled. Jen rolled over and crawled slowly out of the bush. "Jerry?" Her mind began to grasp reality. Had he survived? Like the first Cro-Magnon Woman, Jen slowly pulled her body up. She could feel herself swaying but at least she was standing.

Her eyes began to focus again and her gaze searched for Jerry. Nothing? Where was the body? It just couldn't have totally disappeared? She stumbled toward his position weaving over the terrain still a bit fuzzy.

Then as if in some cartoon, Jerry's head popped up above the ground. Only his head! What the hell, she thought? She rubbed her eyes in disbelief! "No!" she murmured.

"Jen?" he said in relief as they made eye contact. "Help us out. I tackled Tyler and threw us both into this crevasse. Now I can't get my footing. Help?" He actually smiled when he realized how he must look to her. "Honest my whole body is down here and so is Tyler. Damn we were all lucky. Holy crap! I sure am glad that the guy has terrible aim."

"Me too," Jen said surprised to hear her answer making sense. Maybe she didn't have a concussion after all. Thank Heavens.

"He sure as hell had an arsenal of tricks. Glad to see you by the way," Jerry said.

"And you," Jen said.

***

Detective Burger was about to enter Holt's interrogation room. Getting Norton to admit that they had chased an unarmed woman through the woods had been huge. Especially, since it would be easy to prove that he knew exactly who she was from High Vista. Now, it was time to get Holt to admit more information about Henry Holden's murder and conversations. How long had they listened to Henry before they killed him? The surveillance tapes were being listened to right now by the Crime Scene people. He knew that there had to be some answers on those tapes. Brad Holt needed to be opened up and Ernie was just the guy to do it.

Brad seemed to be fairly tired. His head lay on the table when Detective Burger entered the room. "Want a pillow, you prick? Time to wake up, bad boy. The charges just keep adding up. Henry Holden's murder is at the top of the list. Not to mention the two attempts on John Holden. How about arson? Then today you idiots chased an unarmed woman into the woods shooting at her like it was target practice time. Give me a break! Your buddy says it was your fault from the surveillance to the murder. You've been a very busy boy."

Holt jumped up out of his chair like an electric shock hit him! His face became red and Ernie could feel his anger. "That's a fucking lie!" he screamed. "All we did was the surveillance and nothing more. You can't pin no murders on me! Travis didn't tell you nothing. Cop tricks! You're full of them."

Bingo, Burger thought. So we have him admitting to the surveillance charge at least. Now he had to get Holt to confess the rest of it. Murder wouldn't be near as easy. "Why Henry? What in the hell did he do to you? Did he and Billy plan something that was totally against your boss's plans?"

"No. He was cool. We was supposed to make sure that Henry would give his mineral rights to Billy. Everything was all right. Our job was to listen only to Henry's trailer conversations and contact the guy in charge if anything changed."

"Who were you to call?" Burger asked and leaned in closer to Holt.

"I...I don't know. Travis took care of them fucking details. We was pretty well done and laying low when that bitch showed up. We was going to scare her and that was all. She shouldn't have been out there in the woods anyway."

"You mean Ms. Bixler? You mean the lady staying at High Vista who was there when your trailer pulled in?" Burger said hoping to get deeper into the identification piece.

"That's all I'm admitting to. The bitch shouldn't have been in the fucking woods. What the hell was she doing anyway? Snooping?"

"No. I think she was hiking," Burger added casually. Easy does it, he thought. "How many shots did you fire at Ms. Bixler to scare her off?"

"I don't fucking know. We wanted to make sure that she didn't come back," Holt said with a nod of his head.

"So you thought you could teach her a lesson?"

"Yeah, something like that." Holt scratched his chin and aimed his grey eyes at the table. His sandy nest of hair was filthy dirty Burger noticed.

"Then why in the hell did you chase her? You went in pursuit of an unarmed person. Two men with assault rifles! Tell me why the charge of attempted murder wouldn't stick to your sorry ass? You're in deep, Brad, and your buddy, Travis, is willing to let you take the brunt of the charges. He says you murdered Henry. You get that through you thick skull! I'm very willing to let you stand trial for murder in the first degree and attempted murder of Ms. Bixler. You hear me?"

"I'm telling you, we didn't kill Henry. Hell, why would we? He hadn't changed his mind about willing the mineral rights to Billy. He was following the game plan as far as we were concerned. We had no reason I'm telling you!"

"How do you know that Billy was staying on track? We didn't find any listening devices in his trailer. How did you know?" Burger's interest began to peak.

"Well, there must have been some wires at one point; at least that was what we was told. We couldn't listen to one fucking thing from his trailer. It was wired but we couldn't listen. Didn't have the password to open the program. Yeah. The word got out that Billy might be changing his mind. The boss phoned Travis and told him so. We was just listening to Henry that's all."

"Who planted the devices in Billy's trailer?"

"Hell I don't know; it wasn't us. We was paid to listen to Henry only."

"Then you didn't wire Henry's trailer either? Is that correct?"

"We fucking listened and kept both surveillance programs going."

"When did you stop listening to Billy?" Burger asked quickly.

"Hell never; I'm telling you we didn't have the fucking password to open the audio," Holt howled. "In fact, the night before the old coot was killed the boss called to tell us that our job was over and get the hell out. We pulled out and waited at the trailhead for further orders."

"On a cell phone?" Burger asked. "When did Travis hear from the boss again after you moved to the trailhead?"

"Hell, I don't know. It didn't matter at that point. We were told to stay hidden but available and that was it."

"Travis had the cell phone then?"

"Yeah, but we destroyed one cell and bought a new phone at the grocery store. Travis told me that the number always changed so no phone could be identified."

"Where did you destroy the old phone?"

"Travis smashed it and tossed it." Holt sneered with the irony. "I don't know where; didn't care."

That figured thought Burger. Nowadays the throwaway phones really were popular with the criminals. Ernie got up out of his chair and left the room. Chief Marten had just gotten back from the crime scene and was watching through the mirror. "What do you think?" Burger asked the Chief.

Marten stared at Holt intently thinking before answering. "I'd bet that these two shits didn't kill Henry Holden. Neither one is very bright. I do wonder who wired both trailers. Very curious to say the least. Does seem like an inside job in some ways. At least someone in the family or close to the family has to be involved. Not only have we got four thugs doing the messy work but there's a boss or bosses out there cleaning up after them. Motive seems to be tangled in the mineral rights. How far up the chain does this scheme go? I have no idea."

Marten turned and stared at Burger; he had just realized the possible answer to his question. "Could we possibly be dealing with a group of men at the state capitol or oil money in North Dakota? Hell, I hope not," Marten said. "Guess I need to get on the phone and talk with the State Attorney's Office. These crimes could be just the tip of the iceberg. Holy shit," Marten mumbled as he looked back at Brad Holt who quite possibly could be a little fish in a great big ugly pond.

Marten decided to let Ernie handle these idiots for now. He had to try and find Jerry and Jen at this point. There had been a weak signal somewhere near the river basin. No contact but the signal did indicate that they were along the Arkansas River. Marten had sent two officers to the nearest foot bridge crossing that was probably a mile ahead of them. His instructions had been to stand down and wait. His guess would be that both Jerry and Jen knew the foot bridge was coming up. If they had the suspect running, then he just might try to cross on the bridge. It would be the most logical escape route for him. There was no other way across the river for another five miles. The suspect had to be tired by this time, Marten figured. Hell, the guy had been running for the last 24 hours. How much more could he take? James Marten would bet that his two physically fit officers could out run this guy. He wasn't a betting man but he was pretty sure.

"Barb?" he yelled over his shoulder as he inspected the topo. map. Marten tapped his index finger on the little foot bridge icon one more time.

"Yeah, Chief?" Barb appeared in the doorway.

Her brown hair stacked on her head in a 1960's style; she cracked her gum in salute.

"Let me know the minute that Jen and Jerry make contact. They should be coming out in an area where communication is possible. That is, providing we have been following the right signal. Hell, I hope so. Tell the guys waiting near the foot bridge to stay out of sight for me. Will you?"

"Will do," said Barb as she disappeared back into her sanctum with a swirl of her pink skirt and another crack of her gum.

***

Jen grasped Tyler's body as both officers lifted the dog out of the crevasse. Jerry was still wedged into the narrow slit in the boulders. He was able to lift Tyler up into Jen's arms. Getting Jerry out was going to be a little more difficult she thought. From his shoulders down Jerry was below the ground surface. Jen looked around for a way to wedge herself and use her leg muscles to bring him up. There were two rocks fully embedded in the surface near the crevasse. She braced her feet on them spreading her legs slightly apart. The trick would be to push her legs from a bend to straight while holding Jerry's arms from wrists up. They practiced their grip until the tightest hold could be obtained.

"Ready?" Jen said as she began to straighten her legs slowly. Jerry began to rise up out of the crevasse. Relying on her legs had been a good decision. Because their arms were straight, Jen didn't feel stress on her back. Many years of running and pumping weights paid off at this time. Jerry, who weighed at least 225, was out! Tyler immediately began licking his face and wagging. They rested for a few precious minutes letting their breathing become normal again. Their bodies needed a break. The dehydrated food came out and they quickly prepared a meal and ate silently. Each officer needed some time to process the mission.

Finally Jerry said, "I'm thinking that Tyler might like a refresher course before we proceed." He opened the sock bag and gave Tyler another sniff. Now it was time to once again pursue the suspect.

"So, Jerry, let's stay together for a while and track as a team. Maybe we can run him until he's tired," Jen said. She took a big gulp of water and prepared for the next round.

"I agree. He now knows that there are two of us and a dog. No more surprises on our part. Maybe we can force him to hurry. If he wants to stay ahead of us, he won't have time to be shooting at us. Yeah I think you're right. Let's go."

They took off in a full jog. The Arkansas River bank was fairly smooth and easy going. Cathedral cliffs on the right and the river bed on the left would control the route for at least 3 miles, Jen thought. The terrain, once again, would determine how this pursuit would play out. They were directly heading for Leadville ten miles ahead. Hopefully it would end in the next couple of miles. The chances of this guy knowing how far Leadville was had to be slim, Jen mused.

"There he is," Jerry said between breaths. "He's slowed down considerably." Jerry reined Tyler in tight.

No reason to get the dog killed at this point. The guy was spent. Tired with no food or water. "Let's get him," he whispered and went faster.

***

Now, Chief Marten thought, it was just a game of waiting; waiting to see if this pursuit could be put to an end. Catch this guy and maybe Detective Burger could then break one of these suspects into revealing the other players in the game.

Silently, James had been processing the motive and what it would take to orchestrate this scheme on the Holden clan. There had to be plenty of money available. Damn was this the way fracking would control the future? Perish that thought. James Marten was what folks called, 'a good old boy.' He liked his natural gas and oil as much as the next citizen but this kind of shenanigans really wasn't a good sign, he thought. Well, they had to put a stop to the greed that was oozing out of North Dakota right now. The sooner they laid hands on this fucker the better!

Barb's voice boomed from the communication's room, "Chief, get in here!"

CHAPTER 25

HIGH NOON

Jen was moving ahead of Jerry at this point. She was in full run. Seeing the son of the bitch in the distance had really got her blood going. She was madder than hell! Shooting Bill, then launching the grenades was way over the top.

Jerry asked from behind her, "Do you think he'll take the foot bridge coming up?"

Jen's focus reined in as they began to talk strategy. "Good question. It would be his last way out, wouldn't it? We're what, half a mile from the bridge?"

"Yeah. Radio work yet?" Jerry asked.

"Let me try to signal again." Both officers stopped and focused on the radio with hope. "It was static back in the canyon," Jen added. Suddenly the signal took hold; Jen could hear Barb transmitting. They were out there searching for the team! The voice was weak but it was coming in. "Barb? Sgt. Holly calling Code 2, urgent, 10-20 location 10 miles out of Leadville tracking suspect on the Arkansas River bank. We should be coming up on the Cater Rope Bridge 10-23 in five minutes. Come in."

"Jen! Oh my God it's good to hear your voice!" The signal became stronger as Barb adjusted the knobs. "We've been following your static for at least an hour. Two officers are located across the foot bridge on the highway side, 10-61. 10-4"

"Tell them to stay out of sight until suspect decides to cross the bridge. Hopefully, we can trap him on the bridge, 10-76."

"I will alert the officers and Chief Marten. 10-4. Oh…wait a minute, the Chief just walked in!" Barb said quickly.

"This is Chief Marten. So glad to hear from you guys. How far ahead is he, 10-77 ETA?"

"Half a mile," Jen said while trying to catch her breath.

"I take it, you're running. Have you made visual contact?"

"Yes. We think that he's losing energy. The pace is slower now."

"Good. I'm ordering the officers on the other side of the bridge to take cover. Do you read me? Officers?" There was a pause as contact was established with the men on the other side of the bridge.

"Yes, sir. 10-93, setting blockade," confirmed the officers at the bridge. "We are located behind a boulder on the right hand side. The cruiser is back around the curve and out of sight. What are your orders, Chief Marten? 10-4."

"10-23, stand by until you see him approach the middle of the bridge and our team moving in behind him. Approach with caution, 10-4."

Jen then interrupted the orders for a second. "Chief, he may have some more grenades in his possession. We already got to experience the first attack."

"Good Lord," Chief Marten exclaimed. A gasp from Barb in the background could also be heard. "Did you hear that, gentlemen? Approach the suspect with extreme caution. This guy isn't kidding. Make sure that you have your rifles ready. Do you read me?"

"Yes sir, 10-4."

Chief Marten then considered the news about grenade devices and changed his tactic slightly. "Actually, I want one of you to bring the cruiser up on orders and park it blocking the rope bridge after the suspect begins to cross over then use the car as your shield for any fire power that he might send your way. Buena Vista team will keep him on the bridge. I wish I could provide cover for you but…Jerry and Jen, be real careful," he added.

Jen couldn't help but ask at this time. She just needed to know before they risked their lives again. "How is Bill?"

"He's out of surgery and in ICU. Last contact said that he was in critical but stable condition. Barb is in contact with the hospital and will keep us updated." He looked at Barb and sent her a silent nod to go get the latest information. James turned back to the intercom and said, "Now go get this jerk for all of us! 10-4."

Jen knew that the radio channel was still open with the two officers on it. She tested the communication. "This is Sgt. Holly, who am I speaking with?"

"Officers Ryan and Carlton on loan from Salida."

"Well guys, the suspect is just finishing the last curve on our side before the approach to the bridge. I will let you know when he makes up his mind about crossing. Plan B would be that if he continues on then you two join us. Is that all right, Chief?"

"Affirmative. Keep the radio on at all times. Do you read me, Sgt. Holly?"

"10-4." Jen said then locked on the transmit button before she placed the radio back on her belt. Again, they were ready for another encounter. Jen felt the adrenalin rising every moment. She could see the guy hesitate as he made visual contact with the rope bridge. The suspect had to have been weighing the options as he approached it.

The sun sparkled on the river's torrent surface as the bridge swayed like a lazy snake in the breeze. It was one of those bridges where wood slats supported the foot path; thick rope created the handrails stretched some 50 feet across the river. Most of these precarious old bridges had been replaced by the Forest Service. Tourists really had no stomach for these dinosaurs of the early hiking era, especially, if they had children. Jen kind of liked them as long as she had time to inspect their condition. Well, that would be out of the question this time around.

Her thoughts were all focused on the next moments of survival. All those quirks in fate would play out in a few seconds. Would he or wouldn't he cross? And then if he did go for the bridge, what would happen when he realized that it was a trap? Surely he wouldn't jump. Unless you had hidden your head in the sand, you knew that the river current was killing people all over Colorado. Even the rafting tours with experienced guides couldn't guarantee a safe trip right now. Would the suspect heave more grenades at one side or the other? Would he simply charge the cop car in a rage or maybe come back their way where there was no cover for their team? Fate would let it all work out; Jen really had no clue.

Sometimes you just had to trust the future. Trust that you had written your will and paid your debts. Hope that there were more people who believed in your goodness than people you angered. When Jen had become a police officer, she became aware of all the possibilities. It could drive you crazy if you didn't let some of it go. Mothers reduced it to, 'always wear clean underwear.' "Sorry Mom," she murmured to herself. "Let it go."

Jerry then suggested, "Let's give him a little incentive here. Tell the Salida boys that I'm letting shots off in the air to get this party going."

As Jen yelled into the radio, Jerry fired. They all stood frozen for a second to see what would be his choice. The breeze picked up the rope bridge slightly and swung it in slow motion like it had a life of its' own. It could have been a bad sign or maybe it was waving at him to come on down. The suspect chose the bridge! Bingo! Time to move!

Moving across the bridge took both hands for the suspect. He was moving slowly keeping his balance. He looked back over his shoulder to stare at the cops approaching the bridge. He took one hand off the rope rail and fired a shot haphazardly. It was more a signal to tell them not to cross the bridge while he crossed.

The Chief interrupted the tense silence with his order for the officers to pull up the car.

Jen was pretty sure that the suspect couldn't hear anything over the roar of the rapids. He was, however, determined to get to the other side. As he focused on the far bank, the car moved into position. The doors were thrown open and both officers assumed the stance. Jen could see the suspect's shoulders slump in recognition of his dilemma. He was dangling over a death trap of a river on a swaying rope bridge. His eyes became wild as he made his decision. Jail or no jail? Jen could see the realization consume his countenance. Life's most basic decisions could be determined in a flick of an eye!

He grabbed at his vest and threw a grenade toward the car with a scream of rage that penetrated over the top of the river's roar. The flash and explosion dominated the scene as it ascended into the sky. It billowed up into the atmosphere throwing debris and dust toward the car.

Both Jerry and Jen now aimed their rifles at the suspect. Another grenade was released from his arm toward them. They both shoot, simultaneously, at him before they felt the impact of the grenade. They fell to the ground and covered their ears.

The grenade landed in the bridge's main cable anchorage attached to the shore then severed all rope ties from the river bank. The ropes split apart like live tendrils and flew back toward the suspect. Jen looked up in time to see the man's body captured in the tangled ropes. The clump of rope and man fell into the roaring rapids perishing as if some mythical monster had sucked them down. And it was over; he was gone in a flash! All that remained were the attached ropes at the bank on the far side dangling and dancing on the surface of the sun sparkled rapids.

Suddenly the pursuit had new perspective. Fate now brought the officers to the realization that a rescue mission would commence. Jen hit the radio switch quickly. "10-33, suspect in river. Possibly wounded and definitely caught in the current. All officers need to move downriver in search of the suspect who will need help. 10-61, any officer on road from Buena Vista to Salida needs to be on the lookout for suspect. 10-4," she yelled as both teams changed their direction and began to move with the flow of the Arkansas River. Now the current was in control.

Chief Marten came on the radio and issued a quick Code 2 followed by an APB to state patrol and forest service in the surrounding area. He added, "Search and Rescue assistance is now needed. 10-33 in Arkansas River rapids 10-20!"

The race was on! The river team paced themselves so that both sides were directly across from each other. Their eyes wildly searching the waters.

Jen found that she had created a routine in her pursuit. Her stare began in the middle of the river slowly moving to the bank then back to the center again. She became aware of the debris in the current. The water soaked logs drifted like bodies down stream. Their branches with a few green leaves would stick up and wave toward the shore. She began to think about what the suspect had been wearing. Her mind could see a black vest with a red shirt underneath. Blue jeans? No tan khaki pants. Yes, she was sure. The shirt would stand out. She flicked on the radio, "Red shirt, black vest and khaki tan pants, 10-4."

Communication was quiet for the river team while Barb broadcasted out the description of the suspect to other searchers. It was still either a 10-32, man with gun, or a floater. Who knew? The chances of the suspect being alive were definitely less likely at this point thanks to the current. Also, it was pretty clear that both Jen and Jerry had shot him. What were the chances for the guy to be alive, Barb thought as she listened intently?

Chief Marten had moved to the other room so that he could coordinate the rescue. The forest service had calculated that the current could carry a body a mile each four minutes in these waters. That meant that the body could travel through Buena Vista in the next two hours. He made sure that all officers were along the river bank now and informing boaters. He also realized that the rafting tours needed to be alerted from Buena Vista to

Salida. The search had become huge at this point. Dead or alive, this man had to be pulled from the river.

The shoreline had changed from soil to clusters of boulders along the river bed. Jerry and Jen found themselves leaping from one boulder to the next. Their progress had slowed down considerably. There were some larger boulders sticking out in the center of the river with the current running around them. Jen began to notice the river had widened and become somewhat shallow toward the center. She could see the small pebbles on the bottom in places farther out in the white waters.

The roaring current began to foam into white tuffs near the shoreline; the foam was gathering into mounds of white bubbles like soap. Lots of the debris now held tightly to the river banks. Cans and fish paraphernalia nestled into small pools of water trapped along the shoreline. They moved on hoping that this section of river could have slowed down the suspect's progress.

The river finally turned to the right and flowed over a waterfall with determined haste. The water fell about eight feet in all and plummeted with a hefty splash on the rocks below. Jen saw that there was some room behind the waterfall. She pointed instead of yelling.

There was too much force in the falling cascade to be heard. Jerry nodded and indicated that he would go explore the pool. He moved in carefully, gun in hand while paying attention to the slippery moss along the sides of the falls. Jen and Tyler watched him disappear. A few moments later, he came out shaking his head. Too bad, Jen thought. It would have made a great hiding place for a body.

They waved to the Salida boys on the other side and started their progress again. Jen was beginning to feel rather uncomfortable with wet boots. Her boots had started to squeak. She was beginning to feel that a possible blister was forming on her second toe. Ouch.

They were now fighting willow limbs from the shoreline as they moved forward. Pleasant, it was not. The second person got to ward off flinging branches. About 100 feet past the waterfall, the river water again became wider and slower in movement.

There were all sorts of debris caught in the rocks and branches in an overflow area on their side of the river. This area seemed to be the river's dumping ground, a depository, Jen thought. At least the small water pools and rocks made it easier for them to move. It was far enough away from the river flow that they could actually communicate. Jen leaped up on a boulder to get a better view and then stopped dead in her tracks. In a calm small river bank pool was the body. There was no other content in the crystal clear water. The suspect lay face down with arms extended out. He had lost one tennis shoe and sock in his futile escape. She motioned to the Salida boys by pointing down at the body. They nodded their heads and watched. "Over here, Jerry," she yelled.

"Found at last," he said then jumped down into the pool to inspect the body.

Jen pulled out the radio and said, "10-15, suspect

in custody."

Jerry rolled him over and felt for a pulse. He shook his head, no. The man's face was totally gray and the blood from his wounds had long since stopped bleeding. Jen noticed that there were two bullet holes near his heart. Both she and Jerry had landed lethal shots. When one calculated the rough ride down the river currents, maybe to have departed from this world before hand was best. The torrent waters had taken their toll. The body showed signs of being torn and brutalized. Traveling over rocks hadn't been an easy trip for their suspect. She could handle her blister now; a small price to pay to say the least.

"The suspect is dead. Our 10-20 location is approximately 15 miles from Buena Vista. My guess would be fairly close to road 371. We have apparently come full circle back to the car chase area. How strange is that? Suspect, however, will need the coroner's truck this time. 10-4."

"On the way, 10-4," Barb said and went quiet.

Jerry checked the body's back pockets and pulled out a soaked billfold. John Jones did seem to be his actual name. Interesting, Jen thought. The Salida boys called them a few minutes later to tell them that they would be heading back to what was left of their car. Apparently, they had found his shoe back by the falls and had now placed it in a bag. Well John Jones was only missing a sock at this point. Too bad for the choices that he had made. His life had come to a tragic end on a beautiful sunny day.

These two officers now settled in for a long

afternoon. It would be probably an hour before a Forensic Team would find them and comb the area then take pictures. They would bring a body bag and lift Jones out. His final resting place could only be documented at this point; he had floated from torrent water to calm.

Jen thought about his criminal life and saw some parallels to his death. He certainly didn't go down in a blaze of glory but he did go down in a torrent. Jerry, for some reason known only to him, rolled the body back face down.

She could feel her body now starting to relax. It was total relief to know that their mission was over. Jerry and Tyler wandered off onto dry land for a little throw the stick play time. Jen simply moved back on her boulder and sat in the sun. Her face began to absorb the sun's warmth while her body let her know she needed a rest. The aches and pains began to surface; she had ignored the physical stress until this very moment. Lordy, she was tired. Jen took her boots off and placed them along with her socks in the sun. She now let herself begin to consider the stress that the team had experienced.

The mission had truly been a learning experience. It had taught her in many ways why she had become a police woman. The challenges made her feel alive; the mission had created a wealth of experience through team work, not to mention how Jen's confidence in her endurance had improved. It had in many ways felt like an extreme test that went far beyond academy training. Unfortunately, the last test was going to be hard to process, the shooting.

The realization that she had killed someone

suddenly hit home. Yes, one had to take into consideration the circumstances. One had to say that if they hadn't shot him, then he would have killed them. Did it justify how she felt? Jen wasn't sure. No wonder cops had therapists to go see after a shooting. Some guys puffed out their chests and used a shooting as a *Red Badge of Courage*.' No, they said that they didn't have to talk to 'no shrink' but she wondered if late at night, it did bother them. Cops had trouble staying married. There were reasons; reasons beyond the hours of work and temptations. Somehow, Jen could feel a dark cloud covering her heart. Killing for any reason brought anguish followed by turmoil. It was her own turmoil that she had to deal with now. Her mother had once said that a soul created a brilliant light. Each time a person told a lie that light, minutely, dimmed. Jen now had to wonder how dim the light became when a man's life was extinguished.

CHAPTER 26

BELLOWS TO THE RESCUE

Detective Burger knew that some more information had to come from Norton. Holt was as dumb as a fence post. He certainly wasn't in charge of anything. Burger had left Norton sitting in a cell for hours. The guy was looking pretty frustrated. His call to a lawyer hadn't produced any 'suits' coming in the door. Ernie had to wonder about that. He had adopted a wait and see attitude, but now that Jones was a floater, maybe more pressure should be applied. No time like the present.

The last two cops in the office had been sent to the trailer site to search for the remains of the cell phone. He had also placed a call to Bob and Chelsea to stop the morning trash removal just in case. They weren't too happy, but it was a necessary tactic.

Dumpster diving was not anyone's favorite job. However, cell phones did have the data chip; Norton could have missed crushing the chip. The

Crime Lab could then place it in another phone. One could hope.

Burger opened the door and ventured into Norton's interrogation room. "So, big guy, where's your fucking lawyer? Guess we'll have to book you for murder. Holt's been singing the tune of you doing the murder and arson. All he did was sit in the trailer and listen to Henry's conversations while you went around camp killing and burning."

"Now just a minute," Norton said as he pushed his chair back. "You can't get me for murder. Holt and I didn't murder anyone. Where's my lawyer?"

Burger sat down in the chair opposite Norton and leaned back. "You tell me. We haven't locked any doors. No lawyer has walked in and asked to have the privilege to represent you. Quite honestly I'm getting tired of waiting. I'm beginning to think that booking you for first degree murder and the rest of the crimes would work for me. That would be arson, attempted murder on John Holden, Ms. Bixler and first degree on Henry Holden. That should about sum it up."

"Now wait a minute. Brad and I just did surveillance on Henry Holden and then got carried away when Bixler came snooping. We're not good for anything else. I'm telling you," Norton said.

"Well sorry I can't use any of that. You have asked for a lawyer and my hands are tied."

"What if we talked a little more before my lawyer gets here?" Norton asked with a sly smile on his face.

"Are you waiving the right for a lawyer then at this time?" Burger asked.

As if on cue Bellows waltzed in the door waving his hands like a referee. "Don't say another word, Mr. Norton. I've been hired to represent you in this case. Well, actually my firm has asked me to take on the case. I will now need to meet privately with my client." His eyes narrowed as he pulled the lawyer power trip.

Ernie got up with a sigh and moved toward the door. "Let me know when you are ready to give your statement." Burger shut the door and headed for coffee and a break. He had just lifted the coffee pot when Barb emerged from her office.

"Got some interesting information for you, Ernie; might help in the cracking of these two nuts. According to the bank Norton deposited 15,000 bucks in his account before he left North Dakota and Holt only deposited 5,000. Thought that was kind of interesting. You think someone got short changed? Also, the cartridges down by the dumpster belong to the rifles in their trailer. We just got the results back from the Ballistics' Lab and they're sure. Hope that helps," Barb announced then with a dramatic swish of her pink dress, she returned to her inner sanctum.

Ernie replaced the coffee pot and headed for Holt's room. He wanted to get there quickly in case Bellows would be representing both of them. He flew the door open then shut it and sat down. There was a big smile on his face as he stared at Holt. "So how does it feel to not only be arrested for your part in these crimes but to get short changed also?"

"What in the hell are you talking about?" Holt grumbled. About ten minutes later, Burger came back out of Holt's interrogation room and headed toward the Crime Lab. He was checking his notes as he moved swiftly. Charlie Bellows opened Norton's door and looked around for some help. "Hello? Anyone care that we're ready to make a statement?" he asked an empty room. Barb stuck her head out and gave Bellows her coldest stare then said, "I will make sure that Detective Burger will be right with you. We're kind of busy around here today." She shut the door and called Burger's cell to deliver the message privately.

"Thanks Barb. I'll be right there to hear what his majesty has to say. I'm heading into the Chief's office first. A slight delay certainly won't hurt. You might tell them we'll be there shortly."

"Will do," Barb had worked in the office long enough that she could tell something was brewing. Ernie had something going for sure. She wandered over and knocked on the door then opened it and gave the message. Of course she noticed that Bellows looked at his watch and huffed and puffed. Barb quickly shut the door then chuckled as she disappeared. Shortly after Barb's retreat, Burger and Marten came out of the Crime Lab together. They moved to Norton's door, checked the mirror window then went in without a word.

"Gentlemen, I have asked Chief Marten to join us for your statement. Want to make sure that we are all on the same page. Are you ready, Mr. Bellows?"

"Yes."

"I am turning on the recorder." Ernie waited a few seconds for a lead in before he started. "Let the recording show that Mr. Charles Bellows, Mr. Norton's lawyer, is present during this interview. It is July second, 2014. Now, Mr. Norton please state that you have been read your rights and your request for a lawyer has been honored."

Bellows took right over letting it be known that Norton was finished talking. "Mr. Norton will verify that he has indeed been read his rights and I am representing the law firm of Smith, Howard and Bellows."

"Who has hired your law firm? Is Norton paying you directly?" asked Marten not taking his eyes off the notepad in his hands.

"You will need a warrant for any information about the contract between Mr. Norton and our firm. Mr. Norton is a resident of North Dakota and, therefore, has requested our assistance."

"You are aware of the charges that will be brought against Mr. Norton? Shall we read the extent of the list?"

"Yes. Please," Bellows said, "for the record."

"Arson, attempted murder four counts, wiretapping and first degree murder of Henry Holden."

"Please state the specifics of the attempted murder charges," Bellows asked.

"Two attempts on John Holden, one attempt on Ms. Carol Bixler and Ms. Bernie Holden and another attempt today on Ms. Carol Bixler," Marten stated. "How do you plead?"

Burger and Marten hoped that Norton would find his voice at this point and he did. "Not guilty to all of it," he said with satisfaction.

Burger then leaned up and said, " Let the record show that Mr. Norton has in a previous interview before he asked for a lawyer admitted to wiretapping and the attempted murder of Ms. Carol Bixler. He has also stated that Henry Holden, during their surveillance of his private conversations, never strayed from letting his son, Bill Holden, sell the mineral rights on the Holden Ranch when in fact that is a lie."

"That's a pile of crap," Norton yelled. "Holden never said anything differently. He was gonna will it to his son! We didn't listen to Billy's trailer talk; we just recorded on the computer."

"Enough, Mr. Norton. Let me discuss the charges on your behalf," Bellows said.

"Not when they're going to add bullshit to my charges," retorted Norton.

Ernie, trying to keep Norton on a roll added, "That's not true, Mr. Norton. On Monday evening Henry Holden brought Matt Holden to Billy's trailer and they sat down to discuss the agreement. According to the conversation, Henry Holden stated that he wasn't sure that they should sell to the oil company of J Meyer Petro from Texas. Smith, Howard and Bellows Law Firm would have handled the entire transaction. Isn't that correct, Mr. Bellows?"

"Any information about my employment is confidential. You will need a warrant to access any of the firm's business contracts and then there is lawyer-client privilege to protect Mr. Norton's confidentiality," Bellows stated.

"We didn't kill Henry Holden; we just listened to

the son of a bitch. We never heard no conversation from Billy's trailer. It was blocked by another password, not us. Hell, we got orders over the telephone. We just followed orders!" Norton hissed in his defense.

Bellows leapt out of his chair and tried to stop Norton from talking. He yelled over the top trying to shut Norton up! "You'll need to keep your mouth closed, Mr. Norton, if you want my firm to represent you!"

Detective Burger slipped in another verbal jab, "By the way the cartridges found near the dumpster belong to you and Holt. Two more attempted murder charges are being added to your list. You not only listened to Henry's trailer but you tried to keep people out of it by shooting at them. So why should we believe anything that you say? You were obviously the boss."

"No! The boss called us and gave us orders," Norton yelled.

Burger then interjected loudly, "By the way, Holt's not too happy that you took 15,000 and left him with 5,000. He's ready to turn state's evidence. We're about ready to get a statement from him that you killed Henry Holden!"

"Now wait a minute," Bellows yelled! "This interview is over!"

"Find my old cell phone. I threw it in one of the trash cans near where our trailer was parked at High Vista! It would prove that there was a boss!" Norton squealed.

"Who?" Chief Marten yelled.

Bellows began pushing Norton toward the door.

Norton yelled over his shoulder, "Used a damn voice changer gadget! We never knew! I didn't kill Holden, damn it!"

"I demand to see Brad Holt immediately!" Bellows thundered. His face was beet red.

***

Jen and Jerry walked toward the helicopter in the clearing near the crime scene. They were told to head back to the station and not help with the gathering of evidence. Both officers had submitted their rifles to the crime crew. Their statements had been taken and now it was over for them at this specific site. It was protocol.

Jerry eyed Jen as they walked in unison. "How are you feeling?"

Jen knew exactly what he was talking about. The one conversation topic both of them hadn't touched until now. "Have you ever shot someone before?" she asked.

"Bout five years ago. A guy went crazy during a domestic violence call. It all happened so quickly that I just reacted. The girlfriend blamed me and if I hadn't had my partner with me at the time, who knows what might have happened. It was very ugly." Jerry waited for Jen's reaction.

"I'm so sorry. That must have been terrible. I can't imagine," she murmured.

"It makes you aware of the toll that this job can take. I moved to the mountains after it was all over. In the city those types of incidences happen too often. I needed to process," he added.

"Were you able to process?" she asked.

"Not really. Unfortunately, it comes with the job. I can only say that you begin to feel better after time passes. I have known some guys to quit the force because of having to kill someone; others just adjust. Me, I think I landed in the middle of all that. You have to get to the point that you can look at the situation and know that it wasn't avoidable. You have to ask yourself the hard questions. Like, what if he was still alive? What would he do down the road? Would he kill again? Would he have killed one of us?" Jerry looked into Jen's eyes and stopped. He placed his hands on her shoulders. "We had no choice. There comes a time in this job when to kill or be killed is reality just like the path a soldier takes in war. You will need to process it on your own or with the help of someone who is trained to help cops. Don't be afraid to talk it out that's what I did. I will say that we both need to be thankful for each other. I have no doubt that one of us could have easily been killed; you can have my back anytime, partner."

Jen was really thankful for Jerry right now. In the two years that they had worked together, Jerry had never said that much before to her. She was honored by his thoughtfulness and sensitivity.

It would help her especially at night when she would wake up and see the bridge again. Jones would be waiting for her with the grenade in his hand over and over. She would feel that moment when they took the stance and aimed in unison. The sound of rifles firing would quicken her pulse and bring the vision back to her many times she knew.

Maybe that was what processing was really all about. You couldn't change what really happened or manipulate the story. You simply had to play the vision over and over until somehow it became more objective; until you could stand above the action and watch your choice of survival.

A tear fell down Jen's cheek as she said, "Thanks, Jerry, for the advice." He put his arm around her shoulder as they got into the helicopter. The motor started and began to lift them out of the forest. Tomorrow was the 3rd of July. They would move on to other duties.

This case wasn't over by any means, however. Who killed Mr. Holden was still open but Jen did know that the suspect in the woods would no longer bother anyone. Jen wanted to talk with Bix. Bix had been terrorized and stalked; she needed to know that Jones and his friends were no longer a threat. Closure just might be obtainable.

CHAPTER 27

SEARCHING AGAIN

Bix was just finishing her lunch in the Scamp trailer when four police cars zoomed into the park. They didn't have any sirens going but it looked serious. She and Simon watched out the window. Two of the cars stopped near the dumpster at the back of the camp. Simon was doing his quiet, "woof…woof." It was his alarm for medium alert. Bix got her cell off the kitchen table and called Bernie. "What's going on? You see all the cars?"

"Just talked with Chelsea and she said that they're looking for a cell phone that was tossed by the Jones boys in the trash somewhere."

"Wow. So they really need to see all the trash that has been consumed this week. Right?"

"That's what I'm thinking."

"Wonder if they need any help? We could collect all the trash from our sites and give it to them. There are some trash containers that aren't easy to see. What do you think?" Bix asked.

"Maybe moving them wouldn't be a good idea. We could make sure that they know where our containers are located though," Bernie said.

"I see Sgt. Holly out in back checking out the dumpster. I'll go chat." Bix put Simon's leash on and ventured out the door. The group was extremely busy sorting. "Sgt. Holly? We thought that you all might like to know that there are some trash containers around the trailers. They're not quite so obvious," Bix added.

Jen looked up and smiled. "You're trying to make our job easy? Thanks, Bix. Why don't you show me where these containers are and then we can document locations." Sgt. Holly took her cell out of her pocket to take pictures and followed Bix. "By the way, can we talk sometime soon? I'd like to tell you about what happened in the woods and the fact that there will be no more stalking by these criminals," Jen said.

"Sure. I'd like to know the specifics when you can talk," Bix said. "Later then."

As they moved up toward the trailers, the Holdens appeared ready to indicate where their trash was kept. It would have been humorous if the whole matter hadn't been so damn serious, Bix thought. Bernie appeared then and pointed to a metal bear proof container sitting near the picnic table. Sgt. Holly began taking cell pictures. She slowly walked up the row, trailer by trailer, taking the pictures to categorize later. Billy came out last; he motioned to his trash storage container with a flair. Opening the lid and waving his hand. There was a slight smirk on his face. Bix was definitely starting to like Billy.

As he stood with the can lid up waving the smell away, Bix suddenly had a flashback to the morning of Henry's death. She had been standing in about the same place that morning when everyone dashed out to see what had happened. The scene replayed all the chaos of tears flowing and shock. Bix, out of the corner of her eye, had seen BB come rushing out of Billy's trailer but instead of rushing over to Henry's trailer, she stopped and deposited something in the trash then went to Mattie's side. At the time Bix had just thought it a bit odd. Like cleaning was priority. The vision had stuck in Bix's mind. She had dismissed the action by saying that people did odd things. Yet, it hadn't made sense to her.

Bix went in search for Bernie. "Bernie, come here," Bix said. She took Bernie's arm and steered her away from the crowd. "Listen this may seem absolutely stupid but I think they need to check Billy's trash closely. I think BB could be more involved in Henry's murder than we thought. What if she got rid of a container that had poison in it?"

"Well shit! That would be one heck of a find in Billy's trash," Bernie said. "Sgt. Holly, could you come here for a minute? Bix has just remembered something that you need to hear."

They stood apart from the trash container process. Crime scene employees were dumping trash into individual bags then identifying each bag's owner. The three ladies were having a very intense conversation.

As one of the guys from Crime Scene approached Billy's trash, Jen rushed over. She began carefully picking out containers then placing them in a separate bag. Jen pulled out a red plastic juice container and held it up for Bix to look at. There was a nod and Jen then separately bagged that bottle. She pulled one of the crime scene guys to the side and gave him instructions which sent him off to the station with the evidence bag.

Billy, noticing what had happened, walked over to Bernie and Bix. "What was that all about?" Bernie took the lead in the matter. "Bix saw someone put that container in your trash shortly after Dad was discovered."

Billy eyed the two ladies very closely. They could tell that it was registering with him. "It was BB wasn't it?"

Bix replied this time, "Yes."

"Sergeant?" one of the guys yelled coming from the large dumpster near the Commons. He was holding up a clear plastic sack with a crushed phone in it. "We just found this in the trash!"

Excellent," Jen replied. "Make sure that you collect all the trash that isn't food products from that dumpster. We may need to process all of it just in case.

"Okay?"

"We're on it." With that comment the deputy handed the bagged cell phone to Jen and left to finish the job.

Sgt. Holly went back to find Bernie and Bix before she left for the station. They were back watching the bags of trash being lifted into the

Crime Scene truck. The row of large black bags were now lined up with yellow ties and crime scene identification tags meticulous attached. Black ducks in a row, Bix thought as she took a picture. Her vacation needed to be documented so her friends would believe her. It had truly become one strange event to say the least.

"Ladies, I'll let you know what happens soon. I need to inform Detective Burger about your information. He will need to talk to you probably in the next hour. My job is to deliver the trash," she chuckled, "and then maybe get a shower in and a few hours sleep. Thought I'd volunteer for the trash pick up before the shower. I'd still like to talk with you, Bix, sometime soon if that's all right?" she asked.

"Of course it is," Bix said. "By the way, Billy knows. He asked if it had something to do with BB and I couldn't help myself. I said yes."

"Could you tell him not to spread the word until after you all talk with Detective Burger? How this is handled can mean the difference between solving the case or not. Please have that conversation with him right now." Bernie moved away from them and called Billy. "It would probably be best if the three of you met and stayed separate from everyone else until after the meeting with Burger. Don't want the defense claiming that you all spread the word and influenced witnesses. Okay?"

"Consider it done," Bix said. "I'll invite Billy and Bernie over to my place. Tell Detective Burger to join us." As the threesome joined forces, they watched Sgt. Holly take off in one of the squad cars.

The rest of the police team continued loading the trash bags.

Bix began to feel like maybe the good guys were starting to make sense out of this mess. The police did have the two in custody who had fired at her; it began to look hopeful. Henry deserved to rest in peace and his killer needed to be brought to justice. So maybe it was time to take a good hard look at BB and Daddy Dearest. "The spoon!" she said suddenly.

Bernie looked at her not immediately getting it; then the light went on. "And back to the chili. I wonder just whose prints were indeed on that chili spoon; we can only hope. Do the police have her prints?"

"I'll go find something with BB's prints on it just in case Burger needs them," Billy added. "Maybe we can either help eliminate her from the list or make her a prime time suspect."

"See you in a bit," Bernie added. Both Holdens sped off. The police vehicles with trash also moved out.

Bix and Simon headed back toward their trailer. Quite suddenly it had gotten quiet. A break from all the dumpster diving was greatly appreciated. She noticed that the deer had started their late afternoon routine; they began wandering slowly through the camp. Simon watched them silently sniffing the air but being very respectful of their presence. Bix sat down in her lawn chair and pulled Simon up on her lap. He had been a good dog while all the trash chaos was happening. She saw this little doggy moment as his reward for good attendance. The deer were happily lost in their routine and Simon was content.

Bix began to think about all that had happened since last Sunday as she stroked Simon's head. The vortex of events was utterly mystifying. The turmoil from North Dakota had traveled with the Holdens; money and power manipulating life. She could feel the tendrils of corruption crawling beneath the surface. It really felt stark and ugly.

Had the Holdens realized it, Bix wondered. It was so much easier to downplay the circumstances when you were busy scraping out a living. John and Bernie had dismissed the alarming implications that their actions created as they helped the farmers that fateful evening.

John had placed himself in the position to protest against the fracking industry. The lines had been drawn whether that was the intent or not. No wonder Henry had demanded that all the family members needed to be at the family reunion. No wonder that the criminal element had come along to monitor. Henry had been a lot wiser than any of them knew in his attempt to unite them.

Bix began to go down that rabbit hole when a deer simply walked over and sniffed Simon who was sound asleep. It was amazing. The doe had become entirely too bold for its own good; maybe that was the way of the Holden clan. The family had accidentally been forced to take a stand and to seek common ground. They had become conspicuous in North Dakota's economic development. There had to be a future for both ranchers and economic ventures in North Dakota. And just maybe, the

Holdens could play a part in that future. The young deer finally got tired of inspecting Simon and wandered off. Food was much more important in her realm of priorities; Simon was just a passing whim.

Bernie and Billy were now walking toward her. There was lots of conversation being shared. Billy had a hair brush in a bag that he was holding. "Will this do?" he said waving his find. "She always borrowed my brush so I finally bought a new one and left this in the bathroom for her. When she cleared out yesterday, I noticed that BB had left it."

"Perfect," Bix said. She checked her watch. It had been 45 minutes since Jen had taken off for the station. "Maybe we should get out of sight so nobody comes over to chat. Feels funny to be avoiding everyone but still." Bix said. She pulled herself out of the lawn chair and headed for the trailer. Simon followed along ready for his dinner.

"Yeah well this family has had too much avoidance lately anyway," Billy admitted, "and most of it was my fault. Did I insult you, Bix, at any time?"

She thought for a moment and then said, "Not that I can remember." She eyed him for a few seconds, considering the question. "It has been a little tense now and then but that's all. So what do you think about our opinion on your dad's death?" She opened the door of the trailer and motioned them to enter. "Coffee?" she asked while folding up the lawn chair. She brought a chair in for Detective Burger.

"Sounds great," Billy said. "As long as we can

add a little something to the brew," he smiled.

"Bourbon?"

"Exactly." They all sat around the table with elbows resting. "I think that there certainly might be some signs that point toward BB and her dad," Billy ventured. "My romance happened too conveniently now that I think back. Dad started researching the property lines at the County Assessor's Office and here came BB in the same week. It might have been a well thought out plan and I simply walked into it. Unsuspecting and so foolish. Who knew?"

The knock on the door had been expected but they all jumped anyway. Bix got up and peeked out to make sure it was Burger. It was. "Come on in, Detective, we have been expecting you."

"Sorry to intrude again but it sounds like we all might just need to talk. Sgt. Holly told me about BB's possible involvement. The Bellows have shot to the top of the list for a few reasons I might add."

"Coffee plain or with a little added juice?" Bix asked before sitting down. She unfolded the chair for Ernie Burger.

"Just coffee thanks. I take it that you have BB's hair brush in that bag?" he asked. "Or is that another lethal weapon?"

"Just a hair brush. One that BB used when she was living in my trailer," Billy answered.

"If you don't mind, I'll send that evidence back with my driver to take to the lab as we have our conversation. The Chief will phone me the fingerprint results as soon as possible." He took the brush, opened the door and tossed the bag to the officer in the car who left immediately. Returning to the group, Burger settled into the chair. "Do need to tell you that there are some fingerprints that don't match anyone on our records. We do have the immediate family prints but BB wasn't around the day that we got the samples. The juice container and chili spoon prints match each other. So now tell me why you folks have decided to focus on BB?"

"She showed up about the time Dad and I began talking about selling the mineral rights. Some of the court house folks knew what we were doing and finally BB convinced me to talk with her dad about how to make our agreement legal. The papers started flowing until Dad took a step back. He told me that he was sure but that telling the family had to be done before it became absolutely final."

"So your father hadn't signed the papers yet? Bellows knew that Henry would talk with the family on this vacation?" Burger clarified.

"Correct and to sweeten the deal, he began offering the senate race to me. If I got this deal signed then the oil company and his law firm would finance my campaign. At that time it looked like a sweet deal. God, I hate ranching," Billy added. "Sorry, Bernie, but that's the way it's been since I hit my 20's."

"That's okay, Billy. We should have listened to you. The family just couldn't accept it but I think we're coming around," Bernie said giving Billy's knee a pat. "There's no reason you shouldn't still run for the senate. We just need to figure out how to make it happen and convince you to listen to Matt. There's got to be a deal in there some place, brother."

"So your family is willing to help finance the campaign?" Burger questioned. "Did BB know that you were considering running without the law firm and oil being the sole contributors?"

"Only if she listened to our conversation the other night when Dad brought Matt over. However, the door was closed tight; I checked it."

"The two guys we've got in custody tell us that your trailer had been bugged. They claimed that they didn't have the computer password for that program but the boss did. Whoever that boss happens to be. Did BB have a computer or ipad with her for the trip?"

"Actually she did. She had a small laptop in her purse. She made sure it was with her at all times. I wondered at the time what was so damn important," Billy said.

"Okay...well let's go back to the juice container, Ms. Bixler. Tell me what happened?"

"I will if you'll call me Bix."

"Sure. Okay, Bix, in your own words." Burger turned on a recorder and pointed at her to begin.

"Well it was the morning that Mattie found Henry. We all jumped up out of bed and ran over to see why Mattie was screaming and crying. I hadn't been introduced yet to BB at that time but from the description and the fact that she was with Billy, it became obvious. I simply noticed that as Billy and BB came out of their trailer, she paused at the trash can. Actually, Billy had gone ahead then BB stopped and put something in the trash. Anyway, it just seemed odd. Why was throwing a plastic container away more important than finding out what had happened. Well Henry's death became the focus and I promptly forgot. Today when Billy opened the trash lid for Sgt. Holly, I remembered the incident."

Burger added time and dat, so that establishes BB to the container. We have sent the dried ingredients from the container to Denver for verification. The chili spoon did have a small amount of poisonous residue on it, by the way. Tell me about the spoon again, Bernie," Burger asked and then started the recorder.

"Well, Dad was making his famous hotter-than-hell chili in the Commons like he does every year. It takes lots of tasting and added ingredients. Dad was in the middle of taste testing. I noticed BB heading out the screen door about the time I went in. That was before I even knew who she was. Later after the chili was done and Dad and I were cleaning up, I noticed that the spoon was missing. I know it's a small thing but Dad had used that spoon for chili making for years. Matt found it two days later thrown behind the washing machine. Matt had decided to open the water connection on the washer completely so it would fill quickly. He leaned over the machine and there was the spoon. You see, I had been in the Commons looking for the spoon that morning before Matt did his wash. He knew that I was looking for it and there it was."

Burger added date details and then turned off the recorder for the second time. "Okay, so that ties up some loose ends," Ernie said. "So does this conspiracy go deeper? What does the Bellows family have to gain? I'm not sure that I understand

all of that. Is your property that important? I don't
get it," Burger admitted.

"Well, John could probably explain this better,"
Billy began, "but Bellows' law firm is busy
acquiring the river basin property so that they can
sell the water rights to J Meyer Petro and make a
killing financially. The Missouri River water will be
like gold when the fracking on our property gets
going. As for BB? I think she just wanted to be the
wife of a state senator. I'm not too bad of a catch,
you know," Billy added. "And now that I think
about it, BB picked a fight with me when I said that
I was thinking about reversing my opinion and
going with a dry fracking concept. She literally
blew a gasket."

"How much money are we talking about here?"
Burger asked.

"Millions and possibly billions if the law firm
can keep buying along the river basin. Definitely
big bucks to say the least," Billy added.

"So, to go out on a limb and take a chance on the
elimination of Henry and the major land owners in
the Holden family would be plausible?" Burger
asked.

"Yes," Billy said.

"Would it also be fair to say that Smith, Howard
and Bellows could have clout at the State Capitol?
Seems to me that it would take a lot of money to
swing this kind of deal. I need to let you know that
we have contacted the State Attorney General's
Office in North Dakota on this whole situation,"
Burger said then leaned back in his chair to watch
their reactions. If he was looking for surprise, he

was mistaken. The reaction was more like relief.

Bernie was the one who answered. "Good call. There's so much greed and power surfacing right now that we can only hope that the Attorney General is willing to stand up legally."

"You betcha," Billy echoed.

"So I was wondering," Bix hedged. Burger nodded the go-ahead. "Well, being the little bitty fish in a big pond, is Buena Vista and the Holden family going to be able to put these jerks in jail?"

"Good question. I wish we had some type of confession. I mean we have the muscle guys but the crime leaders are still questionable. When you are trying to put away lawyers for crimes it gets hard to say the least. Plus, the money trail and the paper trail could take years to uncover in a scheme this large. Greed, unfortunately, can be one hell of a challenge to prosecute. I think lots of these questions would have to be researched by the State of North Dakota. It would take a bank of money to hire and keep lawyers plus a special task force working. You know what I mean?"

Unfortunately, they did. There was a long pause in the conversation while the group looked deeply into their coffee cups in thought. Bix got up and poured more coffee; she placed the bottle of bourbon on the table. Simon raised his head off his cushion and wondered why it had gotten so quiet. He made sure that Bix was still present and then flopped his head down and went back to sleep.

Billy finally said, "So maybe we need to look at our own problems and not get carried away here. The State of North Dakota would need to decide the larger issues. Almost seems that one could run a campaign on forcing the state, publicly, to investigate this mess." He smiled and looked around the room. "Well, that was spoken as a potential candidate wasn't it? I'm almost ashamed of myself," he said while pouring some more bourbon in his cup.

"Maybe and maybe not, Billy," said Bernie. "You know up until this moment, I've been sort of against your campaign but this whole mess needs to be exposed and pushed. Dad would want that. Dry fracking needs to be explored so the public can learn how to keep their water and still promote fracking. Even if dry fracking proves not possible, oil companies need to be pushed into research. It would be a bonus for your campaign if these two issues were the focus." Bernie paused for a moment and looked around the table as she considered the situation. "Wow. It all takes on a whole new light doesn't it? Dad's murder has got to mean something; some good must come from this whole damn event. Dad's memory deserves that much from us."

"You're exactly right," Bix said. "However, maybe we ought to think more about what we can change here and now. Not that what you're talking about, Billy, isn't totally important. I almost think that I should come and join your campaign. Wonder how many politicians start out supporting a scientific concept?"

"Not many would be my guess," mumbled Burger. "So, Billy, what would you say to meeting with BB and trying to bring out some kind of confession? I mean, who knows how involved she could be in this whole mess. Maybe at the same time, I could bring Bellows into the station for a discussion about his involvement in the mining purchases. Possibly try to convince him to give the case to another law firm. Conflict of interest being our reason for pulling him in might work. What do you think?"

"All I can say is that it will just be a yelling match between BB and me. Let me get this straight. Are you talking about my trailer being wired again only this time for the good guys?"

"Well, now that you mention it," Burger said. "What if we worked on both Daddy and BB at the same time? The wire probably couldn't be used in court but with your testimony, it would be accurate and used as a resource. If BB confessed, she might allow us to use the wire. Who knows? I could place Sgt. Holly and a technician in this trailer, if that's okay, Bix?"

"Sure. Anything to get this mess resolved," Bix said finishing the last of her coffee in one gulp.

"I'm thinking this trailer is a perfect surveillance station because it's the longest distance from Billy's. We could begin moving the equipment into your trailer, Bix, within an hour."

"Fair enough," Bix said.

"Of course you'll need to vacate the trailer since that's police procedure. Do you have somewhere to go for a couple of hours?" he asked.

"Oh, we'll find something to do with her," Bernie added. "Don't worry.

CHAPTER 28

THE PLOT THICKENS

Burger and Billy had taken up the two lawn chairs outside of Bix's trailer. They were obviously organizing what Billy would be asking BB if she agreed to meet. Chief Marten had gone to Bellow's motel. He had asked him to come down to the station so that there could be a clarification of the law firm's actions in this case. To make sure that there was no conflict of interest was the way he had stated it. Marten had noticed that BB wasn't too happy to be left alone without a dinner companion. This information had given Burger and Billy some hope that their plan just might work.

Burger was planted in his lawn chair with straight legs crossed and hands folded over his chest watching Billy talking on his phone while nervously pacing. Billy had his back to Burger as he tried to charm BB into dinner at his trailer.

"But, honey, we do need to meet. You left so

quickly that I felt we hadn't had a chance to talk." There was a pause while Billy listened. "I know that but I never said that I had completely made up my mind. I only said that I was considering John's offer. Look, honey, I don't want to lose you. Everything was so wonderful up until the murder happened. It has really thrown me for a loop. Please, BB, at least come over for dinner. I could call the Italian restaurant and have them deliver. Our wine is still unopened. Please, honey, I really would like a chance to say how sorry I am." Billy listened intently to her response. He pumped his arm in the air a couple of times and said, "Then see you in an hour? Excellent! You won't regret this, BB, I promise."

Billy shut off his phone and smiled. "How much crow can one guy eat in one serving? We've got an hour to get the trailer wired and the food ordered." Both men headed toward Billy's trailer. Burger opened the trailer door and went in to check on the Salida boys' progress with the surveillance equipment. Billy searched to find the cork screw and set the table. Ernie called the restaurant and ordered for them.

The table had been cleared in Bix's trailer and the curtains closed. Sgt. Holly and a police technician named Howie Pierce had arrived in an unmarked van. They were carrying their computer and other paraphernalia into the trailer. Bix did notice that Howie had a supply of Mountain Dew with him. Jen, being a runner, had water. From the kitchen table Bix could see an antenna being aimed at Billy's fifth wheel. The curtain slipped shut when there was obviously a good signal. One could hear the two teams checking and double checking the connections. Their van was now out of sight.

Bix and Bernie were now going around to each trailer and informing the family that Billy's trailer was off limits for this evening. Hope was springing eternal. Lydia and Jim were in the process of telling the kids that this evening was game night inside the pop-up. Bix had gone up to the office and chatted with Chelsea and Bob. Their take on the situation was that just maybe the plot could break wide open tonight.

Bernie and Bix met in front of John and Mattie's trailer. As they entered, they were greeted with enthusiasm. Mattie had been watching out the windows keeping track of the activity. Matt and John tried to ignore everything and were playing cards at their kitchen table.

"So what's happening? Have they arrested Bellows yet? I think he's the one. What do you ladies think?" Mattie asked between breaths.

"Mattie, slow down, honey," John said. "Let the ladies talk." All three pairs of eyes riveted on Bix and Bernie.

Bernie laughed and then began the explanation after sitting down on the couch. "Well, I believe the word is that there will be two stings going on at the same time. Chief Marten and Detective Burger will be trying to take Bellows apart and get as much information as they can about his firm's involvement. At the same time, Billy will be trying to convince BB that he is madly in love with her and needs to know what she knows."

Bix continued where Bernie had left off, "The surveillance center is in my trailer for the evening by the way so you all will have to put up with me tonight and feed me."

"Did you ask for a vacation of murder? I think we could spring for some dinner here, to say the least," John stated after glancing at Mattie.

"Actually, maybe we ought to play cards like it was a normal evening at camp," Mattie suggested. "I'll make popcorn," she offered. "Let Simon stay for crumb sweep up. What's a card game without a dog to clean the floor?" Mattie said. "Just like a normal night at the park, right?" she concluded.

It was decided that poker would be a good excuse for hiding out inside. John decided to spring for pizza and ordered it. The delivery would be around the time that BB arrived. Bernie called Billy to explain what they had decided. Burger then gave his blessing and the camp became fairly quiet and ready for the drama to begin.

Another family had taken over the fire pit tonight. For all intentions, the park looked like business as usual. Bix took Simon out for a quick airing before all the festivities actually started. Her mind was spinning and sorting so many thoughts and feelings. It was a good timeout for her. Simon wandered around in the fenced dog area intent on his own body functions; he was locked in his moment. Bix watched while her thoughts were free to wander. They didn't have time for a true outing. Besides, it wouldn't be long until the pizza arrived. Simon did enjoy pizza crust!

She began thinking about Billy. Bix had to

wonder how he felt right now. Poor guy thought he had found someone to love and now he had to question how much she knew about his father's murder. How ugly was that? What was BB's personal agenda? How powerful was her greed and did it control her goals? Bix contemplated that concept for a moment, then set it aside.

She noticed that the evening was taking on a sundown glow. The deer were gone and the birds were settling in. She could smell dinner being cooked in all various forms throughout the camp. Rows and rows of families were about ready to eat together. The family at the fire pit had just finished organizing their wood. Their empty chairs circled the pit announcing places for maybe 15 observers. The flames would leap and crackle into the immense sky while folks simply talked, simply cared. It was the norm for any good camp agenda, Bix cogitated.

As her thoughts jumped from topic-to-topic, she couldn't help but think about the Holden clan moving on and finding out what life would be like without their patriarch. Right now they felt the loss, past tense. Eventually, the comfort of Henry's irreplaceable history and personal warmth would immerge and replace loss.

There was an ironic strength in that concept. Bix had to chuckle a little. She still found herself thinking of her own mother once in awhile. She'd have a vision of the two of them going shopping or just talking. When her mother had died, Bix had been asked, how close was she? They had been best friends. Over the years Bix had thought about that comment many times. It seemed that Henry had been a best friend to his children. From listening to their comments, Bix knew that his wise-sage advice would be missed.

Bix had watched Lydia and Mattie mother him with affectionate care. The boys and Bernie had relied on his advice. There was now a gap which would soon be filled by a brother, sister or partner; yet each one of them would begin to notice a small voice in the back of their minds; Henry would talk to them from now on in whispers from within. The Holdens would be fine, Bix thought as she opened Mattie and John's trailer door. Just fine.

***

Billy found himself busy cleaning up the kitchen dishes and putting clothes away. When he had walked in, he realized that the place was looking like a bachelor pad. Much of his life had reflected being single. The right woman just hadn't come along. He had to think that being a lonely rancher just didn't attract the right kind of lady. At least not the ladies that he now found himself seeking; of course, maybe it was his spending too much time in the bars. Church wasn't an option either and neither was going on the internet where surreal babes avoided physical relationships by distance. No, that didn't work either. Billy had considered having a talk with Lydia. Maybe she'd have some suggestions other than blind dates. Low and behold, Billy was starting to mature. It wasn't just sex anymore that satisfied him. He found himself wanting someone to share ideas and a future with him. Lord knew BB wasn't that gal either. He had tried to convince himself that she was but in reality, it wasn't there. BB had her own agenda.

Billy examined the room closely to see if he could detect the surveillance devices. Nothing was showing; it looked good. He was nervous about how this would all play out. Billy went over in his mind what he was supposed to ask. The evening weighed heavily on him; it was his responsibility.

He had to wonder if Charlie had planned the senate race and mineral purchases before BB went on the hunt. Maybe, but Charlie had gone to high school with John so it was entirely possible that the scheme would have unfolded regardless of his own need for money. Bellows wasn't a dummy; he could have figured out another ugly scam. Unfortunately, Billy realized that he had just been there and ready to use. His hunger for money and power so easy to read, and then there was his hunger for the right woman.

What if BB really had been involved in his dad's murder? Fuck, he just couldn't think about that now. The guilt brought on a flood of new emotions that overwhelmed him. Hell, he should have stayed away from BB, sex or no sex! She was another woman that he had picked up in a bar. BB had told him that it was her first time in that specific bar and he had bought it. Naturally, her conversation had immediately gone to who she was and her daddy's business. He should have known that it was no accident that she hit on him. It probably was the first time BB had been in that bar, but who knew how many other bars she had frequented. "You're a fool, Billy; get a grip and play this game right tonight," he murmured.

***

Burger sat patiently while Chief Marten finished his conversation with the North Dakota's Attorney General. "Yes sir, I do understand how critical this situation is," Marten said and rolled his eyes. "We definitely will send you a copy of the surveillance on both interviews." Marten paused as he listened again.

"Yes, I have been in contact with our state's Attorney General and he believes that our murder case trumps your case at the present time.

So no, we will not be sending either suspect your way immediately, Mr. Adams. Of course, we have enough evidence to hold them for murder. After our trial, the suspects will be then sent to North Dakota to face your allegations," Marten confirmed. "So you have been investigating that law firm for the last year?" Marten took notes as he listened this time. "And, you have notified Mr. Decker at his Colorado Attorney General's Office? Correct?" He nodded and wrote comments. "Good. Then we're all on the same page. Thank you, Mr. Adams." Marten nodded and waited nervously to end the conversation. "Yes sir…. Thank you, sir. Well let's hope we can get both or one of these people to shed some light on the murder and anything else that will stick. Yes, sir…you too." Chief Marten hung up finally and let out a nice long sigh. "Whew. It sounds exactly like we thought. The case has huge implications. Our murder is only the first domino in a long line that could take years to resolve. Are we ready?"

"I'll check with Sgt. Holly and make sure that we're ready at High Mountain Vista," Burger affirmed.

When Jen's phone rang they were putting the final touches on the computer. Howie was busy double checking the sound quality. The crew in Billy's trailer had finished.

"Sgt. Holly here." She answered.

"Is everything in place and ready?" Burger asked.

"We have an excellent signal and sound quality. Billy has been cleaning and mumbling to himself. I think he's setting the table; the dinner just arrived from the Italian restaurant. They're having lasagna I think; isn't that the Friday night's special?"

"Correct, their specialty. Hate to miss it. Who's over in the High Vista Office tonight?"

"The Salida boys are there. Jerry will be located in the Commons. He should arrive in the next couple of minutes," Jen added then peeked out the window. "Actually, I just saw his unmarked car drive by so we are all in place."

"Let me know when BB arrives. 10-4."

"Will do. And you all do know there's a card game going on in John's trailer? Looks like old home week here."

"Such a deal. I believe its poker and pizza for the rest of the clan," Burger announced.

***

It had been decided in Bix's absence that Five Card Stud Poker was the game of choice. John had searched around for the poker chips and decided that they were in Billy's trailer. However, Mattie had found several boxes of toothpicks to substitute for chips. The pizza had arrived so all was in order for their 'wait and see.' Lydia and Jim had decided to stay with the kids in the pop up trailer to keep them corralled. It had become a quiet night of computer games for them.

"You know," John began, "I remember what Charlie Bellows was like in high school. He was an out-and-out bully with a huge mouth. I'm surprised he went to college since he spent most of his time in detention. I do have to admit the boy did have brains though. He got a scholarship and never looked back on North Dakota until his law firm began practicing in Tioba," John said.

"Wasn't one of the partners established in Texas? I thought Howard had worked for oil companies in their legal department and became filthy rich," Bernie added.

"Now that I think about it, you're right, Bernie. Howard moved here shortly after Bellows arrived back to embrace Tioba. Hadn't been back since he buried his parents that I know of," John said considering the history that he knew. "His daddy was a washed out ranch hand who never made any money himself. When Charlie landed his scholarship, he got the hell out of town. Maybe that's why Charlie never respected the land; his daddy never owned any. They lived in a trailer didn't they, over in the Tioba Hills Park?" John asked.

"I think that's right," Bernie said. "And by the way, I didn't know that Charlie even had a daughter until Billy showed up with her on his arm. She must have been a product of back East."

"So BB hadn't ever been to North Dakota until Charlie came back to join the law firm?" Bix asked. "Where's Charlie's wife?"

"Good question," said John. "Don't know if he's divorced or widowed. I'd say he'd be pretty hard to live with. but who knows?"

"Wonder if he met his partners in law school and they have been staying in touch?" Matt speculated. "Seems like that is a characteristic now what with the internet. The guys I know in agriculture will stay in touch on the internet. I think business trends are now much more open and communicated from state to state. Maybe Charlie, like his daddy, washed out in business then got in contact with college friends. Could be why he's the last name on the billboard," Matt finished.

"Good point, Matt. Maybe we should inform Detective Burger in depth about Charlie's family history. He definitely had some reptiles for relatives," John smiled then popped out of his chair to check Billy's trailer again. "Hate to be like a kid," John confessed, "but how long do you think this will last?"

"As long as it takes Billy to charm a confession out of BB," Bernie said. "Actually, I have no idea.

I'm really glad that our part in this scheme is simply to stay out of sight."

"Do you think the police have officers all around the area?" Mattie asked as she selected a pizza slice.

"I think the Baileys probably have deputies watching the event from the office and there probably are other deputies over at the Commons just in case something goes crazy," Matt said while focusing on adding hot peppers to his pizza. Card time?" he inquired.

"Why not," said Bix while slipping Simon a piece of crust.

"I'll second that," said Mattie.

***

Billy peeked out the window. He was beginning to feel impatient. He finally saw the headlights of a car coming down the road. It was BB's BMW. Billy picked up the cork screw and began opening the wine. His hand was wet; he was perspiring. She'd know if he got too nervous. Billy wiped his hands off on the towel and concentrated on getting himself under control. Couldn't be much worse than riding a bucking bronco, he thought. Billy did a quick inhale, then exhaled, and tried to calm his body. Burger's list of questions began to play through his head. He knew the relationship chemistry would change the game plan in some way. How people reacted and acted was so determined by the moment. It would be so important for him to let patience control the conversation. BB would also have to contribute. Slow and easy, Billy, he thought.

Let it all come together.

BB knocked lightly. He went over and opened the door. Damn, she did look good and smelled good, Billy noticed. "Glad you came; come on in, honey," Billy said as he took her hand. He pulled her close and kissed her tenderly, slowly. "I've missed you, baby," he whispered in her ear. "I'm real sorry we couldn't work things out before. The stress of the situation has been something else; I sure would like to try again."

"Me, too," BB whispered as she tossed her purse on the couch and then melted into his arms. His hands traveled along the curve of her waist. His palms caressed her hips as he pressed his body against hers. She felt so damn good, he thought. Her perfume filled his senses and brought back so many memories of good sex.

***

Sgt. Holly quickly dialed Burger to let him know that BB had arrived. "She just walked into the trailer. They're playing kissy face right now. The surveillance stuff is doing a great job. Here's hoping Billy can do a super job."

"Good. We're still waiting for Bellows to make his appearance. The Chief just got off the phone with North Dakota's Attorney General. Whew, this is some big messy case we got ourselves involved in. Keep me posted," Burger said then hung up.

Jen turned her attention back to the love nest banter. She couldn't imagine what was going through Billy's head right now. What would it be like to know that your ex-lover could have killed your father or been a part of the crime? Denial would probably be huge. You would hope that she hadn't been involved; that the whole plot was her daddy's idea. Could BB really be innocent? Jen found that truly hard to believe.

***

BB, sensing the direction of their inclination, separated them and stared into Billy's eyes as if seeking some answers first. He wasn't quite ready to let her go yet. Fuck, she felt so good. He felt his body becoming hard and so out of control; hopping into bed right now would be incredible. It would be so easy to strip and feel the warmth of her body against his. Letting sex dominate reality; giving them an excuse to forget. A small voice in his head whispered, 'It isn't in the game plan, buddy boy.'

The trailer was wired. The word 'control' finally filled Billy's consciousness. No, this time Billy had to understand the power of responsibility; he owed it to his father's memory. It was up to him to discover how involved BB was in this crime. His body suddenly settled and his resolve began to surface. He could do this.

"Have you changed your mind about anything, Billy? Last time we talked, you had decided to not take Dad's offer. Throw your future away and be a rancher. Henry wouldn't have wanted you to change your mind because of family pressure. Daddy said that Henry's Last Will and Testament is still valid if we can prove that it was his intent. Baby, I do love you but I'm not met to be a rancher's wife. You know that, honey?" She twisted her fingers through his curly red hair then looked at the table fixed with dinner. "This is really sweet. You set the table and everything …and wine."

Billy poured two glasses and handed one to BB. "Here's to a new beginning," he said as they made a toast. The wine had been a nice touch, Billy thought. It gave him time to think. Time to get BB into a frank discussion about what had happened. He pulled her chair out and served the lasagna. "French bread and salad?"

"Of course. Thanks honey."

"You know, BB, this last week has really been terrible for me and my family. I'm really trying to come to grips with my dad's death and the possibility that he was murdered."

"Well, I don't think that he was murdered at all," she said while stuffing some salad in her mouth. "Has anyone considered the fact that he might have accidently drunk or eaten something that didn't agree with him?"

"BB, they're pretty sure that it was poisoning, anti freeze to be exact. People don't just accidently gulp that stuff down. Dad was a lot smarter than that." Billy raised his fork and tried to eat some lasagna.

"Well still…."

They ate for awhile in silence. Billy wasn't getting anywhere so far. He needed to somehow get her trapped into the reality of the case. "The police even think that Dad had been getting small doses of poison for quite some time."

"How?" BB's eyes leveled a cold stare at Billy. Maybe they knew more than she had thought. It was a possibility.

"The chili spoon for starters," Billy continued tentatively. "It was found behind one of the washing machines in the Commons then later there was a juice container found here in my trash with traces of poison. They're checking for finger prints."

"Well, those items could have been thrown away by anyone of the hundreds of tourists in this camp. I mean I don't think it means a whole hell of a lot," BB hissed.

"Don't you think it has to be someone closer to the family?"

BB's fork froze mid-air as she processed that implication. She had to change the topic of the conversation and quick. "Speaking of the family, where are they tonight? Seems pretty quiet around here," she said smugly.

"They're playing poker at John's," Billy said cautiously. The couple avoided looking at each other while the direction of their conversation soaked in. Dinner continued silently.

***

So far Jen couldn't hear anything that would get BB into a confession. The woman was trying to convince Billy that a fucking stranger could have upped and poisoned Holden. BB was going to be a hard nut to crack. Calm down, Jen told herself. "It isn't over yet. Be patient," she mumbled. Her frustration was not lost on Howie, who was quietly sipping his soda. Could end up to be a long night, he thought.

CHAPTER 29

INTERROGATION AND GAMES

Burger shuffled and reviewed the papers in his hands as he waited for Charles Bellows to show up. Naturally, Charlie would be late just to illustrate that he was in charge of the interview. Ernie could sense how important the next couple of hours would be. Two states were now involved in this case. It had gotten much more complicated than he would have liked. So far the police department had acted and reacted professionally. However, it was time to get the case nailed down with some answers. Bellows needed to be tied to Holt and Norton. It had to be more than lawyer client relations. If they could get Bellows to admit to hiring Norton, it would go a long ways toward murder.

Hopefully, tonight BB and Charlie would come clean about poisoning Henry. No one had admitted to any involvement so far. Henry Holden didn't just poison himself and Burger really couldn't see Billy doing the deed. The family was tight. They might have differences but not to the point of murder. Ernie just couldn't see it. No, the evidence was pointing toward the law firm and the Bellows family in particular.

Barb burst through her door and yelled, "Chief! Ernie! I just got some information from the bank in North Dakota. You're going to like it a lot!" She pushed her eye glasses up and sat down in one of the office chairs.

Chief Marten leaned on the door frame with arms crossed expectant of good news.

"Well...on June 26th the law firm of Smith, Howard and Bellows withdrew 20,000 cash from their account. It was labeled for miscellaneous office expenses. That arrogance was a total mistake. Who do you suppose got that money? Hmmmmmmmmmmm?" Barb chortled and smiled.

"Bingo!" Ernie yelled. "We got a connection at last."

"Are you sure?" Marten asked holding his breath.

"Oh, yeah, I'm sure. Checked it five different ways and have the paper trail right here," Barb said waving the emails in the air like a flag. "North Dakota Attorney General's Office had the warrant and I just slipped in for a 'look-see' on what they had. On June 29th Norton deposited $20,000.00 in his account. All done in cash of course," she added. "It's all on the up and up, boss. We got the slimy sucker!" Barb coyly declared and twirled in the office chair displaying her triumph. "And, check out

Holt's cut; Norton is a tight son-of-a-bitch," she giggled and stopped twirling in order to place the emails in Chief Marten's hand.

"These lawyers are really working on moving up the money ladder aren't they?" Ernie commented. "Now to figure out how to get Bellows to admit to some of this. It's pretty obvious that he rushed here to keep Norton from spilling where the money came from," Burger added. His mind was going a million miles an hour. There had to be some type of development that would get Bellows off balance. Some way to push the bastard off the edge. "We need a shock wave to bring him out; something that would start him spinning." The wheels began to turn in the office.

Suddenly, Ernie jumped up out of his chair. "So what if we can get Norton's phone chip to call back the last called number? I wonder whose phone it would ring, BB or Daddy's? I think I'll go check on what the crime team has been able to do with it. I know the phone's toast but if we could get the chip to call the most recent number, it might be interesting!" Barb and Marten watched Ernie rush toward the crime department for help.

"Bellows is pretty damn smart. This worries me. We got one chance with this guy. As soon as he figures that we're setting him up, he'll try to get out of Colorado fast," Marten said quietly more to himself than to Barb. "Extradition papers would do the trick for Bellows. Any lawyer worth a grain of salt could file the papers to get himself back to North Dakota. A state where the court system would look more favorably on him; he would have political pull there. No, tonight is our one shot at this guy," Marten calculated.

"Well, don't you worry boss," Barb said as she patted Marten's shoulder in a motherly fashion. "If anyone can do it, you and Ernie will get the job done. I'd bet money on that," she added with a head shake and a pop of her gum as she walked out of the room.

"Wish I were that confident," Marten grumbled then wandered toward the crime lab to find out what was possible. In an attempt to get any kind of a confession, all the stops had to be taken out. Gimmicks could sometimes work their magic. A glimmer of hope flashed across Marten's countenance. Maybe Barb was right ."So let's see what the crime boys can pull off," Marten proclaimed out loud as he gave himself permission to foresee a positive outcome.

***

The pizza was devoured and Simon had reclined full length on the couch. He, obviously, felt that he had been treated to his full share of crust. One satisfied dog was snoring away soundly. Matt had taken the pizza boxes out to the trash and was just about ready to return. Bix noticed as she peeked out the window, Matt was desperately trying not to look at Billy's trailer. Bix could tell he was having a hard time focusing on that trash. John had gone and gotten his revolver out and placed it on the table. Mattie had just finished cleaning up the kitchen and had seated herself at the poker table; she was dividing up the toothpicks.

Bernie stared at the gun and smirked. "This is like a poker game in Dodge City, John. We're all sitting around waiting for some cowpoke to come into the saloon."

"Well I'm sorry but that's family over there. Have to admit I'm a little nervous. BB could be a stone cold killer as far as any of us know. Charlie, I've known, but BB is totally an unknown to me. She hasn't been in North Dakota long enough for any of us to know her."

"It's all right, John," Mattie patted his hand. "Bernie knows that you're just trying to be careful and you're right we don't know BB. I do think that your little brother has had some experience at handling the ladies, however. Billy hasn't lived in a closet all these years, you know," she stated and gave John a smug look.

Matt came back into the trailer and sat down. "It's all quiet over there. At least they're not having some yelling match. That's an okay situation, right?" he asked.

"I'm sure it is, Matt," Mattie said. "You and Dad need to calm down and play poker. Worrying won't make this evening go any faster. Bernie, deal the damn cards."

"Yes ma'am." Bernie grabbed the deck in a flutter and shuffled furiously. "So each toothpick is a quarter?" she asked and got a nod from each individual at the table. "Ante up," Bernie said before dealing and tossed in a toothpick. Everyone at the table after a little chatter tossed in their ante.

John eyed the crack left in the center of the

curtains. It was getting dark and harder to see Billy's trailer. The good news was that the door was on their side so if anyone ran out, it would be obvious. The porch light was on. He couldn't see the sides of the trailer exactly, but the door was directly across from them.

Bernie then dealt one card down and one card up. Everyone paused to check their hidden card. Bix raised another quarter. Mattie stayed placing her toothpick on the table carefully and waited to see what John would do.

"John, get a grip. I put in my quarter," Mattie said. She kicked him under the table and glanced out the window herself. They did need to keep an eye on the situation as best as they could. She wanted it all over. To go home without knowing what happened to Henry wasn't an option. The family deserved some answers and Mattie really had high hopes that tonight, something would happen to solve the case.

She was, however, relieved that Lydia had stayed with Jim and the kids. If she thought John was nervous, she couldn't imagine how nervous Lydia was. Lydia's little brother was so important to her. As much as she loved Lydia, Mattie couldn't imagine what the tension was like in the pop-up. Calm down, girl, she thought. Stay calm. They needed to do their drama part and play cards. The family would help if need be; they always had. John brought her thoughts back to the table.

"I know, I know. Okay, I'm in," he said and threw in a toothpick.

Matt got up and changed the lighting in the room

so they could see the outline of Billy's trailer better. He pulled the curtain a little farther apart so he could see also. "Dad, put your gun on the floor so it's not so obvious. I'm in and raise one more quarter." He sat back down.

Bernie contributed her toothpick to stay in the game. The group eyed their cards. Bernie then began to deal out the second round of single cards, face up.

"I raise another quarter," Mattie announced. "So they've been in there for an hour according to my watch. I'm sure the bitch will want to eat before they start getting down to brass tacks."

"I wonder if she and Charlie are working together on this scheme?" Bernie questioned. "BB strikes me as the kind of gal who can talk a guy into anything she wants, providing she ends up rich. I'm sure 'daddy' taught her all kinds of tricks."

"I'm thinking that you're exactly right on that one," John said. "I can't see BB ordering the muscle around though but poisoning would be more her game. Well, anyway their game is sure a lot more deadly than our poker," John added.

Bix eyed her third round card and tossed in another toothpick with a sigh. Mattie decided to fold as she said, "I'm not feeling the love here; too rich for me at this point." John quietly tossed in his quarter. His eyes darted around the table slyly.

Matt checked his cards one more time then said, "I call and raise another quarter."

There was a universal moan at the table. "I fold," said Bernie and threw her cards down. Simon looked up to see what was happening. He decided that the noise wasn't alarming. He let his head fall back into slumber.

Mattie examined the money pot and said, "And the plot thickens. Anybody ready for popcorn?"

***

Dinner over, the conversation continued. "You know, BB, the cops are wondering about you and your father. They don't think that my dad accidentally drank anti freeze."

"Now wait a minute!" she shrieked looking him directly in the eyes.

"Hear me out," Billy persisted raising his hand to halt her tirade. "No, they think someone with opportunity or a group killed my father. Someone close enough to him that poisoning him would be easy."

People who would see his murder as a financial gain," Billy went on aggressively. "Charlie's law firm has a lot of bucks already thrown into this fracking deal. Without my father's mineral rights, they all stand to lose big time. My father isn't even buried yet and these people are ready to divide up the land for money. What would stop your father from hiring the hit on my dad? Maybe his law firm is so deep into the buying of the property that murder isn't far-fetched?"

"What?" she yelled pulling her chair back and standing. "How stupid is that? Daddy came to help you and, besides, his firm ordered him to defend those two idiots. Why, I think it was wonderful of Daddy to drive this far and get involved in helping his future son-in-law. Lord knows there isn't a good lawyer in this little town. Billy, he was going to defend you; how can you say that Daddy is the bad guy? I didn't see any of your family jumping up to defend you. Not even Lydia came down to the jail when you were there. Don't be stupid; we're on your side and we're willing to get involved. J Meyer Petro is still willing to throw their money into your campaign. Daddy is going to stand by you no matter what. I didn't see your family ready to hire a lawyer and forfeit money into your defense," she sputtered. "It was my family that got involved when the chips were down!" she yelled placing her hands on her hips. The volume was beginning to elevate as this conversation exploded.

"How involved is that, BB? What do you mean by, no matter what? What do you mean by the chips were down? Are you trying to say that I killed my own father? I don't think so!" retorted Billy while leaning across the table.

"Daddy says that the police need someone to hang this crime on and they're taking a long look at you." BB crossed her arms and plopped down in her chair again. "Face it, this burg of a town needs this crime to go away so the tourist business can move on. It would be incredibly easy to convict you and be done with it!"

"You know I'm not the only suspect here," he argued. "There is one group out there that wonders how involved you are in this scam. Lord knows you had the opportunity to poison my father. Always offering him juice!" Billy blurted out.

"You can't be serious? You're not saying that I

killed Henry are you? My God, are you really that ungrateful and callous?" How could you say that?" BB wailed in disbelief.

"We are all suspect in this murder!" Billy spat out and threw his napkin down on the table. "The police are questioning everyone's motivation and some people are more motivated than others. I have been raked over the coals down at the police station, so I damn well know what it is like to be a suspect. Some people have more to lose in this game than others, like you and your dad!" he yelled. Billy could feel the steam coming out of his ears.

BB picked up her glass of wine and threw it at him. He ducked just in time! "That's crazy talk!" she shrieked. Then BB realized that she might have gone too far and stepped back from her anger. She leaned over and picked up some broken glass pieces trying to get control of the momentum. Her new approach was tempered by what she saw as she retrieved a shard from under the table. There was a new surveillance device underneath! Holy shit, their conversation was being monitored!

***

"Oh, boy, it's getting heated in there," Jen mumbled to Howie.

He nodded and double checked the recording sensors; he didn't want to miss a thing. "Do you think they're going to have a physical fight? Wow, she's hot and I don't mean attractive. Well, she is attractive but you know what I mean. Wow."

"Yes, Howie, I know what you mean," she

teased. "Billy sure is putting it out there. I wonder if he can get her mad enough to say something incriminating?" Jen quipped.

"I think we'll know pretty quick. The tension is sure heating up. You go, boy!" Howie said with a snicker.

***

The police station door flew open as Charlie Bellows entered. His expression was one of agitation. Obviously, he felt that his appearance was unnecessary. "Well, let's get this over with. I have things to do. Time is money as they say. I want to get the hell out of this town within the next couple of days," he grumbled. "What is going on? My clients have done all the interviews that you have required. We have disclosed all the information that is legally necessary so what the hell is your problem?" He shifted his briefcase from hand to hand and checked his watch with a sigh.

"Could we possibly go into one of the interviews rooms? Would you like some coffee?" Burger asked cordially.

"Hell no, I don't want any of that foul brew that you label as coffee. Which one of these uncomfortable rooms are we going to occupy so you can record everything that I say? God, I'm getting tired of your company." Nevertheless, Bellows stomped into the room that Ernie indicated. Bellows' huge sigh echoed through the station.

Barb had come out of her office to observe his obnoxious behavior. She was casually watching with her arms crossed. "Would you like a cup of our toxic brew, Detective Burger?" she asked with sweetness overflowing.

"Yes, please," Ernie said aiming a smile at Barb. "We'll be in our number two comfy interview room." He followed Bellows into the room and shut the door quietly. "Just so you know, Mr. Bellows, we will be recording this interview. Chief Marten will join us in a few moments. He has just finished talking with Mr. Adams, the Attorney General of North Dakota."

Bellows did a double take while he processed that information. Barb tapped on the door and then brought in Ernie's coffee. "Here's your brew, sir," she said, never taking her eyes off Bellows who totally ignored her. With a flutter she was gone. Burger occupied his next few minutes by getting the recorder set up. Finally, Chief Marten entered and sat down beside Ernie. He was intent on the papers that were in his hands as if he were reviewing their contents.

"I believe that Detective Burger should at this point read you your rights and inform you that this interview will be recorded. This interview will be conducted with you as a suspect and not as a lawyer representing clients. Of course, you can request an attorney at any time." Marten and Burger awaited Bellows' decision about requesting another lawyer.

"Oh, please, just get on with it," Bellows mumbled in response.

Marten never took his eyes off the notes in front of him while Burger did his duty. The recorder was on as Ernie finished with, "Let it be known that Mr.

Charles Bellows is fully aware that this interview is
being recorded and has been read his rights on July
3, 2014."

"Can we get on with this outrage?" Bellows
grumbled while checking his watch again.

"I take it that I can interpret your comments as a
'yes' to being recorded?"

"Hell yes," Bellows said and leaned back in his
chair. His eyes were glowing with full blown
contempt. "Let it also be known that as a lawyer,
representing myself, I do not see this interview as
necessary in any way. These officers are crossing
the line into harassment as far as I can determine. I
am representing Mr. Travis Norton and Brad Holt
only at the request of Smith, Howard and Bellows
Law Firm and am not personally involved in this
case in anyway."

"We would have to wonder about that statement,
Mr. Bellows. It would seem that on June 26th your
law firm of Smith, Howard and Bellows, withdrew
20,000 dollars from their bank account and placed
the amount in the miscellaneous fund for office
supplies. According to the bank records that day,
you, Mr. Bellows, withdrew the entire amount in
cash," Chief Marten said. "Is that correct?"

"What of it, you son of a bitch? The firm had
neglected the office supply account for too long.
We decided to replenish the money so supplies
could be bought. I see absolutely nothing wrong
with that other than you all snooping in our business
accounts. You better have had a damn good warrant
is all that I can say!" Bellows face had become
flushed and he seemed slightly uncomfortable. He

began to change his position in the chair, twisting and turning. He checked his watch again. "So now that we have established that my firm needed staples, is there anything else?"

Ernie entered into the conversation at this point. "Matter of fact, yes, there is. Were you aware that Mr. Travis Norton deposited a cash amount on June 29th, 2014? He deposited 15,000 dollars four days after you withdrew the total amount from your law firm account. I find that incredibly interesting and incriminating. Norton then gave Brad Holt 5,000 on June 30th."

"Norton, obviously, was ready to take a vacation and someone decided to give him some money. Giving money freely isn't against the law. The amount is coincidental. What's in a number?" Bellows retorted. "Our firm now has all the office supplies we'll need for the next year. There is absolutely no connection."

"So your shelves are packed with office supplies and you had no contact with Norton and Holt before you became their lawyer? Is that correct?" Burger asked.

"That is correct. I never saw Norton or Holt before."

"You are aware that they both live in North Dakota?"

"I know that since I have started to represent these men," Charlie verified. "They are clients of our law firm and nothing else. It is a big state, you know."

"Speaking of clients, how much business does your firm do with J Meyer Petro from Texas?"

Chief Marten asked while shuffling his notes.

"Well, we represent them in most of their legal interactions with North Dakota. They hire lawyers from each area that they mine. It saves time for them in the long run and enhances the economy of the specific area."

"Yes it does," the Chief said. "According to the Attorney General's Office your law firm collected eight million last year from J Meyer Petro. Is that correct?"

"I...I guess that could be close to our annual fees. The exact amount I do not have at my finger tips. It is a very complicated business relationship."

"Very complicated indeed," added Detective Burger. "Are you aware that one of your junior partners visited the farm of Kevin and Ashley Jensen last June before the 26th? Are you aware that there was an altercation where John and Bernie Holden were present?"

"Absolutely not," Bellows thundered. "I have no idea about that. Our lawyers do not physically fight about lawsuits or any other matter pertaining to J Meyer Petro. That's absurd!" he wailed letting his anger flow.

"Well it might be except that your young lawyer brought along help. Mr. Travis Norton has been identified by both John and Bernie Holden as the man who attacked Kevin Jensen. After the altercation, Mr. Norton crawled over to their vehicle and got in the passenger side. So they came and left in the same vehicle. A vehicle which is being identified as part of Smith, Howard and Bellows car fleet. Mr. Norton has worked for your law firm before hasn't he?"

"I have no idea. I wasn't there or responsible for that situation. I have never met the Jensens or had anything to do with them! To try and say that I hired Norton or knew him, you can't prove that!" Charlie Bellows pounded his fist on the table loudly.

Burger pressed the switch he had in his pocket and suddenly one of Charlie Bellows' cell phones rang.

CHAPTER 30

POKER THEN PLAN B

Bernie dealt the last round of cards face up. Now that she had folded, watching facial expressions was entertaining. Mattie was off concocting popcorn. Bix, John and Matt were the remaining distracted players. The group was getting more agitated by the minute watching nothing. It was too quiet over there.

Bix looked at her poker hand and wondered if two queens could take the pot. She decided to stay in this round and see. "I will raise a quarter." She laid her card down and went over to pet Simon while John considered what to do.

He peeked through the opening in the curtain once more so he could check out Billy's trailer before any card decision. Frustration set in. "Fold. I have a feeling about who has got the cards here and it ain't me. You two can duke it out."

Bix then decided to get some water and peek out

the window herself. She just had to move around. It had gotten dark out there and their visibility of the trailer was far less than it had been. She went back to her chair and sat. "Do you think BB would turn in her father if it came to her confession or would she keep quiet? We're talking murder here. I just don't know."

Bernie thought about the question and then answered, "I think she's pretty stuck on Daddy Dearest. She probably would hate to give up his money. How much do you suppose Bellows offered Billy for the mineral rights? Then how much would Bellows get from J Meyer Petro? He's the middle man here right?"

"I think Bellows' law firm is purchasing as many of the properties along the river as they can then going to sell in one gigantic lump for billions to J Meyer," said Matt. "To control the water and mineral rights is the aggressive move here. I hate to say it but Granddad was a little fish in a great big pond. Smith, Howard and Bellows have certainly gone out on a limb here. Would they go as far as murder, is the question? Greed is quite a motivator."

"I think BB would do anything to become the heir of her daddy's fortune. Wonder if she's more motivated than Daddy?" John questioned as he leaned over to his right and checked the trailer again. "Looks like someone is in the bathroom. At least they're moving around some. She must have said something to keep their game going. Don't you think?"

"I'd say the longer it takes the better chance Billy has," Bernie said. "Well, Matt? What are you thinking here?"

"Raise fifty cents," he said and tossed in two toothpicks.

At that moment Simon raised his head and gave out a low growl from deep in his throat. He looked at everyone for a moment. "Did you have a bad dream, cutie pie?" asked Mattie. She found a piece of pepperoni in the kitchen and gave it to him. He chewed then went back to sleep.

Bernie looked at her watch. She was getting anxious about both games. "Moving along here folks; it's time to see who is going to take home the pot." She figured Matt had the possibility of a flush; Bix, two queens with one already showing.

Bix and Matt checked out their hands now. Bix said, "I'll see your bid and raise you one more quarter." She tossed in the toothpick and waited to see what Matt would do.

"See you and raise you a dollar," Matt said casually.

Well, Bix could see the writing on the wall. Matt either had a flush or he was faking. Somehow, she just couldn't see Matt faking but who knew. She sure as hell didn't know. "Fold," she said.

Matt pulled in the pot. He tossed his cards in and didn't show what he had.

Mattie was the first to object. "Come on. What did you have? Come clean, buddy. Tell your mother or else. Or, no more dinners for you," Mattie came back to the table with a large bowl of popcorn

"Well, if you put it that way, I did have a flush King high." He showed his cards and everyone yowled, "Ahhhhhh!"

John checked his watch and saw that it was only 9:30. "I guess it still is too early for BB to come clean. Mattie, where are your binoculars?"

"Above the bed in the cabinet. Why?"

"Oh I was wondering if we could see more over there with them."

"I'll go get them," she said and disappeared into the bedroom.

"Well, her car is still there so we haven't missed anything," Matt said as he peered out the side window.

The natives were getting restless, Bix thought. She couldn't help the feeling that something wasn't quite right. However, what was right about the whole situation? They were sitting in a trailer playing poker and waiting for BB to confess to murder. Not exactly what one would call a normal evening? Still it seemed awfully quiet over there. Where was the yelling and dishes being thrown? Maybe that was a bit too dramatic, she reconnoitered. Something should be happening, she thought.

"Thanks, honey," John said as he looked through the binoculars and surveyed the whole length of the trailer. "I just don't get it," he mumbled. "I'd think we'd be seeing something."

"So, what if I slipped out?" Matt asked. "Real quiet like. Maybe I could take Simon for his night outing. If that's okay with you, Bix?" Matt asked.

"Go ahead but you both be really careful and don't get too close," Bix said. "That is if it's all right with your mom and dad."

John nodded. "You call me if anything seems out

of order. You hear?"

Matt put the leash on Simon and said, "Yes, sir." John started pacing the minute Matt went out the door. Conversation simply stopped and the poker group waited and listened to every single sound. Tension peaked.

***

A short time earlier BB had picked up the shard and processed who had planted the monitor under the coffee table. So Billy was in on the surveillance; she had no doubt. Maybe the cops were brighter than she thought. Billy was probably trying to save his own sorry ass. Her mind began to formulate quickly a plan. She had to get the hell out of here as soon as possible. BB knew that her dad's law firm was controlling Norton and the other guys. The money to be had in land profits was just too tantalizing. Charlie and friends would be rich beyond anyone's dreams. Therefore, BB just had to wait for her cut of the money. Charlie wouldn't let her down.

She didn't want anything to hinder their actions but Henry just wasn't going to comply; BB had known that all along. Daddy just wasn't listening to her; she had to make it happen. Henry had to go.

BB blew out a calming breath and slowly began, "Billy honey, I'm so sorry. I don't know what's come over me. Let me get us some more wine." She got up and searched for the bottle. "It's just that I'm so stressed about this craziness; we do need to talk calmly." She found the half empty bottle on the kitchen counter. "I need to convince you that I didn't kill your daddy. Let's clean up the stain first and then we can talk. Why don't you get some of that cleaner in the bathroom under the sink? It will take out the stain and I'll pour us some more wine?"

"Okay. That sounds like a deal. I really do want to believe you but there are some questions that I still have." Billy disappeared into the bathroom in search of the cleaner.

BB went to her purse and extracted a small bottle. She peeked around the corner and saw Billy rummaging through the cabinet. She poured two glasses of wine and put a good dose of Flunitrazepam in Billy's glass. Plan B was now beginning for her; there really wasn't any other option. She had to disappear and then let her dad know where she had landed. All she had wanted to do was help her dad get the property and then get her cut of the action.

Putting a little anti-freeze in Henry's juice had been so easy. He thought it was so kind of her to offer him juice every afternoon and look after him. The man certainly was used to being waited on by women. The only trouble was that the old coot was stronger than she figured. He just kept living.

Then this damn vacation had to happen. The whole family in one place was so extreme for her. All of them yelling and trying to convince Billy that he was the bad guy. What in the hell was wrong with trying to scrape out another life? Yes, the spoon had been coated with anti freeze. At that point she had to get rid of Henry. She had to pull out all the stops. It was risky but it had to be done.

Well, there wouldn't be any Billy for her now and no campaign. It probably was for the better. Damn.

Billy came back into the room carrying the cleaner. "Is this the stuff?" he asked.

"Sure is. Let me pour some on and we'll let it soak for awhile. Trade you," she said and gave him his wine glass for the cleaner. Billy immediately began to sip.

He watched BB pouring the stuff on the carpet. "You know, BB, I hope you realize that I'm here to help you in anyway that I can," Billy said softly. "There's very little that we can't work out. I'm sure our future is far more important than the past," Billy said. He was shocked how convincingly his lies flowed. "BB, it just seems that your daddy's law firm has so much to lose if my family doesn't sell their mineral rights. How can you say the lawyers are innocent? The firm sent your dad to be Norton and Holt's attorney. That makes the setup pretty obvious, don't you think?"

"My daddy came to make sure that you weren't convicted of murder first and foremost. Norton and Holt were simply there; it was more business for the firm. That was all."

"And you truly believe that? Didn't Norton work for them now and then? I heard he was their star thug. If they needed to convince some poor rancher that his family was more important than the land, Norton was the man. BB, the fucking problem is that you are too close to your dad. Actually, I think you must be part of the scheme. In fact, I have to wonder how much you know about my dad's murder," Billy added. "Who murdered my dad,

BB?" Billy asked as he slouched onto the couch. His legs felt weak and his head was becoming dizzy. "Who…murdered… my…." Billy was having trouble concentrating; he could feel a headache coming on. What was happening he wondered? He massaged his temples and let the wine glass drop onto the floor. He felt so sleepy…. Billy's eyes closed as he became unconscious. BB sat down and rubbed his neck.

"Billy honey, your daddy was a good man. I would have never hurt him and I've missed you so much." BB started noisily kissing him. She smiled thinking about the monitor under the table. She'd give the cops something to listen to now. "Honey, maybe we should lay down for awhile and finish our discussion in the bedroom." BB began picking up her things quietly. She was now standing in the middle of the room wondering what she should take with her. BB grabbed the flashlight off the counter. "Ooooh Billy, that feels so good," she murmured eyeing the monitor. "Oh honey, you're so hard in there. How about sharing? I've missed our nights in bed. Lordy honey, you're about to explode! Come on, I want some of that. Dessert is in the bedroom then we'll finish our little chat, right honey? What do you think? Oh, baby, that looks so good; I'll take that as a yes," she said as she flipped off comatose Billy.

She made shuffling noises toward the bedroom then threw herself on the bed; the springs squeaked. BB opened the bedroom cabinet and pulled out a bundle of cash then found her tennis shoes under the bed. She slipped off her high heels storing them in her purse. BB tied on her tennis shoes and then locked the trailer's front door. She shut the bedroom door and blew Billy a kiss as she slipped into the bathroom shutting that door quietly. She took the screen off the window, placed it in the tub, hiked her skirt up, leaned out the window, dropped her purse onto the ground and slipped out the window. "You ain't getting none tonight, sweetie," she whispered. The bathroom was on the other side of the trailer. Fortunately, a tree shadowed her escape through the window.

BB turned off the bathroom light and silently moved off into the darkness edging toward the road.

Damn, she thought. She would have to leave her BMW and get a cab somewhere on the highway. She slipped silently from one shadow to the next until she was passing the office. BB could see two cops sitting in the office watching Billy's trailer. Her escape so far was easy. They all figured that she would take her car or say something that would incriminate her. Well, none of that would happen tonight.

As soon as BB got out on the road, she called for a cab to meet her then proceeded to call American Airlines. She wondered how much she'd have to pay to get a ride to Denver. Less than a thousand would probably get the job done. Who wouldn't want to get to Denver to party? Screw this miserable little town. Denver was three hours away; then Mexico was in her destination.

BB speed dialed a number and said, "Hello Momma, I need some help with my bank account." She listened for a moment then responded, "No, nothing like that. Actually, I need my money transferred with no questions asked." BB listened again as she walked the gravel road quickly up to Highway 45. "Tomorrow would be great and, Momma, if anyone should ask, we never talked." BB was now watching the traffic coming down the highway intently looking for her taxi. "Good and thanks, Momma."

A few minutes later a taxi could be seen in the distance. It had the blinker on and pulled over when she waved. "Did you call for a cab, lady?" he asked.

She was in luck; the guy was young enough to want an adventure and not bad looking. BB slid into the cab and said, "Yes, I did and it's your lucky night, baby." BB crossed her legs making sure that the cabby could see plenty. "So how much would it take for you to turn off the meter and drive me to Denver? We could party and definitely have some fun. What's your name, cutie pie?"

"Mark and I think maybe five hundred plus a good time would work. What do you say, honey?" he asked with a smile. "Maybe three hundred up front now just so I can see that you are serious."

"It's Kathy and I'd say you have a deal." She handed him three hundred dollars making sure that her hand touched his and then she leaned back in the cab. Finally, she could relax a little before she figured out how to get rid of this jerk when they hit Denver.

Actually, as she looked at his reflection in the rear view mirror, she noticed he really was good looking. Maybe she did need a fuck before she got on her plane; sort of a bon voyage with a bang. Too bad she hadn't been able to do Billy and given the cops an earful before she left. But that would have been too risky to say the least. No, better to play the game like she did.

The cabby might be a bonus in this whole deal. They could do a fuck in the back seat of the cab at DIA and maybe this whole escape could come off if she made him promise not to tell anyone. She found the plan amusing. One of those discrete pick-up lots that DIA had conveniently constructed would work just fine. A fuck, then a flight was BB's plan. So long Buena Vista!

CHAPTER 31

GOTCHA

The cell phone's ring drained Charlie's complexion when he realized that it wasn't the phone in his pocket. The particular cell phone had been stored in his briefcase that sat on the floor next to him. Business as usual, thought Marten. Charlie probably had individual phones for all his shady dealings. Should be an interesting search, Marten pondered.

"Bingo!" shouted Burger. "Don't you think you ought to answer that, Mr. Bellows? It might be an important call," Ernie said with fake concern showing on his face. He peered over the table to look at the ringing briefcase on the floor.

Bellows wrestled his briefcase open and then silenced the cell. If possible, his whole expression paled completely.

"Let the record show that Mr. Bellows did indeed open his briefcase and extract a ringing phone," Burger added. Ernie's voice had become much more relaxed and almost gleeful.

"You'll need to hand me that phone, sir," Chief James Marten said. "We have the proper warrant for all the phones in your possession." He waved the paper in front of Bellows' face. "Let the record show that Bellows will hand me the cell that rang; he has opened his briefcase and taken the ringing cell phone out of there. I will now have him place the phone in an evidence bag for finger printing." Bellows slowly raised the cell and deposited it into the plastic bag.

Chief Marten examined the display window on the cell phone then verified a detail, "Oh look, Detective Burger, the last call on the bagged phone is from Travis Norton's cell. The same cell phone that is now in our crime lab; the phone that Mr. Norton directed the police to find at High Mountain Vista. This designated cell number from Norton's phone is the number that he called to contact his boss for orders about the Holdens. And look, there is an app on Mr. Bellows' phone to disguise his voice. How convenient is that? Well...well...."

Chief Marten continued, "We need to collect all your other phones now, Mr. Bellows, as the warrant states; all phones in your possession or at your motel room. My goodness, we have a connection. Let's see how many times say in the last month you have called this number for someone that you claim not to know." Marten scrolled down the contacts through the plastic bag. "Looks like about 20 times. Let the record show that Mr. Bellows has been in contact consistently with Travis Norton during the

Holden case."

Let the record also show that we are now offering Mr. Charles Bellows some consideration if he confesses to his part in all the crimes charged against Holt and Norton: various assaults, arson, unlawful surveillance and murder et cetera. A confession would go a long ways to the reduction of impending charges."

Marten leaned toward Bellows to watch him process the offer.

"Let the record show that these crimes were committed in Chaffee County in or near the town of Buena Vista, Colorado. Mr. Charles Bellows has also been implicated in various conspiracy crimes in association with the law firm of Smith, Howard and Bellows. These allegations will be determined and prosecuted by the North Dakota Attorney General, Mr. Allan Adams' Office. Detective Burger, please read Mr. Bellows' his rights and then make the arrest before we proceed."

***

Sgt. Jen Holly suddenly just knew that something was wrong. It had been too quiet in Billy's trailer for the last twenty minutes. If there was sex going on, it was way too quiet. No, this quiet was of another nature. It was the quiet that you heard when no one was home. "Howie, something is wrong. I just know it!"

No more than a minute had passed, when Matt yelled, "Dad! Come quick! Billy's hurt!" Jen threw down her headset and rushed out the door! "Oh, my

God!" she yelled. "Howie, call headquarters!"

She and Matt met at the trailer door and found it locked. They both laid a shoulder into the door that popped open like a soda can! She went immediately to Billy to check for a pulse. Matt searched the trailer. He looked at Jen and shook his head with a 'no.' Jen exhaled a puff of air in relief as she felt Billy's strong pulse. He was completely comatose though.

She grabbed her shoulder radio transmitter and yelled, "This is Sgt. Holly reporting a 10-33 with a 10-52 need at the High Mountain Vista RV Park as soon as possible. Billy Holden is comatose but breathing. Hurry up that ambulance! Code 3, we need an APB out on BB Bellows now!"

Barb hit the interview room door like a charging bull. "Chief, we have a situation! Please join me in the other room now!" There was a shock factor that went through both Burger and Marten. Barb did not charge into interviews ever. Marten got out of the room quickly and shut the door. "Chief, Billy is comatose and BB has escaped. Jen is transmitting now. She has ordered an ambulance and put out an APB on BB!"

"Oh shit, Billy better be all right. Get me Jen on the radio. How in the hell could this have happened! Damnit!" Marten ran for the radio center room as fast as he could go. "Jen? What in the hell happened?"

***

BB had actually enjoyed Mark the Cabby. They

chatted back and forth on I-70 and finally talked sex. She hadn't wanted to stop on the way down but the rest stop just happened. At that point they were at the Chief Hosa Exit which meant they would travel through Denver and then DIA. They were less than an hour from the airport. Besides, she was feeling a little wet between the legs at this point. What the hell?

The backseat tumble had almost had a naïve feel about it. The poor boy was out of his pants by the time he parked and got in the backseat. BB couldn't help but rave, "My-my, sweetie, you are well endowed; you go, boy!" Whip, bang and it was over. BB certainly didn't have to do any foreplay that was for sure. Mark had to have been in his middle 20s and all ready to experience a little raw sex with an older woman. The boy got plenty for his $500 profit; his trip from Buena Vista had been rewarded.

There were a few hints about maybe stopping at a cheap motel but BB put a stop to that. She promised that there would be a next time; she'd call him from the airport when the vacation was over. The only thing he didn't know was that this vacation just might be permanent. The boy would probably have erotic dreams about his blond stranger for awhile. Too funny, she thought. No one could say that she hadn't contributed to the future generation.

Mark delivered her to the Departure Terminal and told her to call him when she got back. Naturally, he had gotten off at the first gate instead of the one flying to Mexico City. BB blew him a kiss then disappeared into the first terminal. Better to walk a little distance than leave too many clues, she thought.

BB had an hour before her flight left. She decided to check in, then go into one of the stores and buy some clothes to change her appearance. Why not, she thought? Dowdy and old would blend in quite nicely, then she could change back when the plane landed on international soil. She was now truly on vacation!

***

"Jen, what happened? Give it to me quick."

"Sir, BB and Billy sounded like they were going to the bedroom for sex. We let it go on for twenty minutes, then I just knew that something had to be wrong. At 10:00 I rushed the trailer door along with Matt Holden who had seen Billy's body in the living room. Billy Holden was comatose with absolutely no reactions but his vital signs were good. I believe that BB used a date rape drug on him. The ambulance medics thought that I was probably right. Anyway, he is being transported to Vail Hospital now."

"Are you checking all the trailers in the park?"

"Yes, sir. We have two rows to go and nothing yet. Jerry has taken the trail out the back but has not seen any tracks so far. We're in contact. Her car is still here by the way."

"No one has seen anything?"

"No, sir. She has disappeared into thin air so far. Maybe someone picked her up on the highway?"

"That would be my guess also, but which way, toward Fairplay or Leadville?"

"Well, I'd go toward I-70 as quickly as I could. Then the question would become Denver or Utah?"

James Marten thought about that question and then realized exactly what he would do. "I think she's headed to DIA as quickly as possible. Keep searching and I'm on it. 10-4."

"10-4…and I am sorry, sir."

"For what? Thank God you aborted the surveillance when you did or she'd be totally out of our reach. Hell, I think we have a chance here." James disconnected. "Barb, get me Chief Nelson in Denver immediately. Make sure that you email out pictures of BB to all counties in Colorado. This is an APB bulletin. Don't leave anyone out."

"I'm on it, Chief," she exclaimed. Barb's hands flew over the computer keys as she talked. The Communications Room exploded with activity. Chief Marten was directing all his deputies on the radio.

Barb was handling the ambulance call and taking down all information that she needed. It was like a dance as the two moved around each other. Ernie Burger finally came out of the interview room and was shocked by the activity.

"What's going on? What happened?" he asked as he entered the room.

"Looks like BB drugged Billy then escaped," Barb said never looking up from her tasks. "It's pure chaos at this point."

"What do you want me to do, boss?" he asked quickly.

"Take all of Bellows' cell phones to the lab and tell them to do a thorough search then monitor any communication. If BB should call any of the phone numbers, let me know immediately! Then go back to Bellows and, real casually, tell him that I'll be in to finish the interview fairly soon. Lie. He must have seen the commotion; tell him there was an accident on the highway. The accident has nothing to do with his case. Let him know that after the interview, he will then be transferred to the jail." Marten looked directly into Ernie's eyes, then said, "I want you then to hightail it to High Mountain Vista and help with the search. We need to comb every inch of that park and the town as soon as possible. Now, get going!"

Ernie Burger shot out the door minutes later. He radioed Barb a code 2! Siren on, Ernie was maybe a minute ETA. Bob and Chelsea were waving at him as he turned in. Ernie rolled down the window and turned off the siren.

"Just wanted you to know that we've been talking and around 10, our dog began to bark. Wasn't much and didn't last long but who knows," Bob said.

"Your dog growl often?" Ernie inquired.

"Just when there's a critter around or a person at the office door."

"I'll take that as a no and go get busy. Thanks." Detective Burger went on down the road. His adrenaline was running high as he approached Billy's trailer.

Howie waved at him and came over to the car. "Sgt. Holly is off helping check the trailers in row

F, I think. So far nobody saw anything. If I didn't know better, I'd say she got on her broom and flew out! Shit!"

Slow down, boy. We'll figure this out. The Chief is betting on Denver right now. How she got on the road is interesting. That is her BMW over there, right?"

"Correct, sir. We would have seen her if she had taken anything out of her car. She was carrying that huge purse by the way."

"Yep, I've seen it. Kind of like carrying a suitcase for sure. You remember anything about it? Color? Design?"

"Think it was brown? Hang on and I'll call Sgt. Holly. See if she remembers anything else about it."

"Jen, come in," Howie said.

"Here. Just about finished with row F. What's up?"

"Detective Burger and I were discussing BB's appearance and he wanted to know if you could describe BB's purse for everyone on speaker."

Jen thought for a moment then said, "It was fairly distinguishable. Light tan with the G design in darker tan for Gucci. I think it had white leather straps with an identification white ID tab hanging from the handles. Cost around 3000 would be my guess if it's an original Gucci."

"Wow. You sure know your purses."

"No. I know expensive if it was a Gucci; that much I do know. Well back to work here. 10-4."

"So who else found Billy other than Jen?" Burger asked Howie.

"It was Matt Holden who was out walking the

dog and checked out one of the windows. He and
Jen broke the door lock a few minutes later. I think
Matt is with the Holden men who are following the
ambulance to Vail Hospital. Most of the ladies are
settled in the office waiting for news."

"Have you moved your equipment out of Miss
Bixler's trailer?

"Not yet but I could do that," Howie said.

"Good idea," Burger commented with a smirk on
his face. "We at least could let these people have
their property back. Think I'll go have a look at
Billy's trailer. Has the Crime Team showed up
yet?"

"On the way. Jen and I stayed out after we saw
Billy. Of course, the medics have had their time in
there. You know how that is, right?" Howie
affirmed.

"Of course." Burger put on his shoe covers and
let himself in. The door was totally wasted. He
could tell from the discarded medical paraphernalia
where Billy had collapsed. Dinner was still on the
table, what was left of it. With rubber gloves on,
Ernie picked up and smelled the discarded wine
glass from the floor. He couldn't tell if the date rape
drug was the cause, but it was a good guess.
Someone had spilled their wine and used cleaner on
the rug in another place. Neat freaks, he thought.
How odd.

He moved into the bedroom and saw a drawer
had been left open but nothing else. He wandered
into the bathroom and saw the screen in the tub.
Good job, BB; she must have crawled out. Ernie
stuck his head out the window and could envision

the escape. Clever. With the whole state on alert, Burger wondered how far she'd get. Well, his guess was that she wouldn't be found near these trailers.

CHAPTER 32

LATE EVENING STILL

"You can't really believe that I was telling Norton to attack the Holden family," Charlie Bellows shouted with an angry red face! "Billy Holden is going to be my future son-in-law. I can't imagine that you would think that double crossing Billy would be of any benefit to Smith, Howard and Bellows. Placing Billy in the state capitol as a senator was the target, not trying to poison his father. I am quite aware that Billy was completely attached to his dad. For you to even imply murder is so totally wrong. How dare you!" Charlie yelped. Bellows flattened his hands on the table and prepared for verbal combat.

"Let's not be so quick to judge our evidence," Chief Marten said. "What about John Holden? Hell, your group tried to drive him off the road even before he got here. I mean, your firm had been quietly trying to destroy the Holdens and you, Mr.

Bellows, was the designated instigator. The one who gave the orders and then crawled back under a rock; we have the proof. Imagine what will happen when we negotiate with Norton or Holt? A little time off for telling us exactly what they know. Norton can identify the law firm since he has worked for it before. So don't try to imply innocence, it won't work." Marten's stare penetrated Charlie.

"You don't think that a man like Norton only works for one group, do you? Hell, he's the slime of the earth. He, obviously, was hired by some other group that wanted in on the action," Charlie said. "More money talks to a guy like that. Remember that the voice on the phone could have been anyone. To assume that it was orchestrated by me is ridiculous!"

"Right, and when we play your phone app, what do you bet that Norton can identify that voice-over? Even a disguised voice has specific characteristics. The sheer number of calls while the Holdens were at High Mountain Vista will convince any jury. No. You are on the hook for arson and attempted murder. You directed the action with the consent of Smith, Howard and Bellows or on your own. Right now it would be far easier to charge you alone with one count of arson and two counts of attempted murder and then to top it off, one count of murder with malice," Marten finished with a satisfied expression.

"I never killed anyone. I never planned any kind of murder! It would make absolutely no sense. Plus, I know nothing about the altercation at the Jensen

Farm. You can't lay those crimes on me. Plus, the farm was in North Dakota and is none of your damn business!" Charlie pointed out by pounding the table.

"But you ordered the Colorado attacks on John Holden including the arson attempt didn't you?" Marten reiterated.

There was a pause in the flow of interrogation. Charlie Bellows was weighing the options. He leaned back in his chair and carefully thought. If he confessed to some of these charges, maybe he could use the confession as leverage when the firm's involvement surfaced. That connection was going to be really ugly, to say the least. North Dakota was going to pick them apart and devour everything except the bones. Some leniency for him just might work in his favor. He had to look at the whole picture at this point. Cover his own ass was now priority. Lord knew his partners were in the process of hanging him out to dry at this very moment.

Bellows took a deep breath and began a new approach. "I was simply following orders to keep my job," Charlie used his victim voice for this venture. He would have to wait and see how it played. "You did notice that my name is last on the billboard? There's a reason for that. If I want to keep my job, I need to follow orders. Coming to Colorado and protecting my future son-in-law was my family priority. It also allowed me to try and keep Norton under control for the firm. You did notice what a hothead that guy is? Control of his crazy actions became more difficult as time went on," Charlie added with compassion registering on his face. "The majority of those calls to Norton were from me trying to stop him. It had gotten out of control with the arson attempt. The man began to not take orders but create his own crimes. I simply couldn't stop him. Norton wanted to literally finish off the Holden family when he was only supposed to monitor their trailers."

Chief Marten checked out the fake tears welling up in Charlie Bellows' eyes. Holy shit, James thought. The man was now playing drama queen. Did he really think that the police were going to buy this story? So maybe, Marten thought, he would throw out some of the fishing line and let Bellows run. Context could reveal a hell of a lot. Maybe enough detail would come out that the DA could reel this jackass in hook, line and sinker. Time to go into the question mode James decided. "Then what you are saying is that Smith and Howard have been sending you instructions since the beginning. What were their first orders and when?"

"It began two years ago. I was to investigate the Holdens as landowners and potential clients. You see, Smith and Howard were looking at the whole river basin and had realized that the water would be sought out by the oil companies. I was directed to explore the possibility of buying the ranches and farms along the basin. My involvement was simply to look at the possibilities. Smith and Howard then began applying pressure on their own. I did what I was told."

James sat there totally surprised how quickly sharks would start eating their own. These guys were dirt. To assume that Bellows was a small player was ludicrous. He reeled in his disgust and kept going. "Who contacted J Meyer Petro?"

"It was Smith who knew the CEO up close and personal. He had worked with him in the Dallas area. They were good old buddies."

"Were you introduced to this man?"

"Yes. Once, but no more. Like I said, my part was to take orders. The firm used my early childhood connections to handle the local people; I was only a mere pawn in the scheme."

Marten could just tell how Bellows was creating his own defense. At least he was smart enough to realize that it would be every man for himself. Just monitoring the trailers my ass, James thought. There were so many nuances to this scam that it was mind-boggling. Well it was time to bring him back down to the crime in Buena Vista. "If all you say is true then who killed Henry Holden?"

"I have no idea. Murder was never discussed through the law firm. It was never the intention of the firm to let this situation be so obvious. Why would the firm want to publicize a secret plan? They wanted to keep the raps on all activities. Murder was never in the game plan. You need to look elsewhere for your answers. We were just trying to scare Henry," Charlie almost pleaded his case at this point. He then continued, "The firm figured that he'd understand the connection between selling the mineral rights and the attempts on John Holden's life. Henry just wouldn't back off, so we kept pushing. We needed his signature on the will, not him out of the picture. Henry was too damn stubborn. The firm never wanted to murder him; we only wanted his mineral rights. We are now left with a case of personal intent to legalize his will. How messy is that? The courts will grind that out for years. That signature meant everything to the firm; it meant a lot of money that is now tied up. We needed to stay ahead of J Meyer Petro to collect on the plan. Henry Holden's murder was the worst news that the firm could possibly get." Charlie, almost out of breath, had finished his diatribe.

"So your involvement centers on intimidating the Holden family and getting Henry Holden's signature? You, however, paid Norton $20,000 and gave the instructions?"

"If I did, and this is just a hypothetical question, plead guilty to some minor charges of illegal wiretapping and intimidation, could there be a deal of some sort offered? Lesser charges might help me in North Dakota; I could be quite helpful to them in proving the larger implications against Smith and Howard's involvement. You know, like I said, I am simply the middle man." Charlie Bellows leaned back in his chair with confidence, hoping that Buena Vista would prosecute in a way that could protect him from the larger crimes.

Chief Marten did have to give Bellows credit. The man could really spin a tale and think quickly. James could see how both states might definitely want to deal with Bellows. Colorado was after only the crimes committed on their soil. Murder, unfortunately, was still out there but all the other stuff could be resolved right now. Yet, Marten wanted it all tied up in one neat confession. One step at a time, he thought. "So you will confess that you had directed and ordered Norton and Holt to run John Holden off the road, spy on any and all conversations in both trailers and the attempted arson? Norton is not capable of staging the arson, Mr. Bellows. You had to have suggested another attempt. I'm not buying it that Norton could think up the arson. No deal." Why did James feel like he was buying a used car right now?

Bellows stared at him for a long moment weighing his options closely. Plead one more minor charge in the State of Colorado for a good defense in North Dakota. It would be worth it if he could use it in his defense and Charlie knew he could with the right lawyer. "Okay. I will also confess to giving an order to stage a minor fire. Again, it was intended to scare John Holden from blocking Henry Holden's wishes about mineral rights. That's all."

"And to shoot at Bernie Holden and Ms. Bixler when they searched Billy Holden's trailer?" James ventured onward.

"Absolutely not! I had nothing to do with those incidences. Norton decided that vengeance was what he wanted. He and Holt then became their own worst enemies. I don't shoot at women, sir. Norton and Holt then went out of control. Their actions were totally and absolutely motivated by their anger and ignorance. The firm, at that point, ordered me to remove them from the High Mountain Vista Park. I thought that hiding them near Mt. Princeton would do the trick. I had no idea that Bixler would then decide to hike that area. I mean, who would have thought that? Norton and Holt were by then making their own decisions and none of them any good. I would have sent them back to North Dakota within a couple of days when things settled down, but no, Bixler had to hike. Those circumstances were out of my control!" Charlie emphasized his denial by raising his voice.

James had let Bellows spin enough. The guy was to the point that he was beginning to look like the victim. Fucking unbelievable. Marten wanted Henry's murder resolved. Somehow this jerk needed to take responsibility for the murder. He had to have sent BB into Billy's life; he had to have helped plan the poisoning…or had he? Suddenly James began to see another alternative here. What if BB had done it on her own to help Daddy? Wow! He began to wonder.

Chief Marten was ready to push for answers; it was time to up the intensity. "Please don't now try to tell me that these two punks planned and carried out the poisoning of Henry Holden. You, obviously, had your hands in that scheme right up to your eyeballs! You murdered Henry Holden, you son of a bitch, or at least instructed someone else to do it!" James had come out of his chair and was yelling at the top of his lungs. The shock of his anger startled Bellows who slide lower in his chair. His mouth flew open as he processed what was happening.

"How did your daughter just happen to meet Billy Holden? Please don't try to tell me that it was a coincidence. I don't believe in them. You set that up so the firm could get closer to Billy Holden and find out what would motivate him. You chose sex and money to feed his ego! How convenient was that? And you sold your daughter to him or was she part of the scam all along?"

"BB knew nothing about the scam! I merely mentioned that she should meet Billy. That he was an up and coming player. Someone with a real future!"

"Right," Marten retorted. "A future that could make you fabulously rich. In fact the whole damn Bellows family would be able to follow the money. BB must have been pretty excited when you leveled with her. When you offered to finance Billy's run for the Senate. How convenient it must have been to sell your daughter or had you two done this before?" Marten's eyes began to glow; he realized BB's potential involvement. "She knew didn't she; she knew it all! My God you guys are sick. How many fucking times has the Bellows family made suckers out of good men? Find a little greed, a little frustration and capitalize on it? You two are really over the top! Did the law firm know what you were up to with BB?"

"I tell you it was all coincidence!" Charlie shot out of his chair and began to nervously pace. "BB just happened to meet Billy at the local bar and fate let it happen. They hit it off and the next thing I knew he was going to be part of the family. I tell you it just happened!" Bellows pivoted and stared directly into Marten's face.

"Like shit it did," Marten hollered! "You had it planned out from the beginning. Holden had to die since he hadn't signed the damn will. It just happened that he had changed his mind like the Holden family has testified?" Marten's anger exploded, "Yeah, Charlie, they have testified that he had indeed changed his mind. You killed Henry Holden!" James pointed an accusing finger in Bellows' face. "It all makes damn good sense to me. You killed him because he had become a threat to your security. You were afraid that he would figure it all out and tell Billy. The evidence is all pointing at you, Mr. Bellows! You killed him!"

"I did not!" Charlie screamed at the top of his lungs. "I had nothing to do with Henry Holden's murder. I…I…." Like a clap of unexpected thunder, Bellows understood the alternative. He then realized exactly where this conversation was heading. It took his breath away. Bellows in a defeated tone quietly said, "I am done talking with you at this time." His mouth locked shut and he glared at James Marten.

CHAPTER 33

NIGHTTIME

For the second time the interview room door flew open and Barb motioned for Chief Marten to join her in the hallway. James had reached a dead end with Bellows at this point. The issue of BB had stopped them cold; Charlie would need time to process what had happened. How much loyalty did criminals possess toward their own offspring? Marten had to wonder. Was going to jail for them worth it or would a parent decide that the kid needed to pay for their own crimes? It would be interesting to see how the Bellows resolved their family dynamics. Well, let Charlie boy stew in his own juices thought James. He was done for awhile.

Barb looked anxious right now. Obviously, they were having another drama. Marten, flashed the 'zip it gesture' to Barb then shut the door securely on Bellows. They walked down the hall to assure no eavesdropping.

"Something has come up that I think will be helpful in finding BB Bellows," she said. "I have just talked with the manager of the Buena Vista Cab Company. He found out that one of his young drivers just let off a blond woman at DIA with the meter off. This former employee was given a large tip to head directly to the airport. Picked her up along Highway 45 near High Mountain Vista. The guy heard the APB on the radio on his way back and called in immediately. He let her off at the East Departure Terminal about an hour ago."

"Excellent. Get on the radio and get me a police helicopter to land on our pad. Let them know that they will need to take off again immediately with two passengers. Hurry!" Barb whirled like a top and disappeared into the Communication Center. He could hear the APB and words like manhunt and Code 2 being murmured.

Marten then connected with Ernie at High Mountain Vista on his phone and ordered Detective Burger to grab Sgt. Holly and report immediately to the helicopter landing pad. "This is a Code 2. You will take off immediately. Your destination will be DIA to apprehend BB Bellows. Any plane leaving the airport within the next hour must be searched immediately, 10-77. Barb will supply a list of flights and times within the next 15 minute. Be ready to pick up on email, 10-4."

A few seconds later Burger called back, "10-76 en route."

James Marten then whirled around and headed for the Communication Room yelling at Barb on the way, "Get me Chief Nelson in Denver right now then research flights leaving DIA within an hour, destinations either international or USA. Send the list to Jen's email."

The web was being spun. Jen and Ernie pulled onto the flight pad five minutes later then turned off their siren, locked the car and jumped into the idling helicopter.

Within seconds the copter was out of Chaffee County and heading to DIA. Both cops put on the copter's headphones and waited to get instructions from Chief Marten. The adrenaline was flowing through both of their bodies. During the short ride to the copter pad neither of them had talked. There were few words needed when you were en route. Jen wasn't sure why Marten had asked for her to accompany Burger but she was definitely pleased.

Marten's voice came into their ears about two minutes later. "Please check your email and make sure that the list of flights has been received."

Jen checked her smart phone and saw a list of 20 some flights that would need to be searched. Lots of details were being organized, she knew.

"Chief Nelson of the Denver Police Department is in contact with the DIA Security. They will be delaying these flights until each plane has been searched. Security will meet your helicopter on the runway. Sgt. Holly, you will handle flights in East Terminal and, Detective Burger, coordinate flights in the West Terminal. Security has delayed the flights until the inspection is over. Move quickly but be thorough. Remember that BB has probably changed her appearance slightly like a wig, sunglasses and various clothes. BB is not dumb by any sense of the imagination. Jen, watch for that purse and spend some time educating Ernie on the specific design and description of that thing. My guess is it's too expensive to toss."

Now it all made sense to Jen. Marten was going with her observational skills. Whatever skill got her in the action was okay by her. She certainly wasn't going to be picky about this assignment. Take the experience and go. Jen took out her pad of paper and began drawing the purse. Ernie nodded as she described it.

"Sir, if I have your permission, I can send the picture of the purse from my phone to the Security email. It might save some time."

"Permission granted. However, send it immediately to Barb and she'll make it happen."

"Yes sir." Jen finished the drawing then placed it in a text to Barb.

A few seconds later, Barb answered that she had received and sent the picture to all the teams involved. Within minutes the helicopter landed at DIA. Security officers swept Burger away in a cart for the other terminal and ran Jen toward the first airplane.

The door of the American Airline plane was open and ready for them to enter. The flight attendants were stationed along the isle. They were talking with the passengers in a friendly manner. The atmosphere was relaxed. Jen moved down the isle slowly eyeing the lady passengers. She tried to keep a calm friendly expression on her face so not to alarm anyone. The attendants had handed her a list of seats where women were flying alone. It was quick and fairly easy. The only problem was that BB wasn't going to Brazil this evening. Well, onto the next plane.

***

Bix, Mattie and Bernie had stayed behind after BB's escape. The police had then gone door-to-door waking people up to do a safety check. Finally the nightmare was over; High Mountain Vista was silent and sleeping. The ladies had decided to wait for information about Billy or BB in Chelsea's office; the cell phone reception was better there and the company reassuring.

Lydia had gone with Matt and John; she had taken her own car, not wanting to spend the entire night at the hospital with the guys. Chelsea's husband, Bob, was sleeping now that the police had left. Jim and kids were asleep in the pop-up; Simon was sleeping on Bix's lap.

Chelsea quietly shut the door to their living quarters then arrived in the office with hot coffee. She had added some chocolate chip cookies on the tray as comfort food. The ladies had arranged the office chairs around a small table by the front windows. Chelsea placed the tray in the center of the table and handed out the napkins. Each lady had their cell phone perched near them ready to pick up. No news was going to get past them.

Mattie's phone rang first; it was John. She jumped on the call. The ladies munched and listened to the one sided conversation. Mattie looked noticeably relieved as she talked. Finally, she disconnected and began to report, "Billy's resting and okay. He woke up about 15 minutes ago. He's got a huge headache and looks pretty groggy but conscious. The doctors do think it was the date rape drug. If so, he'll be released early tomorrow morning for the 4th. They'll get the test results back by morning. He just remembers drinking wine and then passing out. Lydia is on her way back now; she'll come by here first before heading home."

"Wonder if BB raped him before rushing off?" The ladies looked at Bix in mild shock. "Well, BB is pretty devious. Why not, if it suited her? Self-centered people take anything that they can get. She certainly was prepared for any situation; I've got to hand it to her. Tossing the date rape drug in your purse is brilliant, if you're a criminal that is."

"I think her escaping did prove that she is guilty as shit," said Bernie folding a strand of red hair behind her ear. "Sure hope they find her soon. Of course she probably has a disguise ready to put on; her luck just might hold. I find the bitch to be embarrassing to all of womankind. How can you kill an old man to get what you want?" Bernie looked up at the ceiling and said, "Sorry, Dad."

"You can do all of the above if you truly are self centered; always the victim and always right is the motto of people like her," Chelsea answered. "BB was out to get the whole enchilada; money, the senator and power. Consider how her estate would look after Charlie Bellows passes away. Makes you wonder if she would kill her own father if he lasted too long," Chelsea added with cold calculation.

Suddenly the light went on for Bix and Bernie. They pointed at each other across the table and wailed, "The Red Queen!" The description of greed made so much sense now. BB was right there 'running in place.'

"Eeeeeek!" cried Mattie and Chelsea rustling in their chairs as if to distance themselves from the thought. The room fell silent as the group contemplated all that evil.

"Chief Marten said that he'd call us if they apprehended her this evening," Mattie finally said breaking the silence. "The whole state must be looking for her at this time. I just can't see her getting away."

"Are you playing the optimist here, Mattie?" said Bernie. "How evil is she? I hear Colfax Avenue in Denver could hide her pretty easily. Wouldn't put it past that bitch to turn tricks for awhile and disappear underground."

"DIA would be my bet," speculated Bix placing her elbow on the table in contemplation. "She seems to hale from the privileged class. I bet they lived very well back East. BB seems to cherish the expensive comforts." Bix petted Simon as she continued, "If I were she, I'd get myself out of Colorado and maybe the country. BB isn't going to jump into the woods; that would be a stupid move for a city girl. Now, lying on a warm beach might suit her well. I'll bet she has money stashed away and can afford luxury while convincing herself the murder was necessary."

The ladies sipped their coffee in unison processing that concept.

"Agreed," mumbled Chelsea placing her warm coffee cup carefully on her table napkin. "I can see it." She traced the napkin corners with her finger casually and continued, "So here we have both members of the Bellows family involved. Did they work together or separately? I wonder if father and daughter will turn on each other or show some family loyalty?"

"That is the million dollar question," Mattie said while concentrating on a cookie.

"Murder is a huge lump to swallow if you weren't part of the plot all along," Bernie said after reaching for the last cookie. "These are great cookies, Chelsea, homemade?"

"Only the best for my boys," she said. "Personally, I think BB got the idea to poison Henry all by herself. I mean how does poisoning Henry help Charlie Bellows? The will was what he wanted and that takes a live person to sign. Sorry for being so objective but it's true."

"No problem," said Mattie. "We need to be objective so that this thing can get solved. I would have to agree with you, Chelsea. Father and son were solid; Billy wouldn't have let anything happen to Henry. Henry, however, was in BB's way."

"If Henry had decided to not sell the mineral rights, Billy would have stopped pestering him, right?" Bix asked after sneaking Simon the last bite of her cookie.

"Correct," said Bernie. "The family would have stepped up and helped Billy with his career eventually. Family is family and you don't mess with that chemistry."

"So then BB would have become a senator's wife, wouldn't that be enough?' Mattie asked leaning back in her chair.

"Good question but where's her money and power?" Chelsea asked.

"That would be a problem," said Bix. "Married does not mean happily ever after for someone like BB. I think Charlie's empire of millions was her real target. The Bellows family owed her that inheritance; once a victim always a victim you know."

"So where's BB's mother in all of this?" asked Mattie.

"My bet would be that mother, was or is, as evil as BB," Bix answered. "It all fits. Apples never fall far from the gene pool tree. Trust me, that's my retired teacher voice talking of course," Bix added. "The genes are always there, single or married."

Chelsea, with a sparkle in her eye, decided to turn the conversation onto another subject; a subject that she had neglected for too long. "Speaking of mothers, I sure hope Margaret Holden is listening from heaven. I don't know how many times in the last couple of days that I have thought about your mother, Bernie. How pleased that lady would have been watching her children handle this tragedy. Margaret would have been so proud."

"Thanks, Chelsea, that's one huge compliment," Bernie said. "Mom wasn't exactly Wonder Woman, but she sure was super."

Chelsea looked at Bernie and decided to go ahead. She leaned forward in her chair and took a deep breath. "Margaret had you figured out, lady. If you think that your mother didn't know that you were a lesbian, then you hadn't looked closely enough."

"No she didn't," Bernie said sitting up straight as if a shock wave had gone through her.

"Yes she did. We had that exact conversation right here in this room ten years ago." Chelsea smiled knowingly. "Her hope was that you would find peace and then find someone. Your mom was so proud of you. How strong and confident you were on the ranch brought happiness to her heart. There, now I've said it. Something I should have said years ago, Bernie. You go, girl. Your mama was on your side." Chelsea felt the relief of confession; she crossed her arms and happily exhaled.

"We've all known, Bernie," said Mattie in a matter of fact tone. "You think we're so dense that we didn't see?" Mattie placed her hand warmly on Bernie's arm. "The problem is that not talking openly about each other's lives causes discomfort in the Holden family. But, you know how tight lipped the family is about emotions. It has taken me years to get use to how John deals with his emotions. My family was the exact opposite; touchy-feely was my upbringing. It's not that your family feels less but communication has always been hard."

"What's hard?" said Lydia who had just come in the office door. She dragged over the last chair and comfortably sat tossing her car keys on the table.

"Oh how the Holden family handled Bernie's lifestyle. We're discussing Bernie being gay and how emotions seemed to be a big taboo in the

Holden family," Mattie mumbled. "We come to these reunions and walk away with our secrets still hidden."

"Amen to that," said Lydia. "Wish I had been here earlier. The men are just sitting silently holding in their emotions. I finally left after giving Billy a kiss and grumbling something about talking later. Will we? Good question. Thank heavens, he's okay. And then there's poor Bernie…" her gaze landed on Bernie with sympathy as she continued, "who has been waiting for years to hear some kind of support. Jeez, we're a class act. Any more snacks? I'm starving," Lydia said leaning forward in her chair, inspecting an empty plate.

"Coming up," said Chelsea as she disappeared into the kitchen for more refreshments. She couldn't help but think about what a great job she and Bob had. Serving people was wonderful, especially, when the people became close friends.

Chelsea came back into the office as Bix questioned, "You think the Holden family is any different than other families in the Midwest? Maybe we're talking a generation of folks who, I always figured, thought that strength meant silence. You ever thought about that?"

"Sure makes life easier doesn't it? Just go with the flow," said Chelsea as she sat down the replenished tray. She had added some chips this time. The ladies reached and munched.

"Ah the human race in the US of A," Bix mumbled. "My family was in between those two camps just like yours. My father was closed lipped on all things emotional and/ or sexual and kept them under the covers so to speak. When I was a teen and my differences began showing, my mom took me over to meet a couple of neighbor ladies who were most definitely lesbians; it was a fun evening and gave me hope. But of course the Puritan teachings still spread their shadow. Please don't tell me that there weren't gay people on Plymouth Rock? Albeit they must have been way deep in the darkest closet. Poor souls."

Lydia sipped her coffee as if it were nectar. She began to relax and enjoy the easy conversation. "People have come in all sizes since the beginning of time. How they are accepted or not is another topic. So what is the gay life really like, Bix? You seem pretty comfortable in your skin."

"Well I would say that I am comfortable. Colorado suits me and the gay community is far more open here. That's a good thing for me. My Midwest history was very similar to the Holdens. Mom and I never said a word about those gay ladies but when I fell in love the first time, she became uncomfortable with that sexual relationship. Mom had learned from day one the message that straight folks can accept same sex companionship but gay sex is still a closet issue. America seems to treat sex in general with skepticism. Mom finally did accept with the understanding that we would never talk about it. Nowadays, people are becoming more comfortable after realizing that finding someone to love is the true gift."

"Here! Here!" The ladies toasted with coffee, cookies and/ or a chip, then settled comfortably back into their chairs. Bernie knew that she was blushing; it felt wonderful.

Lydia continued, "Look at society practicing the muscle game of intolerance and placing the blame on faith; Jesus knew. After his death, bigots then wrote rigid rules to control their societies and we have tolerated that nonsense ever since. Tolerance is not weakness. Tolerance is not a nasty word, damn it!"

"Well check out how our family has treated Billy speaking of nonsense. Lord help anyone who has different ambitions these days," Mattie added. "Why didn't we all know what his ambitions were? We haven't been able to handle the differences in each other. Having a senator in the family would be a good thing yet it wasn't discussed. How else are you going to change things like fracking? My hope is that the family continues these reunions and makes a point of talking about what's really important. Celebrate Margaret and Henry's legacy."

"Amen!" said Bernie with a smile. "Quite honestly, I will have to apologize to Billy. From the beginning, I was one of the first Holdens to come down on his case. I had no trust and didn't want to hear his explanations about fracking and politics. We make our own troubles, don't we? I was a stupid fool," she said confessing to her share of the blame. Bernie's cell phone suddenly rang finishing their conversation. Her eyes grew large as she looked at the caller ID number. Chief James Marten was on her cell phone.

CHAPTER 34

STILL NOT MORNING

Five planes later Jen was still moving through the aisles. Mexico City was the last international flight on her list. Ernie hadn't done any better either; they had communicated with each other between plane searches. In the back of her mind she had to wonder if the tip had really been solid. There had been no time to ask about the origin although she had confidence in Chief Marten's decisions. Sgt. Holly dismissed that doubt and went back to focusing on her job.

As they entered the plane, Jen did her preliminary scan of the passengers; she felt a chill go up her back. Half way up the left aisle, she focused on a well dressed woman with a cheap black wig; her mother would have called the hair style a pompadour. Maybe something a woman could buy in an airport shop was the thought registering in Jen's mind; some shop where there weren't lots of choices. The woman just didn't fit exactly with her hair perched above the head rest. One high heel stuck out in the aisle nervously twitching away. The majority of passengers were in shorts and bright shirts babbling in excitement. There wasn't any excitement emitted from passenger A12; she was, if anything, trying to look invisible. Jen looked down at her list of single women passengers and there was A12.

Sgt. Holly nudged the security guard and pointed casually at the lady's back; the guard nodded and began his vigilance. They moved at their normal pace but neither of them took their eyes off the lady. Jen could feel her adrenaline pumping as they moved up the isle. Was it BB and did she carry any weapons? If so they would have to be stashed in that purse. Jen finally got close enough to glance under the seat; the tan purse was there! BB had her right hand holding the purse handles. Sgt. Holly nodded at the security guard then moved swiftly.

BB had been ready; she also had known what was coming. She hurled her purse then released it like a heat seeking missile toward Jen's body! The slingshot tan weapon sailed past Jen's head as she dropped down to the aisle floor. The security guard was not so lucky. The heavy purse whacked him squarely in the face. He fell backwards in the isle with his feet flying up in the air. Spewing out of the purse flew miscellaneous projectiles. A skimpy hot pink bikini, top and bottom, floated like a cloud in the cabin air. The top landed on the security guard's chest with cups up. The bottom twirled around the upper cargo hatch handle across the aisle. Blush, lipsticks, billfold, flashlight and tennis shoes spewed out into the plane. Passengers gasped and ducked in shock as the items tumbled down the aisle. It was then a questionable call if one laughed or screamed. No bomb or gun was sighted so the majority of passengers decided to at least chuckle.

Jen pushed BB's shoulders down in the seat and whispered in her ear. "You are under arrest, BB Bellows. You can choose to be totally embarrassed or we can walk off this plane in a more civilized fashion. My guess would be that you will be on the media news tonight. The decision is up to you." Sgt. Holly tightened her hold on BB's shoulder.

The plane passengers had their cell phones aimed in the direction of the altercation now. BB took it all in then gave a slight nod in Jen's direction. She moved out of the seat and walked toward the front exit with her head held high and never looked back.

There was a moan from the security guard as he righted his position and threw the bikini off. Unfortunately, he was left with the task of stuffing the delinquent items back into the purse. The aisle passengers took pity on him and helped gather the propelled contraband. It was obvious that he would have a black eye from the chaos. The tourists clapped as the pilot announced that their departure time was back on schedule. The party atmosphere resumed as soon as BB exited the plane.

Jen placed the handcuffs on BB when they were back on solid ground. Even though BB had taken a swing at the guard, Jen had placed the cuffs in front; she'd hate for there to be pictures of BB tripping in her high heels. Jen went ahead and read BB her rights then escorted her toward the gate never letting go of her. She proceeded to radio Ernie who was now on his way. They walked up the ramp and into a security office before any conversation started.

Jen could feel the anger radiating from BB. Her escape into sun and surf had been swept away in a matter of five minutes. BB sat down in a chair and concentrated on trying to get comfortable before she said anything. It was like watching a hen ruffle feathers before nesting. Jen fully assumed that she would immediately ask for a lawyer, however, BB surprised her.

The faucet of false tears opened and BB sputtered, "It's Smith, Howard and Bellows Law Firm's fault. They forced me into poisoning Henry and having a relationship with Billy Holden. I was only suppose to make Henry sick but the dose that daddy had been told to use by the firm was too strong. It was an accident; I didn't mean to kill him. You have to believe me! We were forced by the firm; they told us that we'd be killed if we didn't carry out their orders. Daddy knew too much and I was just an accessory." BB brought a Kleenex out of her pocket and daubed at her fake flood of tears. "Surely you can identify with how I felt?" She searched Jen's eyes trying to stir up some sympathy. BB now started making sad eyes at the poor security guard who had joined them. He was, of course, mystified by her performance.

Jen realized that her mouth was open in pure shock. BB's drama scene had totally been a surprise. BB now stopped the fake tears and leaned back in the chair. Jen found a legal pad in the office and asked BB, "Will you write down what you have just said. I'm sure that your statement will help your case. I'll leave you alone for a few moments and wait for my partner to arrive." Jen took the handcuffs off. BB rubbed her wrists and sniffed then nodded. Jen got up and left BB with pad and pen. Ernie was outside the door so she joined him.

"Did you hear any of that? The woman just confessed and, yes, I did read BB her rights. So much for a family sticking together. I'd say that her father is screwed and so is his law firm. She never missed a beat."

"Can't say that it surprises me. I got to sit in with the Chief when we interrogated Charlie Bellows. They're both really creepy human beings. Of course, I guess it does take a certain type of individual to commit murder and all the rest of these crimes. However, both of them did know exactly whom to blame for the crime. The law firm has taken a direct hit from both of them. Shouldn't take a DA long to establish their guilt though."

"How did it go in the plane?" Ernie asked as they got ready to call Chief Marten.

"It was like right out of a movie with clothes flying and total chaos. The purse unloaded its contents which included an itsy bitsy pink bikini into the isle. I am sure that the passengers all have it on their cell phones. But leave it to BB to exit with dignity at the end. The Chief won't be amused but shit happens. We got her."

***

Chief James Marten nodded as he listened to the description that his officers related over the phone. It was going to be difficult to absorb the spin that the media would produce. There were many videos out there at this point. Some money conscious passenger was going to get rich. The media's spin would be interesting to say the least. Would it be a positive tone for the police? One never could be confident on that aspect. Now he would have to rely on finesse and hope that Charlie Bellows would decide to say more after he heard BB's confession. Jen had emailed him the video of the actual confession. Hard to believe that BB would be so quick with her testimony. Charlie would absolutely hate it. The man would process and then figure what would work best for him and then BB. An hour later, Chief Marten would get his answer from Charlie.

***

"What do you mean that BB confessed to poisoning Henry Holden? She did no such thing! My daughter is an upstanding citizen. What could she possibly gain from committing that crime? She had Billy in her arms. There is no motive," Bellows yelled!

Marten and Bellows were back in the same interrogation room again. Chief Marten knew that it was time for the final piece of the puzzle. The questions that remained were obvious; was BB acting alone, were the Bellows both in on the murder, and could they really blame the law firm for their actions? He felt confident at this point; Charlie would be forced to come clean. What would be Bellows' choice?

Chief Marten began his approach, "Oh, it's clear to me, BB wanted it all!" Marrying a senator was one thing, but having her hands on the money was something else. Why would she want to wait? Henry was in her way when it came to the money and power," said Marten. "BB knew that Henry wasn't going to sign his will. She knew that Henry's grandson, Matt, was convincing Billy to hold off and let him run on a platform that advocated dry fracking. When the men discussed Billy's political future, BB listened from the trailer bedroom. She heard John and Matt going over the advantages and disadvantages of the fracking issue. She saw how your scheme of purchasing the river basin property could be exposed and the money could dry up. Personally, I don't see BB ready to throw it all away; she doesn't strike me as a very patient woman. What do you think?"

"I think that I would have known if she was planning something as heinous as murder; BB has her limits. Gruesome is not one of her characteristic," Charlie said in a confident tone. "I think you need to look elsewhere for your suspect. Smith and Howard could have easily set something up that we knew nothing about."

James thought that Bellows had no problem dropping his name off the billboard. It was now

Smith and Howard. One could almost taste the defense's case strategy. Marten could hear it being played out like a cheap soap opera. Something to the tune of, poor honest Charlie had been a victim of the two big strong partners who threatened him with a cancellation of his partnership. He would say that blackmail made him do it; the motive would be centered on corporate power. Of course the defense would add in convenient lies about what Charlie did and didn't know. The devil made him do it, James thought. Fortunately, it wouldn't be his problem to get the truth out there to a jury; that's why Marten was a police chief and not a lawyer thank heavens.

Chief Marten let out an audible sigh and continued, "I think it's time that you actually see how devious your daughter can be. You need to know the facts before we go any farther into this subject. The Bellows family isn't going to be able to build a case around being victims." Marten slid his cell phone across the table after pushing the play arrow on the video confession. Charlie Bellows' mouth fell open as he listened and watched BB sobbing away with her fake tears. It would play into any district attorney's hands. 'Cheap' was the word that came into James' mind.

Watching Bellows process what was on the video produced a perverse satisfaction for Marten. It was somehow bitter sweet; James was a father and couldn't image having to stomach the reality of a child wasting their entire future. The video would keep the jury focused on the murder and how truly evil BB could be. She wasn't a victim but a monster. No matter what her motivation had been, the fact remained that she had killed for greed and power. It was all pretty damn horrible, James thought.

Charlie slowly started to come to grips with what he saw on the video. His complexion paled and his eyes began to water. Whether they could blame the firm wasn't as important as the actual confession itself. BB had killed Holden; it was the ugly reality. She had confessed. No matter how anyone clouded the waters, his daughter had committed murder. God help her.

Charlie's voice was quietly compassionate as he began to share some of his memories. "BB was a good child. She was always trying to please me. Straight A student in school and very popular. Well, maybe too popular in some ways. Her damn mother always pushed her socially. My daughter became an overachiever while I began to be away from home too much. Work and playing around became my focus to the point that when I noticed what was happening to BB, it was almost too late." Charlie stared at his folded hands for a moment before continuing.

"The divorce was damn ugly. I'm sure that it took a toll on her. There was an abortion...we got her on the pill...." Charlie looked away into some far distant place as he allowed his thoughts to come and go. "You do the best that you can; we got through it." Charlie let out a sigh of resignation. The pause was long and deeply felt.

Marten began feeling like a therapist. Keep talking, Charlie; it's good for all concerned, the Chief mused.

"BB came to live with me after the dust settled. She was never quite the same again. It was like some light had been turned off. Maybe her innocence was gone. I don't know." Charlie loosened his tie and slouched farther down in the chair. "BB became more determined to find her direction. I…I was never quite sure what that direction was, however. Even after a couple dozen therapists, she never was quite the same." Charlie's voice trailed off escaping into his subconscious leaving the psyche exposed; the quiet was deafening.

Must be lonely in there, James sensed. Retrospect ain't worth much in reality, he thought. Still it was all that an individual had when coping with personal dilemma. The 'ifs' that people created to justify or change an event was really a human quagmire, he admitted. Even the word, 'sorry,' had such a deep pulse. You could never quite bury regrets from your life; you could learn to live with them but never totally bury them. Marten had to admit that he did feel sorry for Bellows at this moment. However, what was said and done is the reality. So be it.

CHAPTER 35

THE FOURTH OF JULY

John Holden pushed Billy out of the Vail Hospital in the mandatory wheel chair. Matt and the attendant followed along. All three men looked tired from the evening's events. Billy's headache had kept pounding until around 3 a.m. John and Matt slept off and on in the hospital chairs. The doctors had confirmed this morning that it was indeed the date rape drug, Flunitrazepam. John surmised that it could have been worse. What if BB had simply shot Billy? The possibilities were, unfortunately, endless. No, this hospital slumber party was truly a relief. It was a small price to pay for keeping your brother alive. They waved to the attendant with his empty wheelchair as Billy walked toward John's truck.

The Holdens piled in with Matt in the backseat. All three men needed a shave and food. They headed for a coffee shop for something to tide them over. Matt took the order and thirty bucks from his dad. As the door shut and the awkward silence settled, John reached inward for his question, "So how are you feeling about the whole thing, Billy? Can I help you?"

Billy Holden cautiously paused to contemplate his answer. The significance of John's inquiry did not escape him. Did John really want him to share his frustrations and horrendous mistakes? He had been so stupid and blind. Nevertheless, could Billy trust John like he had trusted his dad? Intrinsic trust would have to replace years of competitive behavior between these two brothers. Could they develop that kind of relationship? Life had given them a chance; he needed to try.

Billy began his saga. "My God, I sure can pick them, can't I? BB sure knew how to take what she wanted and I was a stupid shit for not seeing what was going on. Fuck, John, am I so desperate that I didn't see the writing on the wall?" He glanced for a second at John then stared out the front window.

Billy's admission shook John down to his roots; their relationship was quickly expanding beyond what he had expected. John reached out to his father for guidance as he began, "Come on, Billy, don't beat yourself up. BB is now going to pay for her actions probably with her own life. She was one deceitful woman as Chief Marten said to us last night. It was her decision to murder our father, not yours. How would you have known what she was capable of? I can't imagine dating these days. I feel so lucky to have found Mattie. Dating out there would scare me to death," John revealed.

"Why is it that I am so unlucky when it comes to love?" Billy continued. "This shit about there's a soul mate waiting for everyone is just getting harder to believe. If that was so, why are 50% of the homes in this country maintained by a single adult? I mean, give me a break. Am I'm so dumb that my father has to get murdered for me to realize the truth? Where is the irony in that? It just isn't fair. It should have been me that got poisoned, not Dad," Billy confessed. The sudden admission, amazingly, freed his pent-up anguish; allowing the words to be spoken was therapeutic he realized.

"Don't say that, Billy. Dad wouldn't have changed the outcome and lived at your expense. You have got to believe that. He believed in you and your future. Billy, it wasn't your fault. How could you have known? You couldn't. Why Dad? I have no idea. I do know that he was a decent man who deserved more. We deserve more; our family deserves more. The preacher at church said that to open up a positive future, you have to get rid of the negatives. Have some faith, little brother; throw the negatives out the window. The Holdens may have been rode hard and put away wet but we'll survive."

Billy, for the first time in a long time, felt that power of family emerging. Could family strength and honor preserve Henry Holden's legacy? Billy found some hope in that thought. Destiny could be positive.

Matt opened the back truck door and placed a cardboard tray on the seat. "Boy, you guys look awful," he said with an amused smile on his face. You look like you've been in the hospital all night."

"Get in here with the cinnamon buns and decent coffee. Lord, I'm starving. They spent the next few minutes devouring the sugar. After they had all sucked down three buns apiece and some coffee, they began to feel better. "Amazing what sugar will do for you," John said as he started the truck and headed toward the highway. "Looks like we'll get back to Mountain Vista before the Denver traffic spills into the mountains and the parade at 10:00," John stated. "Well, gentlemen, happy Fourth of July; now, let's get home in one piece." They toasted the thought with their coffee remains and sat back for the ride.

It took Billy 15 miles of silence to process how he felt right now. "Well, guys, I am going to run for Congress. Dad's sacrifice has to mean something and I think my part of giving back might be more than just satisfying myself. The state does need some guys in the government who aren't just there for the money but for the preservation of North Dakota. That is providing that you will help me; I can't and won't do it without my family's blessing."

"You got it," said John.

"Maybe I can get my tech friends to set up and run your campaign on computer," Matt added. "It's amazing how many ranches and farms get the majority of their news on the computer anymore. Let me see what I can get done when we all head home," Matt said with the satisfaction of being involved.

"Home," said John. "That word sounds good. It's time we took Dad home and buried him next to Mom. To let the neighbors grieve proper for an old friend's passing has to be done. We've done what we can do here. I'm assuming that we'll be making a trip back here to testify in court but our part is done for now."

"You know guys, I think we ought to purchase a memorial bench or fountain and dedicate it in Dad's memory; place it in the park to thank the people of Buena Vista," Billy said. "Besides, it would give us an anchor to come back to each year. Sort of establish our tradition. What do you think?"

"I think it's a great idea. Let me talk with Chief Marten before we leave. I'm sure he'll have some good ideas." John glanced at Billy and smiled. "I'm going to like this new Billy; especially the way you're thinking."

"You mean Senator Holden; the voice of ranchers and oil alike? Works for me," Matt commented, then leaned back in his seat with the feeling that he was truly experiencing the Holden future.

***

Now that the 'wicked witch' had been caught, Lydia and Jim had taken to the idea of the Holdens sponsoring a barbecue. The relief of the capture had calmed the family so they had gone into City Market and purchased a couple briskets. The smoker had been started.

Lydia had placed notices of their offerings in the Commons and with Chelsea in the Office. Chelsea was donating a bowl of potato salad.

Bix had now taken over the oven in the

community kitchen for three peach pies. Bernie was collecting all the leftover vegetables from the Holden's trailers to create a huge salad. Mattie was adding homemade bread done North Dakota style. Other newly arrived guests began to contribute. There was a collection of appetizers and side dishes being deposited in the Commons' refrigerator. The contributions were piling up into quite a feast. The party would be from 2:00 on until the fireworks at dusk.

To make things easier, all food would be left on the tables in the Commons letting anyone come in to eat at their convenience. All you had to bring was your plate and eating utensils; it was an old Indian tipi custom that the Holden family found incredibly convenient. People simply took home their dirty dishes and made life so much easier for the host.

Sgt. Holly found High Mountain Vista bubbling with activity as she entered the park. Jen had just finished her patrol duty at the parade. It was truly wonderful to get back to some ordinary duties around Buena Vista. She would drive to Leadville later for dinner with wine and then watch the fireworks with her mother. Their meeting had been postponed for so long that she was really looking forward to the evening. Her mother was excited to hear the whole story so that she could relate the events to the bridge club. Arlene Holly would then be the center attraction, of course.

Jen had come, unofficially, to talk with Bix. Being stalked by two crazy criminals wasn't anything to take for granted, she knew. Maybe Jen was going to state the obvious to Bix, but it was still something that needed to be done. She saw Bernie with a large basket filled with vegetables. "Hey Bernie, where's Bix?" she yelled out the open car window.

"Hello, Sergeant. Have you been invited yet?' Bernie asked placing her arm on Jen's car window.

"To what?" she inquired.

"We're sponsoring a barbecue starting at 2:00. Grub will be served all afternoon. Bring your own plate."

" Wow, that's a great offer but I am heading over
to Leadville later to see my mom. Thanks for the invitation though; I do appreciate it. Maybe I can stop over before you all leave tomorrow. When are you pulling out?" Jen asked.

"Noon, I think," Bernie answered.

"Good, then see you tomorrow," Jen replied.

"Bix is in the Commons putting a couple of pies together," Bernie said. "She'll be glad to see you."

"So, as the snoop that I am," Jen ventured forward, "I have to ask. How are you and Bix getting along? Is there a romance in your immediate future?" Jen searched Bernie's expression for an answer.

Bernie smiled and said, "Bix and I have lots of history to share. It's all good, Jen. When you get older, truth and trust are so important; you don't have time for drama. Having said that, I will tell you that we are celebrating our good fortune. And speaking of good fortune, working with you, young lady, has been delightful. You've got a great future as a cop; we couldn't have been in better hands."

"Thanks, Bernie. I wish that this case hadn't hurt the Holden family so much; you all didn't deserve what happened. Maybe the future will heal us all. I have a feeling that we do have a connection that will bring closure," she said. She and Bernie nodded and stared for a second into each other's eyes savoring their friendship. Jen then tucked her emotions back inside and headed for the Commons.

Bix had just tossed three pies into the heated oven and glanced at Simon napping near the warm stove on a cushion. She called Simon's assistance, silent help. There was a mess of bowls and utensils to clean up, of course, but the hard part was done. She was filling the sink with hot water and soap when Jen Holly opened the screen door.

"It is going to smell great in here pretty quick," Jen commented while rubbing Simon's back. "This is really a great idea for today. You guys never miss a beat." Jen grabbed a towel to dry the dishes.

"You know that you don't need to do that?" Bix said.

"Needs to be done and I came to talk with you. My mother taught me right. We could always solve the world problems during the evening dishes. I never minded doing them because it was a great time to communicate."

"Sounds like I'd like your mom. So, what's on your mind?" Bix asked.

Jen looked around and realized that Bix and Simon were cooking alone; this was indeed a good opportunity to talk with her privately. "I'd like to share a secret with you, Bix. I joined a rape and assault group years ago to manage my own life. I joined the group because of a stalker event that had haunted me since college. I'd wake up in the middle of the night in panic. Becoming a police officer stopped the vulnerability and helped build back my own confidence, but the shadow never completely disappeared. Since I moved up here, I still go to the meetings in Denver each month like a good habit, weather permitting. If you ever feel the terror hit you, let me know. I could stop by Summit County and pick you up; I'd love some company. Especially, someone who knows how it feels to be hunted for target practice. I'm not making light of the situation, Bix, I just know that there might be some negative baggage left behind."

"Thank you. That is a really nice offer," Bix said while scrubbing out a mixing bowl. She handed it directly to Jen then commented thoughtfully, "I would be honored to ride with you. Right now, I have no idea if this event will be a sleep problem or not but I'm not sure that it matters either way. Bernie and I talked about this subject last night. Murder is never really over, is it? The story never really ends, does it? People's lives change forever."

Jen spun the towel slowly around in the bowl while her mind processed the fundamental fact that their participation in this murder case wasn't over. Closure for the family and Buena Vista was going to be an arduous journey that would touch and define their future. It would someday become their history. "None of us will ever be the same again, even the Red Queen," she avowed and placed the bowl in the cabinet.

THE END

ABOUT THE AUTHOR

The first book that I ever read on my own was a mystery. For some reason while other children were picking up the reading skills, I found myself having nothing but difficulty. The pages were simply blurs of words. The next summer, not to be outdone by my brother, I picked up one of my mother's adult paperback mysteries and faked it. I faked it until one day that summer, comprehension began. Heck with the children's books; I was hooked on mysteries forever!

For 34 years teaching became my profession, Drama and English. The interpretation of the written word motivated me into the educational field; I taught student levels 6th grade through College Prep over the years. Eventually, retirement has blessed me. I now find the time to write mysteries and explore my favorite environment.

I followed my ancestors to Colorado and have spent 30 years in the mountains. The respect that I have for high elevation is incredible. I am addicted to hiking and being outdoors. Writing mysteries and hiking simply blended together into the Colorado Mountain Mystery Caper Series.

Janet McDermott

www.ingramcontent.com/pod-product-compliance
Lightning Source LLC
Chambersburg PA
CBHW051440260626
47162CB00001B/188